**Power and Madness,
Love and Damnation . . .
Robert R. McCammon's**

Tortured by memory, a desperate man finds salvation dancing on the head of a "Pin" . . .

In "Makeup," a Los Angeles punk steals a horror actor's makeup case and finds a new lease on life—and death . . .

"Something Passed By" the earth. Now Johnny and Brenda's little boy lies beyond a vacuum-sealed door, and the clouds are filled with blood . . .

In "Yellachile's Cage," a convicted killer finds wondrous dreams on the wings of a yellow bird . . .

And a special child exacts a brilliantly subtle revenge in "Chico" . . .

Books by Robert R. McCammon

Baal
Bethany's Sin
Blue World
The Night Boat
Stinger
Swan Song
They Thirst
The Wolf's Hour

Published by POCKET BOOKS

BLUE WORLD

ROBERT R. McCAMMON

POCKET BOOKS

New York   London   Toronto   Sydney   Tokyo   Singapore

An *Original* Publication of POCKET BOOKS

POCKET BOOKS, a division of Simon & Schuster Inc.
1230 Avenue of the Americas, New York, NY 10020

ISBN: 0-671-69518-5

First Pocket Books printing April 1990

10 9 8 7 6 5 4 3 2 1

POCKET and colophon are registered trademarks of
Simon & Schuster Inc.

Printed in the U.S.A.

Permissions

Contents

Introduction   ix

Yellowjacket Summer   1

Makeup   25

Doom City   49

Nightcrawlers   65

Pin   91

Yellachile's Cage   101

I Scream Man!   121

He'll Come Knocking at Your Door   131

Chico   151

Night Calls the Green Falcon   163

The Red House   215

Something Passed By   239

Blue World   259

Introduction

Fast Cars, the sign said.

It was in front of a used-car lot in the neighborhood where I grew up. Fast Cars. My friends and I passed it every day on our way to school. Our bikes were the fast cars of our imagination, our Mustangs and Corvettes and Thunderbirds. We longed for four wheels, but we were confined to two and on them we hurtled into the future.

I've built my own fast cars. They're in this book, and they're eager for passengers. They're not made of metal, glass, nuts, and bolts, but rather of the fabric of wonder. All of them have a starting point, and all of them have a destination. You can sit behind the wheel, but I have to steer. Trust me.

We will travel, you and I, across a tortured land where hope struggles to grow like seed in a drought. In this land, a place with no boundaries, we'll run the freeways and back roads and we'll listen to the song of the wheels and peer into windows at lives that might be our own, if we lived in that land. Sometimes we'll have the wind at our backs, and sometimes in our faces. We'll see storms in the distance, whirling closer, and we'll smell the forest and the sea and the hot concrete of the city. Our road will lead us onward, deeper into the tortured land, and as the speedometer revs and the engine roars, we may find strange visions on that twisting highway.

A man who awakens one morning to find a skeleton in bed where his wife had been the night before.

A small-time thief who steals a makeup case, and learns a dead horror star's secret.

A roadside diner, where a Vietnam veteran comes seeking shelter from the storm.

A young man in prison, who finds beauty and hope on the wings of a yellow bird.

Halloween in a very special residential area, where trick-or-treating is deadly serious.

A red house on a street of gray houses, and a breath of sweet fire.

The adventures of a has-been serial hero, who dons his old costume and goes in search of a serial killer.

A priest obsessed by a porno star, and his realization that both of them are being stalked by a third shadow.

We will see worlds within worlds from the windows of our fast car. We might even see the end of the world, and we might sit on a front porch for a while and sip a glass of gasoline on a hot December day.

Some of these roads are tricky. Some of them have sudden curves that want to throw us off into space. Some of them bubble under the blinding sunlight, and some of them freeze beneath the cold white moon. But we have to take them all, if we want to get from here to there. And isn't journeying what life is all about? The question of what lies beyond the dark hills, beyond the steaming forests, beyond the locked door?

The key to a fast car can take you there.

Novels are limousines, stately and smooth. Some of them can ride like tanks, slow and heavy, well-armored. The fast cars of short stories: those are the vehicles that let us zoom close to the ground, with the wind in our hair and the speedometer's needle vibrating on the dangerous edge. Sometimes they're hard to handle; they have minds of their own, and they call for close attention. They can crash and burn so easily, but their sleek power yearns for speed. In such a fast car, we can go anywhere. No locked door can keep us out, and if we want to see what lies around the next bend, or the next hill, all we have to do is steer toward it. We'll be there, roaming through the tortured land, with the lights of other lives and different worlds passing on either side.

I'd like to thank a number of people who have encouraged me in my building of the fast cars in this book. Thank you to Frank Coffey, who published "Makeup," my first short story; to Dave Silva of *The Horror Show,* and Paul and Erin Olson of *Horrorstruck,* for their friendship and encouragement; to Stephen King and Peter Straub for setting the pace, and leaving burning treadmarks on the pavement; to Charles L. Grant for his black-and-white visions; to Joe and Karen Lansdale for true grit; to Tappan King of *Twilight Zone* magazine; to J. N. Williamson and John Maclay for their first publication of "Nightcrawlers"; to Dean R. Koontz, and he knows why; to those good ol' boys Tom Monteleone and Al Sarrantonio; to Ray Bradbury, whose short story "The Lake" made me cry when I was a little boy; to Forrest J. Ackerman, my true father, who raised me on *Famous Monsters of Filmland;* to Tony Gardner; and to Sally, who always stands beside me.

The fast cars are waiting. Listen: their engines are starting up. We have a distance to travel, you and I. Buckle your seat belt. I'll have to steer, because I know the roads. Trust me.

Ready? Then let's go out, in our cocoon of speed, and see what finds us.

ROBERT R. McCAMMON

Yellowjacket Summer

"Car's comin', Mase," the boy at the window said. "Comin' lickety-split."

"Ain't no car comin'," Mase replied from the back of the gas station. "Ain't never no cars comin'."

"Yes there is! Come look! I can see the dust risin' off the road!"

Mase made a nasty sound with his lips and stayed where he was, sitting in the old cane chair that Miss Nancy had said she wouldn't befoul her behind to sit on. Mase was kinda sweet on Miss Nancy, the boy knew, and he was always asking her to come over for a cold CoCola but she had a boyfriend in Waycross and so that wouldn't do. The boy felt a little sorry for Mase sometimes, because nobody in town liked being around him much. Maybe it was because Mase was mean when he got riled, and he drank too much on Saturday nights. He smelled of grease and gasoline too, and his clothes and cap were always dark with stains.

"Come look, Mase!" the boy urged, but Mase shook his head and just sat watching the Braves baseball game on the little portable TV.

Well, there *was* a car, after all, trailing plumes of dust from its tires. But not exactly a car, the boy saw; it was a van with wood trim on its sides. The van had been white before it had met up with four unpaved miles of Highway 241, but

3

now it was reddened by Georgia clay and there were dead bugs spotting the windshield. The boy wondered if any of them were yellowjackets. It was a yellowjacket summer for sure, he thought. Them things were just *everywhere!*

"They're slowin' down, Mase," the boy told him. "I think they're gonna pull in here."

"Lord A'mighty!" He smacked his knee with one hand. "There's three men on base! You go on out and see what they want, hear?"

"Okay," he agreed, and he was almost out the screen door when Mase called, "All they want's a roadmap! They gotta be lost to be in this neck o' nowhere! And tell 'em the gas truck's not due till tomorrow, Toby!"

The screen door slammed shut behind him, and Toby ran out into the steamy July heat as the van pulled up to the pumps.

"There's somebody!" Carla Emerson said as she saw the boy emerge from the building. She released the breath she'd been holding for what seemed like the last five miles, since they'd passed a road sign pointing them to the town of Capshaw, Georgia. The ancient-looking gas station, its roof covered with kudzu and its bricks bleached yellow by a hundred summer suns, was a beautiful sight, especially since the Voyager's tank was getting way too low for comfort. Trish had been driving Carla crazy by saying, "It's on the E, Momma!" every minute or so, and Joe made her feel like a twerp with his doomy pronouncement of "Should've pulled over at the rest stop, Mom."

In the back seat, Joe put aside the *Fantastic Four* comic he'd been reading. "I sure do hope they've got a bathroom," he said. "If I can't pee in about five seconds I'm gonna go out in a burst of glory."

"Thanks for the warning," she told him as she stopped the van next to the dusty pumps and cut the engine. "Go for it!"

He opened his door and scrambled out, trying to keep his bladder from bouncing around too much. He was twelve years old, skinny, and wore braces on his teeth, but he was as intelligent as he was gawky and he figured that someday God would give him a better chance with girls; right now, though, computer games and superhero comics took most of his attention.

He almost ran right into the boy who had hair the color of fire.

"Howdy," Toby said, and grinned. "What can I do for you?"

"Bathroom," Joe told him, and Toby motioned with a finger toward the back side of the gas station. Joe took off at a trot, and Toby called, "Ain't too clean in there, though. Sorry!"

That was the least of Joe Emerson's worries as he hurried around the small brick building, back to where kudzu and stickers erupted out of the thick pine forest. There was just one door, and it had no handle on it, but it was mercifully unlocked. He went in.

Carla had her window rolled down. "Could you fill us up, please? With unleaded?"

Toby kept grinning at her. She was a pretty woman, maybe older than Miss Nancy but not *too* old; her hair was light brown and curly, and she had steady gray eyes set in a high-cheekboned face. Perched in the seat next to her was a little brown-haired girl maybe six or seven. "No gas," he told the woman. "Not a drop."

"Oh." The nervous clenching sensation returned to her stomach. "Oh, no! Well . . . is there another station around here?"

"Yes, ma'am." He pointed in the direction the van was facing. "Halliday's about eighteen or twenty miles. They've got a real nice gas station."

"We're on E!" Trish said.

"Shhhh, honey." Carla touched the little girl's arm. The boy with red, close-cropped hair was still smiling, waiting for Carla to speak again. Through the station's screen door Carla could hear the noise of a crowd roaring on a TV set.

"Bet they got a run," the boy said. "The Braves. Mase is watchin' the game."

Eighteen or twenty miles! Carla thought. She wasn't sure they had enough gas to make it that far, and she sure would hate to run out on a country road. The sun was shining down hot and bright from the fierce blue sky, and the pine woods looked like they went on to the edge of eternity. She cursed herself as a fool for not stopping at that rest station on Highway 84, where there was Shell gasoline and a Burger King, but she'd thought they could fill up ahead and she was in a hurry to get to St. Simons Island. Her husband, Ray, was a lawyer and had flown on to Brunswick for a business meeting several days ago; she and the kids had left Atlanta yesterday morning to visit her parents in Valdosta, then were supposed to swing up through Waycross and meet Ray for a vacation. Stay on the main highway, Ray had told her. You get off the highway, you can get lost in some pretty desolate country. But she thought she'd known her own state, particularly the area she'd grown up in! When the pavement had stopped and Highway 241 had turned to dust a ways back, she'd almost stopped and turned around—but then she'd seen the sign to Capshaw, so she'd kept on going and hoped for the best.

But if this was the best, they were sunk.

In the bathroom, Joe had learned that you spell relief p-e-e. It was not a clean bathroom, true, and there were dead leaves and pinestraw on the floor and the single window was broken, but he would've gone in an outhouse if he'd had to. The toilet hadn't been flushed for a long time, though, and the smell wasn't too pleasant. Through the thin wall he could hear a TV set on. The crack of a bat and the roar of a crowd.

And another sound too. Something that he couldn't identify at first.

It was a low, droning noise. Somewhere close, he thought as he stood at the end of an amber river.

Joe looked up, and his hand abruptly squeezed the river off.

Above his head, the bathroom's ceiling crawled with yellowjackets. Hundreds of them. Maybe thousands. The little winged bodies with their yellow-and-black-striped stingers crawled over and around each other, making a

6

weird droning noise that sounded like a hushed, distant—and dangerous—whisper.

The river would not be denied. It kept streaming. As Joe stared upward with widened eyes, he saw maybe thirty or forty of the yellowjackets take off, buzz curiously around his head, and then fly away through the broken window. A few of them—ten or fifteen, Joe realized—came in for a closer look. His skin crept as the yellowjackets hummed before his face, and he heard their droning change pitch, become higher and faster—as if they knew they'd found an intruder.

More left the ceiling. He felt them walking in his hair, and one landed on the edge of his right ear. The river would not stop, and he knew he must not cry out, *must not must not,* because the noise in this confined place might send the whole colony of them into a stinging frenzy.

One landed on his left cheek and walked toward his nose. Five or six of them were crawling on his sweaty Conan the Barbarian T-shirt. And then he felt some of them land on his knuckles, and—yes—even *there* too.

He fought back a sneeze as a yellowjacket probed his left nostril. A dark, humming cloud of them hung waiting over his scalp.

"Well," Carla said to the red-haired boy, "I don't guess we've got much choice, do we?"

"But we're on E, Momma!" Trish reminded her.

"You 'bout empty?" Toby asked.

"I'm afraid so. We're on our way to St. Simons Island."

"Long way from here." Toby looked off to the right, where a battered old pickup truck with red plastic dice hanging from the rearview mirror was parked. "That's Mase's truck. Maybe he'd drive over to Halliday for you and get you some gas."

"Mase? Who's that?"

"Oh, he owns this place. Always has. Want me to ask him if he'll do it?"

"I don't know. Maybe we could make it ourselves."

Toby shrugged. "Maybe you could, at that." But the way he smiled told Carla that he didn't believe she would, and she didn't believe it herself. Lord, Ray was going to pitch a fit about this!

"I'll ask him, if you like." Toby kicked a stone with the toe of one dirty sneaker.

"All right," Carla agreed. "Tell him I'll pay him five dollars, too."

"Sure thing." Toby walked back to the screen door. "Mase? Lady out here needs some gas pretty bad. Says she'll pay you five dollars to bring her back a few gallons from Halliday."

Mase didn't answer. His face was blue from the TV screen's glow.

"Mase? Did you hear me?" Toby prodded.

"I'm not goin' a damn place until this damn baseball game is over, boy!" Mase finally said, with a terrible scowl. "Been waitin' all week for it! Score's four to two, bottom of the fifth!"

"She's a looker, Mase," Toby said, casting his voice lower. "Almost as pretty as Miss Nancy."

"I said leave me be!" And for the first time Toby saw that Mase had a bottle of beer on the little table beside his chair. It wouldn't do to get Mase riled up, not on a hot day like this in the middle of yellowjacket summer.

But Toby screwed up his courage and tried once more. *"Please*, Mase. The lady needs help!"

"Oh . . ." Mase shook his head. "All right, if you'll just let me finish watchin' this damn game! I'll drive over there for her. God A'mighty, I thought I was gonna have me a peaceful day!"

Toby thanked him and walked back to the van. "He says he'll go, but he wants to watch the baseball game. I'd drive myself, but I just turned fifteen and Mase would whip my tail if I had a wreck. If you like, you can leave the van here. Café to get sandwiches and stuff is just around the bend, walkin' distance. That suit you?"

"Yes, that'd be fine." Carla wanted to stretch her legs, and something cold to drink would be wonderful. But what had happened to Joe? She honked the horn a couple of times and rolled up her window. "Probably fell in," she told Trish.

The yellowjacket had decided not to enter Joe's nostril. Still, there were thirty or more of them on his T-shirt, and he could feel the damned things all in his hair. His teeth were clenched, his face pale and sweating, and yellowjackets were crawling over his hands. Chills ran up and down his spine; he'd read somewhere about a farmer who had disturbed a yellowjacket nest, and by the time they got through with him he was a writhing mass of stung flesh and he'd died on the way to the hospital. At any second he expected a dozen stingers to rip through the skin at the back of his neck. His breathing was harsh and forced, and he was afraid that his knees would buckle and his face would fall into that filthy toilet and then the yellowjackets would go to w—

"Don't move," the red-haired boy said, standing in the bathroom's doorway. "They're all over you. Don't move, now."

Joe didn't have to be told twice. He stood frozen and sweating, and then he heard a low, trilling whistle that went on for maybe twenty seconds. It was a soothing, calming sound, and the yellowjackets started leaving Joe's shirt and flying out of his hair. As soon as they were off his hands, he zipped himself up and he got out of the bathroom with yellowjackets buzzing curiously over his head. He ducked and batted at them, and they flew away.

"Yellowjackets!" he gasped. "Must've been a million in there!"

"Not that many," Toby told him. "It's yellowjacket summer. But don't worry about 'em now. You're safe." He was smiling, and he lifted his right hand.

The boy's hand was covered with them, layer upon layer of them, until it looked as if the hand had grown to grotesque proportions, the huge fingers striped with yellow and black.

Joe stood staring, openmouthed and terrified. The other boy whistled again—this time a short, sharp whistle—and the yellowjackets stirred lazily, humming and buzzing and finally lifting off from his hand in a dark cloud that rose up and flew away into the woods.

"See?" Toby slid his hand into his jeans pocket. "I said you were safe, didn't I?"

"How . . . how . . . did you do—"

"Joe!" It was his mother, calling him. "Come on!"

He wanted to run, wanted to leave tornadoes whirling under his sneakers, but he forced himself to walk at a steady pace around the gas station to where his mother and Trish were out of the Voyager and waiting for him. He could hear the crunch of the other boy's shoes on the gravel, following right behind him. "Hey!" Joe said, his face tightening as he tried to smile. "What's goin' on?"

"We thought we'd lost you! What took you so long?"

Before Joe could answer, a hand was placed firmly on his shoulder. "Got hisself stuck in the bathroom," Toby told her. "Old door oughta be fixed. Ain't that right?" The pressure of his hand increased.

Joe heard a thin buzzing. He looked down, saw that the hand clamped to his shoulder had a yellowjacket lodged between the first and second fingers.

"Mom?" Joe said softly. "I was—" He stopped, because beyond his mother and sister he could see a dark banner— maybe two or three hundred yellowjackets—slowly undulating in the bright sunshine over the road.

"You okay?" Carla asked. Joe looked like he was about to upchuck.

"I think he'll live, ma'am," Toby said, and he laughed. "Just scared him a little, I guess."

"Oh. Well . . . we're going to get a bite to eat and something cold to drink, Joe. He says there's a café right around the bend."

Joe nodded, but his stomach was churning. He heard the boy give a low, weird whistle, so soft that his mother couldn't possibly have heard; the yellowjacket flew off from between the boy's fingers, and the awful waiting cloud of them began to break apart.

"Just 'bout lunchtime!" Toby announced. "Think I'll walk thataway with ya'll."

The sun burned down. A layer of yellow dust seemed to hang in the air. "It's hot, Momma!" Trish complained before they'd walked ten yards away from the gas station, and Carla felt sweat creeping down her back under her pale blue blouse. Joe followed further behind, with the red-haired boy named Toby right on his heels.

The road curved through the pine woods toward the town of Capshaw. It wasn't much of a town, Carla saw in another couple of minutes; there were a few unkempt-looking wood-en houses, a general store with a CLOSED PLEASE COME AGAIN sign in the front window, a small whitewashed church, and a white stone building with a rust-eaten sign that announced it as the CLAYTON CAFÉ. In the gravel parking lot were an old gray Buick, a pickup truck of many colors, and a little red sports car with the convertible top pulled down.

The town was quiet except for the distant cawing of a crow. It amazed Carla that such a primitive-looking place should exist just seven or eight miles off the main highway. In an age of interstates and rapid travel, it was easy to forget that little hamlets like this still stood on the back roads—and Carla felt like kicking herself in the butt for getting them into this mess. Now they were really going to be late getting to St. Simons Island!

"Afternoon, Mr. Winslow!" Toby called, and waved to someone off to the left.

Carla looked. On the front porch of a rundown old house sat a white-haired man in overalls. He sat without moving, and Carla thought he looked like a wax dummy. But then she saw a swirl of smoke rise from his corncob pipe, and he lifted a hand in greeting.

"Hot day today!" Toby said. "It's lunchtime! You comin'?"

"Directly," the man answered.

"Best fetch Miss Nancy, then. Got some tourists passin' through!"

"I can see," the white-haired man said.

"Yeah." Toby grinned at him. "They're goin' to St. Simons Island. Long way from here, huh?"

The man stood up from his chair and went into the house.

"Mom?" Joe's voice was tense. "I don't think we ought to—"

11

"Like your shirt," Toby interrupted, plucking at it. "It's nice and clean."

And then they were at the Clayton Café, and Carla was going inside, her hand holding Trish's. A little sign said WE'RE AIR-CONDITIONED! But if that was so, the air-conditioning was not functioning; it was as hot in the café as it was on the road.

The place was small, with a floor of discolored linoleum and a counter colored mustard yellow. There were a few tables and chairs and a jukebox pushed back against the wall.

"Lunchtime!" Toby called merrily as he followed Joe through the door and shut it behind them. "Brought some tourists today, Emma!"

Something rattled back in the kitchen. "Come say hello, Emma!" Toby urged.

The door to the kitchen opened, and a thin woman with gray hair, a deeply wrinkled face, and somber brown eyes came out. Her gaze went to Carla first, then to Joe, finally lingered on Trish.

"What's for lunch?" Toby asked her. Then he held up a finger. "Wait! I bet I know! Uh . . . alphabet soup, potato chips, and peanut-butter-and-grape-jelly sandwiches! Is that right?"

"Yes," Emma replied, and now she stared at the boy. "That's right, Toby."

"I knew it! See, folks around here used to say I was special. Used to say I knew things that shouldn't be known." He tapped the side of his skull. "Used to say I had the beckonin' touch. Ain't that right, Emma?"

She nodded, her arms limp at her sides.

Carla didn't know what the boy was talking about, but his tone of voice gave her the creeps. Suddenly it seemed way too cramped in this place, too hot and bright, and Trish said, "Ow, Mommy!" because she was squeezing the child's hand too tightly. Carla loosened her grip. "Listen," she said to Toby, "maybe I should call my husband. He's at the Sheraton on St. Simons Island. He'll be real worried if I don't check in with him. Is there a phone I can use somewhere?"

"Nope," Emma said. "Sorry." Her gaze slid toward the wall, and Carla saw an outline there where the pay phone had been removed.

"There's a phone at the gas station." Toby sat down at one of the stools facing the counter. "You can call your husband after lunch. By that time, Mase'll be back from Halliday." He began to spin himself around and around on the stool. "I'm hungry hungry hungry!" he said.

"Lunch is comin' right up." Emma returned to the kitchen.

Carla herded Trish toward one of the tables, but Joe just stood there staring at Toby; then the red-haired boy got off his stool and joined them at the table, turning his chair around so he rested his elbows on the back. He smiled, watching Carla with steady pale green eyes. "Quiet town," she said uneasily.

"Yep."

"How many people live here?"

"A few. Not too many. I don't like crowded places. Like Halliday and Double Pines."

"What does your father do? Does he work around here?"

"Naw," Toby replied. "Can you cook?"

"Uh . . . I guess so." The question had taken her by surprise.

"Raisin' kids, you'd have to cook, wouldn't you?" he asked her, his eyes opaque. "Unless you're rich and you go out to fancy restaurants every night."

"No, I'm not rich."

"Nice van you got, though. Bet it cost a lot of money." He looked over at Joe and said, "Why don't you sit down? There's a chair for you, right beside me."

"Can I get a hamburger, Momma?" Trish asked. "And a Pepsi?"

"Alphabet soup's on the menu today, little girl. Gonna get you a peanut-butter-and-jelly sandwich, too. That suit you?" Toby reached out to touch the child's hair.

But Carla drew Trish closer to her.

The boy stared at her for a moment, his smile beginning to fade. The silence stretched.

"I don't like 'phabet soup," Trish said softly.

"You will," Toby promised. And then his smile came back again, only this time it hung lopsided on his mouth. "I mean . . . Emma makes the best alphabet soup in town."

Carla could not stand to look into the boy's eyes any longer. She shifted her gaze, and then the door opened and two people came into the café. One was the old white-haired man in overalls, and the other was a skinny girl with dirty-blond hair and a face that might've been pretty if it was clean. She was about twenty or twenty-five, Carla thought, and she wore stained khaki slacks, a pink blouse that had been resewn in many places, and a pair of Top Siders on her feet. She smelled bad, and her blue eyes were sunken and shocked. Winslow helped her to a chair at another table, where she sat muttering to herself and staring at her filthy hands.

Neither Carla nor Joe could help but notice the swollen bites that pocked her face, the welts going right up into her hairline.

"My God," Carla whispered. "What . . . *happened* to—"

"Mase called on her," Toby said. "He's sweet on Miss Nancy."

Winslow sat down at a table by himself, lit his pipe, and smoked it in grave silence.

Emma came out with a tray, carrying bowls of soup, little bags of potato chips, and the sandwiches. She began to serve Toby first. "Have to go to the grocery store pretty soon," she said. "We're runnin' low on near 'bout everythin'."

Toby started chewing on his sandwich and didn't reply.

"My bread's got crust," Trish whispered to her mother; sweat clung to her face, and her eyes were round and frightened.

It was so hot in the café that Carla could hardly bear it. Her blouse was soaked with sweat, and now the unwashed smell of Miss Nancy almost sickened her. She felt Toby watching her, and suddenly she found herself wanting to scream. "Excuse me," she managed to say to Emma, "but my little girl doesn't like to eat the crust on bread. Do you have a knife?"

Emma blinked, did not answer; her hand hesitated as she put a bowl of soup in front of Joe. Winslow laughed quietly, a laugh devoid of mirth.

"Sure thing," Toby said as he reached into his jeans pocket. He brought out a folding knife, got the blade extended. "I'll do it," he offered, and started carving the crust away.

"Ma'am? Here's your soup." Emma put a bowl in front of her.

Carla knew she couldn't take a bite of hot soup, not in this already-steaming place. "Can we . . . have something cold to drink, please?"

"Nothin' but water here," Emma said. "Ice machine's broke. Hush up and eat your soup." She moved away to serve Miss Nancy.

And then Carla saw it.

Right there. Spelled out in letters, floating on the top of her alphabet soup.

Boys crazy.

The knife was at work, carving, carving.

Carla's throat was dust-dry, but she swallowed anyway. Her eyes watched the moving blade, so terribly close to her little girl's throat.

"I said, *eat it!*" Emma almost shouted.

Carla understood. She put her spoon into the bowl, churned up the letters so he wouldn't see, then took a mouthful that all but seared her tongue.

"Like it?" Toby asked Trish, holding the blade before her face. "Look at it shine! Ain't it a pretty th—"

He did not finish his sentence, because in that instant hot alphabet soup had been flung into his eyes. But not by Carla. By Joe, who had come out of his daze and now grabbed at the knife as Toby cried out and fell backward from his chair. Even blinded, Toby held off Joe as they fought on the floor, and Carla sat transfixed while precious seconds ticked past.

"Kill him!" Emma screamed. "Kill the little bastard!"

She began beating Toby with the tray she held, but in the confusion most of her blows were hitting Joe. Toby flailed out with the knife, snagging Joe's T-shirt and ripping a hole in it. Then Carla was on her feet too, and Miss Nancy was screaming something unintelligible. Carla tried to grab the boy's wrist, missed, and tried again. Toby shouted and writhed, his face a twisted and terrible rictus, but Joe was holding on to him with all his dwindling strength. "Momma! Momma!" Trish was crying—and then Carla put her foot down on Toby's wrist and pinned the knife hand to the linoleum.

The fingers opened, and Joe snatched up the knife.

Both he and his mother stepped back, and Toby sat up with the fury of hell on his face.

"Kill him!" Emma shouted, red to the roots of her hair. "Put that knife right through his evil heart!" She started to grab the blade, but Joe moved away from her.

Winslow was standing up, still calmly smoking his pipe. "Well," he said quietly, "now you done it. Now you gone and done it."

Toby crawled away from them toward the door, wiping his eyes clear with his forearm. He sat up on his knees, then slowly got to his feet.

"He's crazy as hell!" Emma said. "He's killed everybody in this damned town!"

"Not everybody, Emma," Toby replied. The smile had returned. "Not yet."

Carla had Trish in her arms, and she was so hot she feared she might pass out. All the air was heavy and stagnant, and now Miss Nancy was grinning into her face and pulling at her with her filthy hands.

"I don't know what's going on here," Carla finally said, "but we're getting out. Gas or not, we're leaving."

"Are you? Really?" Toby suddenly inhaled, and let the air out in a long, trilling whistle that made Carla's skin creep. The whistling went on and on. Emma screamed, "Shut him up! Somebody shut him up!"

The whistling abruptly stopped, on an ascending note.

"Get out of our way," Carla said. "We're leaving."

"Maybe. Maybe not. It's yellowjacket summer, lady. Them things are just *everywhere*."

Something touched the café's window. A dark cloud began to grow, to spread across the outside of the glass.

"Ever been stung by a yellowjacket, lady?" Toby asked. "I mean bad, *deep* stung? Stung right to the bone? Stung so bad that you'd scream for somebody to cut your throat and end the misery?"

The windows were darkening. Miss Nancy whimpered, and began to cower under a table.

"It's yellowjacket summer," Toby repeated. "They come when I call 'em. They do what I want 'em to. Oh, I speak their tongue, lady. I've got the beckonin' touch."

"Oh, Jesus." Winslow shook his head. "Now you've gone and done it."

The bright sunlight was going away. Darkness was falling fast. Carla heard the high, thin droning noise from the thousands of yellowjackets that were collecting on the windows, and a trickle of sweat ran down her face.

"State trooper come here once. Lookin' for somebody. I forget who. He says, 'Boy? Where're your folks? How come ain't nobody around here?' And he was gonna put a call through on his radio, but when he opened his mouth I sent 'em in there. They went right smack down his throat. Oh, you should've seen that trooper dance!" Toby giggled at the obscene memory. "They stung him to death from the inside out. But they won't sting me, 'cause I speak their tongue."

The light was almost gone, just a little shard of red-hot sun breaking through when the mass of yellowjackets shifted.

"Well, go on, then," Toby said, and motioned toward the door. "Don't let me stop you."

Emma said, "Kill him right now! Kill him and they'll fly off!"

"Touch me," Toby warned, "and I'll make 'em squeeze through every damned chink in this place. I'll make 'em sting your eyeballs out and go up your ears. And I'll make 'em kill the little girl first."

17

"Why? For God's sake . . . *why?*"

"Because I *can,*" he answered. "Go on. Your van's just a short walk."

Carla set Trish down. She looked into the boy's face for a moment, then took the knife from Joe's hand.

"Give it here," Toby ordered.

She hesitated in the twilight, ran her forearm across her face to mop up some of the sweat, and then she walked to Toby and pressed the blade against his throat. His smile faltered.

"You're going to walk with us," she said, her voice quavering. "You're going to keep them off, or I swear to God that I'll shove this right through your neck."

"I ain't goin' nowhere."

"Then you'll die here with us. I want to live, and I want my children to live, but we're not staying in this . . . this insane asylum. I don't know what you had planned for us but I think I'd rather die. So: which is it?"

"You won't kill me, lady."

Carla had to make him believe she would, though she didn't know what she'd do if the time came. She tensed, drove her hand forward in a short, sharp jab. Toby winced, and a little drop of blood ran down his throat.

"That's it!" Emma crowed. "Do it! Do it!"

A yellowjacket suddenly landed on Carla's cheek. Another on her hand. A third buzzed dangerously close to her left eye.

The one on her cheek stung her, the pain searing and vicious. It seemed to make her entire spine vibrate as if she'd suffered an electric shock, and tears came to her eyes, but she kept the blade against his throat.

"One for one," he said.

"You're going to walk with us," Carla repeated as her cheek started swelling. "If either of my children is hurt, I'll kill you." And this time her voice was steady, though four yellowjackets crawled over her knuckles.

Toby paused. Then he shrugged and said, "Okay. Sure. Let's go."

"Joe, hold on to Trish's hand. Then grab my belt. Don't

let go, and for God's sake don't let her go either." She prodded Toby with the knife. "Go on. Open the door."

"No!" Winslow protested. "Don't go out there! You're crazy, woman!"

"Open it."

Toby slowly turned, and Carla pressed the blade against the pulsing vein in his neck while she grasped his collar with her other hand. He reached out—slowly, very slowly—and turned the doorknob. He pulled the door open, the harsh sunlight blinding Carla for a few seconds. When her vision had returned, she saw a dark, buzzing cloud waiting in the doorway.

"I can put this in your neck if you try to run," she warned him. "You remember that."

"I don't have to run. You're the one they want." And he walked into the cloud of yellowjackets with Carla and her children right behind him.

It was like stepping into a black blizzard, and Carla almost screamed, but she knew that if she did they were all lost; she kept one hand closed around Toby's collar and the knife digging into his neck, but she had to squeeze her eyes shut because the yellowjackets swarmed at her face. She couldn't find a breath, felt a sting and then another on the side of her face, heard Trish cry out as she was stung too. "Get them away, damn it!" she shouted as two more stung her around the mouth. The pain ripped through her face; she could already feel it swelling, distorting, and at that instant panic almost swept her senses away. "Get them away!" she told him, shaking him by the collar. She heard him laugh, and she wanted to kill him.

They came out of the vicious cloud. Carla didn't know how many times she'd been stung, but her eyes were still okay. "You all right?" she called. "Joe? Trish?"

"I got stung in the face," Joe said, "but I'm okay. So is Trish."

"Hush crying!" she told the little girl. Carla's right eyelid had been hit, and the eye was starting to swell shut. More yellowjackets kept humming around her head, pulling at her hair like little fingers.

"Some of 'em don't like to listen," Toby said. "They do as they please."

"Keep walking. Faster, damn you!"

Someone screamed. Carla looked over her shoulder, saw Miss Nancy running in the opposite direction with a swarm of several hundred yellowjackets enveloping her. The younger woman flailed madly at them, dancing and jerking. She took three more steps and went down, and Carla quickly looked away because she'd seen that the yellowjackets completely covered Miss Nancy's face and head. The screams were muffled. In another moment they ceased.

A figure stumbled toward Carla, clutching at her arm. "Help me . . . help me," Emma moaned. The sockets of her eyes were crawling with yellowjackets. She started to fall, and Carla had no choice but to pull away from her. Emma lay twitching on the ground, feebly crying for help.

"You've gone and done it now, woman!" Winslow was standing untouched in the doorway as the thousands of yellowjackets flew in a storm around him. "Damn, you've done it!"

But Carla and the kids were out of the worst of it. Still, whining currents of yellowjackets followed them. Joe dared to look up, and he could no longer see the sun directly overhead.

They reached the gas station, and Carla said, "Oh, my God!"

The van was a solid mass of yellowjackets, and the gas station's sagging old roof was alive with them.

The pickup truck was still there. Over the whining and humming, Carla heard the sound of the baseball game on TV. "Help us!" she cried. "Please! We need help!"

Toby laughed again.

"Call him! Tell him to come out here! Do it *now!*"

"Mase is watchin' the baseball game, lady. He won't help you."

She shoved him toward the screen door. A few yellowjackets were clinging to the screen, but they took off as Toby approached. "Hey, Mase! Lady wants to see you, Mase!"

"Mom," Joe said, his lips swollen and turning blue. "Mom . . ."

She could see a figure in there, sitting in front of the glowing TV screen. The man wore a cap. "Please help us!" she shouted again.

"Mom . . . listen . . ."

"HELP US!" she screamed, and she kicked the screen door in. It fell from its hinges to the dusty floor.

"Mom . . . when I was in the bathroom . . . and he talked to somebody in here . . . I didn't hear anybody *answer* him."

And then Carla understood why.

A corpse sat before the TV. The man was long dead— many months, at least—and he was nothing but a red clay husk with a grinning, eyeless face.

"GET 'EM, MASE!" the boy wailed, and he tore away from Carla's grip. She struck with the blade, caught him across the throat, but not enough to stop him. He shrieked and jumped like a top gone crazy.

Yellowjackets began streaming from the corpse's eye sockets, the cavity where the nose had been, and the straining, terrible mouth. Carla realized with soul-numbing horror that the yellowjackets had burrowed a nest inside the dead man, and now they were pouring out of him by the thousands. They swarmed toward Carla and her children with relentless fury.

She whirled around, picked up Trish under one arm, and shouted, "Come on!" to Joe. She raced toward the van, where thousands more yellowjackets were stirring, starting to fly up and merge into a yellow-and-black-striped wall.

Carla had no choice but to thrust her hand into the midst of them, digging for the door handle.

They covered her hand in an instant, plunged their stingers deep, as if directed by a single malevolent intelligence. Howling with pain, Carla searched frantically for the handle. The sea of yellowjackets flowed up her forearm, up over her elbow, and toward her shoulder, stinging all the way.

Her fingers closed around the handle. She got the door open as yellowjackets attacked her neck, cheeks, and forehead. Both Trish and Joe were sobbing with pain, but all she could do was to throw them bodily into the van. She grabbed up handfuls of yellowjackets and crushed them between her fingers, then struggled in and slammed the door.

Still, there were dozens of them inside. Enraged, Joe started swatting them with his comic book, took off one sneaker and used that as a weapon too. His face was covered with stings, both eyes badly swollen.

Carla started the engine. Used the windshield wipers to brush a crawling mat of the insects aside. And through the windshield she saw the boy, his arms uplifted, his flame-colored hair now turned yellow and black with the yellow-jackets that clung to his skull, his shirt covered with them, and blood leaking from the gash on the side of his neck.

Carla heard herself roar like a beast. She sank her foot to the floorboard.

The Voyager leapt forward, through the storm of yellow-jackets.

Toby saw, and tried to jump aside. But his twisted, hideous face told Carla that he knew he was a step too late.

The van hit him, knocking him flat. Carla twisted the wheel violently to the right and felt a tire wobble as it crunched over Toby's body. Then she was away from the pumps and speeding through Capshaw with Joe hammering at yellowjackets inside the van.

"We made it!" she shouted, though the voice from her mangled lips did not sound human anymore. "We made it!"

The van streaked on, throwing up plumes of dust behind its tires. The treads of the right-front tire were matted with scarlet.

The odometer rolled off the miles, and through the slit of her left eye Carla kept watching the gas gauge's needle as it vibrated over the E. But she did not let up on the accelerator, taking the van around the sudden curves so fast it threatened to fly off the road into the woods. Joe killed the last of the yellowjackets, and then he sat numbly in the back, holding Trish close.

Finally, pavement returned to the road and they came out of the Georgia pines at a three-way intersection. A sign said HALLIDAY . . . 9. Carla sobbed with relief and shot the van through the intersection at seventy miles an hour.

One mile passed. A second, a third, and a fourth. The Voyager started up a hill—and Carla felt the engine kick.

"Oh . . . God," she whispered. Her hands, clamped to the steering wheel, were inflamed and horribly swollen. "No . . . no . . ."

The engine stuttered, and the van's forward progress began to slow.

"No!" she screamed, throwing herself against the wheel in an effort to keep the van going. But the speedometer's needle was falling fast, and then the stuttering engine went silent.

The van had enough steam left to make the top of the hill, and it rolled to a halt about fifteen feet from the declining side. "Wait here!" Carla said. "Don't move!" She got out, staggered on swollen legs to the rear of the van, and put her weight against it, trying to shove it over the hill. The van resisted her. "Please . . . *please,"* she whispered, and kept pushing.

Slowly, inch by inch, the Voyager started rolling forward. She heard a distant droning noise, and she dared to look back.

About four or five miles away, the sky had turned dark. What resembled a massive yellow-and-black-streaked thundercloud was rolling over the woods, bending the pine trees before it.

Sobbing, Carla looked down the long hill that descended in front of the van. At its bottom was a wide S-curve, and off in the green forest were the roofs of houses and buildings.

The droning noise was approaching, and twilight was falling fast.

She heard the muscles of her shoulder crack as she strained against the van. A shadow fell upon her.

The van rolled closer to the decline; then it started rolling on its own, and Carla hobbled after it, grabbed the open door, and swung herself up into the seat just as it picked up real speed. She gripped the wheel, and she told her children to hang on.

What sounded like hail started pelting the roof.

The van hurtled down the hill as the sun went dark in the middle of yellowjacket summer.

Makeup

Stealing the thing was so *easy*. Calvin Doss had visited the Hollywood Museum of Memories on Beverly Boulevard at three A.M., admitting himself through a side door with a hooked sliver of metal he took from the black leather pouch he kept under his jacket, close to the heart.

He'd roamed the long halls—past the chariots used in *Ben-Hur,* past the tent set from *The Sheik,* past the *Frankenstein* lab mock-up—but he knew exactly where he was going. He'd come there the day before, with the paying tourists. And so in ten minutes after he'd slipped into the place he was standing in the Memorabilia Room, foil stars glittering from the wallpaper wherever the beam of his pencil flashlight touched. Before him were locked glass display cases: one of them was full of wigs on faceless mannequin heads; the next held bottles of perfume used as props in a dozen movies by Lana Turner, Loretta Young, Hedy Lamarr; in the next case there were shelves of paste jewelry, diamonds, rubies, and emeralds blazing like Rodeo Drive merchandise.

And then there was the display case Calvin sought, its shelves holding wooden boxes in a variety of sizes and colors. He moved the flashlight's beam to a lower shelf, and there was the large black box he'd come to take. The lid was open, and within it Calvin could see the trays of tubes, little numbered jars, and what looked like crayons wrapped up in waxed paper. Beside the box there was a small white card with a couple of lines of type: *Makeup case once belonging to Jean Harlow. Purchased from the Harlow estate.*

All right! Calvin thought. That's the ticket. He zipped open his metal pouch, stepped around behind the display case to the lock, and worked for a few minutes to find the proper lock-picker from his ample supply.

Easy.

And now it was almost dawn, and Calvin Doss sat in his small kitchenette apartment off Sunset Boulevard, smoking a joint to relax with and staring at the black box that sat before him on a card table. There was nothing to it, really, Calvin thought. Just a bunch of jars and tubes and crayons, and most of those seemed to be so dry they were crumbling to pieces. Even the box itself wasn't attractive. Junk, as far as Calvin was concerned. How Mr. Marco thought he could push the thing to some L.A. collector was beyond him; now, those fake jewels and wigs he could understand, but this . . . ? No way!

The box was chipped and scarred, showing the bare wood beneath the black lacquer at three of the corners. But the lock was unusual: it was a silver claw, a human hand with long sharp fingernails. It was tarnished with age but seemed to work okay. Mr. Marco would appreciate that, Calvin thought. The makeups themselves looked all dried out, but when Calvin unscrewed some of the numbered jars he caught faint whiffs of strange odors: from one a cold, clammy smell, like graveyard dirt; from another the smell of candle wax and metal; from a third an odor like a swamp teeming with reptilian life. None of the makeups carried brand names or any evidence where they'd been bought or manufactured. Some of the crayons crumbled into pieces when he picked them out of their tray, and he flushed the bits down the toilet so Mr. Marco wouldn't find out he'd been tinkering with them.

Gradually the joint overpowered him. He closed the case's lid, snapped down the silver claw, and went to sleep on his sofabed thinking of Deenie.

He awakened with a start. The harsh afternoon sun was streaming through the dusty blinds. He fumbled for his wristwatch. Oh, God! he thought. Two-forty! He'd been told to call Mr. Marco at nine if the job went okay; panic flared within him as he went out to the pay phone at the end of the hall.

Mr. Marco's secretary answered at the antique shop on Rodeo Drive in Beverly Hills. "Who may I say is calling, please?"

"Tell him Cal. Cal Smith."

"Just a moment, please."

Another phone was picked up. "Marco here."

"It's me, Mr. Marco. Cal Doss. I've got the makeup case, and the whole job went like a dream . . ."

"A dream?" the voice asked softly. There was a quiet murmur of laughter, like water running over dangerous rocks. "Is that what you'd call it, Calvin? If that's the case, your sleep must be terribly uneasy. Have you seen this morning's *Times?*"

"No, sir." Calvin's heart was beating faster. Something had gone wrong; something had been screwed up royally. The noise of his heartbeat seemed to fill the telephone receiver.

"I'm surprised the police haven't visited you already, Calvin. It seems you touched off a concealed alarm when you broke into the display case. Ah. Here's the story, page seven, section two." There was the noise of paper unfolding. "A silent alarm, of course. The police think they arrived at the scene just as you were leaving; one of the officers even thinks he saw your car. A gray Volkswagen with a dented left-rear fender? Does that ring a bell, Calvin?"

"My . . . Volkswagen's light green," Cal said, his throat tightening. "I . . . got the banged fender in the Club Zoom's parking lot . . ."

"Indeed? I suggest you begin packing, my boy. Mexico might be nice at this time of year. If you'll excuse me now, I have other business to attend to. Have a nice trip . . ."

"Wait! Mr. Marco! Please!"

"Yes?" The voice was as cold and hard as a glacier now.

"So I screwed up the job. So what? Anybody can have a bad night, Mr. Marco. I've got the makeup case! I can bring it over to you, you can give me the three G's, and then I can pick up my girl and head down to Mexico for . . . *What is it?*"

Mr. Marco had started chuckling again, that cold mirthless laughter that always sent a chill skittering up Calvin's spine. Calvin could envision him in his black leather chair, the armrests carved into faces of growling lions. His broad, moonlike face would be almost expressionless: the eyes dull and deadly, as black as the business end of a double-barreled shotgun, the mouth slightly crooked to one side, parted lips as red as slices of raw liver. "I'm afraid you don't understand, Calvin," he finally said. "I owe you nothing. It seems that you stole the wrong makeup case . . ."

"*What?*" Calvin said hoarsely.

"It's all in the *Times,* dear boy. Oh, don't blame yourself. *I* don't. It was a mistake made by some hopeless idiot at the museum. Jean Harlow's makeup case was switched with one from the Chamber of Horrors. Her case is ebony with diamonds stitched into a red silk lining, supposedly to signify her love affairs. The one you took belonged to a horror-film actor named Orlon Kronsteen, who was quite famous in the late thirties and forties for his monster makeups. He was murdered . . . oh, ten or eleven years ago, in a Hungarian castle he had rebuilt in the Hollywood hills. Poor devil: I recall his headless body was found dangling from a chandelier. So. Mistakes will happen, won't they? Now, if you'll forgive me . . ."

"Please!" Cal said, desperation almost choking him. "Maybe . . . maybe you can sell this horror guy's makeup case?"

"A possibility. Some of his better films—*Dracula Rises, Revenge of the Wolf, London Screams*—are still dredged up for late-night television. But it would take time to find a collector, Calvin, and that makeup case is very hot indeed. *You're* hot, Calvin, and I suspect you will be cooling off shortly up at the Chino prison."

"I . . . I need that three thousand dollars, Mr. Marco! I've got plans!"

"Do you? As I say, I owe you nothing. But take a word of warning, Calvin: go far away, and keep your lips sealed about my . . . uh . . . activities. I'm sure you're familiar with Mr. Crawley's methods?"

"Yeah," Calvin said. "Yes, sir." His heart and head were pounding in unison. Mr. Crawley was Marco's "enforcer," a six-foot-five skeleton of a man whose eyes blazed with bloodlust whenever he saw Calvin. "But . . . what am I going to *do?*"

"I'm afraid you're a little man, dear boy, and what little men do is not my concern. I'll tell you instead what you aren't going to do. You aren't going to call this office again. You aren't to come here again. You aren't ever going to mention my name as long as you live . . . which, if it were up to Mr. Crawley, who is standing just outside my door at this moment, would be less than the time it takes for you to hang up the phone. Which is precisely what *I* am about to do." There was a last chuckle of cold laughter and the phone went dead.

Calvin stared at the receiver for a moment, hoping it might rewaken. It buzzed at him like a Bronx cheer. Slowly he put it back on its cradle, then walked like a zombie toward his room. He heard sirens, and panic exploded within him, but they were far in the distance and receding. What am I going to do? he thought, his brain ticking like a broken record. *What am I going to do?* He closed and bolted his door and then turned toward the makeup case there on the table.

Its lid was open, and Calvin thought that was odd, because he remembered—or thought he remembered—closing it last night. The silver claw was licked with dusty light. Of all the stupid screwups! he thought, anger welling up inside. Stupid, stupid, stupid! He crossed the room in two strides and lifted the case over his head to smash it to pieces on the floor. Suddenly something seemed to bite his fingers and he howled in pain, dropping the case back onto the table; it overturned, spilling jars and crayons.

There was a red welt across Calvin's fingers where the lid had snapped down like a lobster's claw. It bit me! he thought, backing away from the thing.

The silver claw gleamed, one finger crooked as if in invitation.

"I've got to get rid of you!" Calvin said, startled by the sound of his own voice. "If the cops find you here, I'm up the creek!" He stuffed all the spilled makeups back into it, closed the lid, and tentatively poked at it for a minute before picking it up. Then he carried it along the corridor to the back stairway and down to the narrow alley that ran behind the building. He pushed the black makeup case deep inside a garbage can, underneath an old hat, a few empty bottles of Boone's Farm and a Dunkin Donuts box. Then he returned to the pay phone and, trembling, dialed Deenie's apartment number; there was no answer, so he called the Club Zoom. Mike, the bartender, picked up the phone. "How's it goin', Cal?" In the background the Eagles were on the jukebox, singing about life in the fast lane. "Nope, Cal. Deenie's not comin' in today until six. Sorry. You want to leave a message or something?"

"No," Calvin said. "Thanks anyway." He hung up and returned to his room. Where the hell was Deenie? he wondered. It seemed she was never where she was supposed to be; she never called, never let him know where she was. Hadn't he bought her a nice gold-plated necklace with a couple of diamond specks on it to show her he wasn't mad for stringing along that old guy from Bel-Air? It had cost him plenty, too, and had put him in his current financial mess. He slammed his fist down on the card table and tried to sort things out: somehow he had to get some money. He could hock his radio and maybe collect an old pool-hall debt from Corky McClinton, but that would hardly be enough to carry him and Deenie for very long in Mexico. He had to have that three thousand dollars from Mr. Marco! But what about Crawley? That killer would shave his eyebrows with a .45!

What to do, what to do?

First, Calvin reasoned, a drink to calm my nerves. He opened a cupboard and brought out a bottle of Jim Beam and a glass. His fingers were shaking so much he couldn't pour, so he shoved the glass aside and swigged out of the bottle. It burned like hellfire going down. Damn that makeup case! he thought, and took another drink. Damn Mr. Marco: another drink. Damn Crawley. Damn Deenie. Damn the idiot who switched those lousy makeup cases. Damn me for even taking on this screwy job . . .

After he'd finished damning his second and third cousins who lived in Arizona, Calvin stretched out on the sofabed and slept.

He came awake with a single terrifying thought: *The cops are here!* But they weren't, there was no one else in the room, everything was okay. His head was throbbing, and through the small, smog-filmed windows the light was graying into night. What'd I do? he thought. Sleep away the whole day? He reached over toward the Jim Beam bottle, there on the card table beside the makeup case, and saw that there was about a half-swallow left in it. He tipped it to his mouth and drank it down, adding to the turmoil in his belly.

When his fogged gaze finally came to rest on the makeup case, he dropped the bottle to the floor.

Its lid was wide open, the silver claw cupping blue shadows.

"What are you doin' here?" he said, his speech slurred. "I got rid of you! Didn't I?" He was trying to think: he seemed to remember taking that thing to the garbage can, but then again, it might've been a dream. "You're a jinx, that's what you are!" he shouted. He struggled up, staggered out into the hallway to the pay phone again, and dialed the antique shop.

A low, cold voice answered: "Marco Antiques and Curios."

Calvin shuddered; it was Crawley. "This is Calvin Doss," he said, summoning up his courage. "Doss. Doss. Let me speak to Mr. Marco."

"Mr. Marco doesn't want to speak to you."

"Listen, I need my three thousand bucks!"

"Mr. Marco is working tonight, Doss. Stop tying up the phone."

"I just . . . I just want what's comin' to me!"

"Oh? Then maybe I can help you, you little punk. How's about two or three forty-five slugs to rattle around in your brain-pan? I dare you to set foot over here!" The phone went dead before Calvin could say another word.

He put his head in his hands. Little punk. Little man. Little jerk. It seemed someone had been calling him those names all his life, from his mother to the juvenile-home creeps to the L.A. cops. I'm not a little punk! he thought. Someday I'll show them all! He stumbled to his room, slamming his shoulder against a wall in the process, and had to turn on the lights before darkness totally filled the place.

And now he saw that the black makeup case had crept closer to the table's edge.

He stared at it, transfixed by that silver claw. "There's something funny about you," he said softly. "Something reeeeallll funny. I put you in the garbage! Didn't I?" And now, as he watched it, the claw's forefinger seemed to . . . move. To bend. To beckon. Calvin rubbed his eyes. It hadn't moved, not really! Or had it? Yes! No. Yes! No . . .

Had it?

Calvin touched it, then whimpered and drew his hand away. Something had shivered up his arm, like a faint charge of electricity. *"What are you?"* he whispered. He reached out to close the lid, and this time the claw seemed to clutch at his hand, to pull it down into the box itself. He shouted *"Hey!"* and when he pulled his hand back he saw he was gripping one of the jars of makeup, identified by the single number 9.

The lid dropped.

Calvin jumped. The claw had latched itself into place. For a long time he looked at the jar in his hand, then slowly—very slowly—unscrewed the top. It was a grayish-looking stuff, like greasepaint, with the distinct odors of . . . What was it? he thought. Yes. Blood. That and a cold, mossy smell. He dabbed in a finger and rubbed it into the palm of his hand. It tingled, and seemed to be so cold it was hot. He smeared his hands with the stuff. The feeling wasn't unpleasant. No, Calvin decided; it was far from unpleasant. The feeling was of . . . power. Of invincibility. Of wanting to throw himself into the arms of the night, to fly with the clouds as they swept across the moon's grinning face. Feels good, he thought, and smeared some of the stuff on his face. God, if Deenie could only see me now! He began to smile. His face felt funny, filmed with the cold stuff, but different, as if the bone structure had sharpened. His mouth and jaws felt different too.

I want my three thousand dollars from Mr. Marco, he told himself. And I'm going to get it. Yessssssss. I'm going to get it right now.

After a while he pushed aside the empty jar and turned toward the door, his muscles vibrating with power. He felt as old as time, but filled with incredible, wonderful, ageless youth. He moved like an uncoiling serpent to the door, then into the hallway. Now it was time to collect the debt.

He drifted like a haze of smoke through the darkness and slipped into his Volkswagen. He drove through Hollywood, noting the white sickle moon rising over the Capitol Records building, and into Beverly Hills. At a traffic light he could sense someone staring at him from the car beside his; he turned his head slightly, and the young woman at the wheel of her Mercedes froze, terror stitched across her face. When the light changed, he drove on, leaving the Mercedes sitting still.

Yessssss. It was definitely time to collect the debt.

He pulled his car to the curb on Rodeo Drive, two shops down from the royal-blue-and-gold canopy with the lettering MARCO ANTIQUES AND CURIOS. Most of the expensive shops were closed, and there were only a few window-shoppers on the sidewalks. Calvin walked toward the antique shop. Of course the door was locked, a blind pulled down, and a sign that read SORRY WE'RE CLOSED. I should've brought my tool kit! he told himself. But no matter. Tonight he could do magic; tonight there were no impossibilities. He imagined what he wanted to do; then he exhaled and slipped through the doorjamb like a gray, wet mist. Doing it scared the hell out of him, and caused one window-shopper to clutch at his heart and fall like a redwood to the pavement.

Calvin stood in a beige-carpeted display room filled with gleaming antiques: a polished rosewood piano once owned by Rudolph Valentino, a brass bed from the Pickford estate, a lamp with bulbs shaped like roses that had once belonged to Vivien Leigh. Objects of silver, brass, and gold were spotlit by track lights at the ceiling. Calvin could hear Mr. Marco's voice from the rear of the shop, through a door that led back into a short hallway and Marco's office. ". . . that's all well and good, Mr. Frazier," he was saying. "I hear what you're telling me, but I'm not listening. I have a buyer for that item, and if I want to sell it I must make delivery tomorrow afternoon at the latest." There was a few seconds' pause. "Correct, Mr. Frazier. It's not my concern how your people get the Flynn diary. But I'll expect it to be on my desk at two o'clock tomorrow afternoon, is that understood? . . ."

Calvin began to smile. He moved across the room as silently as smoke, entered the hallway, and approached the closed door to Marco's office.

He was about to turn the doorknob when he heard Marco put down his telephone. "Now, Mr. Crawley," Marco said. "Where were we? Ah, yes; the matter of Calvin Doss. I very much fear that we cannot trust the man to remain silent in the face of adversity. You know where he lives, Mr. Crawley. I'll have your payment ready for you when you return . . ."

Calvin reached forward, gripped the doorknob, and wrenched at it. He was amazed and quite pleased when the entire door was ripped from its hinges.

Marco, his three hundred pounds wedged into the chair with the lion faces on the armrests behind a massive mahogany desk, gave out a startled squawk, his black eyes almost popping from his head. Crawley had been sitting in a corner holding a *Hustler* magazine, and now the towering height of him came up like a released spring, his eyes glittering like cold diamonds beneath thick black brows.

Crawley's hand went up under his checked sport coat, but Calvin froze him with a single glance.

Marco's face was the color of spoiled cheese. "Who . . . who are you?" he said, his voice trembling. "What do you want?"

"Don't you recognize me?" Calvin asked, his voice as smooth and dark as black velvet. "I'm Calvin Doss, Mr. Marco."

"Cal . . . vin . . . ?" A thread of saliva broke over Marco's double chins and fell onto the lapel of his charcoal-gray Brooks Brothers suit. "No! It can't be!"

"But it is." Calvin grinned and felt his fangs protrude. "I've come for my restitution, Mr. Marco."

"Kill him!" Marco shrieked to Crawley. "Kill him!"

Crawley was still dazed, but he instinctively pulled the automatic from the holster beneath his coat and stuck it into Calvin's ribs. Calvin had no time to leap aside; Crawley's finger was already twitching on the trigger. In the next instant the gun barked twice, and Calvin felt a distant sensation of heat that just as quickly faded. Behind him, through the haze of blue smoke, there were two bullet holes in the wall. Calvin couldn't exactly understand why his stomach wasn't torn open right now, but this was indeed a night of miracles; he grasped the man's collar and with one hand flung him like a scarecrow across the room. Crawley screamed and slammed into the opposite wall, collapsing to the floor in a tangle of arms and legs. He skittered past Calvin like a frantic crab and ran away along the corridor.

"Crawley!" Marco shouted, trying to get out of his chair. "Don't leave me!"

Calvin shoved the desk forward as effortlessly as if it were the matter of dreams, pinning the bulbous Marco in his chair. Marco began to whimper, his eyes floating in wet sockets. Calvin was grinning like a death's-head. "And now," he whispered, "it is time for you to pay." He reached out and grasped the man's tie, slowly tightening it until Marco's face looked like a bloated red balloon. Then Calvin leaned forward, very gracefully, and plunged his fangs into the throbbing jugular vein. A fountain of blood gushed, dripping from the corners of Calvin's mouth. In another few moments Marco's corpse, which seemed to have lost about seventy-five pounds, slumped down in its chair, its shoulders squashed together and the arms up as if in total surrender.

Calvin stared at the body for a moment, a wave of nausea suddenly rising from the pit of his stomach. He felt light-headed, out of control, lost in a larger shadow. He turned and struggled out to the hallway, where he bent over and retched. Nothing came up, but the taste of blood in his mouth made him wish he had a bar of soap. *What have I done?* he thought, leaning against a wall. Sweat was dripping down his face, plastering his shirt to his back. He looked down at his side, to where there were two holes in his shirt, ringed with powder burns. That should've killed me, he realized. Why didn't it? How did I get in here? Why did I . . . kill Mr. Marco like that? He spat once, then again and again; the taste of blood was maddening. He probed at his gums with a finger. His teeth were all normal now; everything was back to normal.

What did that makeup case turn me into? He wiped the sweat from his face with a handkerchief and stepped back into the office. Yep. Mr. Marco was still dead. The two bullet holes were still in the wall. Calvin wondered where Marco kept his money. Since he was dead, he figured, he wouldn't need it anymore. Right? Calvin leaned over the desk, avoiding the fixed stare from the corpse's eyes, and started going through the drawers. In a lower one, beneath all kinds of papers and other junk, was a white envelope with the name CRAWLEY printed on it. Calvin looked inside. His heart leapt. There was at least five thousand dollars in there; probably the dough Crawley was going to be paid for my murder, Calvin thought. He took the money and ran.

Fifteen minutes later he was pulling into the parking lot beside the Club Zoom. In the red neon-veined light he counted the money, trembling with joy. Fifty-five hundred bucks! It was more money than he had ever seen in his whole life.

He desperately needed some beer to wash away the taste of blood. Deenie would be dancing in there by now, too. He put the money in a back pocket and hurried across the parking lot into the Club Zoom. Inside, strobe lights flashed like crazy lightening. A jukebox thundered from somewhere in the darkness, its bass beat kicking at Calvin's unsettled stomach. A few men sat at the bar or at a scattering of tables, drinking beer and watching the girl onstage who gyrated her hips in a disinterested circle. Calvin climbed onto a bar stool. "Hey, Mike! Gimme a beer! Deenie here yet?"

"Yeah. She's in the back." Mike shoved a mug of beer in front of him and then frowned. "You okay, Cal? You look like you saw a ghost or something."

"I'm fine. Or will be, as soon as I finish this off." He drank most of it in one swallow, swishing it around in his mouth. "That's better."

"What's better, Cal?"

"Nothing. Forget it. Jeez, it's cold in here!"

"You sure you're okay?" Mike asked, looking genuinely concerned. "It must be eighty degrees in here. The air conditioner broke again this afternoon."

"Don't worry about me. I'm just fine. Soon as I see my girl I'll be even better."

"Uh-huh," Mike said quietly. He cleaned up a few splatters of beer from the bar with a rag. "I hear you bought Deenie a present last week. A gold chain. Put you back much?"

"About a hundred bucks. It's worth it, though, just to see that pretty smile. I'm going to ask her to go down to Mexico with me for a few days."

"Uh-huh," Mike said again. Now he was cleaning up imaginary splatters, and finally he looked Calvin straight in the eyes. "You're a good guy, Cal. You never cause any trouble in here, and I can tell you're okay. I just . . . well, I hate to see you get what's coming."

"Huh? What do you mean by that?"

Mike shrugged. "How long have you known Deenie, Cal? A few weeks? Girls like her come and go, man. Here one day, gone the next. Sure she's good-looking; they all are, and they trade on their looks like their bodies are Malibu beachfront properties. You get my drift?"

"No."

"Okay. This is man-to-man. Friend-to-friend, right? Deenie's a taker, Cal. She'll bleed you dry, and then she'll kick you out with the garbage. She's got about five or six guys on the string."

Calvin blinked, his stomach roiling again. "You're . . . you're lying!"

"God's truth. Deenie's playing you, Cal; reeling you in and out like a fish with a hooked gut—"

"You're lying!" Calvin's face flushed; he rose from his seat and leaned over toward the bartender. "You've got no right saying those things! They're lies! You probably want me to give her up so you can have her! Fat chance! I'm going back to see her right now, and you'd better not try to stop me!" He started to move away from the bar, his brain spinning like a top.

"Cal," Mike said softly, his voice tinged with pity, "Deenie's not alone."

But Calvin was already going back behind the stage, through a black curtain to the dressing rooms. Deenie's room was the third door, and as Calvin was about to knock, he heard the deep roll of a man's laughter. He froze, his hand balled into a fist.

"A diamond ring?" the man said. "You're kidding!"

"Honest to God, Max!" Deenie's voice, warmer than Calvin had ever heard it. "This old guy gave me a diamond ring last week! I think he used to work for NBC or ABC or one of those C's. Anyway, he's all washed-up now. Do you know what he wears in bed? Socks with garters! Ha! He said he wanted me to marry him. He must've been serious because that ring brought six hundred bucks at the pawnshop!"

"Oh, yeah? Then where's my share?"

"Later, baby, later. I'll meet you at your place after work, okay? We can do the shower thing and rub each other's backs, huh . . . ?"

There was a long silence in which Calvin could hear his teeth grinding together.

"Sure, babe," Max said finally. "You want to use the black one or the red one tonight?"

Calvin almost slammed his fist through the door. But instead he turned and ran, a volcano about to erupt in his brain; he ran past the bar, past Mike, out the door to his car. I thought she loved me! he raged as he screeched out of the parking lot. She *lied!* She played me for a sucker all the way! He floored the accelerator, gripping the wheel with white-knuckled hands.

By the time he locked himself in his apartment, turned his transistor radio up loud, and flopped down on his sofabed, the volcano had exploded, filling his veins with the seething magma of revenge. *Revenge:* now, there's a sweet word, he thought. It was Satan's battle cry, and now seemed branded into Calvin's heart. How to do it? he wondered. How? How? *Why am I always the little punk?*

He turned his head slightly and gazed at the black makeup case.

It was open again, the silver claw beckoning him.

"You're a jinx!" he screamed at it. But he knew now that it was more. Much, much more. It was weird, evil maybe, but there was power in those little jars: power and perhaps also revenge. *No!* he told himself. No, I won't use it! What kind of nutcake am I turning into, to think that makeup could bring me what I want? He stared at the case, his eyes widening. It was unholy, terrible, something from Lucifer's magic shop. He was aware of the roll of money in his back pocket, and aware also of the bullet holes in his shirt. Unholy or not, he thought, it can give me what I want.

Calvin reached into the makeup case and chose a jar at random. It was numbered 13, and when he sniffed at the cream he found it smelled of dirty brick, rain-slick streets, whale-oil lamps. He dabbed his finger into the reddish-brown goop and stared at it for a moment, the odors making him feel giddy and . . . yes, quite mad.

He smeared it across his cheeks and worked it into the

flesh. His eyes began to gleam with maniacal determination. He scooped out more of it, rubbing it into his face, his hands, his neck. It burned like mad passion.

The lid fell. The claw clicked into place.

Calvin smiled and stood up, stepping to a kitchen drawer. He opened it and withdrew a keen-bladed butcher knife. Now, he thought. Now, me Miss Deenie Roundheels, it's time you got your just desserts, wot? Can't have ladies like you runnin' about in the streets, prancin' and hawkin' your sweet goods to the highest bidder, can we, luv? No, not if I've got a bit to say about it!

And so he hurried out of the apartment and down to his car, a man on an urgent mission of love's revenge.

He waited in the shadows behind the Club Zoom until Deenie came out just after two o'clock. She was alone, and he was glad of that because he had no quarrel with Max; it was the woman—it was Woman—who had betrayed him. She was a beautiful girl with long blond hair, sparkling blue eyes, a sensual pout in a lovely oval face. Tonight she was wearing a green dress, slit to show silky thighs. A sinner's gown, he thought as he watched her slink across the parking lot.

Stepping out of the darkness, he held the knife behind him like a gleaming gift he wanted to surprise her with. "Deenie?" he whispered, smiling. "Deenie, luv?"

She whirled around. "Who's there?"

Calvin stood between darkness and the red swirl of neon. His eyes glittered like pools of blood. "It's your own true love, Deenie," he said. "Your love come to take you to Paradise."

"Calvin?" she whispered, taking a backward step. "What are you doing here? Why . . . does your face look like that?"

"I've brought something for you, luv," he said softly. "Step over here and I'll give it to you. Come on, dearie, don't be shy."

"What's wrong with you, Calvin? You're scaring me."

"Scaring you? Why, whatever for? I'm your own dear Cal, come to kiss you good night. And I've brought a pretty for you. Something nice and bright. Come see."

She hesitated, glancing toward the deserted boulevard.

"Come on," Calvin said. "It'll be the sweetest gift any man ever gave you."

A confused, uncertain smile rippled across her face. "What'd you bring me, Calvin? Huh? Another necklace? Let's see it!"

"I'm holding it behind my back. Come here, luv. Come see."

Deenie stepped forward reluctantly, her eyes as bright as a frightened doe's. When she reached Calvin she held out her hand. "This had better be good, Cal . . ."

Calvin grasped her wrist and yanked her forward. When her head rocked back, he ripped the blade across her offered throat. She staggered and started to fall, but before she did, Calvin dragged her behind the Club Zoom so he could take his own sweet time. When he was finished, he looked down at the cooling corpse and wished he had a pencil and paper to leave a note. He knew what it would say: You Have to be Smart To catch Me. Smart like a Fox. Yours from the Depths of Hell, Cal the Ripper.

He wiped the blade on her body, got in his car, and drove to Hancock Park, where he threw the murder weapon in the LaBrea tarpits. Then a weak, sick feeling overcame him and he sank down into the grass, clutching his knees up close to his body. He was racked with shudders when he realized there was blood all over the front of his shirt. He pulled up handfuls of grass and tried to wipe most of it away. Then he lay back on the ground, his temples throbbing, and tried to think past the pain.

Oh, God! he thought. What kind of a makeup case have I gotten my hands onto? Who made the box? Who conjured up those jars and tubes and crayons? It was magic, yes: but evil magic, magic gone bad and ugly. Calvin remembered Mr. Marco saying it had belonged to a horror-flick actor named Kronsteen, and that Kronsteen was famous for his monster makeups. Calvin was chilled by a sudden terrible thought: how much was makeup and how much was real? Half and half, maybe? When you put on the makeup, the . . . essence of the monster gripped into you like some kind of hungry leech? And then, when it had fed, when it had gorged itself on evil and blood, it loosened its hold on you and fell away? Back there in Marco's office, Calvin thought, I was really part vampire. And then, in the Club Zoom's parking lot, I was part Jack the Ripper. In those jars, he thought, are not just makeups; in those creams and greasepaints there are real monsters, waiting to be awakened by my desires, my passions, my . . . evil.

I've got to get rid of it, he decided. I've got to throw it out before it destroys me! He rose to his feet and ran across the park to his car.

The hallway on his floor was as dark as a werewolf's dreams at midnight. What happened to the damned light bulbs? Calvin thought as he felt his way toward his door. Weren't they burning when I left?

And then a floorboard creaked very softly, down at the hallway's end.

Calvin turned and stared into the darkness, one hand fumbling with his key. He thought he could make out a vague shape standing over there, but he wasn't sure. His heart whacked against his rib cage as he slid the key home.

And he knew it was Crawley a split second before he saw the orange flare from the .45's muzzle. The bullet hit the doorjamb, pricking his face with wood splinters. He shouted in terror, twisted the doorknob, and threw himself into the room. As he slammed the door shut and locked it, another bullet came screaming through the wood, about an inch from the left side of his skull. He spun away from the door, trying to press himself into the wall.

"Where's that five thousand bucks, Doss!" Crawley shouted from the hallway. "It's mine! Give it to me or I'll kill you, you little punk!" A third bullet punched through the center of the door, leaving a hole as big as a fist. Then Crawley began to kick at the door, making it shudder on its aged hinges. Now there were screams and shouts from all over the building, but the door was about to crash in, and soon Crawley would be inside to deliver those two .45 slugs as promised.

Calvin heard a faint *click*.

He whirled around. The silver claw had unlatched itself; the makeup case stood open. He was shaking like a leaf in a hurricane.

The door cracked and whined, protesting the blows from Crawley's shoulder.

Calvin watched it bend inward, almost to the breaking point. Another shot was fired, the bullet shattering a window across the room. He turned and looked fearfully at the makeup case again. It can save me, he thought; that's what I want, and that's what it can do . . .

"I'm gonna blow out your brains when I get in there, Doss!" Crawley roared.

And then Calvin was across the room; he grabbed a jar numbered 15. The thing practically unscrewed itself, and he could smell the mossy, mountain-forest odor of the stuff. He plunged a forefinger into it, hearing the door begin to split down the middle.

"I'm gonna kill you, Doss!" Crawley said, and with his next kick the door burst open.

Calvin whirled to face his attacker, who froze in absolute terror. As Calvin leapt, he howled in animal rage, his claws striping red lines across Crawley's face. They fell to the floor, Calvin's teeth gnashing at the unprotected throat of his prey. He bent over Crawley's remains on all fours, teeth and claws ripping away flesh to the bone. Then he lifted his head and howled with victory. Beneath him Crawley's body twitched and writhed.

Calvin fell back, breathing hard. Crawley looked like something that had gone through a meat grinder, and now his twitching arms and legs were beginning to stiffen. The building was full of racket, screaming and shouting from the lower floors. He could hear a police siren, fast approaching, but he wasn't afraid; he wasn't afraid at all.

He stood up, stepped over a spreading pool of blood, and peered down into Orlon Kronsteen's makeup case. In there was power. In there were a hundred disguises, a hundred masks. With this thing, he would never be called a little punk again. It would be so easy to hide from the cops. So easy. If he desired, it would be done. He picked up a jar numbered 19. When he unscrewed it he sniffed at the white, almost clear greasepaint and realized it smelled of . . . nothing. He smeared it over his hands and face. Hide me, he thought. Hide me. The siren stopped, right outside the building. Hurry! Calvin commanded whatever force ruled the contents of this box. Make me . . . disappear!

The lid fell.

The silver claw clicked into place with a noise like a whisper.

The two LAPD cops, Ortega and Mullinax, had never seen a man as ripped apart as the corpse that lay on the apartment's floor. Ortega bent over the body, his face wrinkled with nausea. "This guy's long gone," he said. "Better call for the morgue wagon."

"What's this?" Mullinax said, avoiding the shimmering pool of blood that had seeped from the slashed stiff. He unlatched a black box that was sitting on a card table and lifted the lid. "Looks like . . . theatrical makeup," he said quietly. "Hey, Luis! This thing fits the description of what was stolen from the Memory Museum last night!"

"Huh?" Ortega came over to have a look. "Christ, Phil! It is! That stuff belonged to Orlon Kronsteen. Remember him?"

"Nope. Where'd that landlady get off to?"

"I think she's still throwing up," Ortega said. He picked up an open jar and smelled the contents, then dropped it back into the case. "I must've seen every horror flick Kronsteen ever starred in." He looked uneasily at the corpse and shivered. "As a matter of fact, amigo, that poor fella looks like what was left of one of Kronsteen's victims in *Revenge of the Wolf*. What could tear a man up like that, Phil?"

"I don't know. And don't try putting the scare in me, either." He turned his head and stared at something else on the floor, over beyond the unmade sofabed. "My God," he said softly. "Look at that!" He stepped forward a few paces and then stopped, his eyes narrowing. "Luis, did you hear something?"

"Huh? No. What is it over there? Clothes?"

"Yeah." Mullinax bent down, his brow furrowing. Spread out before him, still bearing a man's shape, were a shirt, a pair of pants, and shoes. The shoelaces were still tied, the socks in the shoes; the belt and zipper were still fastened as well. Mullinax untucked the shirttail, noting the bloodstains on it and what looked like two cigarette burns, and saw a pair of underwear still in place in the pants. "That's funny," he said. "That's damned funny . . ."

Ortega's eyes were as wide as saucers. "Yeah. Funny. Like that flick Kronsteen did, *The Invisible Man Returns*. He left his clothes just like that when he . . . uh . . . vanished. . . ."

"I think we're going to need some help on this one," Mullinax said, and stood up. His face had turned a pasty gray color, and now he looked past Ortega to the rotund woman in a robe and curlers who stood in the doorway. She stared down at the shredded corpse with dreadful fascination. "Mrs. Johnston?" Mullinax said. "Whose apartment did you say this belonged to?"

"Cal . . . Cal . . . Calvin Doss," she stammered. "He never pays his rent on time."

"You're sure this isn't him on the floor?"

"Yes. He's . . . a little man. Stands about under my chin. Oh, I think my stomach's going to blow up!" She staggered away, her house shoes dragging.

"Man, what a mess!" Ortega shook his head. "Those empty clothes . . . that's straight out of *The Invisible Man Returns*, I'm telling you!"

"Yeah. Well, I guess we can send this thing back to where it belongs." Mullinax tapped his finger on the black makeup case. "You say a horror actor owned it?"

"Sure did. A long time ago. Now I guess all that stuff is junk, huh." He smiled faintly. "The stuff dreams are made of, right? I saw most of that guy's flicks twice, when I was a kid. Like the one about the Invisible Man. And there was another one he did that was really something too, called . . . let's see . . . *The Man Who Shrank*. Now, *that* was a classic."

"I don't know so much about horror films," Mullinax

said. He ran a finger over the silver claw. "They give me the creeps. Why don't you stay up here with our dead friend and I'll radio for the morgue wagon, okay?" He took a couple of steps forward and then stopped. Something was odd. He leaned against the shattered doorjamb and looked at the sole of his shoe. "Ugh!" he said. "What'd I step on?"

Doom City

He awakened with the memory of thunder in his bones.

The house was quiet. The alarm clock hadn't gone off. Late for work! he realized, struck by a bolt of desperate terror. But no, no . . . wait a minute; he blinked the fog from his eyes and his mind gradually cleared too. He could still taste the onions in last night's meatloaf. Friday night was meatloaf night. Today was Saturday. No office work today, thank God. Ah, he thought, settle down . . . settle down . . .

Lord, what a nightmare he'd had! It was fading now, all jumbled up and incoherent but leaving its weird essence behind like a snakeskin. There'd been a thunderstorm last night—Brad was sure of that, because he'd awakened to see the garish white flash of it and to hear the gut-wrenching growl of a real boomer pounding at the bedroom wall. But whatever the nightmare had been, he couldn't recall now; he felt dizzy and disoriented, like he'd just stepped off a carnival ride gone crazy. He did recall that he'd sat up and seen that lightning, so bright it had made his eyes buzz blue in the dark. And he remembered Sarah saying something too, but now he didn't know what it was. . . .

Damn, he thought as he stared across the bedroom at the window that looked down on Baylor Street. Damn, that light looks strange. Not like June at all. More like a white winter light. Ghostly. Kind of made his eyes hurt a little.

Brad got out of bed and walked across the room. He pushed aside the white curtain and peered out, squinting.

What appeared to be a gray, faintly luminous fog hung in the trees and over the roofs of the houses on Baylor Street. It looked like the color had been sucked out of everything, and the fog lay motionless for as far as he could see up and down the street. He looked up, trying to find the sun. It was up there somewhere, burning like a dim bulb behind dirty cotton. Thunder rumbled in the distance, and Brad Forbes said, "Sarah? Honey? Take a look at this."

She didn't reply, nor did she stir. He glanced at her, saw the wave of her brown hair above the sheet that was pulled up over her like a shroud. "Sarah?" he said again, and took a step toward the bed.

And suddenly Brad remembered what she'd said last night, when he'd sat up in a sleepy daze to watch the lightning crackle.

I'm cold, I'm cold.

He grasped the edge of the sheet and pulled it back.

A skeleton with tendrils of brittle brown hair attached to its skull lay where his wife had been sleeping last night.

The skeleton was wearing Sarah's pale blue nightgown, and what looked like dried-up pieces of tree bark—skin, he realized, yes . . . her . . . skin—lay all around, on and between the white bones. The teeth grinned, and from the bed there was the bittersweet odor of a damp graveyard.

"Oh . . ." he whispered, and he stood staring down at what was left of his wife as his eyes began to bulge from their sockets and a pressure like his brain was about to explode grew in his head and blood trickled down from his lower lip where his teeth had pierced.

I'm cold, she'd said, in a voice that had sounded like a whimper of pain. *I'm cold.*

And then Brad heard himself moan, and he let go of the sheet and staggered back across the room, tripped over a pair of his tennis shoes, and went down hard on the floor. The sheet settled back over the skeleton like a sigh.

Thunder rumbled outside, muffled by the fog. Brad stared at one skeletal foot that protruded from the lower end of the sheet, and he saw flakes of dried, dead flesh float down from it to the Sears deep-pile aqua-blue carpet.

He didn't know how long he sat there just staring. He thought he might have giggled, or sobbed, or made some combination of both. He almost threw up, and he wanted to curl up into a ball and go back to sleep again; he did close his eyes for a few seconds, but when he opened them again the skeleton of his wife was still lying in the bed and the sound of thunder was nearer.

And he might have sat there until doomsday if the telephone beside the bed hadn't started ringing.

Somehow, he was up and had the receiver in his hand. Tried not to look down at the brown-haired skull and remember how beautiful his wife—just twenty-eight years old, for God's sake!—had been.

"Hello," he said in a dead voice.

There was no reply. Brad could hear circuits clicking and humming deep in the wires.

"Hello?"

No answer. Except now there might have been—*might* have been—a soft, silken breathing.

"Hello?" Brad shrieked into the phone. "Say something, damn you!"

Another series of clicks; then a tinny, disembodied voice: "We're sorry, but we cannot place your call at this time. All lines are busy. Please hang up and try again later. Thank you. This is a recording . . ."

He slammed the receiver back into its cradle, and the motion of the air made flakes of skin fly from the skull's cheekbones.

Brad ran out of the bedroom, barefoot and in only his pajama bottoms; he ran to the stairs, went down them screaming, "Help! Help me! Somebody!" He missed a step, slammed against the wall, and caught the banister before he broke his neck. Still screaming for help, he burst through the front door and out into the yard, where his feet crunched on dead leaves.

He stopped. The sound of his voice went echoing down Baylor Street. The air was still and wet, thick and stifling. He stared down at all the dead leaves around him, covering brown grass that had been green the day before. And then the wind suddenly moved, and more dead leaves swirled around him; he looked up, and saw bare gray branches where living oak trees had stood before he'd closed his eyes to sleep last night.

"Help me!" he screamed. *"Somebody please help me!"*

But there was no answer; not from the house where the Pates lived, not from the Walkers' house, not from the Crawfords' or the Lehmans'. Nothing human moved on Baylor Street, and as he stood amid the falling leaves on the seventh day of June, he felt something fall into his hair. He reached up, plucked it out, and looked at what he held in his hand.

The skeleton of a bird, with a few colorless feathers sticking to the bones.

He shook it from his hand and frantically wiped his palm on his pajamas—and then he heard the telephone ringing again in his house.

He ran to the downstairs phone, back in the kitchen, picked up the receiver, and said, "Help me! Please . . . I'm on Baylor Street! Please help—"

He stopped babbling, because he heard the clicking circuits and a sound like searching wind, and down deep inside the wires there might have been a silken breathing.

He was silent too, and the silence stretched. Finally he could stand it no longer. "Who is this?" he asked in a strained whisper. "Who's on this phone?"

Click. Buzzzzzz . . .

Brad punched the O. Almost at once that same terrible voice came on the line: "We're sorry, but we cannot place your call at—" He smashed his fist down on the phone's two prongs, dialed 911. "We're sorry, but we cannot—" His fist went down again; he dialed the number of the Pates next door, screwed up, and started twice more. "We're sorry, but—" His fingers went down on about five numbers at once. "We're sorry—"

He screamed and wrenched the telephone from the wall,

threw it across the kitchen, and it broke the window over the sink. Dead leaves began to drift in, and through the glass panes of the back door Brad saw something lying out in the fenced-in backyard. He went out there, his heart pounding and cold sweat beading on his face and chest.

Lying amid dead leaves, very close to its doghouse, was the skeleton of their collie, Socks. The dog looked as if it might have been stripped to the bone in mid-stride, and hunks of hair lay about the bones like snow.

In the roaring silence, Brad heard the upstairs phone begin to ring.

He ran.

Away from the house this time. Out through the backyard gate, up onto the Pates' front porch. He hammered at the door, hollering for help until his voice was about to give out. Then he smashed a glass pane of the door with his fist and, heedless of the pain and blood, reached in and unsnapped the lock.

With his first step into the house, he smelled the graveyard reek. Like something had died a long time ago, and been mummified.

He found the skeletons in the master bedroom upstairs; they were clinging to each other. A third skeleton—Davy Pate, once a tow-headed twelve-year-old boy—lay on the bed in the room with posters of Prince and Quiet Riot tacked to the walls. In a fish tank on the far side of the room there were little bones lying in the red gravel on the bottom.

It was clear to him then. Yes, very clear. He knew what had happened, and he almost sank to his knees in Davy Pate's mausoleum.

Death had come in the night. And stripped bare everyone and everything but him.

But if that were so . . . then who—or *what*—had dialed the telephone? What had been listening on the other end? What . . . oh, dear God, what?

He didn't know, but he suddenly realized that he'd told whatever it was that he was still on Baylor Street. And maybe Death had missed him last night; maybe its scythe had cleaved everyone else and missed him, and now . . . and now it knew he was still on Baylor Street, and it would be coming after him.

Brad fled the house, ran through the dead leaves that clogged the gutters of Baylor Street, and headed east toward the center of town. The wind moved again, sluggishly and heavily; the wet fog shifted, and Brad could see that the sky had turned the color of blood. Thunder boomed behind him like approaching footsteps, and tears of terror streamed down Brad's cheeks.

I'm cold, Sarah had whispered. *I'm cold.* And that was when the finger of Death had touched her, had missed Brad and gone roaming through the night. *I'm cold,* she'd said, and there would never be any warming her again.

He came to two cars smashed together in the street. Skeletons in clothes lay behind the steering wheels. Further on, the bones of a large dog were almost covered by leaves. Above him, the trees creaked and moaned as the wind picked up, ripping holes in the fog and showing the bloody sky through them.

It's the end of the world, he thought. Judgment Day. All the sinners and saints alike turned to bones overnight. Just me left alive. Just me, and Death knows I'm on Baylor Street.

Mommy!"

The sobbing voice of a child pierced him, and he stopped in his tracks, skidding on leaves.

"Mommy!" the voice repeated, echoing and warped by the low-lying fog. "Daddy! Somebody . . . help me!"

It was the voice of a little girl crying somewhere nearby. Brad listened, trying to peg its direction. First he thought it was to the left, then to the right. In front of him, behind him . . . he couldn't be sure. "I'm here!" he shouted. "Where are you?"

The child didn't answer, but Brad could still hear her crying. "I'm not going to hurt you!" he called. "I'm standing right in the middle of the street! Come to me if you can!"

He waited. A flurry of brown, already-decaying leaves fell from overhead—and then he saw the figure of the little girl, hesitantly approaching him through the fog on his right. She had blond hair done up in pigtails with pale blue ribbons, and her pallid face was streaked with tears and distorted by terror; she was maybe five or six years old, wearing pink pajamas and clasping a Smurf doll tightly in her arms. She stopped about fifteen feet away from him, her eyes red and swollen and maybe insane too.

"Daddy?" she whispered.

"Where'd you come from?" he asked, still shocked at hearing another voice and seeing someone else alive on this last day of the world. "What house?"

"Our house," she answered, her lower lip trembling. Her face looked like it was about to collapse. "Over there." She pointed through the fog at a shape with a roof; then her eyes came back to Brad.

"Anyone else alive? Your mother or father?"

The little girl just stared.

"What's your name?"

"Kelly Burch," she answered dazedly. "My tel'phone number is . . . is . . . 555-6949. Could . . . you help me find . . . a p'liceman, please?"

It would be so easy, Brad thought, to curl up in the leaves on Baylor Street and let himself lose his mind; but if there was one little girl still left alive, then there might be other people too. Maybe this awful thing had only happened on Baylor Street . . . or maybe only in this part of town; maybe it was a chemical spill, radiation, something unholy in the lightning, some kind of Army weapon that had backfired. Whatever it was, maybe its effects were only limited to a small part of town. Sure! he thought, and when he grinned, the child abruptly took two steps back. "We're going to be all right," he told her. "I won't hurt you. I'm going to walk to Main Street. Do you want to go with me?"

She didn't reply, and Brad thought she'd truly gone over the edge, but then her lips moved and she said, "I'm looking for . . . for my mommy and daddy. They're gone." She caught back a sob, but new tears ran down her cheeks. "They just . . . they just . . . left bones in their bed and they're gone."

"Come on." He held out his hand to her. "Come with me, okay? Let's see if we can find anybody else."

Kelly didn't come any closer. Her little knuckles were white where she gripped the smiling blue Smurf. Brad heard thunder roaming somewhere to the south, and electric-blue lightning scrawled across the crimson sky like a crack in time. Brad couldn't wait any longer; he started walking again, stopped, and looked back. Kelly stopped too, dead leaves snagged in her hair. "We're going to be all right," he told her again, and he heard how utterly ridiculous he sounded. Sarah was gone; beautiful Sarah was gone, and his life might as well be over. But no, no—he had to keep going, had to at least *try* to make some sense out of all this. He started off once more, east toward Main Street, and he didn't look back, but he knew Kelly was following about fifteen or twenty feet behind.

At the intersection of Baylor and Ashley streets, a police car had smashed into an oak tree. The windshield was layered with leaves, but Brad saw the hunched-over bony thing in the police uniform sitting behind the wheel. And the most terrible thing was that its skeletal hands were still gripping that wheel, trying to guide the car. Whatever had happened—radiation, chemicals, or the devil striding through the streets of his town—had taken place in an instant. These people had been stripped to bones in the blink of a cold eye, and again Brad felt himself balanced precariously on the edge of madness.

"Ask the p'liceman to find Mommy and Daddy!" Kelly called from behind him.

"There's a police station on Main Street," he told her. "That's where we're going to go. Okay?"

She didn't answer, and Brad set off.

They passed silent houses. Near the intersection of Baylor and Hilliard, where the traffic light was still obediently blinking yellow, a skeleton in jogging gear lay sprawled on the ground. Its Nike sneakers were too small for Brad's feet, too large for Kelly's. They kept going, and Kelly cried for a few minutes but then she hugged her doll tighter and stared straight ahead with eyes swollen almost shut.

And then Brad heard it, and his heart pounded with fear again.

Off in the fog somewhere.

The sound of a phone ringing.

Brad stopped. The phone kept on ringing, its sound thin and insistent.

"Somebody's calling," Kelly said, and Brad realized she was standing right beside him. "My tel'phone number is 555-6949."

He took a step forward. Another, and another. Through the fog ahead of him he could make out the shape of a pay phone there on the corner of Dayton Street.

The telephone kept on ringing, demanding an answer.

Slowly Brad approached the pay phone. He stared at the receiver as if it might be a cobra rearing back to strike. He did not want to answer it, but his arm lifted and his hand reached toward that receiver, and he knew that if he heard that silken breathing and the metallic recorded voice on the other end, he might start screaming and never be able to stop.

His hand closed around it. Started to lift it up.

"Hey, buddy!" someone said. "I wouldn't answer that if I was you."

Startled almost out of his skin, Brad whirled around.

A young man was sitting on the curb across the street, smoking a cigarette, his legs stretched out before him. "I wouldn't," he cautioned.

Brad was oddly shocked by the sight of a flesh-and-blood man, as if he'd already forgotten what one looked like. The young man was maybe in his early twenties, wearing scruffy jeans and a dark green shirt with the sleeves rolled up. He had sandy-brown hair that hung to his shoulders, and he looked to have a couple of days' growth of beard. He pulled on the cigarette and said, "Don't pick it up, man. Doom City."

"What?"

"I said . . . Doom City." The young man stood up; he was about six feet, thin and lanky. His workboots crunched leaves as he crossed the street, and Brad saw that he had a patch on the breast pocket of his shirt that identified him as a Sanitation Department workman. As the young man got closer, Kelly pressed her body against Brad's legs and tried to hide behind the Smurf doll. "Let it ring," the young man said. His eyes were pale green, deep-set, and dazed. "If you were to pick that damned thing up . . . Doom City."

"Why do you keep saying that?"

"Because it is what it is. Somebody's tryin' to find all the strays. Tryin' to run us all down and finish the job. Sweep us all into the gutter, man. Close the world over our heads. Doom City." He blew a plume of smoke into the air that hung between them, unmoving.

"Who are you? Where'd you come from?"

"Name's Neil Spencer. Folks call me Spence. I'm a . . ." He paused for a few seconds, staring along Baylor Street. "I *used* to be a garbage man. Till today, that is. Till I got to work and found skeletons sitting in the garbage trucks. That was about three hours ago, I guess. I've been doin' a lot of walking. Lot of poking around." His gaze rested on the little girl, then back to Brad. The pay phone was still ringing, and Brad felt the scream kicking behind his teeth. "You're the first two I've seen with skin," Spence said. "I've been sittin' over there for the last twenty minutes or so. Just waitin' for the world to end, I guess."

"What . . . happened?" Brad asked. Tears burned his eyes. "My God . . . my God . . . what *happened?*"

"Something tore," Spence said tonelessly. "Ripped open. Something won the fight, and I don't think it was who the preachers said was gonna win. I don't know . . . maybe Death got tired of waitin'. Same thing happened to the dinosaurs. Maybe it's happenin' to people now."

"There's *got* to be other people somewhere!" Brad shouted. "We can't be the only ones!"

"I don't know about that." Spence drew on his cigarette one last time and flicked the butt into the street. "All I know is, somethin' came in the night and had a feast, and when it was done it licked the plate clean. Only it's still hungry." He nodded toward the ringing phone. "Wants to suck on a few more bones. Like I said, man . . . Doom City. Doom City here, there, and everywhere."

The phone gave a final shrilling shriek and went silent.

Brad heard the child crying again, and he put his hand on her head, stroked her hair to calm her. He realized he was doing it with his bloody hand. "We've . . . we've got to go somewhere . . . got to *do* something . . ."

"Do what?" Spence asked laconically. "Go where? I'm open to suggestions, man."

From the next block came the distant sound of a telephone ringing. Brad stood with his bloody hand on Kelly's head, and he didn't know what to say.

"I want to take you somewhere, my friend," Spence told him. "Want to show you something real interestin'. Okay?"

Brad nodded, and he and the little girl followed Neil Spencer north along Dayton Street, past more silent houses and buildings.

Spence led them about four blocks to a 7-Eleven store, where a skeleton in a yellow dress splotched with blue and purple flowers lolled behind the cash register with a *National Enquirer* open on its jutting knees. "There you go," Spence said softly. He plucked a pack of Luckies off the display of cigarettes and nodded toward the small TV set on the counter. "Take a look at that, and tell me what we ought to do."

The TV set was on. It was a color set, and Brad realized after a long, silent moment that the channel was tuned to one of those twenty-four-hour news networks. The picture showed two skeletons—one in a gray suit and the other in a wine-red dress—leaning crookedly over a news desk at center camera; the woman had placed her hand on the man's shoulder, and yellow sheets of the night's news were scattered all over the desktop. Behind the two figures were three or four out-of-focus skeletons, frozen forever at their desks as well.

Spence lit another cigarette. An occasional spark of static shot across the unmoving TV picture. "Doom City," Spence said. "Not only here, man. It's everywhere. See?"

The telephone behind the counter suddenly started ringing, and Brad put his hands to his ears and screamed.

The phone's ringing stopped.

Brad lowered his hands, his breathing as rough and hoarse as a trapped animal's.

He looked down at Kelly Burch, and saw that she was smiling.

"It's all right," she said. "You don't have to answer. I found you, didn't I?"

Brad whispered, *"Wha—"*

The little girl giggled, and as she continued to giggle, the laugh changed, grew in intensity and darkness, grew in power and evil until it became a triumphant roar that shook the windows of the 7-Eleven store. "DOOM CITY!" the thing with pigtails shrieked, and as the mouth strained open, the eyes became silver, cold, and dead, and from that awful crater of a mouth shot a blinding bolt of blue-white lightning that hit Neil Spencer and seemed to spin him like a top, throwing him off his feet and headlong through the 7-Eleven's plate-glass window. He struck the pavement on his belly, and as he tried to get up again Brad Forbes saw that the flesh was dissolving from the young man's bones, falling away in chunks like dried-up tree bark.

Spence made a garbled moaning sound, and Brad went through the store's door with such force that he almost tore it from its hinges. His feet slivered with glass, Brad ran past Spence and saw the other man's skull grinning up at him as the body writhed and twitched.

"Can't get away!" the thing behind him shouted. "Can't! Can't! Can't!"

Brad looked back over his shoulder, and that was when he saw the lightning burst from her gaping mouth and hurtle through the broken window at him. He flung himself to the pavement, tried to crawl under a parked car.

Something hit him, covered him over like an ocean wave, and he heard the monster shout in a voice like the peal of thunder. He was blinded and stunned for a few seconds, but there was no pain . . . just a needles-and-pins prickling settling deep into his bones.

Brad got up, started running again. And as he ran he saw the flesh falling from his hands, saw pieces drifting down from his face; fissures ran through his legs, and as the flesh fell away he saw his own bones underneath.

"DOOM CITY!" he heard the monster calling. "DOOM CITY!"

Brad stumbled; he was running on bones, and had left the flesh of his feet behind him on the pavement. He fell, began to tremble and contort.

"I'm cold," he heard himself moan. "I'm cold . . ."

She awakened with the memory of thunder in her bones. The house was quiet. The alarm clock hadn't gone off. Saturday, she realized. No work today. A rest day. But Lord, what a nightmare she'd had! It was fading now, all jumbled up and incoherent. There'd been a thunderstorm last night —she remembered waking up and seeing lightning flash. But whatever the nightmare had been, she couldn't recall now; she thought she remembered Brad saying something too, but now she didn't know what it was . . .

That light . . . so strange. Not like June light. More like . . . yes, like winter light.

Sarah got out of bed and walked across the room. She pushed aside the white curtain and peered out, squinting.

A gray fog hung in the trees and over the roofs of the houses on Baylor Street. Thunder rumbled in the distance, and Sarah Forbes said, "Brad? Honey? Take a look at this."

He didn't reply, nor did he stir. She glanced at him, saw the wave of his dark hair above the sheet that was pulled up over him like a shroud. "Brad?" she said again, and took a step toward the bed.

And suddenly Sarah remembered what he'd said last night, when she'd sat up in a sleepy daze to watch the lightning crackle.

I'm cold, I'm cold.

She grasped the edge of the sheet and pulled it back.

Nightcrawlers

1

"Hard rain coming down," Cheryl said, and I nodded in agreement.

Through the diner's plate-glass windows, a dense curtain of rain flapped across the Gulf gas pumps and continued across the parking lot. It hit Big Bob's with a force that made the glass rattle like uneasy bones. The red neon sign that said BIG BOB'S! DIESEL FUEL! EATS! sat on top of a high steel pole above the diner so the truckers on the interstate could see it. Out in the night, the red-tinted rain thrashed in torrents across my old pickup truck and Cheryl's baby-blue Volkswagen.

"Well," I said, "I suppose that storm'll either wash some folks in off the interstate or we can just about hang it up." The curtain of rain parted for an instant, and I could see the treetops whipping back and forth in the woods on the other side of Highway 47. Wind whined around the front door like an animal trying to claw its way in. I glanced at the electric clock on the wall behind the counter. Twenty minutes before nine. We usually closed up at ten, but tonight—with tornado warnings in the weather forecast —I was tempted to turn the lock a little early. "Tell you what," I said. "If we're empty at nine, we skedaddle. 'Kay?"

"No argument here," she said. She watched the storm for a moment longer, then continued putting newly washed coffee cups, saucers, and plates away on the stainless-steel shelves.

Lightning flared from west to east like the strike of a burning bullwhip. The diner's lights flickered, then came back to normal. A shudder of thunder seemed to come right up through my shoes. Late March is the beginning of tornado season in south Alabama, and we've had some whoppers spin past here in the last few years. I knew that Alma was at home, and she understood to get into the root cellar right quick if she spotted a twister, like that one we saw in '82 dancing through the woods about two miles from our farm.

"You got any love-ins planned this weekend, hippie?" I asked Cheryl, mostly to get my mind off the storm and to rib her too.

She was in her late thirties, but I swear that when she grinned she could've passed for a kid. "Wouldn't *you* like to know, redneck?" she answered; she replied the same way to all my digs at her. Cheryl Lovesong—and I *know* that couldn't have been her real name—was a mighty able waitress, and she had hands that were no strangers to hard work. But I didn't care that she wore her long silvery-blond hair in Indian braids with hippie headbands, or came to work in tie-dyed overalls. She was the best waitress who'd ever worked for me, and she got along with everybody just fine—even us rednecks. That's what I am, and proud of it: I drink Rebel Yell whiskey straight, and my favorite songs are about good women gone bad and trains on the long track to nowhere. I keep my wife happy. I've raised my two boys to pray to God and to salute the flag, and if anybody don't like it he can go a few rounds with Big Bob Clayton.

Cheryl would come right out and tell you she used to live in San Francisco in the late sixties, and that she went to love-ins and peace marches and all that stuff. When I reminded her it was 1984 and Ronnie Reagan was president, she'd look at me like I was walking cow-flop. I always figured she'd start thinking straight when all that hippie-dust blew out of her head.

Alma said my tail was going to get burnt if I ever took a

shine to Cheryl, but I'm a fifty-five-year-old redneck who stopped sowing his wild seed when he met the woman he married, more than thirty years ago.

Lightning crisscrossed the turbulent sky, followed by a boom of thunder. Cheryl said, "Wow! Look at that light show!"

"Light show, my ass," I muttered. The diner was as solid as the Good Book, so I wasn't too worried about the storm. But on a wild night like this, stuck out in the countryside like Big Bob's was, you had a feeling of being a long way off from civilization—though Mobile was only twenty-seven miles south. On a wild night like this, you had a feeling that anything could happen, as quick as a streak of lightning out of the darkness. I picked up a copy of the Mobile *Press-Register* that the last customer—a trucker on his way to Texas—had left on the counter a half-hour before, and I started plowing through the news, most of it bad: those A-rab countries were still squabbling like Hatfields and McCoys in white robes; two men had robbed a Qwik-Mart in Mobile and been killed by the police in a shoot-out; cops were investigating a massacre at a motel near Daytona Beach; an infant had been stolen from a maternity ward in Birmingham. The only good things on the front page were stories that said the economy was up and that Reagan swore we'd show the Commies who was boss in El Salvador and Lebanon.

The diner shook under a blast of thunder, and I looked up from the paper as a pair of headlights emerged from the rain into my parking lot.

2

The headlights were attached to an Alabama state-trooper car.

"Half-alive, hold the onion, extra brown the buns." Cheryl was already writing on her pad in expectation of the order. I pushed the paper aside and went to the fridge for the hamburger meat.

When the door opened, a windblown spray of rain swept in and stung like buckshot. "Howdy, folks!" Dennis Wells peeled off his gray rain slicker and hung it on the rack next to the door. Over his Smokey the Bear trooper hat was a protective plastic covering, beaded with raindrops. He took off his hat, exposing the thinning blond hair on his pale scalp, as he approached the counter and sat on his usual stool, right next to the cash register. "Cup of black coffee and a rare—" Cheryl was already sliding the coffee in front of him, and the burger sizzled on the griddle. "Ya'll are on the ball tonight!" Dennis said; he said the same thing when he came in, which was almost every night. Funny the kind of habits you fall into, without realizing it.

"Kinda wild out there, ain't it?" I asked as I flipped the burger over.

"Lordy, yes! Wind just about flipped my car over three, four miles down the interstate. Thought I was gonna be eatin' a little pavement tonight." Dennis was a husky young man in his early thirties, with thick blond brows over deep-set light brown eyes. He had a wife and three kids, and he was fast to flash a walletful of their pictures. "Don't reckon I'll be chasin' any speeders tonight, but there'll probably be a load of accidents. Cheryl, you sure look pretty this evenin'."

"Still the same old me." Cheryl never wore a speck of makeup, though one day she'd come to work with glitter on her cheeks. She had a place a few miles away, and I guessed she was farming that funny weed up there. "Any trucks moving?"

"Seen a few, but not many. Truckers ain't fools. Gonna get worse before it gets better, the radio says." He sipped at his coffee and grimaced. "Lordy, that's strong enough to jump out of the cup and dance a jig, darlin'!"

I fixed the burger the way Dennis liked it, put it on a platter with some fries, and served it. "Bobby, how's the wife treatin' you?" he asked.

"No complaints."

"Good to hear. I'll tell you, a fine woman is worth her

weight in gold. Hey, Cheryl! How'd you like a handsome young man for a husband?"

Cheryl smiled, knowing what was coming. "The man I'm looking for hasn't been made yet."

"Yeah, but you ain't met *Cecil* yet, either! He asks me about you every time I see him, and I keep tellin' him I'm doin' everything I can to get you two together." Cecil was Dennis' brother-in-law and owned a Chevy dealership in Bay Minette. Dennis had been ribbing Cheryl about going on a date with Cecil for the past four months. "You'd like him," Dennis promised. "He's got a lot of my qualities."

"Well, that's different. In that case, I'm *certain* I don't want to meet him."

Dennis winced. "Oh, you're a cruel woman! That's what smokin' banana peels does to you—turns you mean. Anybody readin' this rag?" He reached over for the newspaper.

"Waitin' here just for you," I said. Thunder rumbled, closer to the diner. The lights flickered briefly once . . . then again before they returned to normal. Cheryl busied herself by fixing a fresh pot of coffee, and I watched the rain whipping against the windows. When the lightning flashed, I could see the trees swaying so hard they looked about to snap.

Dennis read and ate his hamburger. "Boy," he said after a few minutes, "the world's in some shape, huh? Those A-rab pig-stickers are itchin' for war. Mobile metro boys had a little gunplay last night. Good for them." He paused and frowned, then tapped the paper with one thick finger. "This I can't figure."

"What's that?"

"Thing in Florida couple of nights ago. Six people killed at the Pines Haven Motor Inn, near Daytona Beach. Motel was set off in the woods. Only a couple of cinder-block houses in the area, and nobody heard any gunshots. Says here one old man saw what he thought was a bright white star falling over the motel, and that was it. Funny, huh?"

"A UFO," Cheryl offered. "Maybe he saw a UFO."

"Yeah, and I'm a little green man from Mars," Dennis

71

scoffed. "I'm serious. This is weird. The motel was so blown full of holes it looked like a war had been going on. Everybody was dead—even a dog and a canary that belonged to the manager. The cars out in front of the rooms were blasted to pieces. The sound of one of them explodin' was what woke up the people in those houses, I reckon." He skimmed the story again. "Two bodies were out in the parkin' lot, one was holed up in a bathroom, one had crawled under a bed, and two had dragged every piece of furniture in the room over to block the door. Didn't seem to help 'em any, though."

I grunted. "Guess not."

"No motive, no witnesses. You better believe those Florida cops are shakin' the bushes for some kind of dangerous maniac—or maybe more than one, it says here." He shoved the paper away and patted the service revolver holstered at his hip. "If I ever got hold of him—or them—he'd find out not to mess with a 'Bama trooper." He glanced quickly over at Cheryl and smiled mischievously. "Probably some crazy hippie who'd been smokin' his tennis shoes."

"Don't knock it," she said sweetly, "until you've tried it." She looked past him, out the window into the storm. "Car's pullin' in, Bobby."

Headlights glared briefly off the wet windows. It was a station wagon with wood-grained panels on the sides; it veered around the gas pumps and parked next to Dennis' trooper car. On the front bumper was a personalized license plate that said: Ray & Lindy. The headlights died, and all the doors opened at once. Out of the wagon came a whole family: a man and woman, a little girl and boy about eight or nine. Dennis got up and opened the diner door as they hurried inside from the rain.

All of them had gotten pretty well soaked between the station wagon and the diner, and they wore the dazed expressions of people who'd been on the road a long time. The man wore glasses and had curly gray hair, the woman was slim and dark-haired and pretty. The kids were sleepy-eyed. All of them were well-dressed, the man in a yellow sweater with one of those alligators on the chest. They had vacation tans, and I figured they were tourists heading north from the beach after spring break.

"Come on in and take a seat," I said.

"Thank you," the man said. They squeezed into one of the booths near the windows. "We saw your sign from the interstate."

"Bad night to be on the highway," Dennis told them. "Tornado warnings are out all over the place."

"We heard it on the radio," the woman—Lindy, if the license was right—said. "We're on our way to Birmingham, and we thought we could drive right through the storm. We should've stopped at that Holiday Inn we passed about fifteen miles ago."

"That would've been smart," Dennis agreed. "No sense in pushin' your luck." He returned to his stool.

The new arrivals ordered hamburgers, fries, and Cokes. Cheryl and I went to work. Lightning made the diner's lights flicker again, and the sound of thunder caused the kids to jump. When the food was ready and Cheryl served them, Dennis said, "Tell you what. You folks finish your dinners and I'll escort you back to the Holiday Inn. Then you can head out in the morning. How about that?"

"Fine," Ray said gratefully. "I don't think we could've gotten very much further, anyway." He turned his attention to his food.

"Well," Cheryl said quietly, standing beside me, "I don't guess we get home early, do we?"

"I guess not. Sorry."

She shrugged. "Goes with the job, right? Anyway, I can think of worse places to be stuck."

I figured that Alma might be worried about me, so I went over to the pay phone to call her. I dropped a quarter in—and the dial tone sounded like a cat being stepped on. I hung up and tried again. The cat scream continued. "Damn!" I muttered. "Lines must be screwed up."

"Ought to get yourself a place closer to town, Bobby," Dennis said. "Never could figure out why you wanted a joint in the sticks. At least you'd get better phone service and good lights if you were nearer to Mo—"

He was interrupted by the sound of wet and shrieking brakes, and he swiveled around on his stool.

I looked up as a car hurtled into the parking lot, the tires swerving, throwing up plumes of water. For a few seconds I thought it was going to keep coming, right through the window into the diner—but then the brakes caught and the car almost grazed the side of my pickup as it jerked to a stop. In the neon's red glow I could tell it was a beat-up old Ford Fairlane, either gray or a dingy beige. Steam was rising off the crumpled hood. The headlights stayed on for perhaps a minute before they winked off. A figure got out of the car and walked slowly—with a limp—toward the diner.

We watched the figure approach. Dennis' body looked like a coiled spring ready to be triggered. "We got us a live one, Bobby boy," he said.

The door opened, and in a stinging gust of wind and rain a man who looked like walking death stepped into my diner.

3

He was so wet he might well have been driving with his windows down. He was a skinny guy, maybe weighed all of a hundred and twenty pounds, even soaking wet. His unruly dark hair was plastered to his head, and he had gone a week or more without a shave. In his gaunt, pallid face his eyes were startlingly blue; his gaze flicked around the diner, lingered for a few seconds on Dennis. Then he limped on down to the far end of the counter and took a seat. He wiped the rain out of his eyes as Cheryl took a menu to him.

Dennis stared at the man. When he spoke, his voice bristled with authority. "Hey, fella." The man didn't look up from the menu. "Hey, I'm talkin' to *you.*"

The man pushed the menu away and pulled a damp packet of Kools out of the breast pocket of his patched Army fatigue jacket. "I can hear you," he said; his voice was deep and husky, and didn't go with his less-than-robust physical appearance.

"Drivin' kinda fast in this weather, don't you think?"

The man flicked a cigarette lighter a few times before he got a flame, then lit one of his smokes and inhaled deeply. "Yeah," he replied. "I was. Sorry. I saw the sign, and I was in a hurry to get here. Miss? I'd just like a cup of coffee, please. Hot and *real* strong, okay?"

Cheryl nodded and turned away from him, almost bumping into me as I strolled down behind the counter to check him out.

"That kind of hurry'll get you killed," Dennis cautioned.

"Right. Sorry." He shivered and pushed the tangled hair back from his forehead with one hand. Up close, I could see deep cracks around his mouth and the corners of his eyes and I figured him to be in his late thirties or early forties. His wrists were as thin as a woman's; he looked like he hadn't eaten a good meal for more than a month. He stared at his hands through bloodshot eyes. Probably on drugs, I thought. The fella gave me the creeps. Then he looked at me with those eyes—so pale blue they were almost white—and I felt like I'd been nailed to the floor. "Something wrong?" he asked—not rudely, just curiously.

"Nope." I shook my head. Cheryl gave him his coffee and then went over to give Ray and Lindy their check.

The man didn't use either cream or sugar. The coffee was steaming, but he drank half of it down like mother's milk. "That's good," he said. "Keep me awake, won't it?"

"More than likely." Over the breast pocket of his jacket was the faint outline of the name that had been sewn there once. I think it was Price, but I could've been wrong.

"That's what I want. To stay awake as long as I can." He finished the coffee. "Can I have another cup, please?"

I poured it for him. He drank that one down just as fast, then rubbed his eyes wearily.

"Been on the road a long time, huh?"

Price nodded. "Day and night. I don't know which is more tired, my mind or my butt." He lifted his gaze to me again. "Have you got anything else to drink? How about beer?"

"No, sorry. Couldn't get a liquor license."

He sighed. "Just as well. It might make me sleepy. But I

sure could go for a beer right now. One sip, to clean my mouth out."

He picked up his coffee cup, and I smiled and started to turn away.

But then he wasn't holding a cup. He was holding a Budweiser can, and for an instant I could smell the tang of a newly popped beer.

The mirage was there for only maybe two seconds. I blinked, and Price was holding a cup again. "Just as well," he said, and put it down.

I glanced over at Cheryl, then at Dennis. Neither one was paying attention. Damn! I thought. I'm too young to be losin' either my eyesight or my senses! "Uh . . ." I said, or some other stupid noise.

"One more cup?" Price asked. "Then I'd better hit the road again."

My hand was shaking as I picked it up, but if Price noticed, he didn't say anything.

"Want anything to eat?" Cheryl asked him. "How about a bowl of beef stew?"

He shook his head. "No, thanks. The sooner I get back on the road, the better it'll be."

Suddenly Dennis swiveled toward him, giving him a cold stare that only cops and drill sergeants can muster. "Back on the *road?*" He snorted. "Fella, you ever been in a tornado before? I'm gonna escort those nice people to the Holiday Inn about fifteen miles back. If you're smart, that's where you'll spend the night too. No use in tryin' to—"

"No." Price's voice was rock-steady. "I'll be spending the night behind the wheel."

Dennis' eyes narrowed. "How come you're in such a hurry? Not runnin' from anybody, are you?"

"Nightcrawlers," Cheryl said.

Price turned toward her like he'd been slapped across the face, and I saw what might've been a spark of fear in his eyes.

Cheryl motioned toward the lighter Price had laid on the counter, beside the pack of Kools. It was a beat-up silver Zippo, and inscribed across it was NIGHTCRAWLERS with the symbol of two crossed rifles beneath it. "Sorry," she said. "I just noticed that, and I wondered what it was."

Price put the lighter away. "I was in 'Nam," he told her. "Everybody in my unit got one."

"Hey." There was suddenly new respect in Dennis' voice. "You a *vet?*"

Price paused so long I didn't think he was going to answer. In the quiet, I heard the little girl tell her mother that the fries were "ucky." Price said, "Yes."

"How about that! Hey, I wanted to go myself, but I got a high number and things were windin' down about that time anyway. Did you see any action?"

A faint, bitter smile passed over Price's mouth. "Too much."

"What? Infantry? Marines? Rangers?"

Price picked up his third cup of coffee, swallowed some, and put it down. He closed his eyes for a few seconds, and when they opened they were vacant and fixed on nothing. "Nightcrawlers," he said quietly. "Special unit. Deployed to recon Charlie positions in questionable villages." He said it like he was reciting from a manual. "We did a lot of crawling through rice paddies and jungles in the dark."

"Bet you laid a few of them Vietcong out, didn't you?" Dennis got up and came over to sit a few places away from the man. "Man, I was behind you guys all the way. I wanted you to stay in there and fight it out!"

Price was silent. Thunder echoed over the diner. The lights weakened for a few seconds; when they came back on, they seemed to have lost some of their wattage. The place was dimmer than before. Price's head slowly turned toward Dennis, with the inexorable motion of a machine. I was thankful I didn't have to take the full force of Price's dead blue eyes, and I saw Dennis wince. "I *should've* stayed," he said. "I should be there right now, buried in the mud of a rice paddy with the eight other men in my patrol."

"Oh." Dennis blinked. "Sorry. I didn't mean to—"

"I came home," Price continued calmly, "by stepping on the bodies of my friends. Do you want to know what that's like, Mr. Trooper?"

"The war's over," I told him. "No need to bring it back."

Price smiled grimly, but his gaze remained fixed on Dennis. "Some say it's over. I say it came back with the men who were there. Like me. *Especially* like me." Price paused. The wind howled around the door, and the lightning illuminated for an instant the thrashing woods across the highway. "The mud was up to our knees, Mr. Trooper," he said. "We were moving across a rice paddy in the dark, being real careful not to step on the bamboo stakes we figured were planted there. Then the first shots started: *pop pop pop*—like firecrackers going off. One of the Nightcrawlers fired off a flare, and we saw the Cong ringing us. We'd walked right into hell, Mr. Trooper. Somebody shouted, 'Charlie's in the light!' and we started firing, trying to punch a hole through them. But they were everywhere. As soon as one went down, three more took his place. Grenades were going off, and more flares, and people were screaming as they got hit. I took a bullet in the thigh and another through the hand. I lost my rifle, and somebody fell on top of me with half his head missing."

"Uh . . . listen," I said. "You don't have to—"

"I *want* to, friend." He glanced quickly at me, then back to Dennis. I think I cringed when his gaze pierced me. "I want to tell it all. They were fighting and screaming and dying all around me, and I felt the bullets tug at my clothes as they passed through. I know I was screaming too, but what was coming out of my mouth sounded bestial. I ran. The only way I could save my own life was to step on their bodies and drive them down into the mud. I heard some of them choke and blubber as I put my boot on their faces. I knew all those guys like brothers . . . but at that moment they were only pieces of meat. I ran. A gunship chopper came over the paddy and laid down some fire, and that's how I got out. Alone." He bent his face closer toward the other man's. "And you'd better believe I'm in that rice paddy in 'Nam every time I close my eyes. You'd better believe the men I left back there don't rest easy. So you keep your opinions about 'Nam and being 'behind you guys' to yourself, Mr. Trooper. I don't want to hear that bullshit. Got it?"

Dennis sat very still. He wasn't used to being talked to like that, not even from a 'Nam vet, and I saw the shadow of anger pass over his face.

Price's hands were trembling as he brought a little bottle out of his jeans pocket. He shook two blue-and-orange capsules out onto the counter, took them both with a swallow of coffee, and then recapped the bottle and put it away. The flesh of his face looked almost ashen in the dim light.

"I know you boys had a rough time," Dennis said, "but that's no call to show disrespect to the law."

"The law," Price repeated. "Yeah. Right. Bull*shit.*"

"There are women and children present," I reminded him. "Watch your language."

Price rose from his seat. He looked like a skeleton with just a little extra skin on the bones. "Mister, I haven't slept for more than thirty-six hours. My nerves are shot. I don't mean to cause trouble, but when some fool says he *understands,* I feel like kicking his teeth down his throat— because no one who wasn't there can pretend to understand." He glanced at Ray, Lindy, and the kids. "Sorry, folks. Don't mean to disturb you. Friend, how much do I owe?" He started digging for his wallet.

Dennis slid slowly from his seat and stood with his hands on his hips. "Hold it." He used his trooper's voice again. "If you think I'm lettin' you walk out of here high on pills and needin' sleep, you're crazy. I don't want to be scrapin' you off the highway."

Price paid him no attention. He took a couple of dollars from his wallet and put them on the counter. I didn't touch them. "Those pills will help keep me awake," Price said. "Once I get on the road, I'll be fine."

"Fella, I wouldn't let you go if it was high noon and not a cloud in the sky. I sure as hell don't want to clean up after the accident you're gonna have. Now, why don't you come along to the Holiday Inn and—"

79

Price laughed grimly. "Mr. Trooper, the last place you want me staying is at a motel." He cocked his head to one side. "I was in a motel in Florida a couple of nights ago, and I think I left my room a little untidy. Step aside and let me pass."

"A motel in Florida?" Dennis nervously licked his lower lip. "What the hell you talkin' about?"

"Nightmares and reality, Mr. Trooper. The point where they cross. A couple of nights ago, they crossed at a motel. I wasn't going to let myself sleep. I was just going to rest for a little while, but I didn't know they'd come so *fast.*" A mocking smile played at the edges of his mouth, but his eyes were tortured. "You don't want me staying at that Holiday Inn, Mr. Trooper. You really don't. Now, step aside."

I saw Dennis' hand settle on the butt of his revolver. His fingers unsnapped the fold of leather that secured the gun in the holster. I stared at him numbly. My God, I thought. What's goin' on? My heart had started pounding so hard I was sure everybody could hear it. Ray and Lindy were watching, and Cheryl was backing away behind the counter.

Price and Dennis faced each other for a moment, as the rain whipped against the windows and thunder boomed like shellfire. Then Price sighed, as if resigning himself to something. He said, "I think I want a T-bone steak. Extra rare. How 'bout it?" He looked at me.

"A steak?" My voice was shaking. "We don't have any T-bone—"

Price's gaze shifted to the counter right in front of me. I heard a sizzle. The aroma of cooking meat drifted up to me.

"Oh . . . wow," Cheryl whispered.

A large T-bone steak lay on the countertop, pink and oozing blood. You could've fanned a menu in my face and I would've keeled over. Wisps of smoke were rising from the steak.

The steak began to fade, until it was only an outline on the counter. The lines of oozing blood vanished. After the mirage was gone, I could still smell the meat—and that's how I knew I wasn't crazy.

Dennis' mouth hung open. Ray had stood up from the

booth to look, and his wife's face was the color of spoiled milk. The whole world seemed to be balanced on a point of silence—until the wail of the wind jarred me back to my senses.

"I'm getting good at it," Price said softly. "I'm getting very, very good. Didn't start happening to me until about a year ago. I've found four other 'Nam vets who can do the same thing. What's in your head comes true—as simple as that. Of course, the images only last for a few seconds—as long as I'm awake, I mean. I've found out that those other men were drenched by a chemical spray we called Howdy Doody—because it made you stiffen up and jerk like you were hanging on strings. I got hit with it near Khe Sahn. That shit almost suffocated me. It felt like black tar, and it burned the land down to a paved parking lot." He stared at Dennis. "You don't want me around here, Mr. Trooper. Not with the body count I've still got in *my* head."

"You . . . were at . . . that motel, near Daytona Beach?"

Price closed his eyes. A vein had begun beating at his right temple, royal blue against the pallor of his flesh. "Oh, Jesus," he whispered. "I fell asleep, and I couldn't wake myself up. I was having the nightmare. The same one. I was locked in it, and I was trying to scream myself awake." He shuddered, and two tears ran slowly down his cheeks. *"Oh,"* he said, and flinched as if remembering something horrible. "They . . . they were coming through the door when I woke up. Tearing the door right off its hinges. I woke up . . . just as one of them was pointing his rifle at me. And I saw his face. I saw his muddy, misshappen face." His eyes suddenly jerked open. "I didn't know they'd come so fast."

"Who?" I asked him. *"Who* came so fast?"

"The Nightcrawlers," Price said, his face devoid of expression, masklike. "Dear God . . . maybe if I'd stayed asleep a second more. But I ran again, and I left those people dead in that motel."

"You're gonna come with me." Dennis started pulling his gun from the holster. Price's head snapped toward him. "I don't know what kinda fool game you're—"

He stopped, staring at the gun he held.

It wasn't a gun anymore. It was an oozing mass of hot rubber. Dennis cried out and slung the thing from his hand. The molten mess hit the floor with a pulpy *splat*.

"I'm leaving now." Price's voice was calm. "Thank you for the coffee." He walked past Dennis, toward the door.

Dennis grasped a bottle of ketchup from the counter. Cheryl cried out, *"Don't!"* but it was too late. Dennis was already swinging the bottle. It hit the back of Price's skull and burst open, spewing ketchup everywhere. Price staggered forward, his knees buckling. When he went down, his skull hit the floor with a noise like a watermelon being dropped. His body began jerking involuntarily.

"Got him!" Dennis shouted triumphantly. "Got that crazy bastard, didn't I?"

Lindy was holding the little girl in her arms. The boy craned his neck to see. Ray said nervously, "You didn't kill him, did you?"

"He's not dead," I told him. I looked over at the gun; it was solid again. Dennis scooped it up and aimed it at Price, whose body continued to jerk. Just like Howdy Doody, I thought. Then Price stopped moving.

"He's dead!" Cheryl's voice was near-frantic. "Oh God, you killed him, Dennis!"

Dennis prodded the body with the toe of his boot, then bent down. "Naw. His eyes are movin' back and forth behind the lids." Dennis touched his wrist to check the pulse, then abruptly pulled his own hand away. "Jesus Christ! He's as cold as a meat locker!" He took Price's pulse and whistled. "Goin' like a racehorse at the Derby."

I touched the place on the counter where the mirage steak had been. My fingers came away slightly greasy, and I could smell the cooked meat on them. At that instant Price twitched. Dennis scuttled away from him like a crab. Price made a gasping, choking noise.

"What'd he say?" Cheryl asked. "He said something!"

"No he didn't." Dennis stuck him in the ribs with his pistol. "Come on. Get up."

"Get him out of here," I said. "I don't want him—"

Cheryl shushed me. "Listen. Can you hear that?"

I heard only the roar and crash of the storm.

"Don't you *hear* it?" she asked me. Her eyes were getting scared and glassy.

"Yes!" Ray said. "Yes! Listen!"

Then I did hear something, over the noise of the keening wind. It was a distant *chuk-chuk-chuk,* steadily growing louder and closer. The wind covered the noise for a minute, then it came back: CHUK-CHUK-CHUK, almost overhead.

"It's a helicopter!" Ray peered through the window. "Somebody's got a helicopter out there!"

"Ain't nobody can fly a chopper in a storm!" Dennis told him. The noise of rotors swelled and faded, swelled and faded . . . and stopped.

On the floor, Price shivered and began to contort into a fetal position. His mouth opened; his face twisted in what appeared to be agony.

Thunder spoke. A red fireball rose up from the woods across the road and hung lazily in the sky for a few seconds before it descended toward the diner. As it fell, the fireball exploded soundlessly into a white, glaring eye of light that almost blinded me.

Price said something in a garbled, panicked voice. His eyes were tightly closed, and he had squeezed up with his arms around his knees.

Dennis rose to his feet; he squinted as the eye of light fell toward the parking lot and winked out in a puddle of water. Another fireball floated up from the woods, and again blossomed into painful glare.

Dennis turned toward me. "I heard him." His voice was raspy. "He said . . . 'Charlie's in the light.'"

As the second flare fell to the ground and illuminated the parking lot, I thought I saw figures crossing the road. They walked stiff-legged, in an eerie cadence. The flare went out.

"Wake him up," I heard myself whisper. "Dennis . . . dear God . . . *wake him up.*"

4

Dennis stared stupidly at me, and I started to jump across the counter to get to Price myself.

A gout of flame leapt in the parking lot. Sparks marched across the concrete. I shouted, "Get down!" and twisted around to push Cheryl back behind the shelter of the counter.

"What the *hell*—" Dennis said.

He didn't finish. There was the metallic thumping of bullets hitting the gas pumps and the cars. I knew if that gas blew we were all dead. My truck shuddered with the impact of slugs, and I saw the whole thing explode as I ducked behind the counter. Then the windows blew inward with a god-awful crash, and the diner was full of flying glass, swirling wind, and sheets of rain. I heard Lindy scream, and both the kids were crying, and I think I was shouting something myself.

The lights had gone out, and the only illumination was the reflection of red neon off the concrete and the glow of the fluorescents over the gas pumps. Bullets whacked into the wall, and crockery shattered as if it had been hit with a hammer. Napkins and sugar packets were flying everywhere.

Cheryl was holding on to me as if her fingers were nails sunk to my bones. Her eyes were wide and dazed, and she kept trying to speak. Her mouth was working, but nothing came out.

There was another explosion as one of the other cars blew. The whole place shook, and I almost puked with fear.

Another hail of bullets hit the wall. They were tracers, and they jumped and ricocheted like white-hot cigarette butts. One of them sang off the edge of a shelf and fell to the floor about three feet away from me. The glowing slug began to fade, like the beer can and the mirage steak. I put my hand out to find it, but all I felt was splinters of glass and crockery.

A phantom bullet, I thought. Real enough to cause damage and death—and then gone.

You don't want me around here, Mr. Trooper, Price had warned. *Not with the body count I've got in my head.*

The firing stopped. I got free of Cheryl and said, "You stay right *here.*" Then I looked up over the counter and saw my truck and the station wagon on fire, the flames being whipped by the wind. Rain slapped me across the face as it swept in where the window glass used to be. I saw Price lying still huddled on the floor, with pieces of glass all around him. His hands were clawing the air, and in the flickering red neon his face was contorted, his eyes still closed. The pool of ketchup around his head made him look like his skull had been split open. He was peering into hell, and I averted my eyes before I lost my own mind.

Ray and Lindy and the two children had huddled under the table of their booth. The woman was sobbing brokenly. I looked at Dennis, lying a few feet from Price: he was sprawled on his face, and there were four holes punched through his back. It was not ketchup that ran in rivulets around Dennis' body. His right arm was outflung, and the fingers twitched around the gun he gripped.

Another flare sailed up from the woods like a Fourth of July sparkler.

When the light brightened, I saw them: at least five figures, maybe more. They were crouched over, coming across the parking lot—but slowly, the speed of nightmares. Their clothes flapped and hung around them, and the flare's light glanced off their helmets. They were carrying weapons—rifles, I guessed. I couldn't see their faces, and that was for the best.

On the floor, Price moaned. I heard him say "light . . . in the light . . ."

The flare hung right over the diner. And then I knew what was going on. *We* were in the light. We were all caught in Price's nightmare, and the Nightcrawlers that Price had left in the mud were fighting the battle again—the same way it had been fought at the Pines Haven Motor Inn. The

Nightcrawlers had come back to life, powered by Price's guilt and whatever that Howdy Doody shit had done to him.

And we were in the light, where Charlie had been out in that rice paddy.

There was a noise like castanets clicking. Dots of fire arced through the broken windows and thudded into the counter. The stools squealed as they were hit and spun. The cash register rang and the drawer popped open, and then the entire register blew apart and bills and coins scattered. I ducked my head, but a wasp of fire—I don't know what, a bit of metal or glass maybe—sliced my left cheek open from ear to upper lip. I fell to the floor behind the counter with blood running down my face.

A blast shook the rest of the cups, saucers, plates, and glasses off the shelves. The whole roof buckled inward, throwing loose ceiling tiles, light fixtures, and pieces of metal framework.

We were all going to die. I knew it, right then. Those things were going to destroy us. But I thought of the pistol in Dennis' hand, and of Price lying near the door. If we were caught in Price's nightmare and the blow from the ketchup bottle had broken something in his skull, then the only way to stop his dream was to kill him.

I'm no hero. I was about to piss in my pants, but I knew I was the only one who could move. I jumped up and scrambled over the counter, falling beside Dennis and wrenching at that pistol. Even in death, Dennis had a strong grip. Another blast came, along the wall to my right. The heat of it scorched me, and the shock wave skidded me across the floor through glass and rain and blood.

But I had that pistol in my hand.

I heard Ray shout, "Look out!"

In the doorway, silhouetted by flames, was a skeletal thing wearing muddy green rags. It wore a dented-in helmet and carried a corroded, slime-covered rifle. Its face was gaunt and shadowy, the features hidden behind a scum of rice-paddy muck. It began to lift the rifle to fire at me—slowly, slowly . . .

I got the safety off the pistol and fired twice, without

aiming. A spark leapt off the helmet as one of the bullets was deflected, but the figure staggered backward and into the conflagration of the station wagon, where it seemed to melt into ooze before it vanished.

More tracers were coming in. Cheryl's Volkswagen shuddered, the tires blowing out almost in unison. The state-trooper car was already bullet-riddled and sitting on flats.

Another Nightcrawler, this one without a helmet and with slime covering the skull where the hair had been, rose up beyond the window and fired it's rifle. I heard the bullet whine past my ear, and as I took aim I saw its bony finger tightening on the trigger again.

A skillet flew over my head and hit the thing's shoulder, spoiling its aim. For an instant the skillet stuck in the Nightcrawler's body, as if the figure itself was made out of mud. I fired once . . . twice . . . and saw pieces of matter fly from the thing's chest. What might've been a mouth opened in a soundless scream, and the thing slithered out of sight.

I looked around. Cheryl was standing behind the counter, weaving on her feet, her face white with shock. "Get down!" I shouted, and she ducked for cover.

I crawled to Price, shook him hard. His eyes would not open. "Wake up!" I begged him. "Wake up, damn you!" And then I pressed the barrel of the pistol against Price's head. Dear God, I didn't want to kill anybody, but I knew I was going to have to blow the Nightcrawlers right out of his brain. I hesitated—too long.

Something smashed into my left collarbone. I heard the bone snap like a broomstick being broken. The force of the shot slid me back against the counter and jammed me between two bullet-pocked stools. I lost the gun, and there was a roaring in my head that deafened me.

I don't know how long I was out. My left arm felt like dead meat. All the cars in the lot were burning, and there was a hole in the diner's roof that a tractor-trailer truck could've dropped through. Rain was sweeping into my face, and when I wiped my eyes clear I saw them, standing over Price.

There were eight of them. The two I thought I'd killed were back. They trailed weeds, and their boots and ragged clothes were covered with mud. They stood in silence, staring down at their living comrade.

I was too tired to scream. I couldn't even whimper. I just watched.

Price's hands lifted into the air. He reached for the Nightcrawlers, and then his eyes opened. His pupils were dead white, surrounded by scarlet.

"End it," he whispered. "End it . . ."

One of the Nightcrawlers aimed its rifle and fired. Price jerked. Another Nightcrawler fired, and then they were all firing point-blank into Price's body. Price thrashed and clutched at his head, but there was no blood; the phantom bullets weren't hitting him.

The Nightcrawlers began to ripple and fade. I saw the flames of the burning cars through their bodies. The figures became transparent, floating in vague outlines. Price had awakened too fast at the Pines Haven Motor Inn, I realized; if he had remained asleep, the creatures of his nightmares would've ended it there, at that Florida motel. They were killing him in front of me—or he was allowing them to end it, and I think that's what he must've wanted for a long, long time.

He shuddered, his mouth releasing a half-moan, half-sigh. It sounded almost like relief.

The Nightcrawlers vanished. Price didn't move anymore.

I saw his face. His eyes were closed, and I think he must've found peace at last.

5

A trucker hauling lumber from Mobile to Birmingham saw the burning cars. I don't even remember what he looked like.

Ray was cut up by glass, but his wife and the kids were okay. Physically, I mean. Mentally, I couldn't say.

Cheryl went into the hospital for a while. I got a postcard from her with the Golden Gate Bridge on the front. She promised she'd write and let me know how she was doing, but I doubt if I'll ever hear from her. She was the best waitress I ever had, and I wish her luck.

The police asked me a thousand questions, and I told the story the same way every time. I found out later that no bullets or shrapnel were ever dug out of the walls or the cars or Dennis' body—just like in the case of that motel massacre. There was no bullet in me, though my collarbone was snapped clean in two.

Price had died of a massive brain hemorrhage. It looked, the police told me, as if it had exploded in his skull.

I closed the diner. Farm life is fine. Alma understands, and we don't talk about it.

But I never showed the police what I found, and I don't know exactly why not.

I picked up Price's wallet in the mess. Behind a picture of a smiling young woman holding a baby there was a folded piece of paper. On that paper were the names of four men.

Beside one name, Price had written "Dangerous."

I've found four other 'Nam vets who can do the same thing, Price had said.

I sit up at night a lot, thinking about that and looking at those names. Those men had gotten a dose of that Howdy Doody shit in a foreign place they hadn't wanted to be, fighting a war that turned out to be one of those crossroads of nightmare and reality. I've changed my mind about 'Nam because I understand now that the worst of the fighting is still going on, in the battlefields of memory.

A Yankee who called himself Tompkins came to my house one May morning and flashed me an ID that said he worked for a veterans' association. He was very soft-spoken and polite, but he had deep-set eyes that were almost black, and he never blinked. He asked me all about Price, seemed real interested in picking my brain of every detail. I told him the police had the story, and I couldn't add any more to it. Then I turned the tables and asked him about Howdy Doody. He smiled in a puzzled kind of way and said he'd never heard of any chemical defoliant called that. No such thing, he said. Like I say, he was very polite.

But I know the shape of a gun tucked into a shoulder holster. Tompkins was wearing one under his seersucker coat. I never could find any veterans' association that knew anything about him, either.

Maybe I should give that list of names to the police. Maybe I will. Or maybe I'll try to find those four men myself, and try to make some sense out of what's being hidden.

I don't think Price was evil. No. He was just scared, and who can blame a man for running from his own nightmares? I like to believe that, in the end, Price had the courage to face the Nightcrawlers, and in committing suicide he saved our lives.

The newspapers, of course, never got the real story. They called Price a 'Nam vet who'd gone crazy, killed six people in a Florida motel, and then killed a state trooper in a shoot-out at Big Bob's diner and gas stop.

But I know where Price is buried. They sell little American flags at the five-and-dime in Mobile. I'm alive, and I can spare the change.

And then I've got to find out how much courage *I* have.

Pin

I'm going to do it.

Yes. I am.

I hold the pin in my hand, and tonight I'm going to peer into the inner sun.

Then, when I'm filled up with all that glare and heat and my brain is on fire like a four-alarm blaze, I'm going to take my Winchester rifle down to the McDonald's on the corner and we'll see who says what to who when.

There you go, talking to yourself. Well, there's nobody else around, is there, so who am I supposed to talk to? No, no; my friend's here. Right here, in my hand. You know. Pin.

I have a small sharp friend. Oh, look at that little point gleam. It hypnotizes you, Pin does. It says look at me look long and hard and in me you will see your future. It is a very sharp future, and there is pain in it. Pin is better than God, because I can hold Pin. God frets and moans in silence, somewhere . . . up there, somewhere. Way above the ceiling. Damn, I didn't know that crack was there. No wonder this bitching place leaks.

Now, Johnny's an okay guy. I mean, I wouldn't shoot him. He's okay. The others at the stop—bam bam bam, dead in two seconds flat. I don't like the way they clam up when I walk past, like they've got secrets I'm not supposed to know anything about. Like you have secrets when you work on cars all day and fix tires and brake shoes and get that gunk under your fingernails that won't ever wash out? Some secrets. Now, Pin . . . Pin does have secrets. Tonight I'm going to learn them, and I'm going to share my knowledge with those people down on the corner eating their hamburgers in the safe safe world. I'll bet that damn roof doesn't leak I'll make it leak I'll put a bullet right through it, so there.

I'm sweating. Hot in here. Summer night, so what else is new?

Pin, you're so pretty you make me want to cry.

The trick, I think, is not to blink. I've heard about people who did this before. They saw the inner sun, and they went out radiant. It's always dark in here. It's always dark in this town. I think they need a little sunlight, don't you?

Who're you talking to, anyway? Me myself and I. Pin makes four. Hell, I could play bridge if I wanted to. Lucas liked to play bridge, liked to cheat and call you names and what else did you have to do in that place anyway? Oh, those white white walls. I think white is Satan's color, because it has no face. I saw that Baptist preacher on TV and he had on a white shirt with his sleeves rolled up. He said come down the aisle come on come on while you can and I'll show you the door to heaven.

It's a big white door, he said. And he smiled when he said it, and the way he smiled, oh, I knew I just knew he was really saying you're watching me aren't you, Joey? He was really saying, Joey you know all about big white doors, don't you, and how when they swing shut you hear the latch fall and the key rattle and that big white door won't open again until somebody comes and opens it. There was always a long time between the closing and the opening.

I've always wanted to be a star. Like on TV or movies, somebody important with a lot of people nodding around you and saying you make a lot of sense. People like that always look like they know where they're going and they're always in a hurry to get there. Well, I know where I'm going now. Right down to the corner, where the golden arches are. Look out my window, I can see it. There goes a car turning in. Going to be full up on a Saturday night. Full up. My Winchester has a seven-shot magazine. Checkered American walnut. Satin finish. Rubber butt plate. It weighs seven pounds, a good weight. I have more bullets, too. Full up on a Saturday night. Date night, oh yes, I hope she's there that girl you know the one she drives a blue Camaro and she has long blond hair and eyes like diamonds. Diamonds are hard, but you hit one with a bullet and it's not so hard anymore.

Pin, we won't think about her, will we? Nope! If she's there it's fate. Maybe I won't shoot her, and she'll see I'm a nice guy.

Hold Pin close. Closer. Closer still. Up against the right eye. I've thought a long time about this. It was a tough decision. Left or right? I'm right-handed, so it makes sense to use my right eye. I can already see the sun sparkle on the end of Pin, like a promise.

Oh, what I could do with a machine gun. Eliot Ness, Untouchables, tommy-gun-type thing. I sure could send a lot of people behind that big white door, couldn't I? See, the funny thing I mean really funny thing is that everybody wants to go to heaven but everybody's scared to die. That's what I'm going to say when the lights come on and that news guy sticks a microphone in my face. I need to shave first. I need to wear a tie. No, they won't know me with a tie on. I need to wear my gray uniform—gray, now there's a man's color. Pick you up good on TV in gray.

Speak to me, Pin. Say it won't hurt.

Oh, you lying little bitch.

It has to be in the center. In that black part. It has to go in deep. Real deep, and you have to keep pushing it in until you see the inner sun. You know, I'll bet that part's dead anyway. I'll bet you can't even feel any pain in the black part. Just push it in and keep pushing, and you'll see that sunburst and then you can go down and have a hamburger when it's all said and done.

Sweating. Hot night. That fan's not worth a damn, it just makes a racket.

Are you ready?

Closer, Pin. Closer. I never knew the point could look so big. Closer. Almost touching. Don't blink! Cowards blink, nobody can ever say Joey Shatterly's a coward no sir!

Wait. Wait. I think I need a mirror for this.

I smell under my arms. Ban roll-on. You don't want to smell when they turn the lights on you what if it's not the guy but the girl who does the late news the one with big boobs and a smile like frostbite?

No, I don't need to shave I look fine. Oh hell I'm out of Ban. Old Spice that'll do. My dad used to use Old Spice everybody's dad did. Now, that was a good day, when we saw the Reds play the Pirates and he bought me a bag of peanuts and said he was proud of me. That was a good day. Well, he was a fruitcake though a real Marine oh sure. I remember that Iwo Jima crap when he got crazy and drank all the time Iwo Jima Iwo Jima all the time I mean he lived it in his mind a million times. You got sick of hearing who all died at Iwo Jima and how come you ought to be proud to be an American and how things weren't how they used to be. Nothing is, is it? Except Old Spice. They still sell it, and the bottle's still the same. Iwo Jima Iwo Jima. And then he went and did it, put the rope up in the garage and stepped off the ladder and me coming in to get my bike and that grin on his face that said Iwo Jima.

Oh, Ma, I didn't mean to find him. Why didn't you go in there so you could hate yourself?

Now, that was a good day, when we saw the Reds play the Pirates and he bought me a bag of peanuts and said he was proud of me. He was a real Marine.

The black part looks small in the mirror, small as a dot. But Pin's smaller. Sharp as truth. My Winchester holds seven bullets. Magnificent seven I always liked Steve McQueen with that little sawed-off shotgun he died of cancer I think.

Pin, you're so beautiful. I want to learn things. I want to know secrets. In the glare of the inner sun I will walk tall and proud like a Marine on the hot sands of Iwo Jima. Closer, Pin. Closer still. Almost there. Close against the black part, the unblinking black. Look in the mirror, don't look at Pin. Don't blink! Closer. Steady, steady. Don't . . .

Dropped. Don't go down the sink! Get Pin, get it! Don't let it go . . .

There you are. Sweet Pin, sweet friend. My fingers are sweating. Wipe them off nice and neat on a towel. Holiday Inn. When did I stay at a Holiday Inn? When I went and visited Ma oh yes that's right. Somebody else lived in the old house a man and woman I never knew their names and Ma she just sat in that place with the rocking chairs and talked about Dad. She said Leo came to see her and I said Leo is in California and she said you hate Leo don't you? I don't hate Leo. Leo takes good care of Ma, sends her money and keeps her in that place, but I miss the old house. Nothing's how it used to be the whole world is turning faster and faster and sometimes I hold on to my bed because I'm scared the world is going to throw me off like an old shoe. So I hang on and my knuckles get white and pretty soon I can stand up and walk again. Baby steps.

Who blew that horn? Camaro, wasn't it? Blond girl at the wheel? Seven bullets. I'll make a lot of horns blow.

How straight and strong Pin is, like a little silver arrow. How were you made, and who made you? There are millions and millions of pins, but there is only one Pin. My friend, my key to light and truth. You shine and wink, and you say look into the inner sun and take your Winchester to the golden arches where Marines fear to tread.

I'm going to do it.

Yes. I am.

Closer. Closer.

Right up against the black. Shining silver, full of truth. Pin, my friend.

Look at the mirror. Don't blink. Oh . . . sweating . . . sweating. Don't blink!

Closer. Almost there. Silver, filling up the black. Almost. Almost.

You will not blink. No. You will not. Pin will take care of you. Pin will lead you. You. Will. Not. Blink.

Think about something else. Think about . . . Iwo Jima.
Closer. Almost.

One jab. Quick.

Quick.

There.

Ow.

OW. Don't. Don't. *Don't blink.* Don't, okay? Yes. Got it
now. Ow. Hurts. Little bit. Pin, my friend. All silver. Hurts
like truth. Yes it does. Another jab. Quick.

Oh, Jesus. Deeper. Little bit deeper. Oh, don't blink
please please don't blink. Look right there, there yes in the
mirror push it deeper I was wrong the black part isn't dead.

Deeper.

Oh. Oh. Okay. Oh. *Get it out!* No. Deeper. Got to see the
inner sun I'm sweating Joey Shatterly's no coward no sir no
sir. Deeper. Easy, easy. Oh. Streak of light that time. Blue
light. Not a sunburst, a cold moon. Push it in. Oh. Oh.
Hurting. Oh, it hurts. Blue light. Please don't blink push it
in oh oh Dad where's my bike?

OH GOD GET IT OUT GET IT OUT OH IT HURTS
GET IT . . .

No. Deeper.

My face. Twitching. Pain. Cold pain. Twitching. Seven
bullets. Down to the golden arches and deeper still where is
the inner s . . .

Oh . . . it . . . hurts . . . so . . . good . . .

Pin, sliding in. Slow. Cold steel. I love you, Dad. Pin,
show me the truth show me show me show . . .

Deeper. Through the pulse. Center of the unblinking
black. White's turned red. Seven bullets, seven names.
Deeper, to the center of the inner sun.

Oh! There! I saw it! See! Right there! I saw a flash of it push
it deeper into the brain where the inner sun is right there! A
flash of light! Pin, take me there. Pin . . . take me there . . .

Please.

Deeper. Past pain. Cold. Inner sun burning. Makes you
smile. Almost there.

Push it in. Using all of Pin up. A mighty pain.

White light. Flashbulb. Hi, Ma! Oh . . . there . . . right there . . .

Pin, sing to me.

Deeper.

I love you, Dad . . . Ma, I'm so sorry I had to find him I didn't mean to I didn't . . .

One more push. A little one. Pin is almost gone. My eye is heavy, freighted with sight . . .

Pin, sing to me.

Dee

Yellachile's Cage

I kant write too good, but I wanted to get this down. On paper, where it seems more real than it does in your head. A pincil and erasore can be messy things, cant they? Well, I am gone start learnin me how to use that machine up in the liberry. Mister Wheeler say he gone teach me them keys and how to put that ribbon in and all, and he's a truthful man.

Well, now that Im started I dont know where to go. Reckon you should always start at the first, huh? So thats a good place.

I did the crime they said I did, and I never said I didn't. Mans gone cut you, you got to cut him first. I seen the blade grin when he jerked it out of his coat, and thank the Lord I've got a fast hand or Id be sitting in the clouds right now. My momma now, she'd be saying Id be sitting on a hot rock where the sun dont shine. I gave her a lot of trouble, I reckon. Gave everybody a lot of trouble. Well, you don't get in prison for singing too loud in church, thats for damn sure.

I always heard things about the Brickyard. Bricknell Prison's its real name, but nobody inside and few outside call it that. Its the kind of place you hear about when your a kid and you start sassin and crossing the line real early. You know what I mean. Lord, if I had ten cents for every time somebody in Masonville said, "Boy, you gone wind up in the Brickyard yet!" I sure as hell wouldn't have got here in the first place. Masonvilles where I was born and raised, but it aint my home. I never felt much like I had a home. My old man run off when I was a kid. Mama say I look just like him and I got his bad blood too and I say you better quit that talking or Im gone tear this house up. And I would, too. Pretend I was crazy mean just to get her to stop that talking about how bad I was and how bad my old man was and all that such jive. To this day she say I got such a temper I could blow the Brickyard's walls down, but I just pretended to get mad so I could get me some elbow room. Somebody thinks your crazy mean, they aint gone be hanging on your ass ragging you all the time.

Aint much to say about the Brickyard. Its gray, even when the bright sun comes in the winders. Long halls, lots of cages. Always smells like sweat, or piss, or that sick-smelling crap they use to wash down the walls and floors. Toilet backed up in the cell next to mine few days ago, you shoulda seen ol' Duke and Kingman doin the highstep in there and hollerin their heads off. This is an old prison, and at night it moans.

I turned twenty-one a week before they brought me here. Closed the gates behind me on March 24, at sixteen minutes after ten in the mornin. The clocks at the Brickyard work real good, and you remember things like that. Its been seventeen months, twelve days, and four hours since them gates closed and locked, and its been five days since Whitey passed on. I dont say die, cause Im startin to think theres no such thing. These last five days, well, theyve been real strange. I thought and thought of the right word to discribe them but I dont know words so good yet. When I walked in here I couldnt hardly read or write, and now look at me here with a pincil cuttin a buck.

Ive spent time in juve centers and workhomes and crap like that, but you say "Prison" and your talking a different animal. You walk in a prison like the Brickyard and you be twenty-one years old and you better keep a tight ass and your head tucked down real low to the ground or somebody he gone knock it off cause thats his kick. My first day I didnt answer when a plowboy said somethin to me and I got a fist upside my head and a size-ten boot in my jewlls. Im not such a big feller and I learned real quick that playin crazy mean don't go too far in here. Theres plenty who are crazy mean for sure, and they love to do the fandango on your backbone. Anyways, I didnt pay a feller no respect and I was in the hospital bout three hours after the Cap'n dropped me down the chute.

I woke up to somebody pokin the bandage on my head, and I liked to jump out of that bed cause I thought oh Lord they gone bounce me again.

Old man standin next to my bed. Wearing the gray pajamas they give you when your sick or laid up. He say, "Boy, you look like you been killed, buried, and dug up." His voice made me think of my momma's knuckles scrubbin wet clothes on a washboard. He laughed, but I didn't think it was too funny. He say, "Whats your name?" and I told him but he say, "The hell it is! You a Wanda, boy! A fresh-meat, dumb-ass Wanda is what you are!"

Wanda is what they called the new boys at the Brickyard. At least right then. The name changed every few weeks, always some girl's name.

"You a big, bad Wanda, aint you?" he asked, just standing there and grinnin like a black ole fool. He was blacker than me, that African black that's so black you can see blue through the skin. And his eyes were pale amber behind a little pair of wire glasses and he had a tight cap of white hair done in cornrows. His face looked like the bottom of a dried-up mud pond, and I swear there wasnt enough room for another wrinkle. I mean, he was old! Maybe like sixty-five or something, I figured. But he was skinny like me, just walkin bones, and those hospital duds hung on him like a tent.

"Go way and leave me alone," I remember sayin to him. My head was aching fit to bust, I couldnt see straight, and all I wanted to do was sleep.

"Wanda says go way. Think we ought to?" Talkin to somebody else, only there wasnt nobody in the beds around.

"Crazy as hell," I say, and he smile and say, "Yellachile, look at a prime cut of fool."

Well, he holds up somethin out of them gray tent folds and

I saw what it was: a little yella bird. A canary, I guessed it was. My Aunt Mondy had a canary in a cage that she called Sweet Thang and a cat thought it was sweet too cause it gulped it down and didnt leave a feather. He holds it in one hand and its wings are flappin like its fixin to fly and I figured bird shit on my head was about all I needed. I say, "Get that thing outta here!" and he say, "Yes'm, Wanda. Just for you." He put his other hand over it to keep it from flyin off, and back it went into the folds.

And then he leans over real close, and I saw his teeth were as yella as that bird, and he say soft like, "Wanda, you gone be in here for a long time. Cut a brother's throat, didnt you?"

"He tried to cut me first," I said. Didnt bother me that he knew. Aint no privacy in a prison.

"They all sing the same tune. Goes like this: tweet, tweet I didnt do it tweet tweet no sir not me tweet tweet . . ."

"Didnt say I didnt do it," I told him. "Just say I didnt pull the knife first."

"Yeah, and you stuck it in first too. Well, reckon the Brickyard's better than the boneyard, aint it?" He laughed; it was a little chuckle, but it brought a cough out of him and that made another cough come up and another one and then his eyes were full of hurt and he was hackin his lungs out.

"Your sick," I say when he stop that coughin.

"If I was well I wouldnt be in here with the likes of you, would I?" He wheezed a few times, and then whatever it was passed but he had a deep sickness in him. I could tell that right off. The whites of his eyes looked like cups of pus. "Come on, Yellachile," he said to the canary, "let's get on away from Wanda and let her get that beauty sleep she's gone need."

He didnt go too far, just to a bed across the aisle. He laid down on coarse linen like the King of Africa on a gold throne, and the sun was shining in through the bars hot and proper and somebody else was moppin the floor. I sits up and I saw that canary flying round and round over the African's bed, and all of a suddens he reached up and caught that bird and he pulls it to his cheek. Started whistlin to it, makin love sounds to a bird. I knows he's a number-one fool now! But after a while I got to enjoyin the sounds, and it seemed to me that him and the bird were talking back and forth in a language that was older than anythin Id ever heard. I laid my head back on a pillow and slept, and I dreamed of Aunt Mondy's canary flyin in its cage and a catface lookin in.

Well, time passes even in here. You get a routine, and thats how you live. They put me on the garbage detail, which is bout the lowest you can get and not be belly-crawlin, cause a prison's garbage sure aint perfumy. Lot of fellers wanted to fight me cause they heard I figured myself to be bad and suchlike, and plenty of times I got struck out but I hit me a few home runs too and that was all right. You dont fight back in prison, you might as well be sewing a gravesuit. The trick is not to hurt nobody too bad and cause a grudge. Grudges get you killed real quick. Anyway, I got me some friends and a new name. "Wanda" turned into "Wand," cause I'm so skinny, and by that time we were callin new meat "Lucys."

Every cellblock has a different schedool for time in the excercize yard. I was in Block D, and we went out at two-thirty. One day we were out there rappin and shooting some baskets and when we were resting we start talkin bout our first day in. Well, I told em about that old man and the canary, and Brightboy Stubbins say, "Lord, Wand! You done met Whitey and Yellachile!"

"Yellachile's that bird's name, I guess," I said, "but that old man sure aint a whitey!"

"Shush up, boy!" Stretch say. "You dont wanna be disrespectful to Whitey, no sir!"

"Aint being disrespectful," I say. "Aint being nothin. How come the hallboys let that old man keep a bird?" I remembered the Cap'n readin the rules in a roar that quaked my bones. "Aint supposed to be such a thing in here."

"Whitey's special," McCook say. "The hallboys leave him alone."

"Yeah, and you know why." Brightboy leans his head

down, like hes talkin to his shadow. "Whitey's a voodoo man, thass why. Lord, yes! He speaks the conjure tongue!"

I laughed. "Hell, the conjure tongue didnt keep him out of this place, did it?"

They all looked at me like I was a roach on two legs. Stretch put his hand on my shoulder, and Stretch has got a mighty big hand. "You listen up," he says, and the way his eyes were glintin I didnt think we were gonna be friends anymore. "Whitey Latrope is a mighty important feller around here. Dont matter if you dont believe in the power of the conjure tongue. He dont care. But dont you never show disrespect to Whitey, or you gone have to deal with ol' Stretch. Okay?"

I said okay real quick. Wouldnt want to knock heads with Stretch, no sir!

"Whitey Latrope's a voodoo man," Stretch said in that low quiet voice hes got, "and Yellachile aint just a bird. Yellachile knows things, and speaks em to Whitey."

"What things?" I was brave enough to ask.

"Yellachile flies out of his cage at night," Brightboy said, and it was funny to hear such a big man whisper. He looked past me, the sun slamming down on his moon-pie face. I saw he was staring at the tall fence topped with barbed wire, and the fence beyond that, and the gray stone wall that eight men had died tryin to get over, and the brown dusty hills and limp-limbed woods that surrounded the Brickyard for too many miles. "Yellachile flies," he say. His shadow lay across the tight fence mesh. "Out of his cage, through a winder, out of Block A, and gone."

"Gone?" I say. "Gone where?"

"Over the fence. Over the wall. To freedom and back again to his cage before the sun comes up and the whistle blows. And Yellachile tells Whitey where he's flown, and what he's seen out there. Tells him about the towns and the houses all full of light, and the people laughin' in the jukejoints and the music rollin out in the street like silver coins." Brightboy smiled just thinkin about such things, and I saw them in my head and I kind of smiled too. "Oh, that Yellachile goes to some wondrous towns," he said. "Places you never knowed about, but you always dreamed were there."

It was a nice spell, but it didnt hold me too long. "How do you know?" I asked him. "If Whitey's in Block A, how do you know?" There wasnt any mixing between the men in different blocks, see.

"Everybody knows," Stretch answered, and the way he said it let me know I was the big fool. "Besides, they rotate you around here every six months. That's to break up the doodle-dangers and the gangs. I was in Block E with him two years ago. Three cells down from mine."

"Well, I was right crost from him in '81," McCook say. "Block B. Yessir, I could look over there and see that bird flyin round like a little piece of sun every day!"

"Just hold on." Somethin peculiar had come to me, and I ought to say it. "How long's Whitey been in here?"

Stretch said goin on forty years. McCook said thirty-five. Brightboy believed it was between those numbers.

I say, "How long does a bird live? Cant no canary live forty years!"

"Yellachile's always been there," Stretch told me. "Always. Cant die. Whitey's a voodoo man, and Yellachile's his spirit."

That shut me up, but I sure was talkin in myself while we went back to basketball.

I got promoted. Left the garbage cans and got a mop and broom. I had the machine shop, and Lordy there was a lot to sweep up in there! I never could figure out what the machine shop was for. Just men workin on little engines and cogs and gears with plenty of time on their hands. Guess some of them did electrical work round the Brickyard, stuff like that. But one day the rain was pourin down the barred winders and I was sweepin and all of a suddens Pell Donner he say, "Wand! Come on, boy! Whitey's in the shop!"

I followed him, and there he was: the black African with white cornrow hair. Except he looked even skinnier in his prison duds. Looked like his face had grown more wrinkles, and his shirt and trousers hung on him, but I bet there wasnt no size smaller in the laundry. He was standin there with bout ten or eleven men round him, and he had his hands cupped together but I could see Yellachile in the cage of his fingers, every so often flappin his wings and tryin to peek out.

You never seen men with faces like children before if you werent there. And quiet—Lord yes. Even Roughhouse Clayton was quiet, and you couldnt shut him up if you knocked the mouth off his face. Whitey was talkin, and as he talked he kept liftin his hands and blowin little puffs of air in at Yellachile. But somethin was wrong with Whitey's lungs. They gurgled like backed-up drains, and he was havin trouble breathin. I figured cancer, or somethin else wicked.

"Yellachile done some flyin last night," Whitey said, raspy-soft, and his eyes shone behind those glasses like ghost lamps. "Yessir, done some fast and far flyin. Didnt ya?" He looked in at Yellachile, and the little bird cocked its head at him. "Where'd he go, I wonder?"

"Florida. Where it don't rain every night for two months," Billy Davis say.

"Flew to a big city," Junior Murdock say, his voice like a muted New Orleans trumpet. "Where the lights stay on all night long and them ladies parade the streets."

"The country." That was a new man I didnt know. "Over a farm where you can smell the green."

I said it. Dont know why. "Flew to Masonville."

He looked up from Yellachile. The canary's wings fluttered, and Whitey drew the bird against his sunken chest. "Masonville?" he ask. "Who say that?"

Junior Murdock motioned to me with a big black thumb. Somebody else moved aside, and another somebody else, and then I was lookin straight at Whitey and him at me. He nodded, smiled a little bit. "I know you," he say. "You aint a Wanda no more, are you?"

"They call me Wand now."

"I see why. Dont you eat?" he asked.

"Im still growin," I say, and he laugh a coughy laugh and said, "Well, aint we all!"

Then he gets up close in my face, those eyes bright and burnin, and I want to step back from them flames but I dont and all the machines are so quiet I can hear my heart beat. And he says, "Yessir, I do believe Yellachile flew to Masonville last night. Flew right over the heart of town. Lemme check." He lifted the bird to his mouth and gave a few gasping whistles, and then he put the bird to his ear and Yellachile's head cocked but I couldnt hear no song. "Yessir," he say, cupping the canary close again. "Yellachile sure did go to Masonville, and let me tell you what he say: Masonville's a town with two streets, one goin in and one goin out. Masonville's got a park in it, aint a big park, but there are lanterns in it that shed a golden light. Got park benches, and Yellachile he saw lovers on them benches in the golden light. Handsome men and women, they were, talkin of love. And round that park is the town, and in the dark all their lights were on too, so theres never a real dark, and people come and go as they please. The stars shone over Masonville last night, and the moon came up. Such a moon as can only be seen in Masonville. Aint no other place in the world to see it, cause it just bout fills up the sky its so big. Its a warm moon, and Yellachile looked at it from the branch of a pine tree there in that park. Yellachile brought the smell of pine needles on a warm night back with him. There it is." He inhaled. Everybody else did too. "Fresh pine needles," he say. "Bright moon. Handsome men and women in the golden light, under a sky full of stars. That's what Yellachile saw in Masonville. You see it too?"

He was asking me. I said, "Yes sir," and it was the truth.

Whitey smiled. "That makes Yellachile real happy." He stroked the canary with one finger, and the bird lay there content. "Tonight he might fly to Florida. Or over the country, where the land smells green. Never can tell where he'll fly." And then Whitey moved on, and it wasn't until a minute or so had passed that I started smellin machine oil and seein the stone walls again. Overhead was not stars and moon but a tangle of pipes. But just for a few minutes I had been back in Masonville, a long long way from here.

The hallboys came over and broke us up, and we got back to work. Real funny how a simple thing can stay with you. I kept seein Masonville, only after a while I kind of figured out it wasnt the Masonville I knew. No, the real Masonville had a factory in it that went day and night, and the smoke out of its chimneys didnt let you see the stars.

But Whitey had taken me out of the Brickyard for just a few minutes. I was there with Yellachile in the quiet park. No such park in Masonville. Did it matter? I was there. The Masonville in my head was better than the real one. From that moment on I knew the power of voodoo, and why Whitey was so special. He could melt the Brickyard's walls.

I couldnt figure the canary, though. How could a bird live for forty years?

Whitey came through the machine shop a lot of times. Always stopped. The hallboys let him talk, cause they seemed to enjoy it too. One night Yellachile went to Florida, and flew over Miami Beach. That was five hundred miles south, but Yellachile was a spirit and could go anywhere. I closed my eyes and saw all those big hotels and that ocean, and I aint never seen an ocean before cept on TV. Yellachile flew low over the waves, and I could smell the salt air. And one night Yellachile flew to the north and skimmed a field of snow where the tracks of deer led in all directions and the moon shone clear and so cold it made your teeth rattle. Over farms and orchards, deserts, big cities, rivers where barges hooted and tugged, woods lit by no gleam but starlight, islands where the water sounded like music and the air smelled like coconut and cinnamon. All those places and more. One night Yellachile flew through a window into a strip-tease club in New Orleans. Into a boxin arena, where two men battled to the roar of the crowd and the smell of cheap cigars and sweat hung at the roof. To a baseball game on a July night, and Lord I could taste the salted peanut that Yellachile stole from a white man's hand.

I needed to know where Yellachile went every night. I started living to know.

In my cell, after the whistle blew and the lights went out, I lay on my bunk and watched it happen: Yellachile let free from the cage of Whitey's fingers, flyin free and happy in a circle around his cornrowed hair, then flyin out through the bars in a flash of yella. Leavin the world of gray stone and barbed wire, out into the world of light and freedom. Over the Brickyard's turrets, over the fences, over the walls, faster and faster the wings beatin, climbin up to meet the night wind and then a long, slow drift over hazy land that had no beginnin and no end. I did not know the world, but Yellachile did, and Yellachile showed me places I always dreamed were there, far beyond Masonville.

If thats not magic, I dont know what is.

Whitey came one steamin hot day and we all knew things werent right. Knew it first thing. Whitey was havin trouble breathin, and he was coughin bout to burst his lungs. Even Yellachile looked sick, lyin there in his hands not jumpin around like usual. But Whitey came cause he knew how much we wanted to hear, and Id found out he had a route round the prison and the hallboys and even the Cap'n let him alone. The machine-shop work stopped, and we gathers to hear, and he says Yellachile flew a long way last night. Long way, and thats why Yellachile was a little bit tired today. Flew to the Land of the Midnight Sun, he says. Got night and sun at the same time, and its at the top of the world. Yellachile had played in the cool breezes, danced over the ice, and felt the world turnin underneath him. Big old world, it was. So much and so many, worlds inside worlds. Cant you feel that cool wind on your face? Draw a breath. Your lungs are cold, got needles inside em. Aint no heat up there, no drippin wet swelter, no sir. Just cool and quiet, and under the ice life movin in blue water . . .

He fell.

His hands opened. Yellachile fell out, wings flutterin. Hit the floor. Whitey went down too, and I saw the knee that crushed Yellachile.

Better believe we were all right there with him. The hallboys came runnin up too, and somebody tried to turn Whitey over. He was coughing fierce, and stranglin. Through the strangle he say, "Yellachile, Yellachile," like he was callin for a lost baby.

His knee moved. I was closest to him. Yellachile gave an awful smashed twitch. I put my hand around the canary real soft and picked him up. Yellachile twitched, lolled, lay still.

I knew.

Whitey's eyes were on me. He coughed blood out of his mouth, and he say, "My Yellachile!" in such a thunder that I had to press the mangled thing into his hand. Then the hallboys took him away, and I went off behind a greasy machine that spat out cogs and sat there for a long time not sayin nothin, just thinkin.

I cried that night. I aint shamed to admit it. Damn you if you think Im not a man.

I never said nothin. Never. And wasnt a week later that a hallboy came to my cell. Said he was takin me to see Whitey, and that the Cap'n had given the okay.

Whitey's cell had a green curtain cross the bars. I went in, and the hallboy left us alone, just me, the voodoo man and Yellachile.

"Sit down, Wand," Whitey say. Lord, that was a tired voice. Almost used up. The light was dim in here. Somehow I always thought his cell would be full of light, but it wasnt no more than anybody elses. He was sittin at a little desk, and he looked pitiful frail. In front of him was a handkerchief with bloodspots all over it. I sat down on the bunk.

"Say hello, Yellachile." Whitey opened his clasped hands, and the canary flew in a happy circle over his head. It went around three times before Whitey caught it, like he mustve done a thousand times before.

"Yellachiles all fixed now," he say. "Good as new."

"I see that," I told him.

In his hands, the birds wings kept beatin. Its head twitched from side to side. After a little while, he let it wind down. The wings stopped, and the little thing lay without movin.

"I used to work in a jewllry store in Miami," he says. "Long time back. I fixed wristwatches. Aint such a different thing." He laid the yella body on the desktop. My fingers still felt the seam along the underside of the body, and the little gears and cogs inside, the metal rods of the skeleton and wings. In your hands it didn't feel like a bird at all, and up close Id seen how the feathers were fallin out and the yella fabric was wearin away. It had been patched before, many times.

"Still do watch work," he went on. "The hallboys think I can fix anythin. Sometimes I do, sometimes I pull out a gear here, a wheel there, and I say sorry this watch has ticked its last second. Lots of parts inside Yellachile. Needs oil from the machine shop. Sometimes I rub oil on my fingers, just passin through, and that's enough to do the job. I can pick up little spare parts there too." He opened a drawer and pulled out a small metal box. When he lifted the lid, I saw it held tiny gears and wheels—watchwork parts—and tools like dentists use. Also needles and yella fabric. "The Cap'n knows. Hes all right, just talks tough."

I says, "Was there ever a real Yellachile?"

"Always was real!" He almost shouted it. "Still is!" The coughin came up, and he had to wait awhile and spit up a little drool of blood before he could talk again. "Yellachile flew into my cell my first month here. Wasnt much older than you. I trained that bird to fly up and down the cellblock and come back to me." A feeble smile tugged at his mouth. "That's how the voodoo talk started. I let it go on, cause I wasnt no fighter and I come mighty close to gettin my head split open number of times. Them bad boys heard I was a voodoo man and had myself a spirit bird, you damn be sure they left me be." He took Yellachile back with shakin fingers, and at a distance in the dim light it was a sleeping canary again. "Bird died. I kept it secret for a while. If Yellachile was dead, how could I be a voodoo man? Friend of mine on the cellblock, boy name of Tommy Haywood, had a daddy who ran a taxidermy shop in Nashville. See, it was mostly Tommy's idea cause he liked bein friends with a voodoo man. Get yourself lot of cigarettes and extra food that way. So Tommy packed Yellachile in a little box and mailed him up to Nashville, and in the meantimes I tell people Yellachile gone flyin on a long trip. I be goin up to the liberry and readin. Ever heard of the *Nattonal Geographic?*"

I says I believed I had.

"Got em there by the carton load. Course, lot of men here

cant read. Most dont want to. So you tell em stories—beautiful stories, about places theyre never gone see or places theyve been to and wont never see again. Freedom places, far from these walls. You take em out of here for five minutes and you get to be a voodoo man. See?"

I did, but I was heartsick. Lord, what a tumble my soul had taken!

"Yellachile comes back bout a month later. Looked fine but still wasnt done. So I went to work as a watchfixer cause I knew the gears would have to be mighty small. Lots of times I bout gave it up. Fixin the wings to beat was hardest, and that took me a year or more. Workin all night by a candle, night after night. Messed up somethin, you start all over again. What else you got to do in the Brickyard, huh?"

I said I didnt know.

Whitey ran a finger over one of the tiny glass eyes. "Figured it was beyond me. Figured only God can make a bird, and I ought to just go ahead and tell em the truth. I was near bout to . . . but all of a suddens the word comes that somebody down in Block E saw Yellachille flyin over the fence pretty as you please. Somebody else says he seen Yellachile too, sittin on top of the wall like he owned heaven and earth. Fella says he dreamed about Yellachile the night before, saw that bird flyin over his hometown and over the house where his wife and baby were. Yellachile's comin' back, they start sayin. Comin' back from the hand of God."

He lifted his palsied hand and stared at it. Then he reached with that same hand into the metal box and brought out a little silver key. He put that key into a place underneath Yellachile's tailfeathers and gave it a few turns.

There was a tiny clicking, chimy sound. The canary's body twitched, the wings started flappin. Whitey tossed the canary up into the air with a quick snap of his wrist, and the way he did it made it look as if Yellachile had taken off under his own power. The movement of the wings took it a couple of clumsy circles, not like a bird at all if you knew it wasnt and you hadnt seen birds for a while, and just as the body started to fall Whitey reached up and caught it. Whitey held it in the cage of his hands, and the little head seemed to be peckin at the fingers.

"He only sings to me now," Whitey says, and he gave a soft whistle and held Yellachile up to his ear. He listened, smiled, and nodded. "Want to hear where Yellachile went?"

I didnt answer.

He says, "Yellachile flew a long way from here, to a land where there aint no cages: Aint no walls neither. Aint nothin to stop you from goin when you want to go and restin when you want to rest. Says its a mighty big land, and says theres room for everybody. Got peach trees there. Ever smelled peaches in an April breeze? Got rivers there, and all of em flow to the sea, and if you want you can have starlight at high noon and sunshine at midnight. Says theyve been askin about me there, askin why Im so late a-comin. Yellachile told em Id be along pretty soon, but first Ive got me a job to do."

"Job?" I asked. "What kinda job?"

"Buildin a new cage for Yellachile," Whitey says. "This aint it." He held up his hands, with Yellachile moving within. "This was always Yellachile's cage," he says, and he tapped his cornrowed skull. "Always was. Such a cage as that cant never be locked."

I listened. I thought I knew what he was gettin at, but I wasnt sure.

"I need you, Wand," Whitey says, and his eyes were fierce and strong again, though there were flecks of blood on his lips. "You know I do."

"I cant do nothin," I told him.

"Cant do nothin if you say you cant. Your a young boy, and I think youve got some sense." He gave a sly smile. "Maybe not much sense, but its in there. You let me teach you what I know, and you can be Yellachile's cage. I can show you how to fix the gears and keep em oiled. I can show you how to hold Yellachile so wont nobody know he aint real. I can teach you things about the world, boy. Show you them books, and if you cant read em you can look at the pictures til they come alive in your head. I can teach you to listen and hear a mans life story in a sentence. You can keep Yellachile alive . . . and if you do, hes gone take you places you always dreamed were true."

"No," I said. "I couldnt do none of that."

"Why not?" he asked me, and he let it hang.

It was up to me. Now I wont lie and tell you I said yes. I didnt. I got up and left, cause what he was talkin was way beyond me. I wasnt no voodoo man. Didnt particularly care to be, neither. But at night I had trouble sleepin. When I did, I dreamed about Yellachile flyin in the dark, lookin for a place to come down. Just flyin and flyin and no rest in sight, and gettin so tired and weak that the wind shoved it any old direction. Soon Yellachile would be so far from the Brickyard that he couldnt come back, not ever. Then those stone walls and those barbed-wire fences would be our world, and that would be the end of it.

I missed Yellachile so bad. I yearned, and I needed.

Whitey worked on the Brickyard's clocks. Thats why they kept such good time. He told the Cap'n he needed a helper. Lots of clocks in the Brickyard, lots of chances to watch time crawlin past.

It wasnt no easy thing. Whitey tried to give me a lifetime of learnin in eight months. Some of it sank in, some of it I had to do my own way.

I dont show Yellachile so much as he did cause my hands aint as quick. Well, Im learnin. Gonna take time, and Ive sure enough got a lot of that.

I never said I was a voodoo man, but the word gets round. Whitey left Yellachile to me when he passed on, and people want to believe and so thats all right too. Ive had to get glasses, and readin's easier. Still a lot to learn, though, but I feel alive in a way I aint never known before. Feel like I used to be a dead man just walkin around in skin.

Oh, them faces when they see Yellachile! They want to know where Yellachile went last night. They want to hear did Yellachile fly over the turrets and drop a spot on the stones for good measure? Did Yellachile go south, or north, or east, or west? Did he see mountains, rivers, orchards, fields, and hometowns? Did he fly over baseball fields and jukejoints, and did he hear hot jazz music and the silver laughter of women? I say yes, all of those and more. And then I tell them. Not so good as Whitey, but Yellachile's cage is in me now, and I do the best I can.

Somethin in me has been set free from a cage I never knew was there. It flies with Yellachile at night, and we go together on the wind. Sometimes we pass over Masonville, over that park with the golden lamps, on and on and into the world of many worlds that lies before us. It is a mighty big land, and it makes the Brickyard's walls seem like little threads of nothin.

Im gone stop writin now. Gone put these papers away in a safe place. Like I say, Mister Wheeler's helpin me to read and write better, and Im curious bout that old typewriter over there. Maybe I ought to write down some of where Yellachile flies to. Maybe I will.

I aint no voodoo man. Im Yellachile's cage, and thats plenty magic enough.

I Scream Man!

Chimes ring like church bells in the still, hot August night, down at the end of Briarwood Street. I know that sound. I Scream Man! I Scream Man's on his way!

Saturday night. "The Love Boat" is on television, and in the living room the lamps are low. On the floor is the game of Scrabble we've been playing. As usual, I'm losing—which is ridiculous, since I'm an English teacher at the high school and if I know anything, it's how to spell! But the kids always beat me at Scrabble, and Sandra's pretty good at coming up with words that nobody's ever heard of before. It's a good game for a hot summer night.

"Malengine," Sandra says, placing her tiles down on the board. She smiles up at me.

"That's not a word!" Jeff says. "Challenge her, Dad!"

"Challenge her, Dad!" Bonnie echoes.

"Nope. Sorry. It's a word," I tell them. "It means 'something created for the purpose of destruction.' Like a bad engine or something. Sorry, gang." I mentally total up Sandra's points, and I see she's almost got enough to win the game. "We've got to stop her!" I tell my kids. "She's gonna beat us again! Bonnie, you're next! Think hard!"

The screen door is open, and over the noise of the television's laugh track I hear those chimes approaching from along the block. I Scream Man's coming!

Bonnie's small hand plucks up a tile. She considers the

word she's trying to put together in her head, but it won't jell. I can always tell when she's thinking hard, because two small parallel lines surface between her eyes. She has eyes like her mother's—dark green. Jeff has my brown eyes.

I sit down on the floor and wait. "Come on, slowpoke!" Jeff says. "I've got a good word!"

Bonnie says, "Don't rush me! I'm thinkin'!"

"Lord, it's a hot night." Sandra rubs her hand across her forehead. "We've *got* to get that air conditioner fixed."

"We will. Next week. I promise."

"Uh-huh. You said that *last* week. I don't think we can make it the rest of the summer like this. It must be ninety degrees in here!"

"More like a hundred and ninety," Jeff says glumly. "My shirt's stickin' to my back."

I cock my head and listen to the still-distant chimes: *ding ding ding!* When I was a kid, I loved that sound. Now it retains a powerful image of summer, of trees thick and green with summer leaves, of lightning bugs flashing in the dark, of hot dogs turning black over charcoal, and marshmallows charring, charring, char . . .

I Scream Man's on his way!

That's what Bonnie calls him: the I Scream Man. We all call him that now. When I think of him, I think of summer evenings—long, hot nights with nowhere to go and nothing to do. I think of my childhood, and running out into the purple twilight to hand over a quarter for a taste of cool heaven on a stick. Oh, the colors of those frozen ices: robin's-egg blue, banana yellow, grape as deep as a bruise, red the color of fire. I sure do love the I Scream Man!

It *is* hot in the house. "Next week I'll fix the air conditioner," I tell Sandra and she nods. "I promise, okay?"

Something stirs over in the corner, where the stack of newspapers lies. I sit very still, listening, but the sound doesn't repeat. I hear the *ding ding ding!*

"My word," Bonnie announces gravely, "is R . . . A . . . T." And she puts her tiles down on the yellowed board.

"Some word! Anybody can come up with a dumb word like that!" Jeff says with a hint of annoyance.

"Hey, be a sport. Okay, that's a good word, Bonnie. Your turn, Jeff."

He hunkers down on his stomach, his palms cradling his chin. He's a handsome boy. I like to think that he looks like me when I was twelve years old.

Ding ding ding! Getting closer.

"Oh, it's hot!" Sandra fans herself with her hand. "I feel like I'm running a *fever!*"

Again, something rustles in the newspapers. I watch, very carefully. I have good eyes for a man my age. As Jeff ponders his tiles, I see the glint of small, greedy eyes in the corner. "He's coming out again," I tell them in a whisper, and I pick up the pistol on the floor at my side.

I've been waiting for him to make his move. I feel like Gary Cooper in *High Noon*. He pokes his head out, and that's all the target I need. The noise of the pistol seems to shake the house, and more blood splatters the wall in the corner. "Fixed you, you bastard!" I shout gleefully.

As the echo of the gunshot dies, I realize the room is very quiet. Too quiet, I think. They've stopped playing, and they're looking at me as if I'm a stranger. "Hey!" I tell them. "What we need is louder laughter!" So I get up and turn the volume control way up high. The house is full of laughter now, it sounds like a three-ring circus. Sandra said she'd like to take a cruise someday.

"Bermuda," I say, and I put my hand on her shoulder. "That'd be a great place to take a cruise to, wouldn't it? I hear it's always nice and cool in Bermuda."

She doesn't speak for a while. She's having trouble making her mouth work. Then she smiles again and says, "Sssssure! Bermuda would be a great place to visit!"

"Where are you gonna send us?" Jeff asks. "East Podunk? I've got a word." He spells it out as he puts the little tiles down like tombstones: "*D . . . I . . . E . . . D*. That's a neat word, isn't it?"

I'm not sure about that one. It doesn't seem like a very

good word to me. I have an L in my group of letters, and I replace the first D with the L to make LIED. "There," I say. "Now. That's better."

Ding ding ding! The I Scream Man is almost in front of our house, and I can hear him calling, "Vanilla! Chocolate! Double-dip strawberry red!"

It's my turn now. I look at my tiles, and they remind me of teeth. I'm afraid they're going to snap at my fingers when I try to pick them up.

Ding ding ding! "Vanilla! Chocolate! Double-dip strawberry red!"

"Daddy?" Bonnie says in a small, whispery voice. Her eyes are very large in her pale, fragile face. "The I Scream Man is almost here."

"No he's not. He's a long way off. Let's see, now." I'm sweating. Jesus, it's hot!

"Yes he *is* almost here," Bonnie continues. She always was a willful child. It's very hard sometimes to control willful children. But I love her so much. Oh, God, so very very much. And I love Jeff, and I love Sandra with all the life left in my body. I want to take her on a cruise to Bermuda. It's not hot there; the air is always fresh and cool. "He's almost outside, Daddy."

"He is not!" I shout, and my voice cracks. I see Bonnie's face distort, and I hug her close to me before she has a chance to cry. I swore that I would never make my children cry. I'm a good father. I'm so very very proud of my family.

Something touches my shoulder, and my whole body jerks. I look around, and Sandra's face is very close to mine. She says, "Honey? You know the right word, don't you?"

"The right word? What right word?"

"You know," she says, and the sounds of that damned I Scream Man's chimes are about to drive me crazy. She reaches down to my letters; her thin fingers select what she's looking for, and she slowly spells the word out on the board. "There," she says, satisfied. "That's the right word."

The word my wife has spelled out is "radiation."

I stare. My eyes feel like eggs boiling in my skull, and *shut up shut up shut up!*

"Vanilla! Chocolate! Double-dip strawberry red!"

"No," I say. "No *way!* That's not a good word at all!"

The chimes stop. The I Scream Man is outside my front door, and now his call has changed. He says, "Attention! Attention! Bring out your dead!"

"Bring out your dead," Sandra tells me.

"Bring out your dead," Jeff whispers.

And Bonnie leans over and kisses my cheek, and she says in a soft little voice like the mewling of a kitten, "It's time to take us out, Daddy."

"No." I put my arm around her and hold her tight. She feels like a bundle of dry sticks. "No. We've made it together this long. We're going to stay here together. Right here. Right in our own house. There's no radiation *here!* The bombs fell a long way from here! No! We're alive and safe, and we'll be okay if we stay right—"

"Watch him," somebody says. "He's lost it."

I look toward the screen door. Two men in white uniforms stand there; they wear white gloves and gas masks on their faces. They look like monsters, and I reach for my pistol. "Go away!" I warn them, standing up and holding Bonnie under one arm. "Get the hell away from here!"

They back away into the darkness, but I know they're not gone. Oh, no; they're crafty, just like the rats. "Sir?" one of them calls. "It's not safe, sir. You've got to bring out your dead."

They're *crazy!* After those damned bombs fell on New York, Chicago, Dallas, Atlanta, Miami, Houston, and on and on and on, everybody went crazy! Even on my own street, in my hometown where I grew up a child of summer and chased the I Scream Man down the block through the darkness with a quarter in my hand! Oh, God, what's *happened* to people?

"They *smell,* sir," the crazy voice continues. "The heat's . . . about to make them . . ." He hesitates, unsure of how to finish the lie. "Please, sir," he says. "Let us bring them out. We'll put them in the refrigerated truck, and we'll carry them to the—"

"I swear to God I'll blow your head off!" I warn them. And I mean it, too!

But they won't go away, they won't they won't they *won't!* "Sir, you look pretty dosed up yourself. We can get you to the radiation center. Just put down the gun and let's talk, okay? That smell is drawing rats. They're crawling all over the yard and—"

I shoot at him. Once, twice, three times. Bastard! Dirty, lying, crazy bastard! I hope I killed him, because nobody's going to take my wife and children away from me! This is still America, by God!

Something shifts wetly under my arm. Something makes a noise, like gas escaping. I look down. Bonnie. Bonnie. Oh, darling . . . my sweet little dar . . .

For a second, I think I'm losing my mind. Two things that . . . don't look human anymore are arranged around the Scrabble board. There are dead rats everywhere. Static crackles and flickers across the white TV screen—but I can still hear the canned laughter in my head. Laugh louder! I think. Louder! Louder still! Pump your head full of canned laughter and LAUGH!

Under my arm is . . . I don't know. What is it? It's wearing a dress. But it's . . . leaking . . .

The two monsters in white crash through the door. They rip Bonnie out of my arms, but I've still got my pistol. I'll kill them, but one of them shoves me back. I think I step on something that cracks, and then . . .

Oh, I went to sleep. My head's bleeding. I went to sleep, and I dreamed of summer like it used to be, when you could look up and see the moon and there were lights in all the houses, and in the mornings birds sang in the trees and crickets thrummed like harpstrings.

I stand up. There's blood on the corner of the TV set. I hit my head. But the picture's better than ever, and the laughter is deafening.

My wife and kids are gone. Yes. I see that clearly now. The monsters in white took my family. But I've still got my pistol, clamped in my hand. I'll bet they couldn't pry it loose. I've got a strong grip for a man my age.

I SCREAM MAN!

I run out into the street, out into the hot darkness where steam lies close to the ground and the houses look like mausoleums. Things chatter and scurry around my shoes, and I kick them away before they can crawl up my legs.

I still have bullets in my pistol, but I'm not going to waste them on the rats. Oh, no. I'm not a wasteful person.

I listen. I cock my head and try to hear above the laughter.

And there it is, a long way off—maybe on the curve of Windsor Street, or Vernon Circle, or climbing the hill up Hightower Lane.

Ding ding ding!

I Scream Man's on his way!

I know that sound. I know it very, very well.

My wife and children belong with me, at home. Watching television and playing Scrabble. Talking about the trips we're going to take. Dreaming about the future. Having *fun* like families are supposed to. I won't let my family be taken away from me—oh, no.

I call, "I Scream Man!" and listen to the reply of the chimes, like church bells in the night.

I know the way they're going. I can catch them between Lynn and Douglas streets, over where the dark high school stands. But I have to hurry. I have to run very fast.

"I Scream Man!" I call as I take the first step. "Wait for me!" I run faster, with longer strides. I have to catch them, to get my family back.

"Hey, I Scream Man!" I shout, and I hold the pistol like a shiny new coin.

He answers back: *Ding ding ding!*

I am the only child on the street tonight, and I know I'll catch up. I know I will.

He'll Come Knocking at Your Door

1

In the Deep South, Halloween Day is usually shirtsleeve weather. But when the sun begins to sink, there's a foretaste of winter in the air. Pools of shadow deepen and lengthen, and the Alabama hills are transformed into moody tapestries of orange and black.

When Dan Burgess got home from the cement plant in Barrimore Crossing, he found Karen and Jaime working over a tray of homemade candies in the shape of pumpkins. Jaime, three years old and as curious as a chipmunk, was in a hurry to try out the candy. "Those are for the trick-or-treaters, hon," Karen explained patiently, for the third or fourth time. Both mother and daughter were blond, though Jaime had inherited Dan's dark brown eyes. Karen's eyes were as blue as an Alabama lake on a sunny day.

As Dan hugged his wife from behind and peered over her shoulder at the candies, he felt a sense of satisfaction that made life seem deliciously complete. He was a tall man, his face lean and rugged from a life of hard, outdoor labor. He had curly dark brown hair and a beard in need of trimming. "Looks pretty Halloweeny around here, folks!" he drawled, and lifted Jaime into his arms when she reached up for him.

"Punkins!" Jaime said gleefully.

"Hope we get some trick-or-treaters tonight," Dan said. "Hard to tell if we will or not, this far from town." Their home, a rented two-bedroom farmhouse set off the main highway on a couple of acres of rolling woodland, was part of a subdivision of Barrimore Crossing called Essex. The business district of Barrimore Crossing was four miles to the east, and the thirty-five or so inhabitants of the Essex community lived in houses similar to Dan's, comfortable places surrounded by woods where deer, quail, possum, and fox were common sights. At night, Dan could sit on his front porch and see the distant porch lights of other Essex houses up in the hills. It was a quiet, peaceful place. And lucky too, Dan knew. All sorts of good things had happened to them since they'd moved here from Birmingham, after the steel mill shut down in February.

"Might have a few." Karen began to make eyes in the pumpkins with little silver dots of candy. "Mrs. Crosley said they always have a group of kids from town. If we didn't have treats for them, they'd probably egg our house!"

"Hallo'een!" Jaime pointed excitedly toward the pumpkins, wriggling to be set down.

"Oh, I almost forgot!" Karen licked a silver dot from her finger and walked across the kitchen to the cork bulletin board next to the telephone. She took off one of the pieces of paper stuck there by a blue plastic pin. "Mr. Hathaway called at four." She gave him the note, and he set Jaime down. "He wants you to go over to his place for some kind of meeting."

"Meeting?" Dan looked at the note. It said: *Roy Hathaway. His house, 6:30.* Hathaway was the real-estate agent who'd rented them this house. He lived across the highway, up where the valley curved into the hills. "On Halloween? Did he say what for?"

"Nope. He did say it was important, though. He said you were expected, and it was something that couldn't be explained over the phone."

Dan grunted softly. He liked Roy Hathaway, who'd bent over backwards to find them this place. Dan glanced at his new Bulova wristwatch, which he'd won by being the thousandth person to buy a pickup truck from a dealership in Birmingham. It was almost five-thirty. Time enough for a shower and a ham sandwich, and then he'd go see what was so important. "Okay," he said. "I'll find out what he wants."

"Somebody'll be a clown by the time you get back," Karen said, glancing slyly at Jaime.

"Me! Me'll be a clown, Daddy!"

Dan grinned at her and, his heart full, went back to take his shower.

2

Darkness was falling fast as Dan drove his white pickup truck along the winding country road that led to Hathaway's place. His headlights picked out a deer as it bolted in front of the truck. Beyond the ridge of hills to the west, the setting sun tinted the sky a vivid orange.

Meeting, Dan thought uneasily. What was it that couldn't wait? He wondered if it might have something to do with the last rent check. No, no; his days of rubber checks and irate landlords were over. There was plenty of money in the bank. In August, Dan had received a letter that said they'd won five thousand dollars in a contest at the Food Giant store in Barrimore Crossing. Karen didn't even recall filling out an entry slip. Dan had been able to pay off the new truck and buy Karen a color television she'd been wanting. He was making more money than ever before, since his promotion in April from gravel-shoveler to unit supervisor at the cement plant. So money wasn't the problem. What was, then?

He loved the Essex community. It was fresh air and bird songs and a low-lying morning mist that clung like lace in the autumn trees. After the smog and harshness of Birmingham, after the trauma of losing his job and being on unemployment, Essex was a gentle, soul-soothing blessing.

Dan believed in luck. In hindsight, it was even good luck that he'd lost that job at the mill, because if he hadn't he never would have found Essex. One day in May he'd walked into the hardware and sporting-goods store in Barrimore

Crossing and admired a double-barreled Remington shot-gun in a display case. The manager had come over, and they'd talked about guns and hunting for the better part of an hour. As Dan had started to leave, the manager unlocked that display case and said: Dan, I want you to try this baby out. Go ahead, take it! It's a new model, and the Remington people want to know how folks like it. You take it home with you. Bring me back a wild turkey or two, and if you like that gun, tell other folks where they can buy one, hear?

It was amazing, Dan thought. He and Karen were living some kind of fantastic dream. The promotion at the plant had come right out of the blue. People respected him. Karen and Jaime were happier than he'd ever seen them. Just last month, a woman Karen had met at the Baptist church gave them a rich harvest of garden vegetables that would last them through the autumn. The only remotely bad thing that had happened since they'd moved to Essex, Dan recalled, was when he'd made a fool of himself in Roy Hathaway's office. He'd sliced his finger on a sliver of plastic in the pen he was using to sign the lease and had bled all over the paper. It was a stupid thing to remember, he knew, but it had stuck in his mind because he'd hoped it wasn't a bad omen. Now he knew nothing could be further from the truth.

He rounded a corner and saw Roy's house ahead. The front-porch lights were on, and lights showed through most of the windows. The driveway was packed with cars, most of which Dan recognized as belonging to other Essex residents. What's going on? he wondered. A community meeting? On Halloween?

He parked his truck next to Tom Paulsen's new Cadillac and walked up the front-porch steps to the door. As he knocked, a long keening animal cry came from the woods behind Hathaway's house. Bobcat, he thought. The woods are full of 'em.

Laura Hathaway, an attractive gray-haired woman in her mid-fifties, answered the door with a cheerful, "Happy Halloween, Dan!"

"Hi! Happy Halloween." He stepped into the house, and

could smell the aromatic cherry pipe tobacco Roy favored. The Hathaways had some nice oil paintings on their walls, and all their furniture looked new. "What's going on?"

"The men are down in the rumpus room," she explained. "They're having their little yearly get-together." She started to lead him to another door that would take him downstairs. She limped a bit when she walked. Several years ago, Dan understood, a lawn mower had sliced off a few of the toes on her right foot.

"Looks like everybody in Essex is here, with all those cars outside."

She smiled, her kindly face crinkling. "Everybody *is* here, now. Go on down and make yourself at home."

He descended the stairs. He heard Roy's husky voice down there: ". . . Jenny's gold earrings, the ones with the little pearls. Carl, this year it's one of Tiger's new kittens— the one with the black markings on its legs, and that ax you got at the hardware store last week. Phil, he wants one of your piglets and the pickled okra Marcy put in the cupboard . . ."

When Dan reached the bottom of the stairs, Roy stopped talking. The rumpus room, carpeted in bright red because Roy was a Crimson Tide fan, was filled with men from the Essex community. Roy, a hefty man with white hair and friendly, deep-set blue eyes, was sitting in a chair in the midst of them, reading from some kind of list. The others sat around him, listening intently. Roy looked up at Dan, as did the other men, and puffed thoughtfully on his pipe. "Howdy, Dan. Grab yourself a cup of coffee and sit a spell."

"I got your message. What kind of meeting is this?" He glanced around, saw faces he knew: Steve Mallory, Phil Kane, Carl Lansing, Andy McCutcheon, and more. A pot of coffee, cups, and a platter of sandwiches were placed on a table on one side of the room.

"Be with you in a minute," Roy said. While Dan, puzzled at what was so important on Halloween, poured himself a cup of coffee, he listened to Roy reading from the list he held. "Okay, where were we? Phil, that's it for you, I reckon. Next is Tom. This year it's that ship model you put together, a pair of Ann's shoes—the gray ones she bought in Birmingham—and Tom Junior's G.I. Joe doll. Andy, he wants . . ."

Huh? Dan thought as he sipped at the hot black coffee. He looked at Tom, who seemed to have released a breath he'd been holding for a long time. Tom's model of *Old Ironsides* had taken him months to put together, Dan knew. Dan's gaze snagged other eyes that quickly looked away. He noted that Mitch Brantley, whose wife had just had their first child in July, looked ill; Mitch's face was the color of wet cotton. A haze of smoke hung in the air from Roy's pipe and several other smokers' cigarettes. Cups rattled against saucers. Dan looked at Aaron Greene, who stared back at him through strange, glassy eyes. Aaron's wife, Dan had heard, had died of a heart attack last year about this time. Aaron had shown him pictures of her, a robust-looking brunette in her late thirties.

". . . your golf clubs, your silver cufflinks, and Tweety-bird," Roy continued.

Andy McCutcheon laughed nervously. In his pallid, fleshy face his eyes were dark and troubled. "Roy, my little girl loves that canary. I mean . . . she's real attached to it."

Roy smiled. It was a tight, false smile, and something about it started a knot of tension growing in Dan's stomach. "You can buy her another one, Andy," he said. "Can't you?"

"Sure, but she loves—"

"One canary's just like another." He drew at his pipe, and when he lifted a hand to hold the bowl, the overhead light glinted off the large diamond ring he wore.

"Excuse me, gents." Dan stepped forward. "I sure would like for somebody to tell me what this is all about. My wife and little girl are getting ready for Halloween."

"So are we," Roy replied, and blew out a plume of smoke. "So are we." He traced his finger down the list. Dan saw that the paper was mottled and dirty; it looked as if it had been used to wipe out the inside of a garbage can. The writing on it was scrawled and spiky. "Dan," Roy said, and tapped the paper. "This year he wants two things from you. First is a set of fingernail clippings. Your own fingernails. The second is—"

"Hold on." Dan tried to smile, but couldn't find one. "I don't get this. How about starting from the beginning."

Roy stared at him for a long, silent moment. Dan felt other eyes on him, watching him carefully. On the opposite side of the room, Walter Ferguson suddenly began quietly sobbing. "Oh," Roy said. "Sure. It's your first Halloween in Essex, isn't it?"

"Right. And?"

"Sit down, Dan." Roy motioned toward an empty chair near him. "Come on, sit down and I'll tell you."

Dan didn't like the feeling in this room; there was too much tension and fear in here. Walter's sobbing was louder. "Tom," Roy said, "take Walter out for a breath of air, won't you?" Tom muttered an assent and helped the crying man out of his chair. When they had left the rumpus room, Roy struck a kitchen match to relight his pipe and looked calmly at Dan Burgess.

"So tell me," Dan urged as he sat down. He did smile this time, but the smile would not stick.

"It's Halloween," Roy explained, as if speaking to a retarded child. "We're going over the Halloween list."

Dan laughed involuntarily. "Is this a joke, gents? What kind of Halloween list?"

Roy's thick white brows came together as he gathered his thoughts. Dan realized the other man was wearing the same dark red sweater he'd worn the day Dan had signed that lease and cut his finger. "Call it . . . a trick-or-treat list, Dan. You know, we all like you. You're a good man. We can't think of a better neighbor to have in Essex." He glanced around as some of the others nodded. "Essex is a very special place to live, Dan. You must know that by now."

"Sure. It's great. Karen and I love it here."

"We all do. Some of us have lived here for a long time. We appreciate the good life we have here. And in Essex, Dan, Halloween is a very special night of the year."

Dan frowned. "I'm not following you."

Roy produced a gold pocket watch, popped it open to look at the time, then closed it again. When he lifted his gaze, his eyes seemed darker and more powerful than Dan had ever seen them. They made him shiver to his soul. "Do you believe in the Devil?" Roy asked.

Again Dan laughed. "What are we doing, telling spooky stories?" He looked around the room. No one else was laughing.

"When you came to Essex," Roy said softly, "you were a loser. Down on your luck. No job. Your money was almost gone. Your credit rating was zero. You had an old car that was ready for the junkyard. Now I want you to think back on all the good things that have happened to you—all the things you might have taken as a run of good luck—since you've been part of our community. You've gotten everything you've wanted, haven't you? Money's come to you like never before. You got yourself a brand-new truck. A promotion at the plant. And there'll be more good things to come in the years ahead—if you cooperate."

"Cooperate?" He didn't like the sound of that word. "Cooperate how?"

"With the list. Like we all do, every Halloween. Every October thirty-first I find a list just like this one under the welcome mat at the front door. Why I've been chosen to handle it, I don't know. Maybe because I help bring new people in. These items on this list are to be left in front of your door on Halloween. In the morning, they're gone. He comes during the night, Dan, and he takes them away with him."

"This is a Halloween joke, isn't it!" Dan grinned. "Jesus Christ, you gents had me going! That's a hell of an act to put on just to scare the crap out of *me!*"

But Roy's face remained impassive. Smoke seeped from a corner of his wrinkled mouth. "The list," Roy continued evenly, "has to be collected and left out before midnight, Dan. If you don't collect the items and leave them for him, he'll come knocking at your door. And you don't want that, Dan. You really don't."

A chunk of ice seemed to have jammed itself in Dan's

throat, while the rest of his body felt feverish. The Devil in Essex? Collecting things like golf clubs and cufflinks, ship models and pet canaries? "You're crazy!" he managed to say. "If this isn't a damned joke, you've dropped both your oars into the water!"

"It's no joke, and he ain't crazy," Phil Kane said, sitting behind Roy. Phil was a large, humorless man who raised pigs on a farm about a mile away. "It's just once a year. Just on Halloween. Hell, last year alone I won one of them magazine sweepstakes. It was fifteen thousand dollars at one whack! The year before that, an uncle I didn't even know I had died and left me a hundred acres of land in California. We get free stuff in the mail all the time. It's just once a year we have to give him what *he* wants."

"Laura and I go to art auctions in Birmingham," Roy said. "We always get what we want for the lowest bid. And the paintings are always worth five or ten times what we pay. Last Halloween he asked for a lock of Laura's hair and one of my old shirts with blood on it where I cut myself shaving. You remember that trip to Bermuda the real-estate company gave us last summer? I've been given a huge expense account, and no matter what I charge, nobody asks any questions. He gives us everything we want."

Trick-or-treat! Dan thought crazily. He envisioned some hulking, monstrous form lugging off a set of golf clubs, one of Phil's piglets, and Tom's *Old Ironsides*. God, it was insane! Did these men really believe they were making sacrifices to a satanic trick-or-treater?

Roy lifted his eyebrows. "You didn't return the shotgun, did you? Or the money. You didn't refuse the promotion."

"I *earned* that promotion!" Dan insisted, but his voice was strained and weak, and it shamed him.

"You signed the agreement in blood," Roy said, and Dan remembered the drops of blood falling from his cut finger onto the white paper of the lease, right underneath his name. "Whether you knew it or not, you agreed to something that's been going on in Essex for over a hundred years. You can have anything and everything you want, Dan, if you give him what *he* wants on one special night of the year."

"My God," Dan whispered. He felt dizzy and sick. If it *was* true . . . what had he stumbled into? "You said . . . he wants two things from me. The fingernail clippings and what else?"

Roy looked at the list and cleared his throat. "He wants the clippings, and . . . he wants the first joint of the little finger of your child's left hand."

Dan sat motionlessly. He stared straight ahead, and feared for an awful moment that he would start laughing and giggle himself all the way to an asylum.

"It's really not much," Roy said. "There won't be a lot of blood, will there, Carl?"

Carl Lansing, who worked as a butcher at the Food Giant in Barrimore Crossing, raised his left hand to show Dan Burgess. "Not much pain if you do it quick, with a cleaver. One sharp blow'll snap the bone. She won't feel a whole lot of pain if you do it fast."

Dan swallowed. Carl's slicked-back black hair gleamed with Vitalis under the light. Dan had always wondered exactly how Carl had lost the thumb of his left hand.

"If you don't put what he wants in front of your door," Andy McCutcheon said, "he'll come in after them. And then he'll take more than he asked for in the first place, Dan. God help you if he has to knock at your door."

Dan's eyes felt like frozen stones in his rigid face; he stared across the room at Mitch Brantley, who appeared to be either about to faint or throw up. Dan thought of Mitch's new son, and he did not want to think about what might be on the list beside either Mitch's or Walter Ferguson's name. He rose unsteadily from his chair. It was not that he believed the Devil was coming to his house tonight for a bizarre trick-or-treat that frightened him so deeply; it was that he knew *they* believed, and he didn't know how to deal with it.

"Dan," Roy Hathaway said gently, "we're all in this together. It's not so bad. Really it isn't. Usually all he wants are little things. Things that don't matter very much." Mitch made a soft, strangled groaning sound. Dan flinched, but Roy paid no attention. Dan had the sudden urge to leap at

Roy and grab him by the front of that blood-red sweater and shake him until he split open. "Once in a while he . . . takes something of value," Roy said, "but not very often. And he always gives us back so much more than he takes."

"You're crazy. All of you . . . are crazy."

"Give him what he wants." Steve Mallory spoke in the strong bass voice that was so distinctive in the Baptist church choir on Sunday mornings. "Do it, Dan. Don't make him knock at your door."

"Do it," Roy told him. "For your own sake, and for your family's."

Dan backed away from them. Then he turned and ran up the stairs, ran out of the house as Laura Hathaway was coming out of the kitchen with a big bowl of pretzels, ran down the front steps and across the lawn to his pickup. Near Steve Mallory's new silver Chevy, Walter and Tom were standing together. Dan heard Walter sob ". . . not her *ear*, Tom! Dear God, not her whole *ear!*"

Dan got into his truck and left twin streaks of rubber on the pavement as he drove away.

3

Dead leaves whirled through the turbulent, chilly air as Dan pulled up into his driveway, got out and ran up the front-porch steps. Karen had taped a cardboard skeleton to the door. His heart was pounding, and he'd decided to take no chances; if this was an elaborate joke, they could laugh their asses off at him, but he was getting Karen and Jaime out of here.

Halfway home, a thought had occurred to him that had almost made him pull off the road to puke: if the list had demanded a lock of Jaime's hair, would he have given it without question? How about her fingernail clippings? A whole fingernail? An earlobe? And if he had given any of those things, what would be on the trick-or-treat list next year and the year after that?

Not much blood, if you do it quick.

"Karen!" he shouted as he unlocked the door and went in. The house was too quiet. *"Karen!"*

"Lord, Dan! What are you yelling about?" She came into the front room from the hallway, followed by Jaime in clown makeup, an oversize red blouse, patched little blue jeans, and sneakers covered with round yellow happy-face stickers. Dan knew he must look like walking death, because Karen stopped as if she'd run into a wall when she saw him. "What's happened?" she asked fearfully.

"Listen to me. Don't ask any questions." He wiped the sheen of sweat off his forehead with a trembling hand. Jaime's soft brown eyes reflected the terror he'd brought into the house with him. "We're leaving right now. We're going to drive to Birmingham and check into a motel."

"It's Halloween!" Karen said. "We might have some trick-or-treaters!"

"Please . . . don't argue with me! We've got to get out of here right now!" Dan jerked his gaze away from his child's left hand; he'd been looking at the little finger and thinking terrible thoughts. "Right now," he repeated.

Jaime was stunned, about to cry. On a table beside her was a plate with the Halloween candies on it—grinning pumpkins with silver eyes and licorice mouths. "We have to go," Dan said hoarsely. "I can't tell you why, but we have to." Before Karen could say anything else, Dan told her to gather whatever she wanted—toothpaste, a jacket, underwear—while he went out and started the truck. But *hurry!* he urged her. For God's sake, hurry!

Outside, dead leaves snapped at his cheeks and sailed past his head. He slid behind the pickup's wheel, put the key into the ignition, and turned it.

The engine made one long groaning noise, rattled, and died.

Christ! Dan thought, close to panic. He'd never had any problem with the truck before! He pumped the accelerator and tried again. The engine was stone-cold dead, and all the warning lights—brake fluid, engine oil, battery, even gasoline—flashed red on the instrument panel.

Of course, he realized. Of course. He had paid off the

truck with the money he'd won. The truck had been given to him while he was a resident of Essex—and now whatever was coming to their house tonight didn't want him driving that truck *away* from Essex.

They could run for it. Run along the road. But what if they ran into the Halloween visitor, there in the lonely darkness? What if it came up behind them on the road, demanding its trick-or-treat like a particularly nasty child?

He tried the truck again. Dead.

Inside the house, Dan slammed the door and locked it. He went to the kitchen door and locked that too, as his wife and daughter watched him as if he'd lost his mind. Dan shouted, "Karen, check all the windows! Make sure they're shut tight! Hurry, damn it!" He went to the closet and took out his shotgun, got a box of shells off the shelf; he opened the box, put it on the table next to the pumpkin candies, broke open the gun's breech, and stuffed two shells into the chambers. Then he closed the breech and looked up as Karen and Jaime returned, clinging to each other.

"All . . . the windows are shut," Karen whispered, her scared blue eyes flickering back and forth from Dan's face to the shotgun. "Dan, what's wrong with you?"

"Something's coming to our door tonight," he replied. "Something terrible. We're going to have to hold it off. I don't know if we can, but we have to try. Do you understand what I'm saying?"

"It's . . . Halloween," she said, and he saw she thought he was totally cracked.

The telephone! he thought suddenly, and ran for it. He picked up the receiver and dialed for the operator in Barrimore Crossing to call for a police car. *Officer, the Devil's on his way to our house tonight and we don't have his favorite kind of candy.*

But on the other end of the line was a piercing crackle of static that sounded like a peal of eerie laughter. Through the static Dan heard things that made him believe he'd truly hurtled over the edge: the crazy theme music from a Porky Pig cartoon, a crash of cymbals, the military drumming of a marching band, assorted gurgles and gasps and moans as if he'd been plugged into a graveyard party line. Dan dropped the receiver, and it dangled from its cord like a lynched corpse. Have to think, he told himself. Figure things out. Hold the bastard off. Got to hold him off. He looked at the fireplace and felt a new hammerblow of horror. "Dear God!" he shouted. "We've got to block up the chimney!"

Dan got on his knees, reached up the chimney, and closed the flue. There were already pine logs, kindling, and newspapers in the fireplace, ready for the first cold night of the year. He went into the kitchen, got a box of Red Top matches, and put them into the breast pocket of his shirt; when he came back into the room, Jaime was crying and Karen was holding her tightly, whispering, "Shhhhh, darling. Shhhhh." She watched her husband like one would watch a dog with foam on its mouth.

Dan pulled a chair about ten feet from the front door and sat down with the shotgun across his knees. His eyes were sunken into his head and ringed with purple. He looked at his new Bulova watch; somehow, the crystal had shattered. The hands had snapped off.

"Dan," Karen said—and then she too started to cry.

"I love you, honey," he told her. "You know I love both of you, don't you? I swear I do. I won't let him in. I won't give him what he wants. Because if I do that, what will he take next year? I love you both, and I want you to remember that."

"Oh, God . . . Dan . . ."

"They think I'm going to do it and leave it outside the door for him," Dan said. His hands were gripped tightly around the shotgun, his knuckles white. "They think I could take a cleaver and—"

The lights flickered, and Karen screamed. Jaime's wail joined hers.

Dan felt his face contorting with fear. The lights flickered, flickered—and went out.

"He's coming," Dan rasped. "He's coming soon." He stood up, walked to the fireplace, bent down, and struck a match. It took four matches to get the fire going right; its orange light turned the room into a Halloween chamber of horrors, and smoke repelled from the blocked flue swept around the walls like searching spirits. Karen was pressed against the wall, and Jaime's clown makeup was streaming down her cheeks.

Dan returned to the chair, his eyes stinging with smoke, and watched the door.

He didn't know how much longer it was when he sensed something on the front porch. Smoke was filling the house, but the room had suddenly become bone-achingly cold. He thought he heard something scratching out there on the porch, searching around the door for the items that weren't there.

He'll come knocking at your door. And you don't want that. You really don't.

"Dan—"

"Shhhh," he warned her. "Listen! He's out there."

"Him? *Who?* I don't hear—"

There was a knock at the door like a sledgehammer striking the wood. Dan saw the door tremble through the smoke-haze. The knock was followed by a second, with more force. Then a third that made the door bend inward like cardboard.

"Go away!" Dan shouted. "There's nothing for you here!"

Silence.

It's all a trick! he thought. Roy and Tom and Carl and Steve and all the rest are out there in the dark, laughing fit to bust a gut!

But the room was getting viciously cold. Dan shivered, saw his breath float away past his face.

Something scraped on the roof above their heads, like claws seeking a weak chink in the shingles.

"Go away!" Dan's voice cracked. *"Go away, you bastard!"*

The scraping stopped. After a long moment of silence, something smashed against the roof like an anvil being dropped. The entire house groaned. Jaime screamed, and Karen shouted, "What is it, Dan, what is it out there?"

Immediately following was a chorus of laughter from beyond the front door. Someone said, "Okay, I guess that's enough!" A different voice called, "Hey, Dan! You can open up now! Just kiddin'!" A third voice said, "Trick-or-treat, Danny boy!"

He recognized Carl Lansing's voice. There was more laughter, more whooping cries of "Trick-or-treat!"

My God! Dan rose to his feet. It's a joke. A brutal, ridiculous joke!

"Open the door!" Carl called. "We can't wait to see your face!"

Dan almost cried, but there was rage building in him and he thought he might just aim the shotgun at them and threaten to shoot their balls off. Were they all crazy? How had they managed the phone and the lights? Was this some kind of insane initiation to Essex? He went to the door on shaky legs, unlocked it—

Behind him, Karen said suddenly, "Dan, *don't!*"

—and opened the door.

Carl Lansing stood on the porch. His black hair was slicked back, his eyes as bright as new pennies. He looked like the cat that had swallowed the canary.

"You damned fools!" Dan raged. "Do you know what kind of scare you people put into me and my family? I ought to shoot your damned—"

And then he stopped, because he realized Carl was standing alone on the porch.

Carl grinned. His teeth were black. "Trick-or-treat," he whispered, and raised the ax that he'd been holding behind his back.

With a cry of terror, Dan stumbled backward and lifted the shotgun. The thing that had assumed Carl's shape oozed across the threshold; orange firelight glinted off the upraised ax blade.

Dan squeezed the shotgun's trigger, but the gun didn't go off. Neither barrel would fire. Jammed! he thought wildly, and broke open the breech to clear it.

There were no shells in the shotgun. Jammed into the chambers were Karen's pumpkin candies.

"Trick-or-treat, Dan!" the thing wailed. *"Trick-or-treat!"*

Dan struck into the Carl-thing's stomach with the butt of

the shotgun. From its mouth sprayed a mess of yellow canary feathers, pieces of a kitten, and what might have been a piglet. Dan hit it again, and the entire body collapsed like an exploding gasbag. Then Dan grabbed Karen's hand in a frantic blur of motion and was pulling her with him out the door. She held on to Jaime, and they ran down the porch steps and across the grass, along the driveway and the road and toward the main highway with the Halloween wind clutching around them.

Dan looked back, saw nothing but darkness. Jaime shrieked in tune with the wind. The distant lights of other Essex houses glinted in the hills like cold stars.

They reached the highway. Dan shouldered Jaime, and still they ran into the night, along the roadside where the high weeds caught at their ankles.

"Look!" Karen cried. "Somebody's coming, Dan! Look!"

He did. Headlights were approaching. Dan stood in the middle of the road, frantically waving. The vehicle—a gray Volkswagen van—began to slow down. At the wheel was a woman in a witch costume, and two children dressed like ghosts peered out the window. People from Barrimore Crossing! Dan realized. Thank God! "Help us!" he begged. "Please! We've got to get out of here!"

"You in trouble?" the woman asked. "You have an accident or something?"

"Yes! An accident! Please, get us to the police station in Barrimore Crossing! I'll pay you! Just please get us there!"

The woman looked at them uncertainly, glanced over at her own costumed kids, and then motioned toward the back. "Okay, get in."

They gratefully scrambled into the back seat, and the woman accelerated. Karen cradled her sobbing child, and Dan's voice shook as he said, "We're all right now. We're all right." The two ghost-children stared curiously at them over the seat.

"You have a car accident?" the woman asked, and looked in the rearview mirror as Dan nodded. "Where's your car?" One of the children giggled softly.

And then something wet and sticky hit Dan's cheek and drooled down his face. He touched the liquid and looked at his fingers. Spit, he thought. That looks like—

Another drop hit his forehead.

He looked up, at the roof of the van.

The van had teeth. Long, jagged fangs were protruding from the wet gray roof of the van, and now they were rising from the floorboard too, drooling saliva.

Dan heard his wife scream, and then he started to laugh—a terrible, uncontrollable laughter that sent him spinning off the edge of sanity.

"Trick-or-treat, Dan," the thing behind the wheel said.

And Dan's last coherent thought was that the Devil sure could come up with one hell of a Halloween costume.

The fanged jaws slammed together and began to grind back and forth.

And then the van, now looking more like a huge cockroach, crawled off the road and began to scurry across a field toward the dark hills where the Halloween wind shrieked in triumph.

Chico

"Everythin'," Marcus Salomon said as he took another swig of wisdom, "is shit." He finished his beer and thunked the bottle down on the beat-up little table beside his chair. The noise spooked a roach from its hiding place under the lip of an overflowing ashtray, and it fled for a safer haven. "Jesus!" Salomon shouted, because the roach—a shiny black one perhaps two inches long—had leapt to the arm of his chair and was skittering madly along it. Salomon whacked at it with his beer bottle, missed, the roach ran down the chair and got to the floor and shot toward one of many cracks along the baseboard. Salomon had a bulging beer belly and a number of jiggling chins, but he was still fast; at least, faster than the roach had anticipated. Salomon slid out of the chair, stomped across the room, and smashed his foot down on the roach before it could squeeze into the crack.

"Little bastard!" he seethed. "Little bastard!" He settled his weight down, and there was a satisfying *crunch* that changed his sneer to a grin. "Got your ass, didn't I?" He ground his shoe down, as if grinding a cigarette butt, and then he lifted his foot to look at the carnage. The roach had been torn almost in half, its abdomen crushed into the floorboards. A single leg feebly twitched. "That's what you get, you little bastard!" Salomon said—and it was no sooner spoken than another black roach shot out of a baseboard crack and ran past its dead mate in the opposite direction.

Salomon bellowed with rage—a shout that shook the flimsy walls and the dirty glass in the open fire-escape window—and stomped after it. This one was faster and more cunning, trying to get under the threadbare brown rug between the apartment's front room and the narrow hallway leading to the rear. But Salomon was an experienced killer; though he missed twice, his third stomp stunned the roach and made it lose its course. The fourth stomp mashed it, and the fifth one burst it open. Salomon settled his two hundred and thirty-seven pounds on the roach, grinding it into the boards. Someone hammered on the floor from below, probably with the end of a broom, and a voice shouted, "Stop that noise up there! You're breakin' the damn place down!"

"I'll break your ass, monkey lips!" Salomon hollered back at old Mrs. Cardinza in the apartment below.

And then came the frail, almost frantic voice of Mr. Cardinza: "You don't talk to my wife like that! I'll call the police on you, you bastard!"

"Yeah, call the cops!" Salomon shouted, and stomped the floor again. "Maybe they'll want to talk to that nephew of yours about who's sellin' all the drugs in this building! Go on and call 'em!" That quieted the Cardinzas, and Salomon stomped on the floor above their heads with both feet, his weight making the boards shriek and moan. And now Bridger, the drunk next door, started up: "Shut your mouths over there! Let a man sleep, damn you to hell!"

Salomon stalked to the wall and pounded on it. The apartment was thick with the steamy heat of mid-August, and sweat glistened on Salomon's face and wet through his T-shirt. "You go to Hell! Who you tellin' to go to Hell? I'll come over there and kick your skinny ass, you—" A motion caught his attention: a roach zooming over the floor like a haughty black limousine. "Sonofabitch!" Salomon shrieked, and he took two strides after the insect and brought his shoe down on it like Judgment Day. He pressed hard, his teeth gritted and sweat dripping from his chins: a *crunch,* and Salomon smeared the roach's insides across the floor.

Another movement caught the corner of his eye. He

turned, a wall of belly, and looked at what he considered a roach of a different kind. "What the hell do *you* want?"

Chico, of course, didn't answer. He had crawled into the room on his hands and knees and now he sat on his haunches, his oversize head cocked slightly to one side.

"Hey!" Salomon said. "Want to see somethin' pretty?" He grinned, showing bad teeth.

Chico grinned too. In his fleshy brown face one eye was deep-set and dark, and the other was pure white—a dead, blind stone.

"Real pretty! Want to see it?" Salomon nodded, still grinning, and Chico grinned and nodded in emulation. "Come on over here, then. Right here." He pointed to the glistening yellow insides of the crushed roach that lay on the floor.

Chico crawled, eager and unaware, toward Salomon. The man stepped back. "Right there," Salomon said, and touched the glinting mess with his shoe. "It tastes like candy! Yum-yum! Go on and lick it!"

Chico was over the yellow smear. He looked at it, looked quizzically up at Salomon with his single dark eye.

"Yum-yum!" Salomon said, and rubbed his belly.

Chico lowered his head and stuck out his tongue.

"Chico!"

The woman's voice, shrill and nervous, stopped him before he reached the smear. Chico lifted his head and sat up, looking at his mother. The weight of his head began to instantly strain his neck and make his skull tilt to one side.

"Don't do that," she told him, and shook her head. *"No."*

Chico's eye blinked. His lips pursed; he mouthed *no* and crawled away from the dead roach.

Sophia trembled. She glared at Salomon, her thin arms dangling at her sides and her hands gripped into fists. "How could you do such a thing?"

He shrugged; his grin had gotten a little meaner, as if his mouth was a wound made by a very sharp knife. "I'm just kiddin' with him, that's all. I wasn't goin' to let him do it."

"Come here, Chico," Sophia said, and the twelve-year-old boy crawled quickly to his mother. He rested his head against her leg, like a dog might, and she touched his curly black hair.

"You take everythin' too serious," Salomon told her, and he kicked the crushed roach into a corner. He enjoyed killing them; picking up the dead ones was Sophia's job. "Shut up!" he bellowed through the wall at Bridger, who was still shouting about a man never being able to get any sleep in this festering hellhole. Bridger fell silent, knowing when not to push his luck. In the apartment below, the Cardinzas were quiet too, lest the ceiling cave in on their heads. But other noises swarmed into the apartment, both from the open window and from the guts of the tenement itself: the relentless, maddening roar of traffic on East River Drive; a man and woman shouting curses at each other in the garbage-strewn square of concrete that the city called a "park"; a boom box blasting, turned up to its highest notch; the choked chugging of overloaded pipes; and the chatter of fans that were utterly useless in the sweltering heat. Salomon sat down in his favorite chair, the one that had a caved-in seat and springs hanging out the bottom. "Bring me a beer," he said.

"Get it yourself."

"I said . . . bring me a beer." His head turned, and he stared at Sophia with eyes that threatened destruction.

Sophia held his gaze. She was a small dark-haired woman with a lifeless face, but her mouth tightened and she didn't move; she looked like a tough reed, arching itself against an oncoming storm.

Salomon worked his big knuckles. "If I have to get out of this chair," he said quietly, "you're goin' to be real sorry."

She'd been sorry before; once he'd slapped her across the face so hard her ears had rung like Santa Maria's bells for three days. Another time, he'd thrown her against a wall and he might have broken her ribs had Bridger not threatened to go for the police. The worst time, though, was when he'd kicked Chico and left a bruise on the boy's shoulder for a week. She had gotten them into this mess, not Chico, and anytime Chico was hurt, it carved her heart to pieces.

Salomon placed his hands on the armrests, in preparation to hoist his body out of the chair.

Sophia turned and walked the four steps into what served as a kitchen. She opened the stuttering refrigerator, which held a mixture of leftovers, things in sacks, and bottles of the cheapest beer Salomon could find. Salomon settled himself back in his chair, paying no attention to Chico crawling mindlessly back and forth across the floor. A big, useless roach, Salomon thought. Somebody ought to squash the little bastard. Put him out of his misery. Hell, wouldn't that be better than bein' deaf, dumb, and half-blind? Anyway, Salomon reasoned, the kid was empty in the head. Couldn't even walk. Just crawled around, a moron on hands and knees. Now, if he could get out and hustle some money somewhere, it might be different, but as far as Salomon could see, all Chico did was take up room, shit, and eat. "You ain't nothin'," he said, and looked at the boy. Chico had found his customary corner, and was crouched there, grinning.

"How come you think everythin's so damned funny?" Salomon sneered. "You go to work on those loadin' docks like I do every night and you won't grin so damn much!"

Sophia brought him his beer, and he jerked it out of her hand, unscrewed the cap, and spun it away. He swigged beer down his throat. "Tell him to stop it," he told her.

"Stop what?"

"That grinnin'. Tell him to stop it, and to stop lookin' at me."

"Chico's not hurtin' you."

"It hurts me to look at his damn ugly face!" Salomon shouted. He saw a dark flash: a roach running past Chico's foot along the cracked baseboard. A drop of sweat dripped down Salomon's nose, and he wiped it off before it reached the tip. "Burnin' up," he said. "I can't take this heat. Makes my head ache." Lately his head had been aching a lot. It was this place, he thought. It was these dirty walls and fire-escape window. It was Sophia's long black hair, streaked with gray at age thirty-two, and Chico's remote grin. He needed a change, something different to keep him from going crazy. Why the hell had he ever taken in this woman and her idiot child anyway? The answer was clear enough: to fetch him his beer, wash his clothes, and spread her legs when he wanted them spread. Nobody else would have her, and the welfare people were about a signature away from putting Chico in a home with other idiots like him. Salomon ran the chilly bottle over his forehead. When he glanced at Chico in the corner, he saw the boy still grinning. Chico could sit like that for hours. That grin; there was something about it that grated Salomon's nerves. A big black roach suddenly ran up the wall behind Chico, and like a fuse it set off Salomon's charge. "Damn it to Hell!" he shouted, and he flung the half-full bottle of beer.

Sophia screamed. The bottle hit just below the roach, and about six or seven inches over Chico's swollen skull. It didn't break, but splattered beer everywhere. The bottle fell and rolled, and the roach darted up the wall and winnowed into a crack. Chico sat perfectly still, grinning.

"You're crazy!" Sophia shouted. "You're crazy!" She knelt down, putting her arms around her son, and Chico's skinny brown arms embraced her.

"Make him stop lookin' at me!" Salomon was on his feet, his belly and chins trembling with rage—toward Chico, toward the black, shiny roaches that it seemed he had to kill over and over again, toward the crack-crazed walls and the roar of noise on East River Drive. "I'll bash his face in, I swear it!"

Sophia grasped Chico's chin. His head was heavy, resisting her. But then she got his face turned away from Salomon, and Chico rested his head against her shoulder and gave a soft, strengthless sigh.

"I'm goin' to take a leak," Salomon announced. He was ashamed; not of throwing the bottle at Chico, but of wasting beer. He left the room, went out the door and toward the community bathroom at the end of the hall.

Sophia rocked her son. "Shut up that screamin'!" Somebody shouted from along the corridor. A radio blasted rap music between the walls. A bittersweet smell drifted to her: someone free-basing in one of the abandoned apartments that now served the addicts and dealers. The noise of a distant siren caused a panicked scuttling beyond the door across the hall, but the siren faded and the scuttling ceased. How she'd come to this, she didn't know. No, no; that wasn't right, she decided. She knew very well. It was a story of poverty and abuse from her father—or, at least, the man her mother had said was her father. The story included turning tricks at age fourteen in Spanish Harlem, needles and cocaine and picking the pockets of tourists on 42nd Street. It was a story that, once spun out, could not be reeled back in. There had been corners of decision, and Sophia had always taken the dark street. She had been young then, and drawn to a thrill. Who Chico's father was, she didn't really know; maybe the salesman who said he was from Albany and whose wife had gone cold; maybe the hustler on 38th Street who wore pins through his nose; maybe any one of a number of faceless johns who passed like shadows through her semiconsciousness. But she knew it was her sin that had swollen the infant's head in her womb and turned him into a silent sufferer. That, and the time she'd been kicked down a flight of stairs with the baby in her arms. Such was life. She feared Salomon, but she feared losing Chico too. He was all she had, and all she'd ever have. Salomon might be cruel and brutal, but he wouldn't throw them out into the street, nor would he beat them too badly; he enjoyed her welfare check too much, with the allowance she got for having a retarded child. She loved Chico; he needed her, and she would not turn him over to the cold hands of an institution.

Sophia leaned her head against Chico's and closed her eyes. She had dreamed of having a child, when she was a very young girl. And in those dreams that child was a perfect, happy, healthy boy, and he was full of love and goodness and . . . yes . . . and miracles. She smoothed Chico's hair, and she felt his fingers on her cheek. Sophia opened her eyes and looked at him, at his single dark eye and the dead white one. His fingers floated across her face, and she grasped his hand and gently held it. He had long, slim fingers. The hands of a doctor, she thought. A healer. If only . . . if only . . .

Sophia looked through the window. In the sultry gray clouds over the East River there was a splinter of blue. "Goin' to be a change," she whispered in Chico's ear. "Won't always be like this. Goin' to be a change, when Jesus comes. It'll happen in an instant, when you least expect it. Oh, he'll come in white robes and he'll put his hands on you, Chico. He'll put his hands on both of us, and oh we're goin' to fly so high up over this world. Do you believe that?"

Chico stared at her with his good eye, and his grin flickered off and on.

"It's promised," she whispered. "All things made new. All bodies whole, and everybody set free. You and me, Chico. You and me."

The door opened and thudded shut. Salomon said, "What're you whisperin' about? Me?"

"No," she said. "Not you."

"Better not be. I might have to whip some ass." It was a hollow threat, and they both knew it. Salomon belched like a bass drumbeat. As he walked across the floor, another roach skittered past in front of him. "Damn it! Where are all these bastards comin' from?" He knew the walls must be full of the things, but no matter how many he killed, they were all over the place. A second roach, larger than the first, shot from under Salomon's chair. Salomon bellowed, stepped forward, and stomped down. The roach, its back broken, spun in circles. Salomon's shoe came down again, and when it lifted, the roach lay in an oozing yellow mass. "Things are drivin' me crazy!" he said. "Everywhere I look, there's another one!"

"It's the heat," Sophia told him. "They always come out in the heat."

"Yeah." He wiped sweat off his neck and glanced at Chico. There was that grin again. "What's so funny? Come on, moron! What's so damned funny?"

"Don't talk to him like that! He can understand your voice!"

"The hell he can!" Salomon grunted. "He got a big hole where his brain ought to be!"

Sophia stood up. Her stomach was clenching, but there was life in her face now, and her eyes glittered. Being so near Chico—touching him—always made her feel so strong, so . . . hopeful. "Chico's my son," she said with quiet strength. "If you want us to leave, we will. Just say the word and we'll get out."

"Right. Tell me another one!"

"We've lived on the streets before." Her heart pounded, but the words were seething out of her. "We can do it again."

"Yeah, I'll bet the welfare people would love that!"

"Everything's going to work out," Sophia said, and her heart kicked; for the first time in a long, long while, she actually believed it. "You'll see. Everything's going to work out."

"Uh-huh. Show me another miracle, and I'll make you a saint." He laughed hollowly, but his laughter was forced. Sophia wasn't backing down from him this time. She was standing with her chin lifted and her backbone straight. Sometimes she got like this, but it didn't last for long. Another roach ran across the floor, almost under Salomon's feet, and he stomped for it but it was a fast one.

"I mean it," Sophia said. "My son is a human being. I want you to start treatin' him like one."

"Yeah, yeah, yeah." He waved her off. He didn't like talking to her when she sounded strong; it made him feel weak. Anyway, it was too hot to fight. "I've gotta get ready for work," he said, and he began pulling off his wet T-shirt as he walked into the hallway. His mind was already turning toward endless rows of crates coming off a conveyor belt, and trucks rumbling up to take them away. It was work, he knew, that he would do for the rest of his days. Everythin' is shit, he told himself. Even life itself.

Sophia stood in the room, with Chico crouched in his corner. Her heart was still beating hard. She had expected a blow, and been prepared to take it. Perhaps it would fall later . . . or perhaps not. She looked down at Chico; his face was peaceful, his head tilted far to one side, as if he heard music she could never hear. She looked out the window, at the clouds over the river. Not much blue in that sky. But maybe tomorrow. Salomon was going to work. He would need his dinner. Sophia went into the kitchen to make him a sandwich from the leftovers in the refrigerator.

Chico remained in his corner for a while longer. Then he stared at something on the floor, and he crawled to it. His head lolled, and he had a moment of difficulty when its weight threatened to capsize him.

"You want mustard?" Sophia called.

Chico picked up the dead roach that Salomon had just crushed. He held it in his palm, looked at it closely with his good eye. Then he closed his palm and grinned.

"What?" Salomon asked.

Chico's hand trembled just a little bit.

He opened his palm, and the roach skittered over his fingers, dropped to the floor, and darted into a baseboard fissure.

"Mustard!" Sophia said. "On your sandwich!"

Chico crawled to the next dead roach. He picked it up, closed his palm around it. He grinned, his eye glittering. The roach squeezed between his fingers, darted away. Gone, back into the wall.

"Yeah," Salomon decided. He sighed, heavy-laden. "Whatever."

The relentless roar of traffic on East River Drive came through the fire-escape window. A boom box blared at its highest volume. Pipes chugged and moaned, fans chattered uselessly against the heat, and roaches returned to the cracks.

Night Calls the
Green Falcon

1

Never Say Die

He was in the airplane again, falling toward the lights of Hollywood.

Seconds ago the craft had been a sleek silver beauty with two green-painted propellers, and now it was coming apart at the seams like wet cardboard. The controls went crazy, he couldn't hold the stick level, and as the airplane fell he clinched his parachute pack tighter around his chest and reached up to pop the canopy out. But the canopy was jammed shut, its hinges red with clots of rust. The propellers had seized up, and black smoke whirled from the engines. The plane nosed toward the squat, ugly buildings that lined Hollywood Boulevard, a scream of wind passing over the fuselage.

He didn't give up. That wasn't his way. He kept pressing against the canopy, trying to force the hinges, but they were locked tight. The buildings were coming up fast, and there was no way to turn the airplane because the rudder and ailerons were gone too. He was sweating under his green suit, his heart beating so hard he couldn't hear himself think. There had to be a way out of this; he was a never-say-die type of guy. His eyes in the slits of the green cowl ticked to the control panel, the jammed hinges, the dead stick, the smoking engines, back to the control panel in a frantic geometry.

The plane trembled; the port-side engine was ripping

away from the wing. His green boots kicked at the dead rudder pedals. Another mighty heave at the canopy, another jerk of the limp control stick—and then he knew his luck had, at long last, run out. It was all over.

Going down fast now, the wings starting to tear away. Klieg lights swung back and forth over the boulevard, advertising somebody else's premiere. He marked where the plane was going to hit: a mustard-yellow five-floored brick building about eight blocks east of the Chinese Theater. He was going to hit the top floor, go right into somebody's apartment. His hands in their green gloves clenched the armrests. No way out . . . no way out . . .

He didn't mourn for himself so much, but someone innocent was about to die, and that he couldn't bear. Maybe there was a child in that apartment, and he could do nothing but sit in his trap of straps and glass and watch the scene unfold. No, he decided as the sweat ran down his face. No, I can't kill a child. Not another one. I *won't*. This script has to be rewritten. It wasn't fair, that no one had told him how this scene would end. Surely the director was still in control. Wasn't he? "Cut!" he called out as the mustard-yellow building filled up his horizon. "Cut!" he said again, louder —then screamed it: *"Cut!"*

The airplane crashed into the building's fifth floor, and he was engulfed by a wall of fire and agony.

2

An Old Relic

He awoke, his flesh wet with nightmare sweat and his stomach burning with the last flames of an enchilada TV dinner.

He lay in the darkness, the springs of his mattress biting into his back, and watched the lights from the boulevard— reflections of light—move across the cracked ceiling. A fan stuttered atop his chest of drawers, and from down the hall he could hear the LaPrestas hollering at each other again. He lifted his head from the sodden pillow and looked at his alarm clock on the table beside his bed: twenty-six minutes past twelve, and the night had already gone on forever.

His bladder throbbed. Right now it was working, but sometimes it went haywire and he peed in his sheets. The laundromat on the corner of Cosmo Street was not a good place to spend a Saturday night. He roused himself out of bed, his joints clicking back into their sockets and the memory of the nightmare scorched in his mind. It was from Chapter One of *Night Calls the Green Falcon,* RKO Studios, 1949. He remembered how he'd panicked when he couldn't get the plane's canopy up, because he didn't like close places. The director had said, "Cut!" and the canopy's hinges had been oiled and the sequence had gone like clockwork the second time around.

The nightmare would be back, and so would the rest of them—a reel of car crashes, falls from buildings, gunshots, explosions, even a lion's attack. He had survived all of them, but they kept trying to kill him again and again. Mr. Thatcher at the Burger King said he ought to have his head looked at, and maybe that was true. But Mr. Thatcher was only a kid, and the Green Falcon had died before Mr. Thatcher was born.

He stood up. Slid his feet into slippers. Picked his robe off a chair and shrugged into it, covering his pajamas. His eyes found the faded poster taped to the wall: NIGHT CALLS THE GREEN FALCON, it said, and showed an assemblage of fistfights, car crashes, and various other action scenes IN TEN EXCITING CHAPTERS! the poster promised. STARRING CREIGHTON FLINT, "THE GREEN FALCON."

"The Green Falcon has to piss now," he said, and he unlocked the door and went out into the hallway.

The bathroom was on the other side of the building. He trudged past the elevator and the door where the LaPrestas were yelling. Somebody else shouted for them to shut up, but when they got going there was no stopping them. Seymour, the super's cat, slinked past, hunting rats, and the old man knocked politely at the bathroom's door before he entered. He clicked on the light, relieved himself at the urinal, and looked away from the hypodermic needles that were lying around the toilet. When he was finished, he picked up the needles and put them in the trashcan, then washed his hands in the rust-stained sink and walked back along the corridor to his apartment.

Old gears moaned. The elevator was coming up. It opened when he was almost even with it. Out walked his next-door neighbor, Julie Saufley, and a young man with close-cropped blond hair.

She almost bumped into him, but she stopped short. "Hi, Cray. You're prowlin' around kinda late, aren't you?"

"Guess so." Cray glanced at the young man. Julie's latest friend had pallid skin that was odd in sun-loving California, and his eyes were small and very dark. Looks like an extra in a Nazi flick, Cray thought, and then returned his gaze to Julie, whose dark brown hair was cut in a Mohawk and decorated with purple spray. Her spangled blouse and short leather skirt were so tight he couldn't fathom how she could draw a breath. "Had to use the bathroom," he said. Didn't that just sound like an old fool? he asked himself. When he was forty years younger such a statement to a pretty girl would have been unthinkable.

"Cray was a movie star," Julie explained to her friend. "Used to be in . . . what did they call them, Cray?"

"Serials," he answered. Smiled wanly. "Cliff-hangers. I was the—"

"I'm not paying you for a tour of the wax museum, baby." The young man's voice was taut and mean, and the sound of it made Cray think of rusted barbed wire. A match flared along the side of a red matchbook; the young man lit a cigarette, and the quick yellow light made his eyes look like small ebony stones. "Let's get done what we came here for," he said, with a puff of smoke in Cray Flint's direction.

"Sure." Julie shrugged. "I just thought you might like to know he used to be famous, that's all."

"He can sign my autograph book later. Let's go." Spidery white fingers slid around her arm and drew her away.

Cray started to tell him to release her, but what was the

use? There were no gentlemen anymore, and he was too old and used-up to be anyone's champion. "Be careful, Julie," he said as she guided the man to her apartment.

"My name's Crystal this week," she reminded him. Got her keys out of her clutch purse. "Coffee in the morning?"

"Right." Julie's door opened and closed. Cray went into his room and eased himself into a chair next to the window. The boulevard's neon pulse painted red streaks across the walls. The street denizens were out, would be out until dawn, and every so often a police car would run them into the shadows, but they always returned. The night called them, and they had to obey. Like Julie did. She'd been in the building four months, was just twenty years old, and Cray couldn't help but feel some grandfatherly concern for her. Maybe it was more than that, but so what? Lately he'd been trying to help her get off those pills she popped like candy, and encouraging her to write to her parents back in Minnesota. Last week she'd called herself Amber; such was the power of Hollywood, a city of masks.

Cray reached down beside his chair and picked up the well-worn leather book that lay there. He could hear the murmur of Julie's voice through the paper-thin wall; then her customer's, saying something. Silence. A police car's siren on the boulevard, heading west. The squeak of mattress springs from Julie's apartment. Over in the corner, the scuttling of a rat in the wall. Where was Seymour when you needed him? Cray opened his memory book, and looked at the yellowed newspaper clipping from the Belvedere, Indiana *Banner* of March 21, 1946, that said HOMETOWN FOOTBALL HERO HOLLYWOOD-BOUND. There was a picture of himself, when he was still handsome and had a headful of hair. Other clippings—his mother had saved them—were from his high-school and college days, and they had headlines like BOOMER WINS GYMNASTIC MEDAL and BOOMER BREAKS TRACK-MEET RECORD. That was his real name: Creighton Boomershine. The photographs were of a muscular, long-legged kid with a lopsided grin and the clear eyes of a dreamer.

Long gone, Cray thought. Long gone.

He had had his moment in the sun. It had almost burned him blind, but it had been a lovely light. He had turned sixty-three in May, an old relic. Hollywood worshiped at the altar of youth. Anyway, nobody made his kind of pictures anymore. Four serials in four years, and then—

Cut, he thought. No use stirring up all that murky water. He had to get back to bed, because morning would find him mopping the floor in the Burger King three blocks west, and Mr. Thatcher liked clean floors.

He closed the memory book and put it aside. On the floor was a section of yesterday's L.A. *Times;* he'd already read the paper, but a headline caught his attention: FLIPTOP KILLER CHALLENGES POLICE. Beneath that was a story about the Fliptop, and eight photographs of the street people whose throats had been savagely slashed in the last two months. Cray had known one of them: a middle-aged woman called Auntie Sunglow, who rocketed along the boulevard on roller skates singing Beatles songs at the top of her lungs. She was crazy, yes, but she always had a kind tune for him. Last week she'd been found in a trash dumpster off Sierra Bonita, her head almost severed from her neck.

Bad times, Cray mused. Couldn't think of any worse. Hopefully the police would nail the Fliptop before he—or she—killed again, but he didn't count on it. All the street people he knew were watching their backs.

Something struck the wall in Julie's apartment. It sounded like it might have been a fist.

Cray heard the springs squalling, like a cat being skinned alive. He didn't know why she sold her body for such things, but he'd learned long ago that people did what they had to do to survive.

There was another blow against the wall. Something crashed over. A chair, maybe.

Cray stood up. Whatever was going on over there, it sounded rough. Way too rough. He heard no voices, just the awful noise of the springs. He went to the wall and pounded on it. "Julie?" he called. "You all right?"

No answer. He put his ear to the wall, and heard what he thought might have been a shuddering gasp.

The squall of the springs had ceased. Now he could hear only his own heartbeat. "Julie?" He pounded the wall again. "Julie, answer me!" When she didn't respond, he knew something was terribly wrong. He went out to the corridor, sweat crawling down his neck, and as he reached out to grip the doorknob of Julie's apartment he heard a scraping noise that he knew must be the window being pushed upward.

Julie's window faced the alley. The fire escape, Cray realized. Julie's customer was going down the fire escape.

"Julie!" he shouted. He kicked at the door, and his slipper flew off. Then he threw his shoulder against it, and the door cracked on its hinges but didn't give way. Again he rammed into the door, and a third time. On the fourth blow the door's hinges tore away from the wood and it crashed down, sending Cray sprawling into the apartment.

He got up on his hands and knees, his shoulder hurting like hell. The young man was across the untidy room, still struggling with the reluctant windowsill, and he paid Cray no attention. Cray stood up, and looked at the bed where Julie lay, naked, on her back.

He caught his breath as if he'd been punched in the stomach. The blood was still streaming from the scarlet mass of Julie Saufley's throat, and it had splattered across the yellow wall like weird calligraphy. Her eyes were wet and aimed up at the ceiling, her hands gripped around the bars of the iron bedframe. Without clothes, her body was white and childlike, and she hardly had any breasts at all. The blood was everywhere. So red. Cray's heart was laboring, and as he stared at the slashed throat he heard the window slide up. He blinked, everything hazy and dreamlike, and watched the young blond man climb through the window onto the fire escape.

Oh, God, Cray thought. He wavered on his feet, feared he was about to faint. Oh, my God . . .

Julie had brought the Fliptop Killer home to play.

His first impulse was to shout for help, but he squelched it. He knew the shout would rob his breath and strength, and right now he needed both of them. The LaPrestas were still fighting. What would one more shout be? He stepped forward. Another step, and a third one followed. With the rusty agility of a champion gymnast, he ran to the open window and slid out to the fire escape.

The Fliptop Killer was about to go down the ladder. Cray reached out, grasped the young man's T-shirt in his freckled fist, and said hoarsely, *"No."*

The man twisted toward him. The small black eyes regarded him incuriously: the emotionless gaze of a clinician. There were a few spatters of blood on his face, but not many. Practice had honed his reflexes, and he knew how to avoid the jetting crimson. Cray gripped his shirt; they stared at each other for a few ticks of time, and then the killer's right hand flashed up with an extra finger of metal.

The knife swung at Cray's face, but Cray had already seen the blow coming in the tension of the man's shoulder, and as he let go of the shirt and scrambled backward, the blade hissed past.

And now the Fliptop Killer stepped toward him—a long stride, knife upraised, the face cold and without expression, as if he were about to cut a hanging piece of beef. But a woman screamed from an open window, and as the man's head darted to the side Cray grasped the wrist of his knife hand and shouted, "Call the po—"

A fist hit him in the face, crumpling his nose and mashing his lips. He pitched back, stunned—and he fell over the fire escape's railing into empty space.

3

A Red Matchbook

His robe snagged on a jagged edge of metal. The cloth ripped, almost tore off him, and for three awful seconds he was dangling five floors over the alley, but then he reached upward and his fingers closed around the railing.

The Fliptop Killer was already scrambling down the fire

escape. The woman—Mrs. Sargenza, bless her soul—was still screaming, and now somebody else was hollering from another window and the Fliptop Killer clambered down to the alley with the speed and power of a born survivor.

Cray pulled himself up, his legs kicking and his shoulder muscles standing out in rigid relief. He collapsed onto his knees when he'd made it to the landing's safety. He thought he might have to throw up enchiladas, and his stomach heaved, but mercifully there was no explosion. Blood was in his mouth, and his front teeth felt loose. He stood up, black motes buzzing before his eyes. Looked over the edge, gripping hard to the railing.

The Fliptop Killer was gone, back to the shadows.

"Call the police," he said, but he didn't know if Mrs. Sargenza had heard him, though she disappeared from her window and slammed it shut. He was trembling down to his gnarly toes, and after another moment he climbed back into the room where the corpse was.

Cray felt her wrist for a pulse. It seemed the sensible thing to do. But there was no pulse, and Julie's eyes didn't move. In the depths of the wound he could see the white bone of her spine. How many times had the killer slashed, and what was it inside him that gave him such a maniacal strength? "Wake up," Cray said. He pulled at her arm. "Come on, Julie. Wake up."

"Oh, Jesus!" Mr. Myers from across the hall stood in the doorway. His hand went to his mouth, and he made a retching sound and staggered back to his apartment. Other people were peering in. Cray said, "Julie needs a doctor," though he knew she was dead and all a doctor could do was pull the bloodied sheet over her face. He still had her hand, and he was stroking it. Her fingers were closed around something; it worked loose and fell into Cray's palm.

Cray looked at it. A red matchbook. The words GRINDERSWITCH BAR printed on its side, and an address just off Hollywood and Vine, three blocks over.

He opened the red matchbook. Two matches were missing. One of them had been used to light the Fliptop Killer's cigarette, out in the hallway. The Fliptop Killer had been to the Grinderswitch, a place Cray had walked past but never entered.

"Cops are on their way!" Mr. Gomez said, coming into the room. His wife stood at the door, her face smeared with blue anti-aging cream. "What happened here, Flint?"

Cray started to speak, but found no words. Others were entering the room, and suddenly the place with its reek of blood and spent passions was too tight for him; he had a feeling of suffocation, and a scream flailed behind his teeth. He walked past Mr. Gomez, out the door, and into his own apartment. And there he stood at the window, the brutal neon pulse flashing in his face and a red matchbook clenched in his hand.

The police would come and ask their questions. An ambulance without a siren would take Julie's corpse away, to a cold vault. Her picture would be in the *Times* tomorrow, and the headline would identify her as the Fliptop Killer's ninth victim. Her claim to fame, he thought, and he almost wept.

I saw him, he realized. *I saw the Fliptop. I had hold of the bastard.*

And there in his hand was the matchbook Julie had given him. The bartender at the Grinderswitch might know the Fliptop. The bartender might *be* the Fliptop. It was a vital clue, Cray thought, and if he gave it up to the police it might be lost in shufflings of paper, envelopes, and plastic bags that went into what they called their evidence storage. The police didn't care about Julie Saufley, and they hardly cared about the other street victims either. No, Julie was another statistic—a "crazy," the cops would say. The Fliptop Killer loved to kill "crazies."

Julie had given him a clue. Had, perhaps, fought to keep it with her dying breath. And now what was he going to do with it?

He knew, without fully knowing. It was a thing of instincts, just as his long-ago gymnastic training, track-and-field, and boxing championships were things of instinct.

Inner things that, once learned and believed in, could never be fully lost.

He opened the closet's door.

A musty, mothball smell rolled out. And there it was, on its wooden hanger amid the cheap shirts and trousers of an old dreamer.

It had once been emerald green, but time had faded it to more of a dusky olive. Bleach stains had mottled the flowing green cape, and Cray had forgotten how that had happened. Still, he'd been a good caretaker: various rips had been patched over, the only really noticable mar a poorly stitched tear across the left leg. The cowl, with its swept-back, crisply winglike folds on either side of the head and its slits for the eyes, was in almost perfect condition. The green boots were there on the floor, both badly scuffed, and the green gloves were up on the shelf.

His Green Falcon costume had aged, just like its owner. The studio had let him keep it after he came out of the sanatarium in 1954. By then serials were dying anyway, and of what use was a green suit with a long cape and wings on the sides of its cowl? In the real world, there was no room for Green Falcons.

He touched the material. It was lighter than it appeared, and it made a secret—and dangerous—whispering noise. The Green Falcon had made mincemeat out of a gallery of villains, roughnecks, and killers every Saturday afternoon in the cathedrals of light and shadow all across America. Why, then, could the Green Falcon not track down the Fliptop Killer?

Because the Green Falcon is dead, Cray told himself. Forget it. Close the door. Step back. Leave it to the police.

But he didn't close the door, nor did he step back. Because he knew, deep at his center, that the Green Falcon was not dead. Only sleeping, and yearning to awaken.

He was losing his mind. He knew that clearly enough, as if somebody had thrown ice water in his face and slapped him too. But he reached into the closet, and he brought the costume out.

The siren of a police car was approaching. Cray Flint began to pull the costume on over his pajamas. His body had thinned, not thickened, with age; the green tights were loose, and though his legs were knotty with muscles, they looked skinny and ill-nourished. His shoulders and chest still filled out the tunic portion of the costume, though, but his thin, wiry arms had lost the blocky muscularity of their youth. He got the costume zipped up, worked his feet into the scuffed boots, then put on the cape and laced it in place. The dust of a thousand moth wings shimmered gold against the green. He lifted the gloves off the shelf, but discovered the moths had enjoyed an orgy in them and they were riddled with holes. The gloves would have to stay behind. His heart was beating very hard now. He took the cowl off its hanger. The police car's siren was nearing the building. Cray ran his fingers over the cowl, which still gleamed with a little iridescence, as it had in the old days.

I shouldn't do this, he told himself. *I'm going crazy again, and I'm nothing but an Indiana boy who used to be an actor . . .*

I shouldn't . . .

He slipped the cowl over his head and drew its drawstring tight. And now he saw the world through cautious slits, the air coming to his nostrils through small holes and smelling of mothballs and . . . yes, and something else. Something indefinable: the brassy odor of a young man's sweat, the sultry heat of daredevilry, maybe the blood of a split lip incurred during a fight scene with an overeager stuntman. Those aromas and more. His stomach tightened under the green skin. *Walk tall and think tall,* he remembered a director telling him. His shoulders pulled back. How many times had he donned this costume and gone into the battle against hoodlums, thugs, and murderers? How many times had he stared Death in the face through these slits, and walked tall into the maelstrom?

I'm Creighton Flint, he thought. And then he looked at the faded poster that promised a world of thrills and saw STARRING CREIGHTON FLINT, "THE GREEN FALCON."

The one and only.

NIGHT CALLS THE GREEN FALCON

The police car's siren stopped.

It was time to go, if he was going.

The Green Falcon held the matchbook up before his eye slits. The Grinderswitch was a short walk away. If the Fliptop Killer had been there tonight, someone might remember.

He knew he was one stride away from the loony bin, and if he went through that door dressed like this there was no turning back. But if the Green Falcon couldn't track down the Fliptop, nobody could.

It was worth a try. Wasn't it?

He took a deep breath, and then the one stride followed. He walked out into the hallway, and the residents gathered around Julie Saufley's door saw him and every one of them recoiled as if they'd just seen a man from Mars. He didn't hesitate; he went past them to the elevator. The little numerals above the door were on the upward march. The policemen were coming up, he realized. It would not be wise to let them see the Green Falcon.

"Hey!" Mr. Gomez shouted. "Hey, who the hell are *you?*"

"He must be nuts!" Mrs. LaPresta said, and her husband —in a rare moment—agreed.

But Cray was already heading toward the door marked STAIRS. The cape pinched his neck and the mask was stuffy; he didn't remember the costume being so uncomfortable. But he pulled open the door and started quickly down the stairway, the matchbook clenched in his hand and the smell of Julie's blood up his nostrils.

He was puffing by the time he reached the ground floor. But he crossed the cramped little lobby, went out the revolving door and onto Hollywood Boulevard, where the lights and the noise reminded him of a three-ring circus. But he knew full well that shadows lay at the fringes of those lights, and in those shadows it was dangerous to tread. He started walking west, toward Vine Street. A couple of kids zipped past him on skateboards, and one of them gave a fierce tug at his cape that almost strangled him. Horns were honking as cars passed, and ladies of the night waved and jiggled their wares from the street corner. A punk with his hair in long red spikes peered into Cray's eyeholes and sneered. "Are you for *real,* man?" The Green Falcon kept going, a man with a mission. A black prostitute jabbed her colleague in the ribs, and both of them hooted and made obscene noises as he passed. Here came a group of Hare Krishnas, banging tambourines and chanting, and even their blank eyes widened as they saw him coming. But the Green Falcon, dodging drunks and leather-clad hustlers, left them all in the flap of his cape.

And then there was the Grinderswitch Bar, jammed between a porno theater and a wig shop. Its blinking neon sign was bright scarlet, and out in front of the place were six big Harley-Davidson motorcycles. Cray paused, fear fluttering around in the pit of his stomach. The Grinderswitch was a place of shadows; he could tell that right off. There was a meanness even in the neon's buzz. Go home, he told himself. Forget this. Just go home and—

Do what? Vegetate? Sit in a lousy chair, look at clippings, and reflect on how lucky you are to have a job sweeping the floor at a Burger King?

No. He was wearing the armor of the Green Falcon now, and why should he fear? But still he paused. To go into that place would be like walking into a lion's den after rolling around in fresh meat. Who was Julie Saufley, anyway? His friend, yes, but she was dead now, and what did it matter? Go home. Put the costume back on its hanger and forget. He looked at the door, and knew that beyond it the monsters waited. Go home. Just go home.

4

One-Eyed Skulls

He swallowed thickly. *Walk tall and think tall,* he told himself. If he did not go in, the very name of the Green Falcon would be forever tainted. Pain he could take; shame he could not.

He grasped the door's handle, and he entered the Grinderswitch.

The six motorcycle owners, husky bearded men wearing black jackets that identified them as members of the ONE-EYED SKULLS gang, looked up from their beers. One of them laughed, and the man sitting in the center seat gave a low whistle.

The Green Falcon paid them no attention. Bass-heavy music pounded from ceiling-mounted speakers, and on a small upraised stage a thin blond girl wearing a G-string gyrated to the beat with all the fervor of a zombie. A few other patrons watched the girl, and other topless girls in G-strings wandered around with trays of beers and cheerless smiles. The Green Falcon went to the bar, where a flabby man with many chins had halted in his pouring of a new set of brews. The bartender stared at him, round-eyed, as the Green Falcon slid onto a stool.

"I'm looking for a man," Cray said.

"Wrong joint, Greenie," the bartender answered. "Try the Brass Screw, over on Selma."

"No, I don't mean that." He flushed red under his mask. Trying to talk over this hellacious noise was like screaming into a hurricane. "I'm looking for a man who might have been in here tonight."

"I serve beer and liquor, not lonely-hearts-club news. Take a hike."

Cray glanced to his left. There was a mug on the bar full of GRINDERSWITCH matchbooks. "The man I'm looking for is blond, maybe in his early or mid-twenties. He's got pale skin and his eyes are very dark—either brown or black. Have you seen anybody who—"

"What are the hell are you doin' walking around in a friggin' green suit?" the bartender asked. "It's not St. Patrick's Day. Did you jump out of a nuthouse wagon?"

"No. Please, try to think. Have you seen the man I just described?"

"Yeah. A hundred of 'em. Now I said move it, and I'm not gonna say it again."

"He took one of those matchbooks," Cray persisted. "He

might have been sitting on one of these stools not long ago. Are you sure you—"

A hand grasped his shoulder and swung him around. Three of the bikers had crowded in close, and the other three watched from a distance. A couple of go-go dancers rubbernecked at him, giggling. The bass throbbing was a physical presence, making the glasses shake on the shelves behind the bar. A broad, brown-bearded face with cruel blue eyes peered into Cray's mask; the biker wore a bandanna wrapped around his skull and a necklace from which rusty razor blades dangled. "God Almighty, Dogmeat. There's somebody *inside* it!"

The biker called Dogmeat, the one who'd whistled as Cray had entered, stepped forward. He was a burly, gray-bearded hulk with eyes like shotgun barrels and a face like a pissed-off pit bull. He thunked Cray on the skull with a thick forefinger. "Hey, man! You got some screws loose or what?"

Cray smelled stale beer and dirty armpits. "I'm all right," he said with just a little quaver in his voice.

"I say you *ain't*," Dogmeat told him. "What's wrong with you, comin' into a respectable joint dressed up like a Halloween fruitcake?"

"Guy was just on his way out," the bartender said. "Let him go." The bikers glared at him, and he smiled weakly and added, "Okay?"

"No. Not okay," Dogmeat answered. He thunked Cray's skull again, harder. "I asked you a question. Let's hear you speak, man."

"I'm . . . looking for someone," Cray said. "A young man. Blond, about twenty or twenty-five. Wearing a T-shirt and blue jeans. He's got fair skin and dark eyes. I think he might have been in here not too long ago."

"What're you after this guy for? He steal your spaceship?" The others laughed, but Dogmeat's face remained serious. Another thunk of Cray's skull. "Come on, that was a joke. You're supposed to laugh."

"Please," Cray said. "Don't do that anymore."

"Do what? This?" Dogmeat thunked him on the point of his chin.

"Yes. Please don't do that anymore."

"Oh. Okay." Dogmeat smiled. "How about if I do this?" And he flung his half-full mug of beer into Cray's face. The liquid blinded Cray for a few seconds, then washed out of his mask and ran down his neck. The other One-Eyed Skulls howled with laughter and clapped Dogmeat on the back.

"I think I'd better be going." Cray started to get up, but Dogmeat's hand clamped to his shoulder and forced him down with ridiculous ease.

"Who are you supposed to be, man?" Dogmeat asked, feigning real interest. "Like . . . a big bad superhero or somethin'?"

"I'm nobo—" He stopped himself. They were watching and listening, smiling with gap-toothed smiles. And then Cray straightened up his shoulders, and it came out of him by instinct. "I'm the Green Falcon," he said.

There was a moment of stunned silence, except for that thunderous music. Then they laughed again, and the laughter swelled. But Dogmeat didn't laugh; his eyes narrowed, and when the laughter had faded he said, "Okay, Mr. Green Falcon, sir. How about takin' that mask off and . . . like . . . let's see your secret identity." Cray didn't respond. Dogmeat leaned closer. "I *said*, Mr. Green Falcon, sir, that I want you to take your mask off. Do it. *Now.*"

Cray was trembling. He clenched his fists in his lap. "I'm sorry. I can't do that."

Dogmeat smiled a savage smile. "If you won't, I will. Hand it over."

Cray shook his head. No matter what happened now, the die was cast. "No. I won't."

"Well," Dogmeat said softly, "I'm really sorry to hear that." And he grasped the front of Cray's tunic, lifted him bodily off the stool, twisted and threw him across a table eight feet away. Cray went over the table, crashed into a couple of chairs, and sprawled to the floor. Stars and rockets fired in his brain. He got up on his knees, aware that Dogmeat was advancing toward him. Dogmeat's booted foot drew back, the kick aimed at the Green Falcon's face.

5

The Star and Question Mark

A shriek like the demons of hell singing Beastie Boys tunes came from the speakers. "Christ!" Dogmeat shouted, clapping his hands to his ears. He turned, and so did the other One-Eyed Skulls.

A figure stood over at the record's turntable near the stage, calmly scratching the tone arm back and forth across the platter. The Green Falcon pulled himself up to his feet and stood shaking the explosions out of his head. The figure let the tone arm skid across the record with a last fingernails-on-chalkboard skreel, and then the speakers were silent.

"Let him be," she said in a voice like velvet smoke.

The Green Falcon's eyes were clear now, and he could see her as well as the others did. She was tall—maybe six-two or possibly an inch above that—and her amazonian body was pressed into a tigerskin one-piece bathing suit. She wore black high heels, and her hair was dyed orange and cropped close to her head. She smiled a red-lipped smile, her teeth startlingly white against her ebony flesh.

"What'd you say, bitch?" Dogmeat challenged.

"Gracie!" the bartender said. "Keep out of it!"

She ignored him, her amber eyes fixed on Dogmeat. "Let him be," she repeated. "He hasn't done anything to you."

"Lord, Lord." Dogmeat shook his head with sarcastic wonder. "A talkin' female monkey! Hey, I ain't seen you dance yet! Hop up on that stage and shake that black ass!"

"Go play in somebody else's sandbox," Gracie told him. "Kiddie time's over."

"Damned right it is." Dogmeat's cheeks burned red, and he took a menacing step toward her. "Get up on that stage! Move your butt!"

She didn't budge.

Dogmeat was almost upon her. The Green Falcon looked

around, said, "Excuse me," and lifted an empty beer mug off a table in front of a pie-eyed drunk. Then he cocked his arm back, took aim, and called out, "Hey, Mr. Dogmeat!"

The biker's head swiveled toward him, eyes flashing with anger.

The Green Falcon threw the beer mug, as cleanly as if it were a shot put on an Indiana summer day. It sailed through the air, and Dogmeat lifted his hand to ward it off, but he was way too late. The mug hit him between the eyes, didn't shatter but made a satisfying clunking sound against his skull. He took two steps forward and one back, his eyes rolled to show the bloodshot whites, and he fell like a chopped-down sequoia.

"Sonofabitch!" the brown-bearded one said, more in surprise than anything else. Then his face darkened like a storm cloud and he started toward the Green Falcon with two other bikers right behind him.

The Green Falcon stood his ground. There was no point in running; his old legs would not get him halfway to the door before the bikers pulled him down. No, he had to stand there and take whatever was coming. He let them get within ten feet, and then he said in a calm and steady voice, "Does your mother know where you are, son?"

Brown Beard stopped as if he'd run into an invisible wall. One of the others ran into him and bounced off. *"Huh?"*

"Your mother," the Green Falcon repeated. "Does she know where you are?"

"My . . . my mother? What's she got to do with this, man?"

"She gave birth to you and raised you, didn't she? Does she know where you are right now?" The Green Falcon waited, his heart hammering, but Brown Beard didn't answer. "How do you think your mother would feel if she could see you?"

"His mother wouldn't feel nothin'," another of them offered. "She's in a home for old sots up in Oxnard."

"You shut up!" Brown Beard said, turning on his companion. "She's not an old sot, man! She's just . . . like . . . a little sick. I'm gonna get her out of that place! You'll see!"

"Quit the jawin'!" a third biker said. "We gonna tear this green fruit apart or not?"

The Green Falcon stepped forward, and he didn't know what he was about to say, but lines from old scripts were whirling through his recollection like moths through klieg lights. "Any son who loves his mother," he said, "is a true American, and I'm proud to call him friend." He held his hand out toward Brown Beard.

The other man stared at it and blinked uncertainly. "Who . . . who the hell *are* you?"

"I'm the Green Falcon. Defender of the underdog. Righter of wrongs and champion of justice." *That's not me talking,* he realized. *It's from* Night Calls the Green Falcon, *Chapter Five.* But he realized also that his voice sounded different, in a strange way. It was not the voice of an old man anymore; it was a sturdy, rugged voice, with a bass undertone as strong as a fist. It was a hero's voice, and it demanded respect.

No one laughed.

And the biker with the brown beard slid his hand into the Green Falcon's, and the Green Falcon gripped it hard and said, "Walk tall and think tall, son."

At least for a few seconds, he had them. They were in a thrall of wonder, just like the little children who'd come to see him during the public-relations tour in the summer of 1951, when he'd shaken their hands and told them to respect their elders, put up their toys, and do right: the simple secret of success. Those children had wanted to believe in him, so badly; and now in this biker's eyes there was that same glimmer—faint and faraway, yes—but as clear as a candle in the darkness. This was a little boy standing here, trapped in a grown-up skin. The Green Falcon nodded recognition, and when he relaxed his grip, the biker didn't want to let go.

"I'm looking for a man who I think is the Fliptop Killer," the Green Falcon told them. He described the blond man who'd escaped from the window of Julie Saufley's apartment. "Have any of you seen a man who fits that description?"

Brown Beard shook his head. None of the others offered information either. Dogmeat moaned, starting to come around. "Where is he?" Dogmeat mumbled. "I'll rip his head off."

"Hey, this joint's about as much fun as a mortician's convention," one of the bikers said. "Women are ugly as hell too. Let's hit the road."

"Yeah," another agreed. "Ain't nothin' happenin' around here." He bent down to help haul Dogmeat up. Their leader was still dazed, his eyes roaming in circles. The bikers guided Dogmeat toward the door, but the brown-bearded one hesitated.

"I've heard of you before," he said. "Somewhere. Haven't I?"

"Yes," the Green Falcon answered. "I think you probably have."

The man nodded. Pitched his voice lower, so the others couldn't hear: "I used to have a big stack of *Batman* comics. Read 'em all the time. I used to think he was *real,* and I wanted to grow up just like him. Crazy, huh?"

"Not so crazy," the Green Falcon said.

The other man smiled slightly, a wistful smile. "I hope you find who you're lookin' for. Good luck." He started after his friends, and the Green Falcon said, "Do right."

And then they were gone, the sounds of their motorcycles roaring away. The Green Falcon glanced again at the bartender, still hoping for some information, but the man's face remained a blank.

"You want a beer, Greenie?" someone asked, and the Green Falcon turned to face the tall black go-go dancer.

"No, thank you. I've got to go." To where, he didn't know, but the Grinderswitch was a dead end.

He had taken two steps toward the door when Gracie said, "I've seen him. The guy you're after." The Green Falcon abruptly stopped. "I know that face," Gracie went on. "He was in here maybe two, three hours ago."

"Do you know his name?"

"No. But I know where he lives."

His heart kicked. "Where?"

"Well . . . he might live there or he might not," she amended. She came closer to him, and he figured she was in her late twenties, but it was hard to tell with all the makeup. "A motel on the Strip. The Palmetto. See, I used to . . . uh . . . work there. I was an escort." She flashed a quick warning glance at the bartender, as if she just dared him to crack wise. Then back to the Green Falcon again. "I used to see this guy hanging out around there. He comes in here maybe two or three times a week. Asked me out one time, but I wouldn't go."

"Why not?"

She shrugged. "Too white. Amazin' Grace doesn't have to go out with just anybody. I choose my own friends."

"But you remember seeing him at the Palmetto?"

"Yeah. Or at least somebody who fits that description. I'm not saying it's the same guy. Lots of creeps on the Strip, and those hot-springs motels lure most of them one time or another." She licked her lower lip; the shine of excitement was in her eyes. "You really think he's the Fliptop?"

"I do. Thank you for telling me, miss." He started toward the door, but again her husky voice stopped him.

"Hey, hold on! The Palmetto's about ten or twelve blocks east. You got a car?"

"No."

"Neither do I, but there's a cabstand down the street. I'm just clocking out. Right, Tony?"

"You're the star," the bartender said with a wave of his hand.

"You want some company, Greenie? I mean . . ." She narrowed her eyes. "You're not a crazy yourself, are you?" Gracie laughed at her own question. "Hell, sure you are! You've *got* to be! But I'm heading that way, and I'll show you the place if you want. For free."

"Why would you want to help me?" he asked.

Gracie looked wounded. "I've got civic pride, that's why! Hell, just because I strut my butt in this joint five nights a week doesn't mean I'm not a humanitarian!"

The Green Falcon considered that, and nodded. Amazin' Grace was obviously intelligent, and she probably enjoyed the idea of a hunt. He figured he could use all the help he could get. "All right. I'll wait while you get dressed."

She frowned. "I *am* dressed, fool! Let's go!"

They left the Grinderswitch and started walking east along the boulevard. Gracie had a stride that threatened to leave him behind, and his green suit drew just as many double-takes as her lean ebony body in its tigerskin wrapping. The cabstand was just ahead, and a cab was there, engine running. A kid in jeans and a black leather jacket leaned against the hood; he was rail-thin, his head shaved bald except for a tuft of hair in the shape of a question mark on his scalp.

"You got a fare, kid," Gracie said as she slid her mile-long legs in. "Move it!"

The kid said, "I'm waitin' for—"

"Your wait's over," Gracie interrupted. "Come on, we don't have all night!"

The kid shrugged, his eyes vacant and disinterested, and got behind the wheel. As soon as the Green Falcon was in, the kid shot away from the curb with a shriek of burning rubber and entered the flow of westbound traffic.

"We want to go to the Palmetto Motel," Gracie said. "You know where that is?"

"Sure."

"Well, you're going the wrong way. And start your meter, unless we're going to ride for free."

"Oh. Yeah." The meter's arm came down, and the mechanism started ticking. "You want to go east, huh?" he asked. And without warning he spun the wheel violently, throwing the Green Falcon and Gracie up against the cab's side, and the vehicle careened in a tight U-turn that narrowly missed a collision with a BMW. Horns blared and tires screeched, but the kid swerved into the eastbound lane as if he owned Hollywood Boulevard. And the Green Falcon saw a motorcycle cop turn on his blue light and start after them, at the same time as a stout Hispanic man ran out of a Chock Full O'Nuts coffee shop yelling and gesturing frantically.

"Must be a caffeine fit," Gracie commented. She heard

the siren's shrill note and glanced back. "Smart move, kid. You just got a blue-tailed fly on your ass."

The kid laughed, sort of. The Green Falcon's gut tightened; he'd already seen the little photograph on the dashboard that identified the cabdriver. It was a stout Hispanic face.

"Guy asked me to watch his cab while he ran in to pick up some coffee," the kid said with a shrug. "Gave me a buck, too." He looked in the rearview mirror. The motorcycle cop was waving him over. "What do you want me to do, folks?"

The Green Falcon had decided, just that fast. The police might be looking for him since he'd left the apartment building, and if they saw him like this they wouldn't understand. They'd think he was just a crazy old man out for a joyride through fantasy, and they'd take the Green Falcon away from him.

And if anyone could find the Fliptop Killer and bring him to justice, the Green Falcon could.

He said, "Lose him."

The kid looked back, and now his eyes were wide and thrilled. He grinned. "Roger wilco," he said, and pressed his foot to the accelerator.

The cab's engine roared, the vehicle surged forward with a power that pressed the Green Falcon and Gracie into their seats, and the kid whipped around a Mercedes and then up onto the curb, where people screamed and leapt aside. The cab, its exhaust pipe spitting fire, rocketed toward the plate-glass window of a lingerie store.

Gracie gave a stunned little cry, gripped the Green Falcon's hand with knuckle-cracking force, and the Green Falcon braced for impact.

6

Handful of Straws

The kid spun the wheel to the left, and the cab's fender knocked sparks off a brick wall as it grazed past the window. Then he veered quickly to the right, clipped away two parking meters, and turned the cab off Hollywood onto El Centro Avenue. He floorboarded the gas pedal.

"Let me outta here!" Gracie shouted, and she grasped the door's handle but the cab's speedometer needle was already nosing past forty. She decided she didn't care for a close acquaintance with asphalt, and anyway, the Green Falcon had her other hand and wasn't going to let her jump.

The motorcycle cop was following, the blue light spinning and the siren getting louder. The kid tapped the brakes and swerved in front of a gasoline truck, through an alley, and behind a row of buildings, then back onto El Centro and speeding southward. The motorcycle cop came out of the alley and got back on their tail, again closing the gap between them.

"What's your name?" the Green Falcon asked.

"Me? Ques," he answered. "Because of—"

"I can guess why. Ques, this is very important." The Green Falcon leaned forward, his fingers clamped over the seat in front of him. "I don't want the policeman to stop us. I'm—" Again, lines from the scripts danced through his mind. "I'm on a mission," he said. "I don't have time for the police. Do you understand?"

Ques nodded. "No," he said. "But if you want to give the cop a run, I'm your man." The speedometer's needle was almost to sixty, and Ques was weaving in and out of traffic like an Indy racer. "Hold on," he said.

Gracie screamed.

Ques suddenly veered to the left, almost grazing the

fenders of cars just released from a red light at the intersection of El Centro and Fountain Avenue. Outraged horns hooted, but then the cab had cleared the intersection and was speeding away. Ques took a hard right onto Gordon Street, another left on Lexington, and then pulled into an alley behind a Taco Bell. He drew up close to a dumpster and cut the headlights.

Gracie found her voice: "Where the hell did you learn to drive? The Demolition Derby?"

Ques got himself turned around in the seat so he could look at his passengers. He smiled, and the smile made him almost handsome. "Close. I was a third-unit stunt driver in *Beverly Hills Cop II*. This was a piece of cake."

"I'm getting out right here." Gracie reached for the door's handle. "You two never saw me before, okay?"

"Wait." The Green Falcon grasped her elbow. The motorcycle cop was just passing, going east on Lexington. The siren had been turned off, and the blue light faded as he went on.

"Not in the clear yet," Ques said. "There'll be a lot of shellheads looking for us. We'd better sit here awhile." He grinned at them. "Fun, huh?"

"Like screwing in a thornpatch." Gracie opened the door. "I'm gone."

"Please don't go," the Green Falcon said. "I need you."

"You need a good shrink is what you need. Man, I must've been crazy myself to get into this! You thinking you could track down the Fliptop!" She snorted. "Green Falcon, my ass!"

"I need you," he repeated firmly. "If you've got connections at the Palmetto, maybe you can find someone who's seen him."

"The Fliptop?" Ques asked, his interest perked again. "What about that sonofabitch?"

"I saw him tonight," the Green Falcon said. "He killed a friend of mine, and Gracie knows where he might be."

"I didn't say that, man. I said I knew where I'd seen a guy who looked like the guy who's been coming into the Grinderswitch. That's a big difference."

"Please stay. Help me. It's the only lead I've got."

Gracie looked away from him. The door was halfway open and she had one leg out. "Nobody cares about anybody else in this city," she said. "Why should I stick around and get my ass in jail . . . or *worse?*"

"I'll protect you," he answered.

She laughed. "Oh, yeah! A guy in a green freaksuit's going to protect me! Wow, my mind feels so much better! Let me go." He hesitated, then did as she said. She sat on the seat's edge, about to get out. About to. But a second ticked past, and another, and still she sat there. "I live on Olympic Boulevard," she said. "Man, I am a *long* way from home."

"Green Falcon, huh?" Ques asked. "That what you call yourself?"

"Yes. That's . . ." A second or two of indecision. "That's who I am."

"You got information about the Fliptop, why don't you give it to the cops?"

"Because . . ." *Why not, indeed?* he asked himself. "Because the Fliptop's killed nine times and he's going to kill again. Maybe tonight, even. The police aren't even close to finding him. *We* are."

"No, we're not!" Gracie objected. "Just because I saw a guy at a motel a few times doesn't mean he's the Fliptop! You've got a handful of straws, man!"

"Maybe I do. But it's worth going to the Palmetto to find out, isn't it?"

"You just don't want to go to the cops because you're afraid they'll pitch you into the nuthouse," Gracie said, and the way the Green Falcon settled back against the seat told her she'd hit the target. She was silent for a moment, watching him. "That's right, isn't it?"

"Yes," he said, because he knew it was. "I . . ." He hesitated, but they were listening and he decided to tell it as it had been, a long time ago. "I've spent some time in a sanatarium. Not recently. Back in the early fifties. I had a nervous breakdown. It . . . wasn't a nice place."

"You used to be somebody, for real?" Ques inquired.

"The Green Falcon. I starred in serials." The kid's face

showed no recognition. "They used to show them on Saturday afternoons," Cray went on. "Chapter by chapter. Well, I guess both of you are too young to remember." He clasped his hands together in his lap, his back bowed. "Yes, I used to be somebody. For real."

"So how come you went off your rocker?" Gracie asked. "If you were a star and all, I mean?"

He sighed softly. "When I was a young man I thought the whole world was one big Indiana. That's where I'm from. Some talent scouts came through my town one day, and somebody told them about me. Big athlete, they said. Won all the medals you can think of. Outstanding young American and all that." His mouth twitched into a bitter smile. "Corny, but I guess it was true. Heck, the world was pretty corny back then. But it wasn't such a bad place. Anyway, I came to Hollywood and I started doing the serials. I had a little talent. But I saw things . . ." He shook his head. "Things they didn't even know about in Indiana. It seemed as if I was on another world, and I was never going to find my way back home. And everything happened so fast . . . it just got away from me, I guess. I was a star—whatever that means—and I was working hard and making money, but . . . Cray Boomershine was dying. I could feel him dying, a little bit more every day. And I wanted to bring him back, but he was just an Indiana kid and I was a Hollywood star. The Green Falcon, I mean. Me. Cray Flint. Does that make any sense to you?"

"Not a bit," Gracie said. "Hell, *everybody* wants to be a star! What was wrong with you?"

His fingers twined together, and the old knuckles worked. "They wanted me to do a public-relations tour. I said I would. So they sent me all across the country . . . dressed up like this. And the children came out to see me, and they touched my cape and they asked for my autograph and they said they wanted to grow up just like me. Those faces . . . they gave off such an innocent light." He was silent, thinking, and he drew a deep breath and continued because he could not turn back. "It was in Watertown, South Dakota. April 26, 1951. I went onstage at the Watertown

Palace theater, right after they showed the tenth and final chapter of *Night Calls the Green Falcon*. That place was packed with kids, and all of them were laughing and happy." He closed his eyes, his hands gripped tightly together. "There was a fire. It started in a storeroom in the basement." He smelled acrid smoke, felt the heat of flames on his face. "It spread so *fast*. And some of the kids . . . some of them even thought it was part of the show. Oh, God . . . oh, my God . . . the walls were on fire, and children were being crushed as they tried to get out . . . and I heard them screaming! 'Green Falcon! Green Falcon!'" His eyes opened, stared without seeing. "But the Green Falcon couldn't save them, and fourteen children died in that fire. He couldn't save them. Couldn't." He looked at Ques, then to Gracie, and back again, and his eyes were wet and sunken in the mask's slits. "When I came out of the sanatarium, the studio let me keep the costume. For a job well done, they said. But there weren't going to be any more Green Falcon serials. Anyway, everybody was watching television, and that was that."

Neither Ques nor Gracie spoke for a moment. Then Gracie said, "We're going to take you home. Where do you live?"

"Please." He put his hand over hers. "I can find the Fliptop Killer. I know I can."

"You *can't*. Give it up."

"What would it hurt?" Ques asked her. "Just to drive to that motel, I mean. Maybe he's right." He held up his hand before she could object. "*Maybe*. We could drive there and you could ask around, and then we'll take him home. How about it?"

"It's crazy," she said. "And *I'm* crazy." But then she pulled her leg back in and shut the door. "Let's try it."

The Palmetto Motel was a broken-down stucco dump between Normandie and Mariposa, on the cheap end of Hollywood Boulevard. Ques pulled the cab into the trash-strewn parking lot, and he spoke his first impression: "Place is a crack gallery, folks." He saw shadowy faces peering through the blinds of second-floor windows, and blue firelight played across a wall. "Bullet holes in a door over there." He motioned toward it. "From here on we watch our asses." He stopped the cab next to a door marked OFFICE and cut the engine.

"It's sure enough gone to hell since I worked here," Gracie said. "Nothing like addicts to junk a place up." Not far away stood the hulk of a car that looked as if it had been recently set afire. "Well, let's see what we can see." She got out, and so did the Green Falcon. Ques stayed behind the wheel, and when Gracie motioned him to come on, he said nervously, "I'll give you moral support."

"Thanks, jerkoff. Hey, hold on!" she said, because the Green Falcon was already striding toward the office door. He grasped the knob, turned it, and the door opened with a jingle of little bells. He stepped into a room where lights from the boulevard cut through slanted blinds, and the air was thick with the mingled odors of marijuana, a dirty carpet, and . . . What else was it?

Spoiled meat, he realized.

And that was when something stood up from a corner and bared its teeth.

The Green Falcon stopped. He was looking at a stocky black-and-white pit bull, its eyes bright with the prospect of violence.

"Oh, shit," Gracie whispered.

Soundlessly the pit bull leapt at the Green Falcon, its jaws opened for a bone-crushing bite.

7

The Watchman

The Green Falcon stepped back, colliding with Gracie. The pit bull's body came flying toward him, reached the end of its chain, and its teeth clacked together where a vital member of the Green Falcon's anatomy had been a second before. Then the dog was yanked back to the wall, but it immediately regained its balance and lunged again. The Green Falcon stood in front of Gracie, picked up a chair to ward the beast off, but again the chain stopped the pit bull short of contact. As the animal thrashed against its collar, a figure rose up from behind the counter and pulled back the trigger on a double-barreled shotgun.

"Put it down," the man told the Green Falcon. He motioned with the shotgun. "Do it or I swear to God I'll blow your head off." The man's voice was high and nervous, and the Green Falcon slowly put the chair down. The pit bull was battling with its chain, trying to slide its head out of the collar. "Ain't nobody gonna rob me again," the man behind the counter vowed. Sweat glistened on his gaunt face. "You punks gonna learn some respect, you hear me?"

"Lester?" Gracie said. The man's frightened eyes ticked toward her. "Lester Dent? It's me." She took a careful step forward, where the light could show him who she was. "Sabra Jones." The Green Falcon stared at her. She said, "You remember me, don't you, Lester?"

"Sabra? That really you?" The man blinked, reached into a drawer, and brought out a pair of round-lensed spectacles. He put them on, and the tension on his face immediately eased. "Sabra! Well, why didn't you say so?" He uncocked the shotgun and said, "Down, Bucky!" to the pit bull. The animal stopped its thrashing, but it still regarded the Green Falcon with hungry eyes.

"This is a friend of mine, Lester. The Green Falcon." She said it with all seriousness.

"Hi." Lester lowered the shotgun and leaned it behind the counter. "Sorry I'm a little jumpy. Things have changed around here since you left. Lot of freaks in the neighborhood, and you can't be too careful."

"I guess not." Gracie glanced at a couple of bullet holes in the wall. Flies were buzzing around the scraps of hamburger in Bucky's feed bowl. "Used to be a decent joint. How come you're still hanging around here?"

Lester shrugged. He was a small man, weighed maybe a

hundred and thirty pounds, and he wore a Captain America T-shirt. "I crave excitement. What can I say?" He looked her up and down with true appreciation. "Life's being pretty good to you, huh?"

"I can't complain. Much. Lester, my friend and I are looking for somebody who used to hang around here." She described the man. "I remember he used to like Dolly Winslow. Do you know the guy I mean?"

"I think I do, but I'm not sure. I've seen a lot of 'em."

"Yeah, I know, but this is important. Do you have any idea what the guy's name might have been, or have you seen him around here lately?"

"No, I haven't seen him for a while, but I know what his name was." He grinned, gap-toothed. "John Smith. That's what all their names were." He glanced at the Green Falcon. "Can you breathe inside that thing?"

"The man we're looking for is the Fliptop Killer," the Green Falcon said, and Lester's grin cracked. "Do you know where we can find Dolly Winslow?"

"She went to Vegas," Gracie told him. "Changed her name, the last I heard. No telling where she is now."

"You're lookin' for the Fliptop Killer?" Lester asked. "You a cop or somethin'?"

"No. I've got . . . a personal interest."

Lester drummed his fingers on the scarred countertop and thought for a moment. "The Fliptop, huh? Guy's a mean one. I wouldn't want to cross his path, no sir."

"Anybody still around who used to hang out here?" Gracie asked. "Like Jellyroll? Or that weird guy who played the flute?"

"That weird guy who played the flute just signed a million-dollar contract at Capitol Records," Lester said. "We should all be so weird. Jellyroll's living uptown somewhere. Pearly's got a boutique on the Strip, makin' money hand over fist. Bobby just drifted away." He shook his head. "We had us a regular club here, didn't we?"

"So everybody's cleared out?"

"Well . . . not everybody. There's me, and the Watchman."

"The Watchman?" The Green Falcon came forward, and the pit bull glowered at him but didn't attack. "Who's that?"

"Crazy old guy, lives down in the basement," Lester said. "Been here since the place was new. You won't get anything out of him, though."

"Why not?"

"The Watchman doesn't speak. Never has, as far as I know. He goes out and walks, day and night, but he won't tell you where he's been. You remember him, don't you, Sabra?"

"Yeah. Dolly told me she saw him walking over on the beach at Santa Monica one day, and Bobby saw him in downtown L.A. All he does is walk."

"Can he speak?" the Green Falcon asked.

"No telling," Lester said. "Whenever I've tried talkin' to him, he just sits like a wall."

"So why do you call him the Watchman?"

"You know the way, Sabra." Lester motioned toward the door. "Why don't you show him?"

"You don't want to see the Watchman," she said. "Forget it. He's out of his mind. Like me for getting into this. See you around, Lester." She started out, and Lester said, "Don't be such a stranger."

Outside, Gracie continued walking to the cab. The Green Falcon caught up with her. "I'd like to see the Watchman. What would it hurt?"

"It would waste my time and yours. Besides, he's probably not even here. Like I said, he walks all the time." She reached the cab, where Ques was waiting nervously behind the wheel.

"Let's go," Ques said. "Cars have been going in and out. Looks like a major deal's about to go down."

"Hold it." The Green Falcon placed his hand against the door before she could open it. "If the Watchman's been here so long, he might know something about the man we're looking for. It's worth asking, isn't it?"

"No. He doesn't speak to *anybody.* Nobody knows where he came from, or who he is, and he likes it that way." She glanced around, saw several figures standing in a second-floor doorway. Others were walking across the lot toward a black Mercedes. "I don't like the smell around here. The faster we get out, the better."

The Green Falcon stepped back and let her get into the cab. But he didn't go around to the other door. "I'm going to talk to the Watchman," he said. "How do I get to the basement?"

She paused, her eyelids at half-mast. "You're a stubborn fool, aren't you? There's the way down." She pointed at a door near the office. "You go through there, you're on your own."

"We shouldn't leave him here," Ques said. "We ought to stay—"

"Shut up, cueball. Lot of bad dudes around here, and I'm not getting shot for anybody." She smiled grimly. "Not even the Green Falcon. Good luck."

"Thanks for your help. I hope you—"

"Can it," she interrupted. "Move out, Ques."

He said, "Sorry," to the Green Falcon, put the cab into reverse, and backed out of the lot. Turned left across the boulevard and headed west.

And the Green Falcon stood alone.

He waited, hoping they'd come back. They didn't. Finally he turned and walked to the door that led to the Palmetto Motel's basement, and he reached for the knob.

But somebody came out of another room before he could open the door, and the Green Falcon saw the flash of metal.

"Hey, *amigo*," the man said, and flame shot from the barrel of the small pistol he'd just drawn.

8

Yours Truly

The Hispanic man lit his cigarette with the flame, then put the pistol-shaped lighter back into his pocket. "What kinda party you dressed up for?"

The Green Falcon didn't answer. His nerves were still jangling, and he wasn't sure he could speak even if he tried.

"You lookin' for a score or not?" the man persisted.

"I'm . . . looking for the Watchman," he managed to say.

"Oh. Yeah, I should've figured you were. Didn't know the old creep had any friends."

Somebody called out, "Paco! Get your ass over here *now!*"

The man sneered. "When I'm ready!" and then he sauntered toward the group of others who stood around the Mercedes.

The Green Falcon went through the door and into darkness.

He stood on a narrow staircase, tried to find a light switch, but could not. Two steps down and his right hand found a light bulb overhead, with a dangling cord. He pulled it, and the light bulb illuminated with a dim yellow glow. The concrete stairs descended beyond the light's range, the walls made of cracked gray cinder block. The Green Falcon went down, into a place that smelled as damp and musty as a long-closed crypt. Halfway down the steps, he halted.

There had been a sound of movement over on the right. "Anyone there?" he asked. No answer, and now the sound had ceased. Rats, he decided. Big ones. He came to the bottom of the stairs, darkness surrounding him. Again he felt for a light switch, again with no reward. The smell was putrid: wet and decaying paper, he thought. He took a few steps forward, reaching out to both sides; his right arm brushed what felt like a stack of magazines or newspapers. And then the fingers of his left hand found a wall and a light switch, and when he flicked it, a couple of naked bulbs came on.

He looked around at the Watchman's domain.

The basement—a huge, cavernous chamber—might have put the periodicals department of the L.A. Public Library to shame. Neat stacks of books, newspapers, and magazines were piled against the walls and made corridors across the basement, their turns and windings as intricate as a carefully constructed maze. The Green Falcon had never seen anything like it before; there had to be thousands—no, hundreds of thousands—of items down here. Maps of Los Angeles, Hollywood, Santa Monica, Beverly Hills, and other municipalities were mounted on the walls, tinged with green mold but otherwise unmarred. Here stood a stack of telephone books six feet tall, there were multiple stacks of old *Hollywood Reporter*s. The place was an immense repository of information, and the Green Falcon was stunned because he'd never expected anything like this. A bank of battered filing cabinets stood against one wall, more newspapers stacked on top of them. There had to be thirty years of accumulated magazines and papers just in this part of the basement alone, and the chamber stretched the length of the motel. He couldn't restrain his curiosity; he went to one of the filing cabinets, which had precise little alphabet letters identifying their contents, and opened a drawer. Inside were hundreds of notebook pages covered with what appeared to be license-plate numbers and the make and color of the cars that carried them, all written in an elegant, almost calligraphic handwriting. Another drawer held lists of items found in various trashcans at scores of locations and dates. A third drawer bulged with pages that seemed to record the routes of pedestrians through the city streets, how long to the second they stayed in this or that store or restaurant, and so forth.

And it dawned on the Green Falcon that this was exactly what the Watchman did: he watched, recorded, filed away, all to the service of some bizarre inner logic, and he'd been doing it for years.

Something moved, back beyond the room in which the Green Falcon stood. There was a quick rustling sound of papers being disturbed . . . then silence. The Green Falcon wound his way through the maze, found another light switch that illuminated two more bulbs at the rear of the basement. Still more periodicals, maps, and filing cabinets stood in that area of the basement as well, but there was a cot too, and a desk with a blue blotter.

And a man in a long, dirty olive coat, huddled up with his back wedged into a corner, and his Peter Lorre eyes looked as if they were about to pop from their sockets.

"Hello," the Green Falcon said quietly. The man, gray-bearded and almost emaciated, trembled and hugged his knees. The Green Falcon walked closer and stopped, because the Watchman was shaking so hard he might have a heart attack. "I've come to talk to you."

The Watchman's mouth opened in his sallow face, gave a soft gasp, and closed again.

"I'm looking for someone you might help me find." The Green Falcon described the man. "I think he might be the Fliptop Killer, and I understand a man fitting that description used to come around here. He might have been friends with a girl named Dolly Winslow. Do you know the man I'm talking about?"

Still no response. The Watchman looked as if he were about to jump out of his skin.

"Don't be afraid. I'm the Green Falcon, and I wish you no harm."

The Watchman was so terrified there were tears in his eyes. The Green Falcon started to speak again, but he realized the futility of it. The Watchman was a human packrat, and Amazin' Grace had been right: there was nothing to be gained here.

He almost took off his mask and threw it aside in disgust. What had made him think he could track down the Fliptop? he asked himself. A red matchbook from a dead girl's hand? A glimpse of the killer's face, and an ill-founded yearning for a counterfeit past? It was ridiculous! He was standing in a motel's dank basement with a drug deal going on over his head, and he'd better get out of here as fast as he could before he got his throat cut. "I'm sorry to have bothered you," he told the Watchman, and he started walking toward the stairs. He heard the Watchman gasp and crawl across the floor, and he looked back to see the man rummaging with frantic speed inside an old mildewed cardboard box.

This is no place for me, the Green Falcon realized. In fact, there was no place at all left for the Green Falcon, but Cray Flint's mop was waiting at the Burger King.

He kept going to the stairs, burdened with age.

"'Dear Davy,'" the voice rang out. "'I am sorry I can't

come to Center City this summer, but I'm working on a new mystery . . .'"

The Green Falcon stopped.

"'. . . and I'm very busy. I just wanted you to know that I appreciate your letter, and I like to hear from my fans very much. Enclosed is something I want you to have, and I hope you'll wear it with pride. Remember to respect your elders, put up your toys, and do right . . .'"

He turned, his heart pounding.

"'Yours truly, the Green Falcon.'" And the Watchman looked up, smiling, from the yellowed, many-times-folded letter in his hands. "You signed it," he said. "Right here. Remember?" He held it up. Then scrambled to the box again, rummaged, and came up with an old wallet covered in multicolored Indian beads. He flipped it open and showed what was pinned inside. "I kept it all this time. See?"

The plastic button said THE GREEN FALCONEERS. "I see." Cray's voice cracked.

"I did right," Davy said. "I always did right."

"Yes." The Green Falcon nodded. "I know you did."

"We moved from Center City." Davy stood up; he was at least six inches taller than the Green Falcon. "My dad got a new job, when I was twelve. That was . . ." He hesitated, trying to think. "A long time ago," he decided. A frown slowly settled on his deeply lined face. "What happened to you?"

"I got old," the Green Falcon said.

"Yes, sir. Me too." His frown started to slip away, then took hold again. "Am I still a Falconeer?"

"Oh, yes. That's a forever thing."

"I thought it was," Davy said, and his smile came back.

"You've got a nice collection down here." The Green Falcon walked amid the stacks. "I guess gathering all this takes a lot of time."

"I don't mind. It's my job."

"Your job?"

"Sure. Everybody's got a job. Mine is watching things, and writing them down. Keeping them, too."

"Have you actually read all these papers and magazines?"

"Yes, sir. Well . . . most of them," he amended. "And I remember what I read, too. I've got . . . like . . . a Kodak in my brain."

Did he mean a photographic memory? the Green Falcon wondered. If so, might he recall the man Gracie remembered? "Davy," he said in his heroic voice, "I've come to you because I need your help. I'm trying to find the Fliptop Killer. Have you heard of him?"

Davy nodded without hesitation.

"Can you think of a man like the one I described? A man who was a friend of—"

"Dolly Winslow," Davy finished for him. "Yes, sir. I remember him. I never liked him, either. He laughed at people when he didn't think they were looking."

So far, so good. The Green Falcon felt sweat on the back of his neck. "I want you to concentrate very hard, like a good Falconeer. Did you ever hear the man's name?"

Davy rubbed his mouth with the back of his hand, and his eyes took on a steely glint. He walked to a filing cabinet, bent down, and opened the bottom drawer. Looked through dozens of envelopes. And then he pulled one of them out, and he brought it to the Green Falcon. On it Davy had written: *23.* "Dolly's room," he said. "He cleaned his wallet out in her trashcan one night."

The Green Falcon went to the desk and spilled the envelope's contents out on the blotter. There was a torn-open Trojan wrapper, two dried-up sticks of Doublemint gum, a few cash-register receipts, a ticket stub to a Lakers game, and . . .

"His name's Rod Bowers. It's on the library card," Davy said. "His address too."

The library card had been torn into quarters, but Davy had taped it back together again. And there were the name and address: Rodney E. Bowers, 1416 D Jericho Street, Santa Monica.

"That was over a year ago, though. He might not be there now," Davy said.

The Green Falcon's hands were shaking. Davy had taped

together another piece of paper: a receipt that had been torn into many fragments. On that receipt was the name of a business: The House of Blades. On December 20, 1986, Rodney Bowers had bought himself a Christmas present of a John Wayne Commemorative Hunting knife.

"Did I do right?" Davy asked, peering over the Green Falcon's shoulder.

"You sure did, son." He grasped the younger man's arm. "You're . . ." He said the first thing that came to mind: "The number-one Falconeer. I have to go now. I've got a job to do." He started striding, his pace quick, toward the stairs.

"Green Falcon, sir?" Davy called, and he paused. "I'll be here if you ever need my help again."

"I'll remember," the Green Falcon answered, and he climbed the stairs with the taped-together library card and the House of Blades receipt gripped in his hand.

He went through the door into the parking lot—and instantly heard someone shouting in Spanish. Somebody else was hollering from the second floor, and there were other angry voices. The man named Paco was standing next to the Mercedes, and suddenly he drew a pistol—not a cigarette lighter this time, but a .45 automatic. He shouted out a curse and began firing into the Mercedes, glass from the windshield exploding into the air. At the same time, two men got out of another car, flung themselves flat on the pavement, and started spraying Paco with gunfire. Paco's body danced and writhed, the .45 going off into the air.

"Kill 'em!" somebody yelled from the second floor. Machine-gun fire erupted, and bullets ricocheted off the concrete in a zigzagging line past the Green Falcon.

Oh, my God! Cray thought. And he realized he'd come out of the basement into the middle of a drug deal gone bad.

The two men on the pavement kept firing. Now figures were sprinting across the parking lot, shooting at the men on the second floor. Machine-gun bullets cut one of them down, and he fell in a twitching heap. The Green Falcon backed up, hit the wall, and stayed there—and then a man in a dark suit turned toward him, a smoking Uzi machine gun in his hand, his face sparkling with the sweat of terror. He lifted the weapon to spray a burst at the Green Falcon.

9

Hell or High Water

A black-and-white streak shot across the parking lot, and the pit bull hit the gunman like a miniature locomotive. The man screamed and went down, the Uzi firing an arc of tracers into the sky. And Lester ran past, stopped almost in front of the Green Falcon, fired a shotgun blast at another man, and then skidded on his belly behind the protection of a car.

The Green Falcon ran toward the street—and was almost struck by a cab that whipped into the lot with a shriek of burning rubber.

Ques hit the brake, and Gracie shouted, "Come on, fool!" as she threw the door open. The Green Falcon heard a bullet hiss past his head, and then he grasped the door and hung on as Ques reversed out of the lot and sped away on Hollywood.

Gracie pulled the Green Falcon in, and they got the door closed, but Ques still kept a leaden foot on the accelerator. "Slow down!" she told him. "We don't want the cops stopping us!" He didn't respond, and she slapped him on the question mark. *"Slow down!"*

Ques did, but only by a little. "They had guns," he said shakily. *"Real* guns!"

"What'd you expect drug dealers to carry? Slingshots?" She looked at the Green Falcon. "You in one piece?" He nodded, his eyes huge behind his mask. "We were circling the block, waiting for you to come out. We figured you'd never get out of this neighborhood alive. We were almost right, huh?"

"Yes," he croaked.

"Welcome to the big city. You find the Watchman?"

"I did." He drew a couple of deep breaths, could still smell the gunsmoke. "And something else too." He gave the library card to Ques. "That's where we're going. I think it's the Fliptop Killer's name and address."

"Not *that* again!" Gracie protested. "Man, we're taking you home!"

"No. We're going to Santa Monica. You don't have to get out of the cab if you don't want to—in fact, I'd rather you didn't. But I'm going to find the Fliptop, with you or without you."

"It'll be without me, all right," she answered, but the way he'd said that let her know he was through talking about it. The man had a mission, and he was going to do it come hell or high water. She settled back into her seat, muttering, and Ques turned toward the Santa Monica Freeway.

The address was near the beach, so close they could smell the sea. The building was dark-bricked, one of those old art-deco places that probably used to be a hotel when Santa Monica was young. Ques pulled the cab to a halt in front of it and cut the engine.

"I want both of you to stay here," The Green Falcon said. "I'm going in alone." He started to get out, but Gracie caught his arm.

"Hey, listen. If the Fliptop's really in there, this is the time to call the cops. No joke."

"I don't know that he's in there. It's an old library card; he might have moved. But if he's there, I've got to see his face for myself. Then we can call the police."

"She's right," Ques told him. "Listen, it's crazy to go in there. You don't have a gun or anything."

"The Green Falcon," he said adamantly, "never carries a gun."

"Yeah, and the Green Falcon's only got one life, fool!" Gracie didn't release her grip. "Playtime's over. I mean it. This isn't some old serial, this is real life. You know what reality is?"

"Yes, I do." He turned the full wattage of his gaze on her. "The reality is that . . . I think I'd rather die as the Green

Falcon than live as an old man with a screwed-up bladder and a book of memories. I want to walk tall, just once more. Is that so terrible?"

"It's nuts," she answered. "And *you're* nuts."

"So I am. I'm going." He pulled loose from her and got out of the cab. He was scared, but not as much as he thought he'd be. It wasn't as bad as indigestion, really. And then he went up the front steps into the building, and he checked the row of mailboxes in the alcove.

The one for apartment D had BOWERS on it.

Apartments A, B, and C were on the first floor. He climbed the stairs, aided by a red-shaded light fixture on the wall, and stood before Apartment D's door.

He started to knock. Stopped his hand, the fist clenched. A thrill of fear coursed through him. He stood there facing the door, and he didn't know if he could do it or not. He wasn't the Green Falcon; there was no such entity, not really. It was all a fiction. But Julie's death was not a fiction, and neither was what he'd been through tonight to reach this door. The sane thing was to back off, go down those stairs, get to a phone, and call the police. Of course it was.

He heard a car's horn blare a quick tattoo. The cab, he thought. Ques, urging him to come back?

He knocked at the door and waited. His heart had lodged in his throat. He tensed for a voice, or the sudden opening of the door.

The stairs creaked.

He heard the cab's horn again. This time Ques was leaning on it, and suddenly the Green Falcon knew why.

He turned, in awful slow motion, and saw the shadow looming on the wall.

And there he was: the young blond, dark-eyed man who'd slashed Julie's throat. Coming up the staircase, step by step, not yet having seen the Green Falcon. But he would, at any second, and each step brought them closer.

The Green Falcon didn't move. The killer's weight made the risers moan, and he was smiling slightly—perhaps, the Green Falcon thought, musing over the feel of the blade piercing Julie's flesh.

And then the Fliptop Killer looked up, saw the Green Falcon at the top of the stairs, and stopped.

They stared at each other, standing not quite an arm's length apart. The killer's dark eyes were startled, and in them the Green Falcon saw a glint of fear.

"I've found you," the Green Falcon said.

The Fliptop Killer reached to his back, his hand a blur. It returned with the bright steel of the hunting knife, taken from a sheath that must fit down at his waistband. He moved fast, like an animal, and the Green Falcon saw the blade rising to strike him in the throat or chest.

"It's him!" Gracie shouted as she burst into the alcove and to the foot of the steps.

The killer looked around at her—and it was the Green Falcon's turn to move fast. He grasped the man's wrist and struck him hard in the jaw with his right fist, and he felt one of his knuckles break, but the killer toppled backward down the stairs.

The man caught the railing before he'd tumbled to the bottom, and he still had hold of the knife. A thread of blood spilled from his split lower lip, his eyes dazed from a bang of his skull against a riser. The Green Falcon was coming down the steps after him, and the Fliptop Killer struggled up and backed away.

"Watch out!" the Green Falcon yelled as Gracie tried to grab the man's knife. The killer swung at her, but she jumped back and the blade narrowly missed her face. But she had courage, and she wasn't about to give up; she darted in again, clutching his arm to keep the knife from another slash. The Green Falcon tensed to leap at the man, but suddenly the killer struck Gracie in the face with his left fist and she staggered back against the wall. Just that fast, the man fled toward the front door.

The Green Falcon stopped at Gracie's side. Her nose was bleeding and she looked about to pass out. She said, "Get the bastard," and the Green Falcon took off in pursuit.

Out front, the Fliptop Killer ran to the parked cab. Ques tried to fight him off, but a slash of the blade across Ques's shoulder sprayed blood across the inside of the windshield;

the Fliptop Killer looked up, saw the man in the green suit and cape coming after him. He hauled Ques out of the cab and leapt behind the wheel.

As the cab's tires laid down streaks of rubber, the Green Falcon grasped the edge of the open window on the passenger side and just had an instant to lock his fingers, broken knuckle and all, before the cab shot forward. Then he was off his feet, his body streamlined to the cab's side, and the vehicle was roaring north along serpentine Jericho Street at fifty miles an hour.

The Green Falcon hung on. The killer jerked the wheel back and forth, slammed into a row of garbage cans, and kept going. He made a screeching left turn at a red light that swung the Green Falcon's body out from the cab's side and all but tore his shoulders from their sockets, but still the Green Falcon hung on. And now the Fliptop Killer leaned over, one hand gripping the wheel, and jabbed at the Green Falcon's fingers with the knife. Slashed two of them, but the Green Falcon's right hand darted in and clamped around the wrist. The cab veered out of its lane, in front of a panel truck whose fender almost clipped the Green Falcon's legs. The killer thrashed wildly, trying to get his knife hand free, but the Green Falcon smashed his wrist against the window's frame and the fingers spasmed open; the knife fell down between the seat and the door.

Beachfront buildings and houses flashed by on either side. The cab tore through a barricade that said WARNING—NO VEHICLES BEYOND THIS POINT.

The Green Falcon tried to push himself through the window. A fist hit his chin and made alarm bells go off in his brain. And then the Fliptop Killer gripped the wheel with both hands, because the cab was speeding up a narrow wooden ramp. The Green Falcon had the taste of blood in his mouth, and now he could hear a strange thing: the excited shouts of children, the voices of ghosts on the wind. His fingers were weakening, his grip about to fail; the voices, overlapped and intermingled, said *Hold on, Green Falcon, hold on. . . .*

And then, before his strength collapsed, he lunged

through the window and grappled with the Fliptop Killer as the cab rocketed up onto a pier and early-morning fishermen leapt for their lives.

Fingers gouged for the Green Falcon's eyes, could not get through the mask's slits. The Green Falcon hit him in the face with a quick boxer's left and right, and the killer let go of the wheel to clench both sinewy hands around the Green Falcon's throat.

The cab reached the end of the pier, crashed through the wooden railing, and plummeted into the Pacific Ocean twenty feet below.

10

Nightmare Netherworld

The sea surged into the cab, and the vehicle angled down into the depths.

The Fliptop Killer screamed. The Green Falcon smashed him in the face with a blow that burst his nose, and then the sea came between them, rising rapidly toward the roof as the cab continued to sink.

The last bubbles of air exploded from the cab. One headlight still burned, pointing toward the bottom, and for a few seconds the instrument panel glowed with weird phosphorescence. And then the lights shorted out, and darkness claimed all.

The Green Falcon released his prey. Already his lungs strained for a breath, but still the cab was sinking. One of the killer's thrashing legs hit his skull, a hand tearing at his tunic. The Green Falcon didn't know which was up and which was down; the cab was rotating as it descended, like an out-of-control aircraft falling through a nightmare netherworld. The Green Falcon searched for an open window but found only the windshield's glass. He slammed his fist against it, but it would take more strength than he had to break it.

Cut, he thought. Panic flared inside him, almost tore loose the last of the air in his lungs. *Cut!* But there was no director here, and he had to play this scene out to its end. He twisted and turned, seeking a way out. His cape was snagged around something—the gearshift, he thought it was. He ripped the cape off and let it fall, and then he pulled his cowl and mask off and it drifted past him like another face. His lungs heaved, bubbles coming out of his nostrils. And then his flailing hands found a window's edge; as he pushed himself through, the Fliptop Killer's fingers closed on his arm.

The Green Falcon grasped the man's shirt and pulled him through the window too.

Somewhere below the surface, he lost his grip on the Fliptop Killer. His torn tunic split along the seams, and left him. He kicked toward the top with the legs that had won a gold medal in his junior-year swim meet, and as his lungs began to convulse his head broke the surface. He shuddered, drawing in night air.

People were shouting at him from the pier's splintered rail. A wave caught him, washed him forward. The rough surface of a barnacled piling all but ripped the green tights off his legs. Another wave tossed him, and a third. The fourth crashed foam over him, and then a young arm got him around the neck and he was being guided to the beach.

A moment later, his knees touched sand. A wave cast him onto shore and took the last tatters of his Green Falcon costume back with it to the sea.

He was turned over. Somebody trying to squeeze water out of him. He said, "I'm all right," in a husky voice, and he heard someone else shout, "The other one washed up over here!"

Cray sat up. "Is he alive?" he asked the tanned face. "Is he alive?"

"Yeah," the boy answered. "He's alive."

"Good. Don't let him go." Cray snorted seaweed out of his nostrils. "He's the Fliptop Killer."

The boy stared at him. Then shouted to his friend, "Sit on that dude till the cops get here, man!"

It wasn't long before the first police car came. The two

officers hurried down to where Cray sat at the edge of the land, and one of them bent down and asked his name.

"Cray Fl . . ." He stopped. A piece of green cloth washed up beside him, was pulled back again just as quickly. "Cray Boomershine," he answered. And then he told them the rest of it.

"This guy got the Fliptop!" one of the kids standing nearby called to his friend, and somebody else repeated it and it went up and down the beach. People crowded around, gawking at the old man who sat in his pajamas on the sand.

The second police car came, and the third one brought a black go-go dancer and a kid with a question mark on his scalp and a bandage around his shoulder. They pushed through the crowd, and Gracie called out, "Where is he? Where's the Green Fal—"

She stopped, because the old man standing between two policemen was smiling at her. He said, "Hello, Gracie. It's all over."

She came toward him. Didn't speak for a moment. Her hand rose up, and her fingers picked seaweed out of his hair. "Lord have mercy," she said. "You look like a wet dog."

"You got that sucker, didn't you?" Ques watched the cops taking the Fliptop, in handcuffs, to one of the cars.

"We got him," Cray said.

A TV news truck was pulling onto the beach. A red-haired woman with a microphone and a guy carrying a video camera and power pack got out, hurrying toward the center of the crowd. "No questions!" a policeman told her, but she was right there in Cray's face before she could be restrained. The camera's lights shone on him, Gracie, and Ques. "What happened here? Is it true that the Fliptop Killer was caught tonight?"

"No questions!" the policeman repeated, but Gracie's teeth flashed as she grinned for the camera.

"What's your name?" the woman persisted. She thrust the microphone up to Cray's lips.

"Hey, lady!" Ques said. The microphone went to him. "Don't you recognize the Green Falcon?"

The newswoman was too stunned to reply, and before she

could find another question, a policeman herded her and the cameraman away.

"We're going to the station and clear all this mess away," the officer who had hold of Cray's elbow said. "All three of you. Move it!"

They started up the beach, the crowd following and the newswoman trying to get at them again. Gracie and Ques got into one of the police cars, but Cray paused. The night air smelled sweet, like victory. The night had called, and the Green Falcon had answered. What would happen to him, Gracie and Ques from this moment on, he didn't know. But of one thing he was certain: they had done right.

He got into the police car, and realized he still wore his green boots. He thought that maybe—just maybe—they still had places to go.

The police car carried them away, and the TV news truck followed.

On the beach, the crowd milled around for a while. Who was he? somebody asked. The Green Falcon? Did he used to be somebody? Yeah, a long time ago. I think I saw him on a rerun. He lives in Beverly Hills now, went into real estate and made about ten million bucks, but he still plays the Green Falcon on the side.

Oh, yeah, somebody else said. I heard that too.

And at the edge of the ocean a green mask and cowl washed up from the foam, started to slip back into the waves again.

A little boy picked it up. He and his dad had come to fish on the pier this morning, before the sun came up and the big ones went back to the depths. He had seen the cab go over the edge, and the sight of this mask made his heart beat harder.

It was a thing worth keeping.

He put it on. It was wet and heavy, but it made the world look different, kind of.

He ran back to his dad, his brown legs pumping in the sand, and for a moment he felt as if he could fly.

The Red House

I've got a story to tell, like everybody else in the world. Because that's what makes up life, isn't it? Sure. Everybody's got a story—about somebody they met, or something that's happened to them, something they've done, something they want to do, something they'll never do. In the life of everybody on this old spinning ball there's a story about a road not taken, or a love that went bad, or a ghost of some kind. You know what I mean. You've got one too.

Well, I want to tell you a story. Trouble is, there are so *many* things I remember about Greystone Bay. I could tell you about what Joey Hammers and I found in the wreck of an old Chevy down where the blind man lives amid the junked cars. I could tell you about the time the snakes started coming out of old lady Farrow's faucets, and what she did with them. I could tell you about that Elvis Presley impersonator who came to town, and went crazy when he couldn't get his makeup off. Oh, yeah, I know a lot about what goes on in Greystone Bay. Some things I wouldn't want to tell you after the sun goes down, but I want to tell you a story about *me*. You decide if it's worth the telling.

My name's Bob Deaken. Once upon a time, I was Bobby Deaken, and I lived with my Mom and Dad in one of the clapboard houses on Accardo Street, up near South Hill. There are a lot of clapboard houses up there, all the same shape and size and color—kind of a slate gray. A tombstone color. All of them have identical windows, front porches, and concrete steps leading up from the street. I swear to God, I think all of them have the same cracks in those steps, too! I mean, it's like they built one of those houses and took a black-and-white picture of it and said, "This is the ideal house for Accardo Street," and they put every one together just the same right down to the warped doors that stick in the summer and hang when it's cold. I guess Mr. Lindquist figured those houses were good enough for the Greeks and Portuguese, Italians and Poles who live in them and work at his factory. Of course, a lot of plain old Americans live on Accardo Street too, and they work for Mr. Lindquist like my dad does.

Everybody up on Accardo pays rent to Mr. Lindquist, see. He owns all those houses. He's one of the richest men in Greystone Bay, and his factory churns out cogs, gears, and wheels for heavy machinery. I worked as a "quality controller" there during summer break from high school. Dad got me the job, and I stood at a conveyor belt with a few other teenage guys and all we did day after day was make sure a certain size of gear fit into a perfect mold. If it was one hair off, we flipped it into a box and all the rejects were sent back to be melted down and stamped all over again. Sounds simple, I guess, but the conveyor belt pushed thousands of gears past us every hour and our supervisor, Mr. Gallagher, was a real bastard with an eagle eye for bad gears that slipped past. Whenever I had a complaint about the factory, Dad said I ought to be thankful I could get a job there at all, times being so bad and all; and Mom just shrugged her shoulders and said that Mr. Lindquist probably started out counting and checking gears somewhere too.

But you ask my Dad what kind of machines all those gears, cogs, and wheels went into, and he couldn't tell you. He'd worked there since he was nineteen years old, but he still didn't know. He wasn't interested in what they did, or where they went when the crates left the loading docks; all he did was make them, and that's the only thing that mattered to him—millions and millions of gears, bound for

unknown machines in faraway cities, a long way off from
Greystone Bay.

South Hill's okay. I mean, it's not the greatest place, but
it's not a slum either. I guess the worst thing about living on
Accardo Street is that there are so many houses, and all of
them the same. A lot of people are born in the houses on
Accardo Street, maybe move two or three doors away when
they get married, and they have kids who go to work at Mr.
Lindquist's factory, and then their kids move two or three
doors away and it just goes on and on. Even Mr. Lindquist
used to be Mr. Lindquist Junior, and he lives in the same big
white house that his grandfather built.

But sometimes, when my Dad started drinking and
yelling and Mom locked herself in the bathroom to get away
from him, I used to go up to the end of Accardo Street. The
hulk of what used to be a Catholic church stands up there;
the church caught on fire in the late seventies, right in the
middle of one of the worst snowstorms Greystone Bay ever
saw. It was a hell of a mess, but the church wasn't completely destroyed. The firemen never found Father Marion's
body. I don't know the whole story, but I've heard things I
shouldn't repeat. Anyway, I found a way to climb up to what
was left of the old bell tower, and the thing creaked and
moaned like it was about to topple off, but the risk was
worth it. Up there you could see the whole of Greystone
Bay, the way the land curved to touch the sea, and you got a
sense of where you were in the world. And out there on the
ocean you could see yachts, workboats, and ships of all
kinds passing by, heading for different harbors. At night
their lights were especially pretty, and sometimes you could
hear a distant whistle blow, like a voice that whispered,
Follow me.

And sometimes I wanted to. Oh, yeah, I did. But Dad said
the world beyond Greystone Bay wasn't worth a shit, and a
bull should roam his own pasture. That was his favorite
saying, and why everybody called him "Bull." Mom said I
was too young to know my own mind; she was always on my
case to go out with "that nice Donna Raphaelli," because
the Raphaellis lived at the end of the block and Mr.

Raphaelli was Dad's immediate supervisor at the factory. Nobody listens to a kid until he screams, and by then it's too late.

Don't let anybody tell you the summers aren't hot in Greystone Bay. Come mid-July, the streets start to sizzle and the air is a stagnant haze. I swear I've seen seagulls have heat strokes and fall right out of the sky. Well, it was on one of those hot, steamy July mornings—a Saturday, because Dad and I didn't have to work—when the painters pulled up onto Accardo Street in a white truck.

The house right across the street from ours had been vacant for about three weeks. Old Mr. Pappados had a heart attack in the middle of the night, and at his funeral Mr. Lindquist gave a little speech because the old man had worked at the factory for almost forty years. Mrs. Pappados went west to live with a relative. I wished her luck on the day she left, but Mom just closed the curtains and Dad turned the TV up louder.

But on this particular morning in July, all of us were on the front porch trying to catch a breeze. We were sweltering and sweating, and Dad was telling me how this was the year the Yankees were going to the World Series—and then the painters pulled up. They started setting up their ladders and getting ready to work.

"Going to have a new neighbor," Mom said, fanning herself with a handkerchief. She turned her chair as if to accept a breeze, but actually it was to watch the house across the street.

"I hope they're *American*," Dad said, putting aside the newspaper. "God knows we've got enough foreigners living up here already."

"I wonder what job Mr. Lindquist has given our new neighbor." Mom's glance flicked toward Dad and then away as fast as a fly can escape a swatter.

"The line. Mr. Lindquist always starts out new people on the line. I just hope to God whoever it is knows something about baseball, because your son sure don't!"

"Come on, Dad," I said weakly. It seems like my voice was always weak around him. I had graduated from high school in May, was working full time at the factory, but Dad had a way of making me feel twelve years old and stupid as a stone.

"Well, you don't!" he shot back. "Thinkin' the *Cubs* are gonna take the Series? Crap! The Cubs ain't never gonna get to the—"

"I wonder if they have a daughter," Mom said.

"Hey, don't you talk when I'm talkin'. What do you think I am, a wall?"

The painters were prying their paint cans open. One of them dipped his brush in.

"Oh, my God," Mom whispered, her eyes widening. "Would you *look* at that?"

We did, and we were stunned speechless.

The paint was not the bland gray of all the other clapboard houses on Accardo Street. Oh, no—that paint was as scarlet as a robin's breast. Redder than that: as red as the neon signs down where the bars stand on Harbor Road, crimson as the warning lights out on the bay where the breakers crash and boom on jagged rocks. Red as the party dress of a girl I saw at a dance but didn't have enough nerve to meet.

Red as a cape swirled before the eyes of a bull.

As the painters began to cover the door of that house with screaming-scarlet, my dad came up out of his chair with a grunt as if he'd been kicked in the rear. If there was anything he hated in the world, it was the color red. It was a Communist color, he'd always said. *Red* China. The *Reds*. *Red* Square. The *Red* Army. He thought the Cincinnati Reds was the lousiest team in baseball, and even the sight of a red shirt drove him to ranting fits. I don't know what it was, maybe something in his mind or his chemistry, maybe. He just went into a screaming rage when he saw the color red.

"Hey!" he yelled across the street. The painters stopped working and looked up, because his shout had been loud enough to rattle the windows in their frames. "What do you think you're doin' over there?"

"Ice-skatin'," came the reply. "What does it look like we're doin'?"

"Get it off!" Dad roared, his eyes about to explode from his head. "Get that shit off right *now!*" He started down the concrete steps, with Mom yelling at him not to lose his temper, and I knew somebody was going to get hurt if he got his hands on those painters. But he stopped at the edge of the street, and by this time people were coming out of their houses all around to see what the noise was all about. It was no big deal, though; there was always some kind of yelling and commotion on Accardo Street, especially when the weather turned hot and the walls of those clapboard houses closed in like cages. Dad hollered, "Mr. Lindquist owns these houses, you idiots! Look around! You see any of the others painted Commie red?"

"Nope," one of them replied, while the other kept on painting.

"Then what the hell are you doin'?"

"Followin' Mr. Lindquist's direct orders," the painter said. "He told us to come up here to 311 Accardo Street and paint the whole place Firehouse Red." He tapped one of the cans with his foot. "This is Firehouse Red, and that's 311 Accardo." He pointed to the little metal numbers up above the front door. "Anymore questions, Einstein?"

"These houses are *gray!*" Dad shouted, his face blotching with color. "They've been gray for a hundred years! You gonna paint every house on this street Commie red?"

"Nope. Firehouse Red. And we're just painting this place right here. Inside and outside. But that's the only house we're supposed to touch."

"It's right in front of my *door!* I'll have to look at it! My God, a color like that *screams* to be looked at! I can't stand that color!"

"Tough. Take it up with Mr. Lindquist." And then he joined the other painter in the work, and when Dad returned to the house he started throwing around furniture and cursing like a madman. Mom locked herself in the bathroom with a magazine, and I went up to the church to watch the boats go by.

As it turned out, on Monday Dad gathered his courage to go see Mr. Lindquist on his lunch break. He only got as far as Mr. Lindquist's secretary, who said she'd been the one to call Greystone Bay Painters and convey the orders. That was all she knew about it. On the drive home, Dad was so mad he almost wrecked the car. And there was the red house, right across the street from our own gray, dismal-looking clapboard house, the paint still so fresh that it smelled up the whole street. "He's trying to get to me," Dad said in a nervous voice at dinner. "Yeah. Sure. Mr. Lindquist wants to get rid of me, but he don't have the guts of his father. He's afraid of me, so he paints a house Commie red and sticks it in my face. Sure. That's what it's got to be!" He called Mr. Raphaelli up the street to find out what was going on, but learned only that a new man had been hired and would be reporting to work in a week.

I tell you, that was a crazy week. Like I say, I don't know why the color red bothered my dad so much; maybe there's a story in that too, but all I know is that my dad started climbing the walls. It took everything he had to open the front door in the morning and go to work, because the morning sunlight would lie on the walls of that red house and make it look like a four-alarm fire. And in the evening, the setting sun set it aflame from another direction. People started driving along Accardo Street—*tourists,* yet!—just to take a look at the gaudy thing! Dad double-locked the doors and pulled the shades as if he thought the red house might rip itself off its foundations at night and come rattling across the street after him. Dad said he couldn't breathe when he looked at that house, the awful red color stole the breath right out of his lungs, and he started going to bed early at night with the radio tuned to a baseball game and blaring right beside his head.

But in the dark, when there was no more noise from the room where my mom and dad slept in their separate beds, I sometimes unlocked the front door and went out on the porch to stand in the steamy night. I wouldn't dare tell my mom or dad, but . . . I *liked* the red house. I mean, it looked like an island of life in a gray sea. For a hundred years there had been only gray houses on Accardo Street, all of them exactly the same, not a nail or a joint different. And now *this*. I didn't know why, but I was about to find out in a big way.

Our new neighbors came to the red house exactly one week after the house had been painted. They made enough noise to wake the rich folks in their mansions up on North Hill, hollering and laughing on an ordinarily silent Saturday morning, and when I went out on the porch to see, my folks were already out there. My dad's face was almost purple, and there was a mixture of rage and terror in his eyes. My mom was stunned, and she kept rubbing his arm and holding him from flinging himself down the steps.

The man had crew-cut hair the color of fire. He wore a red-checked shirt and trousers the shade of Italian wine. On his feet were red cowboy boots, and he was unloading a U-Haul trailer hooked to the back of a beat-up old red station wagon. The woman wore a pink blouse and crimson jeans, and her shoulder-length hair glinted strawberry blond in the strong morning light. A little boy and little girl, about six and seven, were scampering around underfoot, and both of them had hair that was almost the same color of the house they'd come to inhabit.

Well, suddenly the man in red looked up, saw us on the porch, and waved. "Howdy!" he called in a twanging voice that sounded like a cat being kicked. He put aside the crimson box he'd been carrying, strode across the street in his red cowboy boots and right up the steps onto our porch, and he stood there grinning. His complexion looked as if he'd been weaned on ketchup.

"Hello," my mom said breathlessly, her hand digging into Dad's arm. He was about to snort steam.

"Name's Virgil Sikes," the man announced. He had thick red eyebrows, an open, friendly face, and light brown eyes that were almost orange. He held a hand out toward my dad. "Pleased to meet you, I'm sure."

Dad was trembling; he looked at Virgil Sikes' hand like it was a cow flop in a bull's pasture.

I don't know why. I guess I was nervous. I didn't think. I just reached out and shook the man's hand. It was hot, like he was running a high fever. "Hi," I said. "I'm Bobby Deaken."

"Howdy, Bobby!" He looked over his shoulder at the woman and two kids. "Evie, bring Rory and Garnett up here and meet the Deakens!" His accent sounded foreign, slurred and drawled, and then I realized it was Deep South. He grinned wide and proud as the woman and two children came up the steps. "This is my wife and kids," Virgil said. "We're from Alabama. Long ways from here. I reckon we're gonna be neighbors."

All that red had just about paralyzed my dad. He made a croaking sound, and then he got the words out, "Get off my porch."

"Pardon?" Virgil asked, still smiling.

"Get off," Dad repeated. His voice was rising. "Get off my porch, you damned redneck hick!"

Virgil kept his smile, but his eyes narrowed just a fraction. I could see the hurt in them. He looked at me again. "Good to meet you, Bobby," he said in a quieter voice. "Come on over and visit sometime, hear?"

"He will *not!*" Dad told him.

"Ya'll have a good day," Virgil said, and he put his arm around Evie. They walked down the steps together, the kids right at their heels.

Dad pulled free from my mother. "Nobody around here lives in a red house!" he shouted at their backs. They didn't stop. "Nobody with any sense *wants* to! Who do you think you are, comin' around here dressed like that? You a Commie or somethin'? You hick! Why don't you go back where you belong, you damned—" And then he stopped suddenly, because I think he could feel me staring at him. He turned his head, and we stared at each other in silence.

I love my dad. When I was a kid, I used to think he hung the moon. I remember him letting me ride on his shoulders. He was a good man, and he tried to be a good father—but at that moment, on that hot July Saturday morning, I saw that there were things in him that he couldn't help, things that had been stamped in the gears of his soul by the hands of ancestors he never even knew. Everybody has those things in them—little quirks, meannesses, and petty things that don't get much light; that's part of being human. But when you love somebody and you catch a glimpse of those things you've never seen before, it kind of makes your heart pound a little harder. I saw also, as if for the first time, that my dad had exactly the same shade of blue eyes as my own.

"What're *you* lookin' at?" Dad asked, his face all screwed up and painful.

He looked so old. There was gray in his hair, and deep lines on his face. So old, and tired, and very much afraid.

I dropped my gaze like a dog about to be kicked, because my dad always made me feel weak. I shook my head and got back inside the house quick.

I heard my mom and dad talking out there. His voice was loud, but I couldn't make out what he was saying; then, gradually, his voice settled down. I lay on my bed and stared at a crack in the ceiling that I'd seen a million times. And I wondered why I'd never tried to patch it up in all those years. I wasn't a kid anymore; I was right on the edge of being a man. No, I hadn't patched that crack because I was waiting for somebody else to do it, and it was never going to get done that way.

He knocked on the door after a while, but he didn't wait for me to invite him in. That wasn't his way. He stood in the doorway, and finally he shrugged his big heavy shoulders and said, "Sorry. I blew my top, huh? Well, do you blame me? It's that damned red house, Bobby! It's makin' me crazy! I can't even think about nothin' else! You understand that, don't you?"

"It's just a red house," I said. "That's all it is. Just a house with red paint."

"It's *different!*" he replied sharply, and I flinched. "Accardo Street has been just fine for a hundred years the way it used to be! Why the hell does it have to change?"

"I don't know," I said.

"Damned right you don't know! 'Cause you don't know about *life!* You get ahead in this world by puttin' your nose to the wheel and sayin' 'yes sir' and 'no sir' and toein' the line!"

"Whose line?"

"The line of anybody who pays you money! Now, don't you get smart with me, either! You're not man enough yet that I can't tear you up if I want to!"

I looked at him, and something in my face made him wince. "I love you, Dad," I said. "I'm not your enemy."

He put a hand to his forehead for a minute, and leaned against the doorframe. "You don't see it, do you?" he asked quietly. "One red house is all it takes. Then everything starts to change. They paint the houses, and the rent goes up. Then somebody thinks Accardo Street would be a nice place to put condos that overlook the bay. They bring machines in to do the work of men at the factory—and don't you think they don't have machines like that! One red house and everything starts to change. God knows I don't understand why Mr. Lindquist painted it. He's not like his old man was, not by a long shot."

"Maybe things need to change," I said. "Maybe they *should* change."

"Yeah. Right. And where would *I* be? Where else am I going to find work, at my age? Want me to start collectin' garbage the tourists leave down at the beach? And where would *you* be? The factory's your future too, y'know."

I took a step then, over the line into forbidden territory. "I'd still like to go to college, Dad. My grades are good enough. The school counselor said—"

"I've told you we'll talk about that later," Dad said firmly. "Right now we need the extra money. Times are tough, Bobby! You've got to pull your weight and toe the line! Remember, a bull should roam his own pasture. Right?"

I guess I agreed. I don't remember. Anyway, he left my room and I lay there for a long time, just thinking. I think I remember hearing a boat's whistle blow, way off in the distance, and then I fell asleep.

On Monday morning we found out where Virgil Sikes was assigned. Not the line. Not the loading dock. He came right into the big room where my dad worked on one of the machines that smoothed and polished the gears until they were all exactly the same, and he started working on a machine about twenty feet away. I didn't see him, because I worked on the loading dock that summer, but my dad was a nervous wreck at the end of the day. Seems Virgil Sikes was wearing all red again; and, as we were to learn, that's the only color he *would* wear, crimson right down to his socks.

It began to drive my dad crazy. But I know one thing: the first week Virgil Sikes worked at the factory, I carted about twenty more crates than usual off that loading dock. The second week, the factory's quota was up by at least thirty crates. I know, because my sore muscles took count.

The story finally came from Mr. Raphaelli: Virgil Sikes had hands as fast as fire, and he worked like no man Mr. Raphaelli had ever seen before. Rumor was circulating around the factory that Sikes had labored in a lot of different factories along the coast, and in every one of them he'd boosted production by from twenty to thirty percent. The man was never still, never slowed down or even took a water break. And somehow Mr. Lindquist had found out about him and hired him away from a factory down South, but to come to Greystone Bay Virgil Sikes had asked one thing: that the house he live in be painted as bright a red—inside and out—as the painters could find.

"That redneck's a lot younger than me," Dad said at dinner. "I could do that much work when I was his age!" But all of us knew that wasn't true; all of us knew nobody at the factory could work like that. "He keeps on like this, he's gonna blow up his damn machine! Then we'll see what Lindquist thinks about him!"

But about a week after that, word came down to assign Virgil Sikes to *two* polishers at the same time. He handled them both with ease, his own speed gearing up to match the machines.

The red house began to haunt my dad's dreams. Some nights he woke up in a cold sweat, yelling and thrashing around. When he got drunk, he ranted about painting our house bright blue or yellow—but all of us knew Mr. Lindquist wouldn't let him do that. No, Virgil Sikes was special. He was different, and that's why Mr. Lindquist let him live in a red house amid the gray ones.

And one night when Dad was drunk he said something that I knew had been on his mind for a long time. "Bobby boy," he said, placing his hand on my shoulder and squeezing, "what if somethin' *bad* was to happen to that damn Commie-red house over there? What if somebody was to light a little bitty fire, and that red house was to go up like a—"

"Are you *crazy?"* Mom interrupted. "You don't know what you're saying!"

"Shut up!" he bellowed. "We're talkin' man-to-man!" And that started another yelling match. I got out of the house pretty quick, and went up to the church to be alone.

I didn't go back home until one or two in the morning. It was quiet on Accardo Street, and all the houses were dark. But I saw a flicker of light on the red house's porch. A match. Somebody was sitting on the porch, lighting a cigarette.

"Howdy, Bobby," Virgil Sikes' voice said quietly, in its thick Southern drawl.

I stopped, wondering how he could see it was me. "Hi," I said, and then I started to go up the steps to my own house, because I wasn't supposed to be talking to him and he was kind of spooky anyway.

"Hold on," he said. I stopped again. "Why don't you come on over and sit a spell?"

"I can't. It's way too late."

He laughed softly. "Oh, it's *never* too late. Come on up. Let's have us a talk."

I hesitated, thought of my room with the cracked ceiling. In that gray house, Dad would be snoring, and Mom might be muttering in her sleep. I turned around, walked across the street and up to the red house's porch.

"Have a seat, Bobby," Virgil offered, and I sat down in a chair next to him. I couldn't see very much in the dark, but I knew the chair was painted red. The tip of his cigarette glowed bright orange and Virgil's eyes seemed to shine like circles of flame.

We talked for a while about the factory. He asked me how I liked it, and I said it was okay. Oh, he asked me all sorts of questions about myself—what I liked, what I didn't like, how I felt about Greystone Bay. Before long, I guess I was telling him everything about myself—things I suppose I'd never even told my folks. I don't know why, but while I was talking to him, I felt as comfortable as if I were sitting in front of a warm, reassuring fireplace on a cold, uncertain night.

"Look at those stars!" Virgil said suddenly. "Did you ever see the like?"

Well, I hadn't noticed them before, but now I looked. The sky was full of glittering dots, thousands and thousands of them strewn over Greystone Bay like diamonds on black velvet.

"Know what most of those are?" he asked me. "Worlds of fire. Oh, yes! They're created out of fire, and they burn so bright before they go out—so very bright. You know, fire creates and it destroys too, and sometimes it can do both at the same time." He looked at me, his orange eyes catching the light from his cigarette. "Your father doesn't think too highly of me, does he?"

"No, I guess not. But part of it's the house. He can't stand the color red."

"And I can't stand to live *without* it," he answered. "It's the color of fire. I like that color. It's the color of newness, and energy . . . and change. To me, it's the color of life itself."

"So that's why you wanted the house changed from gray to red?"

"That's right. I couldn't live in a gray house. Neither could Evie or the kids. See, I figure houses are a lot like the people who live in them. You look around here at all these gray houses, and you know the people who live there have got gray souls. Maybe it's not their choice, maybe it is. But what I'm sayin' is that *everybody* can choose, if he has the courage."

"Mr. Lindquist wouldn't let anybody else paint their house a different color. You're different because you work so good."

"I work so good because I live in a red house," Virgil said. "I won't go to any town where I can't live in one. I spell that out good and proper before I take a man's money. See, I've made my choice. Oh, maybe I won't ever be a millionaire and I won't live in a mansion—but in my own way, I'm rich. What more does a man need than to be able to make his own choices?"

"Easy for you to say."

"Bobby," Virgil said quietly, "everybody can choose what color to paint their own house. It don't matter who you are, or how rich or poor—*you're* the one who lives inside the walls. Some folks long to be red houses amid the gray, but they let somebody else do the paintin'." He stared at me in the dark. His cigarette had gone out, and he lit another with a thin red flame. "Greystone Bay's got a lot of gray houses in it," he said. "Lots of old ones, and ones yet to be."

He was talking in riddles. Like I say, he was kind of spooky. We sat for a while in silence, and then I stood up and said I'd better be getting to bed because work came early the next morning. He said good night, and I started across the street.

It wasn't until I was in my room that I realized I hadn't seen any matches or a lighter when Virgil had lit that second cigarette. Was I crazy—or had the flame been growing from his index finger?

Lots of old ones, Virgil had said. *And ones yet to be.*

I went to sleep with that on my mind.

And it seemed like I'd just closed my eyes when I heard my dad say, "Up and at 'em, Bobby! Factory whistle's about to blow!"

The next week, the loading dock moved at least thirty-five more crates over quota. We could hardly keep up with them as they came out of the packing room. Dad couldn't believe how fast Virgil Sikes worked; he said that the man moved so fast between those two machines that the air got hot and Virgil's red clothes seemed to smoke.

One evening we came home and Mom was all shook up. It seems she got a telephone call from Mrs. Avery from two houses up Accardo. Mrs. Avery had gone nosing around the red house, and had looked into the kitchen window to see Evie Sikes standing over the range. Evie Sikes had turned all the burners on, and was holding her face above them like an ordinary person would accept a breeze from a fan. And Mrs. Avery swore she'd seen the other woman bend down and press her forehead to one of the burners as if it was a block of ice.

"My God," Dad whispered. "They're not *human*. I knew something was wrong with them the first time I saw them! Somebody ought to run them out of Greystone Bay! Somebody ought to burn that damned red house to the ground!"

And this time Mom didn't say anything.

God forgive me, I didn't say anything either.

Lots of old ones. And ones yet to be.

Rumor got around the factory: Virgil Sikes was going to be in charge of three polishing machines. And somebody in that department was going to get a pink slip.

You know how rumors are. Sometimes they hold a kernel of truth, most times they're just nervous air. Whatever the case, Dad started making a detour to the liquor store on the way home from work three nights a week. He broke out in a sweat when we turned onto Accardo and had to approach the red house. He could hardly sleep at night, and sometimes he sat in the front room with his head in his hands, and if either Mom or I spoke a word, he blew up like a firecracker.

And finally, on a hot August night, his face covered with sweat, he said quietly, "I can't breathe anymore. It's that red house. It's stealin' the life right out of me. God Almighty, I can't *take* it anymore!" He rose from his chair, looked at me, and said, "Come on, Bobby."

"Where are we going?" I asked him as we walked down

the steps to the car. Across the street, the lights of the red house were blazing.

"You don't ask questions. You just do as I say. Get in, now. We've got places to go."

I did as he said. And as we pulled away from the curb I looked over at the red house and thought I saw a figure standing at the window, peering out.

Dad drove out into the sticks and found a hardware store still open. He bought two three-gallon gasoline cans. He already had a third in the back. Then he drove to a gas station where nobody knew us and he filled up all three cans at the pumps. On the way home, the smell of the gasoline almost made me sick. "It has to be done, Bobby," Dad said, his eyes glittering and his face blotched with color. "You and me have to do it. Us men have to stick together, right? It's for the good of both of us, Bobby. Those Sikes people aren't *human*."

"They're different, you mean," I said. My heart was hammering, and I couldn't think straight.

"Yes. Different. They don't belong on Accardo Street. We don't need any red houses on our street. Things have been fine for a hundred years, and we're going to make them fine again, aren't we?"

"You're . . . going to kill them," I whispered.

"No. Hell, no! I wouldn't kill anybody! I'm gonna set the fire and then start yellin'. They'll wake up and run out the back door! Nobody'll get hurt!"

"They'll know it was you."

"You'll say we were watchin' a movie on TV. So will your mom. We'll figure out what to say. Damn it, Bobby, are you with me or against me?"

I didn't answer because I didn't know what to say. What's wrong and what's right when you love somebody?

Dad waited until all the lights had gone out on Accardo Street. Mom sat with us in the front room; she didn't say anything, and she wouldn't look at either of us. We waited until the Johnny Carson show was over. Then Dad put his lighter in his pocket, picked up two of the gas cans, and told me to get the third. He had to tell me twice, but I did it. With all the lights off but the glow of the TV, I followed my father out of the room, across the street, and quietly up to the red house's porch. Everything was silent and dark. My palms were sweating, and I almost dropped my gas can going up the steps.

Dad started pouring gas over the red-painted boards, just sloshing it everywhere. He poured all the gas out from two cans, and then he looked at me standing there. "Pour yours out!" he whispered. "Go on, Bobby!"

"Dad," I said weakly. "Please . . . don't do this."

"Christ Almighty!" He jerked the can from my hand and sloshed it over the porch too.

"Dad . . . please. They don't mean any harm. Just because they're different . . . just because they live in a house that's a different *color*—"

"They shouldn't be different!" Dad told me. His voice was strained, and I knew he was right at the end of his rope. "We don't like different people here! We don't *need* different people!" He started fumbling for his lighter, took from his pocket a rag he'd brought from the kitchen.

"Please . . . don't. They haven't hurt us. Let's just forget it, okay? We can just walk away—"

His lighter flared. He started to touch the flame to the rag.

Lots of old ones, I thought. *And ones yet to be.*

Me. Virgil Sikes had been talking about *me.*

I thought about gears at that instant. Millions and millions of gears going down a conveyor belt, and all of them exactly the same. I thought about the concrete walls of the factory. I thought about the machines and their constant pounding, damning rhythm. I thought about a cage of gray clapboard, and I looked at my dad's scared face in the orange light and realized he was terrified of what lay outside the gray clapboards—opportunity, choices, chance, *life.* He was scared to death, and I knew right then that I could not be my father's son.

I reached out and grabbed his wrist. He looked at me like he'd never seen me before.

And I heard my voice—stronger now, the voice of a stranger—say, *"No."*

Before Dad could react, the red-painted front door opened.

And there was Virgil Sikes, his orange eyes glittering. He was smoking a cigarette. Behind him stood his wife and two kids—three more pairs of orange, glowing eyes like campfires in the night.

"Howdy," Virgil said in his soft Southern drawl. "Ya'll havin' fun?"

My dad started sputtering. I still had hold of his wrist.

Virgil smiled in the dark. "One less gray house in Greystone Bay, Bobby."

And then he dropped the cigarette onto the gas-soaked boards at his feet.

The flames caught, burst up high. I tried to grab Virgil, but he pulled back. Then Dad was pulling me off the porch as the boards began to explode into flame. We ran down into the street, and both of us were yelling for the Sikes to get out the back door before the whole house caught.

But they didn't. Oh, no. Virgil took one of the children in his arms and sat down in a red chair, and his wife took the other and sat down beside him in the midst of the flames. The porch caught, hot and bright, and as we watched in fascinated horror, we saw all four of the Sikeses burst into flame; but their fire-figures were just sitting there in the chairs, as if they were enjoying a nice day at the beach. I saw Virgil's head nod. I saw Evie smile before fire filled up her face. the children became forms of flame—happy fires, bouncing and kicking joyfully in the laps of their parents.

I thought something then. Somthing that I shouldn't think about too much.

I thought: *They were always made of fire. And now they're going back to what they were.*

Cinders spun into the air, flew up and glittered like stars, worlds on fire. The four figures began to disintegrate. There were no screams, no cries of pain—but I thought I heard Virgil Sikes laugh like the happiest man in the world.

Or something that had *appeared* to be a man.

Lights were coming on all up and down Accardo Street. The fires were shooting up high, and the red house was almost engulfed. I watched the sparks of what had been the Sikes family fly up high, so very high—and then they drifted off together over Greystone Bay, and whether they winked out or just kept going, I don't know. I heard the siren of a fire truck coming. I looked at my dad, looked long and hard, because I wanted to remember his face. He looked so small. So small.

And then I turned and started walking along Accardo Street, away from the burning house. Dad grabbed at my arm, but I pulled free as easily as if I were being held by a shadow. I kept walking right to the end of Accardo—and then I just kept walking.

I love my mom and dad. I called them when the workboat I signed onto got to a port up the coast about thirty miles. They were okay. The red house was gone, but of course the firemen never found any bodies. All that was left was the red station wagon. I figured they'd haul that off to where the junked cars are, and the blind old man who lives there would have a new place to sleep.

Dad got into some trouble, but he pleaded temporary insanity. Everybody on Accardo knew Bull was half-crazy, that he'd been under a lot of pressure and drank a lot. Mr. Lindquist, I heard later, was puzzled by the whole thing, like everybody else, but the clapboard houses were cheap and he decided to build a white brick house across from my folks. Mr. Lindquist had wanted to get rid of those clapboard things and put up stronger houses for the factory workers anyway. This just started the ball rolling.

My folks asked me to come back, of course. Promised me everything. Said I could go to college whenever I wanted. All that stuff.

But their voices sounded weak. I heard the terror in those voices, and I felt so sorry for them, because they knew the walls of their cage were painted gray. Oh, I'll go back to Greystone Bay sometime—but not until later. Not until I've found out who I am and what I am. I'm Bob Deaken now.

I still can't figure it out. Was it planned? Was it happenstance? Did those creatures that loved fire just fit me into their lives by accident, or on purpose? You know, they say the Devil craves fire. But whatever the Sikeses were, they unlocked me from a cage. They weren't evil. Like Virgil Sikes said: Fire creates as well as it destroys.

They're not dead. Oh, no. They're just . . . somewhere else. Maybe I'll meet them again sometime. Anything's possible.

I may not be a red house. I may be a blue one, or a green one, or some other color I haven't even seen yet. But I know I'm not a gray house. I know that for sure.

And that's my story.

Something Passed By

1

Johnny James was sitting on the front porch, sipping from a glass of gasoline in the December heat, when the doom-screamer came. Of course doomscreamers were nothing new; these days they were as common as blue moons. This one was of the usual variety: skinny-framed, with haunted dark eyes and a long black beard full of dust and filth. He wore dirty khaki trousers and a faded green Izod shirt, and on his feet were sandals made from tires with the emblem still showing: Michelin. Johnny sipped his Exxon Super Unleaded and pondered that the doomscreamer's outfit must be the yuppie version of sackcloth and ashes.

"Prepare for the end! Prepare to meet your Maker!" The doomscreamer had a loud, booming voice that echoed in the stillness over the town that stood on the edge of Nebraskan cornfields. It floated over Grant Street, where the statues of town fathers stood, past the Victorian houses at the end of King's Lane that had burned with such beautiful flames, past the empty playground at the silent Bloch school, over Bradbury park where paint flaked off the grinning carousel horses, down Koontz Street where the businesses used to thrive, over Ellison Field where no bat would ever smack another softball. The doomscreamer's voice filled the town, and ignited the ears of all who remained: "No refuge for the wicked! Prepare for the end! Prepare! Prepare!"

Johnny heard a screen door slam. His neighbor in the white house across the way stood on his own porch loading a rifle. Johnny called, "Hey! Gordon! What're you doin', man?"

Gordon Mayfield continued to push bullets into his rifle. Between Johnny and Gordon, the air shimmered with hazy heat. "Target practice!" Gordon shouted; his voice cracked, and his hands were shaking. He was a big fleshy man with a shaved head, and he wore only blue jeans, his bare chest and shoulders glistening with sweat. "Gonna do me some target practice!" he said as he pushed the last shell into the rifle's magazine and clicked the safety off.

Johnny swallowed gasoline and rocked in his chair. "Prepare! Prepare!" the doomscreamer hollered as he approached his end. The man was standing in front of the empty house next to Gordon's, where the Carmichael family had lived before they fled with a wandering evangelist and his flock on his way to California. "Prepare!" The doomscreamer lifted his arms, sweat stains on his Izod, and shouted to the sky, "O ye sinners, prepare to—"

His voice faltered. He looked down at his Michelins, which had begun to sink into the street.

The doomscreamer made a small terrified squeak. He was not prepared. His ankles had sunk into the gray concrete, which sparkled like quicksilver in a circle around him. Swiftly he sank to his waist in the mire, his mouth open in a righteous O.

Gordon had lifted the rifle to put a bullet through the doomscreamer's skull. Now he realized a pull of the trigger would be wasted energy, and might even increase his own risk of spontaneous combustion. He released the trigger and slowly lowered his gun.

"Help me!" The doomscreamer saw Johnny, and lifted his hands in supplication. "Help me, brother!" He was up to his alligator in the shimmering, hungry concrete. His eyes begged like those of a lost puppy. "Please . . . help me!"

Johnny was on his feet, though he didn't remember standing. He had set the glass of gasoline aside, and he was about to walk down the porch steps, across the scorched yard, and offer his hand to the sinking doomscreamer. But he paused, because he knew he'd never get there in time, and when the concrete pooled like that, you never knew how firm the dirt would be either.

"Help me!" The doomscreamer had gone down to his chin. He stretched, trying to claw his way out, but quicksilver offers no handholds. "For God's sake, hel—" His face went under. His head slid down, and the concrete swirled through his hair. Then—perhaps two seconds later—his clawing hands were all that was left of him, and as they slid down after him, the street suddenly solidified again in a ripple of hardening silver. Concrete locked around the ex-doomscreamer's wrists, and his hands looked like white plants growing out of the center of the street. The fingers twitched a few times, then went rigid.

Gordon went down his steps and walked carefully to the upthrust hands, prodding his path with the rifle's barrel. When he was certain, or as certain as he could be, that the street wouldn't suck him under too, he knelt beside the hands and just sat there staring.

"What is it? What's going on?" Brenda James had come out of the house, her light brown hair damp with sweat. Johnny pointed at the hands, and his wife whispered, "Oh, my God."

"Got on a nice wristwatch," Gordon said after another moment. He leaned closer, squinting at the dial. "It's a Rolex. You want it, Johnny?"

"No," Johnny said. "I don't think so."

"Brenda? You want it? Looks like it tells good time."

She shook her head and grasped Johnny's arm.

"It'd be a waste to leave it out here. First car that comes along, no more watch." Gordon glanced up and down the street. It had been a long time since a car had passed this way, but you never knew. He decided, and took the Rolex off the dead man's wrist. The crystal was cracked and there were flecks of dried concrete on it, but it was a nice shiny watch. He put it on and stood up. "Happened too fast to do anythin' about. Didn't it, Johnny?"

"Yeah. Way too fast." His throat was dry. He took the last

sip of gasoline from the glass. His breath smelled like the pumps at Lansdale's Exxon Station on deLint Street.

Gordon started to walk away. Brenda said, "Are you . . . are you just going to *leave* him there?"

Gordon stopped. He looked down at the hands, wiped his brow with his forearm, and returned his gaze to Brenda and Johnny. "I've got an ax in my garage."

"Just leave him there," Johnny said, and Gordon nodded and walked up his porch steps, still testing the earth with the rifle's barrel. He sighed with relief when he reached the porch's sturdy floor.

"Poker game at Ray's tonight," Gordon reminded them. "You gonna make it?"

"Yeah. We'd planned on it."

"Good." His gaze slid toward the white hands, then quickly away again. "Nothin' like winnin' a little cash to take your mind off your troubles, right?"

"Right," Johnny agreed. "Except you're the one who usually wins all the money."

"Hey, what can I say?" Gordon shrugged. "I'm a lucky dude."

"I thought I'd bring J.J. tonight," Brenda offered in a high, merry voice. Both Johnny and Gordon flinched a little. "J.J. needs to get out of the house," Brenda went on. "He likes to be around people."

"Uh . . . sure." Gordon glanced quickly at Johnny. "Sure, Brenda. Ray won't mind. See you folks later, then." He darted another look at the white hands sticking out of the street, and then he went into his house and the screen door slammed behind him.

Brenda began to sing softly as Johnny followed her into their house. An old nursery song, one she'd sung to J.J. when he was just an infant: *"Go to sleep, little baby, when you wake I'll give you some cake and you can ride the pretty little poneeee . . ."*

"Brenda? I don't think it's a good idea."

"What?" She turned toward him, smiling, her blue eyes without luster. "What's not a good idea, hon?"

"Taking J.J. out of his room. You know how he likes it in there."

Brenda's smile fractured. "That's what *you* say! You're always trying to hurt me, and keep me from being with J.J. Why can't I take J.J. outside? Why can't I sit on the porch with my baby like other mothers do? Why can't I? Answer me, Johnny?" Her face had reddened with anger. *"Why?"*

Johnny's expression remained calm. They'd been over this territory many times. "Go ask J.J. why," he suggested, and he saw her eyes lose their focus, like ice forming over blue pools.

Brenda turned away from him and strode purposefully down the corridor. She stopped before the closed door to J.J.'s room. Hanging on a wall hook next to the door was a small orange oxygen tank on a backpack, connected to a clear plastic oxygen mask. Brenda had had much practice in slipping the tank on, and she did it with little difficulty. Then she turned on the airflow and strapped the hissing oxygen mask over her nose and mouth. She picked up a crowbar, inserting it into a scarred furrow in the doorjamb of J.J.'s room. She pushed against it, but the door wouldn't budge.

"I'll help you," Johnny said, and started toward her.

"No! No, I'll do it!" Brenda strained against the crowbar with desperate strength, her oxygen mask fogging up. And then there was a small cracking noise followed by a *whoosh* that never failed to remind Johnny of a pop top coming off a vacuum-sealed pack of tennis balls. Air shrilled for a few seconds in the hallway, the suction staggering Johnny and Brenda off balance, and then the door to J.J.'s room was unsealed. Brenda went in, and lodged the crowbar between the doorjamb and the door so it wouldn't trap her when the air started to leak away again, which would be in less than two minutes.

Brenda sat down on Johnny Junior's bed. The room's wallpaper had airplanes on it, but the glue was cracking in the dry, airless heat and the paper sagged, the airplanes falling to earth. "J.J?" Brenda said. "J.J? Wake up, J.J." She

245

reached out and touched the boy's shoulder. He lay nestled under the sheet, having a good long sleep. "J.J, it's Momma," Brenda said, and stroked the limp dark hair back from the mummified, gasping face.

Johnny waited in the corridor. He could hear Brenda talking to the dead boy, her voice rising and falling, her words muffled by the oxygen mask. Johnny's heart ached. He knew the routine. She would pick up the dry husk and hold him—carefully, because even in her madness she knew how fragile J.J. was—and maybe sing him that nursery rhyme a few times. But it would dawn on her that time was short, and the air was being sucked out of that room into a vacuum-sealed unknown dimension. The longer the door was left open, the harder the oxygen was pulled into the walls. If you stayed in there over two or three minutes, you could feel the walls pulling at you, as if they were trying to suck you right through the seams. The scientists had a name for it: the "pharaoh effect." The scientists had a name for everything, like "concrete quicksand" and "gravity howitzers" and "hutomic blast," among others. Oh, those scientists were a real smart bunch, weren't they? Johnny heard Brenda begin to sing, in an oddly disconnected, wispy voice: *Go to sleep, little baby, when you wake I'll give you some cake . . ."*

It had happened almost two months ago. J.J. was four years old. Of course, things were crazy by then, and Johnny and Brenda had heard about the "pharaoh effect" on the TV news, but you never thought such a thing could ever happen in your own house. J.J. had gone to bed, like any other night, and sometime before morning all the air had been sucked out of his room. Just like that. All gone. Air was the room's enemy; the walls hated oxygen, and sucked it all into that unknown dimension before it could collect. They both had been too shocked to bury J.J., and it was Johnny who'd realized that J.J.'s body was rapidly mummifying in the airless heat. So they let the body stay in that room, though they could never bring J.J. out because the corpse would surely fall apart after a few hours of exposure to oxygen.

Johnny felt the air swirling past him, being drawn into

J.J.'s room. "Brenda?" he called. "You'd better come on out now."

Brenda's singing died. He heard her sob quietly. The air was beginning to whistle around the crowbar, a dangerous sound. Inside the room, Brenda's hair danced and her clothes were plucked by invisible fingers. A storm of air whirled around her, being drawn into the walls. She was transfixed by the sight of J.J.'s white baby teeth in his brown, wrinkled face: the face of an Egyptian prince. "Brenda!" Johnny's voice was firm now. "Come on!"

She drew the sheet back up to J.J.'s chin; the sheet crackled like a dead leaf. Then she smoothed his dried-out hair and backed toward the door with insane winds battering at her body.

They both had to strain to dislodge the crowbar. As soon as it came loose, Johnny grasped the door's edge to keep it from slamming shut. He held it, his strength in jeopardy, as Brenda squeezed through. Then he let the door go. It slammed with a force that shook the house. Along the door's edge was a quick *whoooosh* as it was sealed tight. Then silence.

Brenda stood in the dim light, her shoulders bowed. Johnny lifted the oxygen tank and backpack off her, then took the mask from her face. He checked the oxygen gauge; have to fill it up again pretty soon. He hung the equipment back on its hook. There was a shrill little steampipe whistle of air being drawn through the crack at the bottom of the door, and Johnny pressed a towel into it. The whistle ceased.

Brenda's back straightened. "J.J. says he's fine," she told him. She was smiling again, and her eyes glinted with a false, horrible happiness. "He says he doesn't want to go to Ray's tonight. But he doesn't mind that we go. Not one little bit."

"That's good," Johnny said, and he walked to the front room. When he glanced at his wife, he saw Brenda still standing before the door to the room that ate oxygen. "Want to watch some TV?" he asked her.

"TV. Oh. Yes. Let's watch some TV." She turned away from the door and came back to him.

Brenda sat down on the den's sofa, and Johnny turned on

the Sony. Most of the channels showed static, but a few of them still worked: on them you could see the negative images of old shows like "Hawaiian Eye," "My Mother the Car," "Checkmate," and "Amos Burke, Secret Agent." The networks had gone off the air a month or so ago, and Johnny figured these shows were just bouncing around in space, maybe hurled to Earth out of the unknown dimension. Their eyes were used to the negative images by now. It beat listening to the radio, because on the only station they could get, Beatles songs were played backward at half-speed, over and over again.

Between "Checkmate" and a commercial for Brylcreem Hair Dressing—"A Little Dab'll Do Ya!"—Brenda began to cry. Johnny put his arm around her, and she leaned her head against his shoulder. He smelled J.J. on her: the odor of dry corn husks, burning in the midsummer heat. Except it was almost Christmastime, ho ho ho.

Something passed by, Johnny thought. That's what the scientists had said, almost six months ago. *Something passed by.* That was the headline in the newspapers, and on the cover of every magazine that used to be sold over at Sarrantonio's newsstand on Gresham Street. And what it was that passed by, the scientists didn't know. They took some guesses, though: magnetic storm, black hole, time warp, gas cloud, a comet of some material that kinked the very fabric of physics. A scientist up in Oregon said he thought the universe had just stopped expanding and was now crushing inward on itself. Somebody else said he believed the cosmos was dying of old age. Galactic cancer. A tumor in the brain of Creation. Cosmic AIDS. Whatever. The fact was that things were not what they'd been six months ago, and nobody was saying it was going to get better. Or that six months from now there'd be an Earth, or a universe where it used to hang.

Something passed by. Three words. A death sentence.

On this asylum planet called Earth, the molecules of matter had warped. Water had a disturbing tendency to explode like nitroglycerine, which had rearranged the intestines of a few hundred thousand people before the scientists figured it out. Gasoline, on the contrary, was now safe to drink, as well as engine oil, furniture polish, hydrochloric acid, and rat poison. Concrete melted into pools of quicksand, the clouds rained stones, and . . . well, there were other things too terrible to contemplate, like the day Johnny had been with Marty Chesley and Bo Duggan, finishing off a few bottles at one of the bars on Monteleone Street. Bo had complained of a headache, and the next minute his brains had spewed out of his ears like gray soup.

Something passed by. And because of that, anything could happen.

We made somebody mad, Johnny thought; he watched the negative images of Doug McClure and Sebastian Cabot. We screwed it up, somehow. Walked where we shouldn't have. Done what we didn't need to do. We picked a fruit off a tree we had no business picking, and . . .

God help us, he thought. Brenda made a small sobbing sound.

Sometime later, red-bellied clouds came in from the prairie, their shadows sliding over the straight and empty highways. There was no thunder or lightning, just a slow, thick drizzle. The windows of the James house streamed crimson, and blood ran in the gutters. Pieces of raw flesh and entrails thunked down onto the roofs, fell onto the streets, lay steaming in the heat-scorched yards. A blizzard of flies followed the clouds, and buzzards followed the flies.

2

"Read 'em and weep, gents," Gordon said, showing his royal flush. He swept the pot of dimes and quarters toward him, and the other men at the round table moaned and muttered. "Like I say, I'm a lucky dude."

"Too lucky." Howard Carnes slapped his cards down—a measly aces and fours—and reached for the pitcher. He poured himself a glassful of high-octane.

"So I was sayin' to Danny," Ray Barnett went on, speaking to the group as he waited for Gordon to shuffle and deal. "What's the use of leavin' town? I mean, it's not like there's gonna be anyplace different, right? Everything's screwed up." He pushed a plug of chewing tobacco into his mouth and offered the pack to Johnny.

Johnny shook his head. Nick Gleason said, "I heard there's a place in South America that's normal. A place in Brazil. The water's still all right."

"Aw, that's bullshit." Ike McCord picked up his newly dealt cards and examined them, keeping a true poker face on his hard, flinty features. "The whole damn Amazon River blew up. Bastard's still on fire. That's what I heard, before the networks went off. It was on CBS." He rearranged a couple of cards. "Nowhere's any different from here. The whole world's the same."

"You don't know everything!" Nick shot back. A little red had begun to glow in his fat cheeks. "I'll bet there's someplace where things are normal! Maybe at the north pole or somewhere like that!"

"The north pole!" Ray laughed. "Who the hell wants to live at the damned north pole?"

"I could live there," Nick went on. "Me and Terri could. Get us some tents and warm clothes, we'd be all right."

"I don't think Terri would want to wake up with an icicle on her nose," Johnny said, looking at a hand full of nothing.

Gordon laughed. "Yeah! It'd be ol' Nick who'd have an icicle hangin' off somethin', and it wouldn't be his nose!" The other men chortled, but Nick remained silent, his cheeks reddening; he stared fixedly at his cards, which were just as bad as Johnny's.

There was a peal of high, false, forced laughter from the front room, where Brenda sat with Terri Gleason, Jane McCord and her two kids, Rhonda Carnes and their fifteen-year-old daughter, Kathy, who lay on the floor listening to Bon Jovi tapes on her Walkman. Elderly Mrs. McCord, Ike's mother, was needlepointing, her glasses perched on the end of her nose and her wrinkled fingers diligent.

"So Danny says he and Paula want to go west," Ray said. "I'll open for a quarter." He tossed it into the pot. "Danny says he's never seen San Francisco, so that's where they want to go."

"I wouldn't go west if you paid me." Howard threw a quarter in. "I'd get on a boat and go to an island. Like Tahiti. One of those places where women dance with their stomachs."

"Yeah, I could see Rhonda in a grass skirt! I'll raise you a quarter, gents." Gordon put his money into the pot. "Couldn't you guys see Howard drinkin' out of a damn coconut? Man, he'd make a monkey look like a prince char—"

From the distance came a hollow *boom* that echoed over town and cut Gordon's jaunty voice off. The talking and forced laughter ceased in the front room. Mrs. McCord missed a stitch, and Kathy Carnes sat up and took the Walkman earphones off.

There was another *boom,* closer this time. The house's floor trembled. The men sat staring desperately at their cards. A third blast, further away. Then silence, in which hearts pounded and Gordon's new Rolex ticked off the seconds.

"It's over," old Mrs. McCord announced. She was back in her rhythm again. "Wasn't even close."

"I wouldn't go west if you paid me," Howard repeated. His voice trembled. "Gimme three cards."

"Three cards it is." Gordon gave everybody what they needed, then said, "One card for the dealer." His hands were shaking.

Johnny glanced out the window. Far away, over the rotting cornfields, there was a flash of jagged red. The percussion came within seconds: a muffled, powerful *boom.*

"I'm bumpin' everybody fifty cents," Gordon announced. "Come on, come on! Let's play cards!"

Ike McCord folded. Johnny had nothing, so he folded too. "Turn 'em over!" Gordon said. Howard grinned and showed his kings and jacks. He started to rake in the pot, but

Gordon said, "Hold on, Howie," as he turned over his hand and showed his four tens and a deuce. "Sorry, gents. Read 'em and weep." He pulled the coins toward himself.

Howard's face had gone chalky. Another blast echoed through the night. The floor trembled. Howard said, "You're cheatin', you sonofabitch."

Gordon stared at him, his mouth open. Sweat glistened on his face.

"Hold on, now, Howard," Ike said. "You don't want to say things like—"

"You must be helpin' him, damn it!" Howard's voice was louder, more strident, and it stopped the voices of the women. "Hell, it's plain as day he's cheatin'! Ain't nobody's luck can be as good as his!"

"I'm not a cheater." Gordon stood up; his chair fell over backward. "I won't take that kind of talk from any man."

"Come on, everybody!" Johnny said. "Let's settle down and—"

"I'm not a cheater!" Gordon shouted. "I play 'em honest!" A blast made the walls moan, and a red glow jumped at the window.

"You always win the big pots!" Howard stood up, trembling. "How come you always win the big pots, Gordon?"

Rhonda Carnes, Jane McCord, and Brenda were peering into the room, eyes wide and fearful. "Hush up in there!" old Mrs. McCord hollered. "Shut your traps, children!"

"Nobody calls me a cheater, damn you!" Gordon flinched as a blast pounded the earth. He stared at Howard, his fists clenched. "I deal 'em honest and I play 'em honest, and by God, I ought to . . ." He reached out, his hand grasping for Howard's shirt collar.

Before his hand could get there, Gordon Mayfield burst into flame.

"Jesus!" Ray shrieked, leaping back. The table upset, and cards and coins flew through the air. Jane McCord screamed, and so did her husband. Johnny staggered backward, tripped, and fell against the wall. Gordon's flesh was aflame from bald skull to the bottom of his feet, and as his plaid shirt caught fire, Gordon thrashed and writhed. Two burning deuces spun from the inside of his shirt and snapped at Howard's face. Gordon was screaming for help, the flesh running off him as incandescent heat built inside his body. He tore at his skin, trying to put out the fire that would not be extinguished.

"Help him!" Brenda shouted. "Somebody help him!" But Gordon staggered back against the wall, scorching it. The ceiling above his head was charred and smoking. His Rolex exploded with a small *pop*.

Johnny was on his knees in the protection of the overturned table, and as he rose he felt Gordon's heat pucker his own face. Gordon was flailing, a mass of yellow flames, and Johnny leapt up and grasped Brenda's hand, pulling her with him toward the front door. "Get out!" he yelled. "Everybody get out!"

Johnny didn't wait for them; he pulled Brenda out the door, and they ran through the night, south on Silva Street. He looked back, saw a few more figures fleeing the house, but he couldn't tell who they were. And then there was a white flare that dazzled his eyes and Ray Barnett's house exploded, timbers and roof tiles flying through the sultry air. The shock wave knocked Brenda and Johnny to the pavement; she was screaming, and Johnny clasped his hand over her mouth because he knew that if he started to scream it was all over for him. Fragments of the house rained down around them, along with burning clumps of human flesh. Johnny and Brenda got up and ran, their knees bleeding.

They ran through the center of town, along the straight thoroughfare of Straub Street, past the Spector Theatre and the Skipp Religious Bookstore. Other shouts and screams echoed through the night, and red lightning danced in the cornfields. Johnny had no thought but to get them home, and hope that the earth wouldn't suck them under before they got there.

They fled past the cemetery on McDowell Hill, and there was a crash and *boom* that dropped Johnny and Brenda to their knees again. Red lightning arced overhead, a sickly-sweet smell in the air. When Johnny looked at the cemetery again, he saw there was no longer a hill; the entire rise had been mashed flat, as if by a tremendous crushing fist. And then, three seconds later, broken tombstones and bits of coffins slammed down on the plain where a hill had stood for two hundred years. *Gravity howitzer,* Johnny thought; he hauled Brenda to her feet, and they staggered on across Olson Lane and past the broken remnants of the Baptist church at the intersection of Daniels and Saul streets.

A brick house on Wright Street was crushed to the ground as they fled past it, slammed into the boiling dust by the invisible power of gravity gone mad. Johnny gripped Brenda's hand and pulled her on, through the deserted streets. Gravity howitzers boomed all across town, from Schow Street on the west to Barker Promenade on the east. The red lightning cracked overhead, snapping through the air like cat-o'-nine-tails. And then Johnny and Brenda staggered onto Streiber Circle, right at the edge of town, where you had a full view of the fields and the stars, and kids used to watch, wishfully, for UFOs.

There would be no UFOs tonight, and no deliverance from the Earth. Gravity howitzers smashed into the fields, making the stars shimmer. The ground shook, and in the glare of the red lightning Johnny and Brenda could see the effect of the gravity howitzers, the cornstalks mashed flat to the ground in circles twelve or fifteen feet around. The fist of God, Johnny thought. Another house was smashed to rubble on the street behind them; there was no pattern or reason for the gravity howitzers, but Johnny had seen what was left of Stan Haines after the man was hit by one on a sunny Sunday afternoon. Stan had been a mass of bloody tissue jammed into his crumpled shoes, like a dripping mushroom.

The howitzers marched back and forth across the fields. Two or three more houses were hit, over on the north edge of town. And then, quite abruptly, it was all over. There was the noise of people shouting and dogs barking; the sounds seemed to combine, until you couldn't tell one from the other.

Johnny and Brenda sat on the curb gripping hands and trembling. The long night went on.

3

The sun turned violet. Even at midday the sun was a purple ball in a white, featureless sky. The air was always hot, but the sun itself no longer seemed warm. The first of a new year passed, and burning winter drifted toward springtime.

Johnny noticed them in Brenda's hands first. Brown freckles. Age spots, he realized they were. Her skin was changing. It was becoming leathery, and deep wrinkles began to line her face. At twenty-seven years of age, her hair began to go gray.

And sometime later, as he was shaving with gasoline, he noticed his own face: the lines around his eyes were going away. His face was softening. And his clothes: his clothes just didn't fit right anymore. They were getting baggy, his shirts beginning to swallow him up.

Of course Brenda noticed it too. How could she not, though she tried her best to deny it. Her bones ached. Her spine was starting to bow over. Her fingers hurt, and the worst was when she lost control of her hands and dropped J.J. and a piece of him cracked off like brittle clay. One day in March it became clear to her, when she looked in the mirror and saw the wrinkled, age-freckled face of an old woman staring back. And then she looked at Johnny and saw a nineteen-year-old boy where a thirty-year-old man used to be.

They sat on the porch together, Johnny fidgety and nervous, as young folks are when they're around the gray-haired elderly. Brenda was stopped and silent, staring straight ahead with watery, faded blue eyes.

"We're goin' in different directions," Johnny said in a voice that was getting higher-pitched by the day. "I don't know what happened, or why. But . . . it just did." He reached out, took one of her wrinkled hands. Her bones felt fragile, birdlike. "I love you," he said.

She smiled. "I love you," she answered in her old woman's quaver.

They sat for a while in the purple glare. And then Johnny went down to the street and pitched stones at the side of Gordon Mayfield's empty house while Brenda nodded and slept.

Something passed by, she thought in her cage of dreams. She remembered her wedding day, and she oozed a dribble of saliva as she smiled. *Something passed by.* What had it been, and where had it gone?

Johnny made friends with a dog, but Brenda wouldn't let him keep it in the house. Johnny promised he'd clean up after it, and feed it, and all the other stuff you were supposed to do. Brenda said certainly not, that she wouldn't have it shedding all over her furniture. Johnny cried some, but he got over it. He found a baseball and bat in an empty house, and he spent most of his time swatting the ball up and down the street. Brenda tried to take up needlepoint, but her fingers just weren't up to it.

These are the final days, she thought as she sat on the porch and watched his small body as he chased the ball. She kept her Bible in her lap, and read it constantly, though her eyes burned and watered. The final days were here at last, and no man could stop the passage of their hours.

The day came when Johnny couldn't crawl into her lap, and it hurt her shoulders to lift him, but she wanted him nestled against her. Johnny played with his fingers, and Brenda told him about paradise and the world yet to be. Johnny asked her what kind of toys they had there, and Brenda smiled a toothless grin and stroked his hair.

Something passed by, and Brenda knew what it was: time. Old clocks ticking down. Old planets slowing in their orbits. Old hearts laboring. The huge machine was winding to a finish now, and who could say that was a bad thing?

She held him in her arms as she rocked slowly on the front porch. She sang to him, an old, sweet song: *"Go to sleep, little baby, when you wake . . ."*

She stopped, and squinted at the fields.

A huge wave of iridescent green and violet was undulating across the earth. It came on silently, almost . . . yes, Brenda decided. It came on with a lovely grace. The wave rolled slowly across the fields, and in its wake it left a gray blankness, like the wiping clean of a schoolboy's slate. It would soon reach the town, their street, their house, their front porch. And then she and her beautiful child would know the puzzle's answer.

It came on, with relentless power.

She had time to finish her song: ". . . *I'll give you some cake and you can ride the pretty little poneeee.*"

The wave reached them. It sang of distant shores. The infant in her arms looked up at her, eyes glowing, and the old woman smiled at him and stood up to meet the mystery.

Blue World

1

His cowboy boots clocked on the wet pavement, where streams of neon oozed like the rivers of hell.

A fog had drifted over San Francisco, blanking out the stars. With it had come a stinging drizzle, and diamonds of Pacific rain glittered in the man's sandy-blond crew-cut hair. He walked along Broadway, east into the heart of the tawdry Tenderloin, brushing past grinning Japanese businessmen, hayseed gawkers, and tourists with a taste for the wild life.

Here it was to be tasted. The neon signs and gaudy flashing lights stood like the gates into another world, announcing the wares that lay within the dark domains. The man in the cowboy boots stopped, a gust of wind riffling the knee-length brown canvas coat he wore. His dark brown, hollow-socketed eyes scanned the signs: *Girls and Boys Live Onstage! Dominant Females in Black Leather! Sorority Girls in Heat! All Sizes, All Flavors!*

At the outer corners of his eyes were three small crimson teardrops, tattooed on the smooth pale flesh as if he were weeping drops of blood.

He went on, past the open doors that bellowed loud rock drumbeats and snared knots of gaping Japanese. His thumbs hooked in the ornate silver buckle of his belt, and his pace began to slow.

Just past the *All Nude! All Crude Honeys!* parlor was the

sign he'd been seeking. It announced *Porno Queens Want to Meet Ya* and had glossy pictures of attractive though heavily made-up young women covering the front window. Captions identified some of them, names like Tasha Knotty, Kitt Cattin, Easee Breeze, and Paula Bunyan. The man, who was of indeterminate age, possibly in his late twenties, regarded the photographs for a moment. Then he looked down at the sill, where dead flies lay and one was still feebly kicking.

This must be the place.

He strode through a red door into a corridor where a burly Chicano man sat reading a *Slash Maraud* comic book behind a caged-in ticket booth. "Ten bucks," the Chicano said in a bored voice. He didn't put aside the comic. "You want to meet anybody special?"

"Yes," the cowboy said in a toneless, whispery voice. "Easee Breeze."

The sound—like the hiss of a snake—made the Chicano look up. He stared at the tattooed teardrops.

"You see somethin' you don't like, *amigo?*"

"No. No, man." The Chicano shook his head and sat up a little straighter. The crew-cut guy was lean, about six-two or six-three, and he looked like a dude you didn't want to mess with. "Yeah, Easee's in here, man. You want to party?"

"Maybe. Easee was in a movie called *Super Slick,* wasn't she?"

"She's been in a lot of flicks, man. She's a *star!*"

"I know that. I saw her in *Super Slick.*" He glanced toward another red door further along the corridor. From beyond it was a bass-heavy boom. "I want to meet her."

"You go in there and sit down, man. Enjoy the show. If Easee's onstage, you ring her number. If she's not, she'll be up in a few minutes. Ten bucks. Okay?" He tentatively tapped the countertop.

The cowboy took a wallet from the inside of his duster, opened it, brought out a ten-dollar bill, and slid it through the bars. A light sheen of sweat had begun to glisten on his bony face.

"Tippin's extra, man," the Chicano said. "Easee ain't cheap."

"Neither am I." The cowboy smiled faintly, but it was a cold smile. Then he strode on toward the door, and the Chicano hit a switch that unlocked it. The cowboy went through, and the door locked again as it swung shut.

Speakers in the red-velvet-covered walls emitted a steady drumbeat. Three rows of tattered theater seats, where four other men sat in a smoky gloom, faced a large plate-glass window. Behind the glass gyrated three nude women, each with a numbered card hanging between her breasts. Easee Breeze was not among the dancers, and the cowboy took a seat on the back row and propped his boots up to wait.

After another moment one of the other men pressed a little button on the armrest of his chair. There were five alarm-bell rings, and the thin redhead with the numeral 5 on her card put on a false smile that looked like a death's-head grimace and came out through a barred door to meet her date. The redhead led the grinning, beer-bellied tourist through another doorway at the other side of the room.

"Hope ya'll have fun!" the cowboy shouted just before the door closed.

The dancing started again. Two more men—kids, really, probably college students—entered the room and took their seats, giggling and whispering nervously. The cowboy paid them no attention; he just sat back, watched the bouncing boobs, and waited.

A couple more girls reemerged from the back room and started listlessly dancing. Neither of them was the one the cowboy sought. The pounding rhythm, the red walls, the dim light, made him sleepy, as if he were sitting in a huge womb. But after four minutes or so he slid his boots off the seat back and leaned forward, smiling with renewed interest.

A slender, pretty blond had joined the dancers, and was grinding energetically. Around her neck was a card with the numeral 2 on it. He started to press his button—but before he could, two rings came over the speakers. The cowboy looked around, startled, and saw one of the college kids sheepishly getting to his feet.

At once the cowboy was up, and he strode to the kid before Easee Breeze came out from behind the window. He clamped his hand firmly on the kid's shoulder. "Easee's *my* date, dude. Sit yourself down."

The blood drained out of the kid's face. He sat down fast, and the cowboy turned his best smile on Easee Breeze.

She didn't touch him, but she gave him a wary smile and motioned him to follow. They went through the door, into a narrow red-lit corridor lined with cubicles. Moans and moist sucking noises came from behind some of the closed doors. A huge bald-headed man came along the corridor, jingling a ring of keys. "Twelve and thirteen," the man said, tapping the doors.

"Listen," Easee said, turning to the cowboy. She had produced a little tube of lip balm from somewhere, and she dabbed a bit on her index finger and swabbed her lips. "I'm kinda tired, okay? Like my jaws are really cramping bad."

"I'm sorry to hear that, Easee," the cowboy said sympathetically.

Her eyes were pale blue, and they shone glassily. She had a cocaine stare, the painted eyes of a Kewpie doll. Easee's lips were very red, and she kept working the balm in. "I'll give you half-rate for half time. Fifty dollars for three minutes. Okay?"

"Three minutes will be plenty long enough," the cowboy answered, and paid the bald-headed guy with two twenties and two fives.

"Good. I'm just about pooped. What's your name?"

He glanced quickly at the bald-headed dude, who had returned along the aisle to his seat at the alley door. On that door was a sign reading THIS WAY OUT. "Travis," he said. "Like that guy at the Alamo."

"The Alamo what?" Easee asked. He didn't respond. "I like your tattoos," she said. "They're funky."

"Yeah, aren't they."

She motioned him into cubicle twelve, and she closed his door and then entered the next cubicle.

Between them was a thin piece of wallboard with a hole cut through it at crotch level. "Want me to get you up?" she asked. On her side was a little plastic trashcan, a chair, a stopwatch on a chain, and a box of Kleenex. She started the watch ticking.

"No. I'm ready." The cowboy had dropped his pants, and he pushed through the hole.

Easee sat down in the chair and began, examining her chipped fingernail polish as she worked. "You ever see any of my movies, Travis?" she asked him between licks.

"I saw *Super Slick*. You were real good in it."

"Thank you." Silence, while Easee labored. "What was your favorite part?"

"When you went down on three guys. That was hot."

"Yeah, I liked that too. Travis, do you like what I'm doing now?"

"Sure." He smiled, his cheek pressed against the wallboard. "Keep it up."

She glanced at the stopwatch. God, time crawled in this dump! Well, this was a temporary thing anyway. She was on her way back to L.A. on Friday. Her agent had a three-day film job lined up for her, and then she was flying to Hawaii to meet a rich Arab. Those Arab guys smelled a little bit, but they loved porno because they couldn't get it in Arabia. Anyway, the Arabs always had a lot of money to throw around, and she'd even known two actresses who'd married sheiks and gone to live over there. Easee figured that was the life, lying around in a country that was just like a big Malibu Beach, doing your thing for some Arab and living in a castle. It could happen to her. Anything was possible.

"Bite it," Travis requested. "Harder. Come on, Easee. Harder."

She worked, staring at the stopwatch.

"I'm a big fan of yours, Easee," Travis said. "I saw you in *Hustler* last month. Harder. That ain't *bitin'!* I saw you in *Hustler*. That was a real good layout. Man, I'd like to have me a job takin' them pictures. I sure would."

She grunted. The second hand crept.

"I saw you at the Triple-X in L.A.," he told her. "When you signed autographs. You signed my book."

Something was wrong with the stopwatch, she thought. She felt him tremble, and pulled out a Kleenex.

"I love you, Easee," Travis said. "Wait a minute. Hold on." He scraped back through the hole. "I love you," he repeated. "Hear me?"

"Sure," she said. And put her mouth to the hole. "Come on, Travis. Let's finish our party."

"We will. Just hold on." He removed the Colt .45 pistol from his silver-buckled gunbelt. It was intricately filigreed and had a mother-of-pearl handle. On the belt were loops holding at least thirty bullets. "I dream about you all the time. Hot dreams."

"Come on, baby. Travis?" She heard a metallic *click*. What the hell was the freak doing? "Come *on,* man!"

"Open wide," he said, and he shoved the Colt's barrel through the hole. "I loved Cheri Dane too," he told her, and heard her gag.

He pulled the trigger.

The gunshot boomed hollowly, and the Colt bucked in his hand.

He heard her body thump off the chair. When he pulled the gun back in, its barrel was red and dripping.

Then, quickly, Travis zipped his fly and kicked the cubicle's door open.

It banged out and tore off its flimsy hinges. The bald-headed dude was on his feet, a fleshy mountain of shock. One of the other cubicles opened; an Oriental girl peered out, saw the Colt, screamed shrilly, and slammed the door shut. A man looked out from another door, his jowly face contorted with horror.

Travis shot him. The bullet hit the man's collarbone and knocked him off his feet. The whole cubicle collapsed, cheap walls folding in like cardboard. And then Travis, his eyes shining and glazed, began to stride toward the alley door, and as he walked he fired randomly through the cubicle doors. The shots boomed in the narrow space, sending bits of wallboard flying. The place was a bedlam of screams and calls for God. The bald-headed man was reaching into his pocket, and his hand came out with a switchblade.

"No," Travis said calmly, and shot him through the throat. The dude strangled and fell back, the knife clattering to the linoleum. Travis brushed the bleeding bulk aside, but as he started to open the door a hand caught him by the hair and jerked his head back.

"You bastard!" the man gasped, eyes holes of rage and terror. "I'll kill you, you lousy bas—"

Travis's fingers moved on a hidden switch at the Colt's handle. Four inches of serrated blue steel slid out from the mother-of-pearl, and Travis plunged the blade into the man's fleshy cheek and tore brutally across it and out the mouth.

The man screamed, grasped his ripped face, and thunked to his knees.

Travis darted through the doorway and into the alley. The smell of blood and gunsmoke was up his nostrils, charging through his bones and nerves like a primal drug. He wiped the blade off on a discarded Burger King bag, triggered the switch again, and the knife slid back to its hidden sheath. Then he spun the pistol around his finger and returned it to the holster with a gunfighter's grace.

He began to run, buttoning his coat as the wind whipped its folds around him. His face was pale and sweating, but his eyes were lazy and sated.

He ran on, away from the screams. The night and fog took him.

2

Jesus wept.

A timeless reaction, the slimly built blond man mused as he read today's study in the philosophical textbook. Jesus wept almost two thousand years ago, and would certainly shed tears today. But tears alone would change nothing, the man knew. If Jesus had wept at the immensity of spiritual poverty in the world, thrown up his hands and given up humanity as a lost cause, then the world and mankind would have truly been consumed by darkness. No, it was one thing to cry, but there had to be courage too.

He finished the passage he was reading, closed the textbook, and put it aside. The strong afternoon sunlight slanted through the window blinds and painted the beige wall where a crucifix and figure of Christ were mounted. A bookcase was filled with scholarly works on such subjects as redemption, the logic of religion, Catholicism and the third world, and temptation. Next to the bookcase was a portable TV hooked up to a VCR, and a collection of tapes, among them the titles *Victory over Sin*, *The Challenge of Urban Priesthood*, and *The Road Warrior*.

He rose from his chair and returned the textbook to its exact place in the bookcase. He checked his wristwatch: twelve minutes before three. At three he was on duty in the confessional. But he had time yet. He walked into the small kitchen, poured himself a cup of cold black coffee from the pot he'd made this morning, and took it back to the den with him. On the fireplace's mantel, a clock ticked politely. In the den's corner was the man's ten-speed bicycle, its front tire mounted on a little set of ratchets and gears so he could do his stationary riding. He went to the window and opened the blinds, staring down onto Vallejo Street as the sunlight washed into his face.

He had the soft features of a choirboy, his eyes gentle and dark blue, his thinning blond hair brushed back from his high forehead and allowed to grow a little long in back. He was thirty-three years old, but he might have passed for five years younger. Small lines were beginning to creep from the corners of his eyes, and deeper lines bracketed his mouth. He had a long, aristocratic nose and a strong square chin, and he stood at just under six-feet-one. His skin was pale, because he didn't get out much, but his strict regimen of bike riding and jogging on a treadmill kept his weight at one hundred and seventy pounds. He was a man of discipline and organization, and he knew deep in his heart that he would have trouble living in the outside world, with its dissonance and disorders and riotous confusion. He was born for the meditative life of a priest, with its rituals and cerebral passions. He had been a priest for more than twelve years, and before that a student of priestly disciplines.

Over a squatty gray building he could see a large red X, a symbol on a building on Broadway. He could also see part of another sign: *Girls and Boys*. Monsignor McDowell, at their conference this morning, had told him there was a shooting in one of the flesh parlors last night, but the details were unknown. The young priest had never walked down that street, a block away from the Cathedral of St. Francis, and thinking about its dens of lust and corruption made his stomach churn.

Well, everyone in the world had free choice as to what to do with his life. That was part of the majestic beauty of God's creation. But the young priest wondered often why God allowed such carnality and sin to survive. Surely mankind would be better served if all those places were leveled to the ground. He stared at the huge red X for a moment longer, then grunted, shook his head, and turned away.

He sipped at his coffee and regarded the half-finished jigsaw puzzle that lay on a table nearby. It was a picture of thousands of multicolored jelly beans, and he'd been working on it steadily for about two weeks. He saw where two more pieces fitted, and slipped them into their notches.

Then it was time to go. He went into the bathroom, brushed his teeth, and gargled with Scope. Then he put on his dark shirt and white collar over his undershirt, went to the closet and got his black suit jacket. At the top of the closet was a shelf holding a dozen jigsaw puzzles in their boxes, some with the shrinkwraps still unbroken. He kissed his rosary, said a quick prayer before the Cross, put a pack of Certs in his pocket, and went out his apartment door. On the breast pocket of his jacket was a little plastic tag that identified him as Father John Lancaster.

Outside his door, a carpeted corridor led him from the rectory to a staircase. He descended it, went through another door and into the administrative wing of the church, where his own office and the other offices were.

Father Darryl Stafford, a dark-haired man in his early forties, came out of his office to the water fountain and saw Lancaster. "Hi, John. Almost that time, huh?"

"Almost." John checked his watch. Two minutes before three. "I'm running a little late."

"You? Late? Never happen." Stafford took off his glasses and wiped the lenses on a white handkerchief. "I've got the preliminary budget figures almost ready. If you want to go over them tomorrow, my schedule's clear."

"Fine. How about nine o'clock sharp?"

"Nine sharp it is." Stafford returned the glasses to his face. He had large, owlish, intelligent eyes. "You heard about the commotion last night, I guess?"

"I heard about it. That's all." John took a couple of steps toward the next door, feeling the pull of the confessional.

But Father Stafford was starved for conversation. "I talked to Jack this morning." Jack Clayton was a police officer who patrolled the area. "He says two people were killed and one wounded. A lunatic shot up one of those parlors and ran out the back door. He got away. Somebody described the guy pretty well, though, and Jack left the report with me. He wants us to keep a lookout for . . . Now get this." He smiled with a hint of wickedness. "A man with red tears tattooed on his cheeks. Face cheeks, I mean."

"It's a relief to know I won't have to be pulling anybody's pants down," John said, and then he grasped the door's handle and hurried into the church as Stafford said, "You and me both, pal!"

The chimes began to ring, announcing confessional. John's shoes clicked on the white marble at the front of the church, and he was aware of several people sitting in the pews, but he kept his head down, his face away from them. He entered the confessional booth, closed the door, and sat down on a bench covered with red velvet. Then he slid open the small grilled partition between his cubicle and the next, popped a Cert into his mouth, and waited for the chimes to cease. He took his wristwatch off and placed it on a little shelf where he could see it. Confessional was over at four-thirty, and at five-thirty he had a dinner appointment with the mayor's council on the homeless problem in the area.

As the chimes echoed away, the first person entered the cubicle and knelt down. A bearded mouth pressed toward the grille, and a man's Hispanic-accented voice said, "Forgive me, Father, for I have sinned."

It was the beginning of the ritual, and John listened. The man was an alcoholic, and had stolen money from his wife to buy liquor, then beaten her when she complained. John nodded, said occasionally, "Yes, go on," but his gaze kept straying to the wristwatch. The man left, armed with his Hail Marys, and the next person—an elderly woman—entered.

"Yes, go on," John told her, as her rubbery red lips moved on the other side of the grille.

When the woman left, John put another Cert into his mouth. The next person—a man with a terrible wheeze in his lungs—left body odor behind him. There was a pause of about ten or twelve minutes before the next person, also a man, entered, and in that time John wondered if he was going to be able to pick up his other suit from the cleaners before five-thirty. Then he brought his mind back on track and tried to concentrate on a rambling tale of infidelities and misspent passions. But John wanted to listen; he honestly did. It was just that the seat was hard and the red velvet was thin, the confessional's walls were starting to close around him, and he was aware of his stomach rumbling from the cold coffee. After a while the ritual became just that—a ritual. John would say, "Yes, go on," and the confessor would continue with a list of sins and miseries that became terribly, sadly commonplace. He felt freighted with human ills, contaminated by the knowledge of good and evil. It was if Sin and the Devil reigned full sway over the world, and even the walls of the church creaked and showed hairline cracks against such hideous pressure. But John clasped his hands together, sucked on a Cert, and said, "Yes, go on."

The man said, "Father, I'm through," and sighed as if the telling had shrunk fifty pounds off him.

"Go with the grace of Christ," John told him, and the sinner left.

More came and went. The watch showed four-sixteen. John waited, thinking about his report to be given to the mayor's council tonight. He needed to look over it again, to make sure he hadn't made any errors in the figures. Another two minutes crept past, and no one else came in. John shifted uncomfortably on the bench. Surely somebody could invent a more comfortable way to—

The cubicle's door opened. Someone entered and knelt down.

John smelled a musky, cinnamony perfume. It was a welcome aroma, clearing away the last traces of body odor the third confessor had brought in. John took a deep breath of the perfume. He'd never smelled anything quite like it.

"Anybody in there?" a young woman's voice asked. A long, red-polished fingernail tapped the grille.

"Yes, go on," John said.

There was a pause. "Go *on?* Shit, I haven't *started* yet."

"Please don't curse," John said sternly.

"So who's cursin'?" The woman hesitated again. Then: "Debbie, you're one stupid jerk to think this would do a damn bit of good!"

She was talking to herself. He let that curse word slip past, because Darryl used it all the time and even the monsignor was prone to it. "It might do some good," John said. "If you're sincere."

"Oh, sincere!" She laughed softly. She had a smoky voice with a strange accent. "Father, sincere's my middle name!"

"I'm listening," John told her.

"Yeah, but is *God* listenin'?" she asked pointedly.

"I believe He is."

"Good for you."

John waited. The young woman didn't say anything else for a moment. Gathering her thoughts? John wondered. She certainly sounded bitter, torn up internally, in need of confession. Her accent, he'd figured out, was Southern: Deep South, maybe Georgia, Alabama, or Louisiana. Whoever she was, she was a long way from home.

"I don't have anything to confess," she said suddenly. "I'm okay. It's just . . . well . . ." She trailed off. "This is harder'n I thought it was gonna be."

"Take your time," he advised, but as he said it he glanced at the watch.

There was a longer pause. Then: "A friend of mine is dead."

John didn't reply, urging her to continue by his silence.

"She got killed. I told her not to work that scuzzbox. I *told* her not to! Janey never listened to a damn thing anybody ever told her! Hell, you tell her not to do it and that just makes her want to even worse!" She laughed harshly. "Listen to me, babblin' on like I'm really *talkin'* to somebody!"

"Go on," John said quietly.

"Janey was somebody. Hell, she was a movie star! She did five flicks in two weeks, and I swear to God that's got to be a record. We went to Acapulco together last year, and we met these two Mexican lifeguards. So Janey says, Debbie, let's make us a Mexican double-decker sandwich and really get it on."

John's eyes had widened. The girl on the other side laughed, softly now, a laugh of remembrances. "Janey liked to live," the girl said. "She wrote poetry. Most of it was crap, but some of it . . . some of it you could tell her was good and really mean it. Oh, Jesus . . ."

He heard something break inside her. Just that quick, the tough shell cracked. The girl began to sob—the heart-crushed sobbing of a lost child. He wanted to soothe her, reach through the grille between them and touch her, but of course that was forbidden. The girl caught back another soft sob. He heard her open her purse and fumble in it. There was the sound of a Kleenex being pulled out.

"Damn, my mascara's all over the place," she said. "I got it on this white cloth over here."

"That's all right."

"Looks expensive. Man, you holy guys really know how to spend the bucks, don't you?"

John heard her fighting against more tears. "I'm not such a holy guy," he said.

"Sure you are. You're plugged into God's hotline, aren't you? If you aren't, then you're in the wrong job."

He didn't respond. He had stopped looking at the wristwatch.

"Some freak killed my friend," she went on quietly. "I called Janey's folks. They live in Minnesota. You know what that sonofabitch told me? He says: We have no daughter. Then he hung up in my face. I even called before the rates went down, and that's what he has to say!" She hesitated, battling a sob. Her voice had gotten full of grit and fire. "The county's gonna bury her. That shit she had for an agent said she was just a lost investment. You ever hear anything to beat that?"

"No," John said. "I never have."

She blew her nose into the Kleenex and snuffled. "Shits," she said. "Dirty, rotten shits."

"When did your friend die? I can look into the funeral arrangements if you—"

"Janey hated the Catholics," she interrupted. "No offense meant. She just thought you guys were screwin' everything up by not lettin' people use birth control and all. So, thanks, but no thanks." She snuffled again. "It happened last night, over on Broadway. Janey was workin'. A freak shot her. That's all I know."

"Oh." The realization hit him that Janey's death was connected with the shooting at the porno parlor. And if Janey had been working over there, then this girl on the other side of the booth was probably involved in that business too. His heart had started beating a little harder, and her musky scent filled his nostrils. "I've never been over there," he said.

"You ought to walk the strip sometime. It'll give you an education."

"I don't believe I want that kind of knowledge." He sat up a little straighter.

"Hell, you're a *man*, aren't you? And sex makes the world swing round."

"Not my world." He had the sensation of things getting out of control, of damp heat at the base of his spine.

"Everybody's world," she said. "Why does a priest hide his head in books all day, and take cold showers ten times a day? God made the world, right? He made sex too."

"Miss . . ." he began, but he didn't know what he was going to say. He just wanted to stop her. "That'll be enough," he managed.

She laughed again. "Can't stand the heat, huh? I figured you guys were pretty close to the edge."

Had it shown in his voice that quickly? he wondered. And shame hit him, hard and fast. He thought her perfume must be drugging him or something, because his brain gears were clogging up.

She leaned close to the grille. He could see her full, slightly parted red lips, the same color as her nails.

"Anybody ever asks you," she whispered in that smoky, knowing voice, "you can tell them you met a real-live movie star. Debra Rocks. That's me. I've got a movie showin' on the strip. Tell all your friends." He watched as her tongue slid wetly along her lower lip, and he realized she was getting a real thrill out of baiting him. The realization angered him, but it started the clockwork mechanism that neither praying nor spiritual literature nor philosophical contemplation could halt. His groin began to throb.

She pulled her mouth away from the grille. "Sorry," she said. Her voice had changed, gotten softer again. "It's in my bones. Listen . . . all I'm askin' is that you . . . like . . . say a prayer or somethin' for Janey. Okay?"

"Okay," John answered. His voice sounded as if he'd been gargling with glass.

"I feel a lot better now," Debra Rocks said, and then she got up and John heard the booth's door open and close. Then the click of high heels on the marble floor. She was walking fast, in a hurry to go somewhere—or just in a hurry to get out of the church. The chimes began to ring, signaling the end of confession.

John had a sheen of sweat on his face, and his insides felt as hot as a blast furnace. She would be almost to the door by now, about to return to the street. The chimes rang on. He was not supposed to leave the confessional until they ended, at exactly four-thirty. But his hand reached for the latch, grasped it, and hung there. The pounding at his crotch was almost unbearable, a pain that he'd thought he'd forgotten.

He glanced at the watch. The seconds were moving too fast. The chimes went on.

John turned the handle and stepped out.

A slim girl with long black or dark brown hair, wearing a tight red dress, was just reaching for the door. It opened, letting in a glare of chilly sunlight, and then Debra Rocks was out the door and it closed behind her.

There were two more chimes. Then silence.

John took a deep breath, his heart hammering. He could still smell her perfume, and he thought it must be caught in his clothes. The palms of his hands were slick with cold sweat. He thought he might be about to faint, but surely he was made of stronger stuff than that. His black slacks had bulged at the crotch, and he knew he had to get to his bathroom shower and turn on that freezing water *fast*.

"God help me," he whispered as he hurried out of the sanctuary.

3

Just when he least expected it, he would catch a hint of her fragrance. He was sitting in the Scaparelli Seafood Restaurant in North Beach, with Monsignor McDowell on his right and the mayor's chief aide on his left, when he smelled it in the garlic-and-rosemary sauce. He was reading his report on the homeless figures and the soup kitchen's budget when he caught it, and he quickly sniffed his fingers as if he were scratching his nose. Her scent was everywhere, yet nowhere.

And gradually it dawned on him that her aroma lingered in his mind.

A dark-haired woman wearing a red dress came in, and snagged his attention while the mayor's aide was talking to him. John watched the woman, holding hands with a date or her husband, as she neared the table and passed it, and he heard her say something to the man in a voice that was nothing like Debra Rocks'.

"See what I mean?" the aide, a somber-faced man named Vandervolk, asked him. John nodded yes, without really understanding the question.

"No, we do *not* see what you mean!" McDowell said quickly, his crusty, age-spotted face growing deep wrinkles as he scowled. "Either we get the matching funds, or we'll have to shut down to half of what we're doing now. That's the bottom line." He glared with his ice-blue eyes at John Lancaster.

The conversation went on, edging toward heat, and John's attention drifted in and out. He sipped red wine and smelled her. He clasped his hands, and saw her lips behind the grille. He heard a woman laugh, and he looked around so fast McDowell said, "John, what the *hell* is wrong with you, boy?"

"Nothing. Sorry. I was thinking about something else." When McDowell got mad, you better pay heed.

"Well, think about the business at hand!" the monsignor ordered, and continued his debate with Vandervolk and the other three men at the table.

John tried to. But it was a difficult task. He kept seeing swirls of red from the corners of his eyes, and then he was gone again. He had taken three cold showers—bang bang bang, one right after the other. Then he'd sat down and concentrated on his jigsaw puzzle, still dripping wet and shivering. He'd gotten four pieces mashed down into the wrong grooves before he gave it up. And then, as if in a sleepwalker's daze, he'd found himself standing at the window, stark naked and broken out in goosebumps, staring at that red X in the sky.

I've got a movie showin' on the strip, she'd said.

"Isn't it, Father Lancaster?"

John looked, alarmed, into the monsignor's face.

"Isn't it?" McDowell asked again, his eyes threatening rage.

"Yes, sir, it certainly is," John answered, and McDowell smiled and nodded.

"We'll tackle the porno problem at a later date," Vandervolk said. "As both you gentlemen are well aware, the mayor is doing everything possible to clean that area up. But those people have got smart lawyers, and they slam the First Amendment in your face like a hot skillet."

"Well, get better lawyers then!" McDowell thundered. "Pay 'em more! For going on twenty-five years I've had to sit on the edge of that filth and watch it grow like a cancer! You know, somebody went crazy over there last night and killed some people! Probably was teased to madness by some—dare I say—whore with the morals of a packrat. When is the mayor going to get that filth out of my parish?"

John had lifted a fork of whitefish to his mouth. Now he paused and looked at McDowell. Looked at him long and hard, as the old monsignor continued to rage about the porno district. He thought he saw a callous face behind that age-spotted flesh that he'd never seen before. McDowell hit the table with his fist and made the silverware jump.

"She was a person," John said.

McDowell's mouth stopped. He stared at John. "What?"

John had spoken without thinking. He was trembling inside. He put the fork down, the whitefish uneaten. "She was . . . I mean, she must've been a person. The girl who was shot."

"What do you know about it?" McDowell challenged.

Now was the moment to tell him about Debra Rocks. Here it was. But John reached for his glass of wine, and the moment slid forever past.

"I say load 'em all up on a garbage barge and send them to sea!" McDowell stormed on. "Maybe you can get a good fishing reef in the bargain."

John felt a little sick. It was the wine, he thought. Debra Rocks' scent welled out of it. Someone opened a red menu two tables away. John thought he was sweating under his clothes, and his collar seemed too tight, starched way too stiff. It was rubbing blisters on the back of his neck. And then, terrifyingly fast, the image of Debra Rocks, faceless, and a second faceless girl on the beach with two Mexican lifeguards came into his mind and leeched there and he thought, simply, *I'm going crazy.*

"What did you say?" Vandervolk asked him.

"I said . . . this wine's making me feel a little hazy." He hadn't thought he'd spoken, and this new laxness of his discipline frightened him on a deep, primeval level. He felt like a clock without hands, his insides wound up and running but his face totally blank. The taste of garlic was powerful in his mouth, and he suddenly realized how cockeyed this was: men arguing about feeding the homeless from underbudgeted soup kitchens while eating twenty-dollar meals off blue bone china. Something was skewed here, and very wrong, and that awareness coupled with the steamy image of Debra Rocks on a sun-splashed beach made him fear for a second that he was going to be spun off the very earth.

"Where would they go?" John asked, with an effort.

"Where would who go?" The monsignor was wiping his plate with a bread crust.

"The women in the porno district. Where would they go if everything shut down?"

"Not *if*. When." McDowell frowned, the lines knotting between his bushy white eyebrows. "That's a strange question, John."

"It may be." He looked around, uneasily, at the other men. "But I think it's a fair question. What would happen to the women?"

"They'd be forced to find decent jobs, for one thing," McDowell said. "And the important thing is that the filth would be off the streets where schoolchildren wouldn't have to see it every day."

"I know that's important, but . . . ." He paused, trying to figure out how to say this. "It seems to me . . . that maybe we ought to consider the women—and men too—who work over there. I mean . . . it's one thing to say they'd be forced to find decent jobs, and it's another to believe that they really *would* find them. I don't think the city would spring for a fund to reeducate prostitutes and go-go dancers, a lot of whom are probably hooked on drugs." He glanced at Vandervolk, who had stony eyes. Then back to McDowell, who sat with the bread crust frozen at his mouth. "They wouldn't exactly become Catholics overnight." He tried for a smile, but his face felt rubbery. "I guess . . . sir . . . that what I'm trying to say is . . . who'll take those people in when we throw them out?"

A silence stretched. McDowell chewed on the bread and washed it down with a long swallow of wine. "Your question," he answered finally, "is not based on the greater good. Those people have chosen their own paths, and we're not responsible for them."

"We're not?" John asked, and in his voice—and soul— there was a deep puzzlement and hurt.

"No," McDowell said. He put his wineglass down. "We were talking about the homeless problem. How did we get off on this subject?"

No one told him he had sidetracked the conversation himself. The dinner and discussion went on, but from that point no questions were fielded to Father Lancaster. And that was fine with him, because he concentrated on finishing his wine and trying—unsuccessfully—to banish Debra Rocks' voice from his fevered brain.

I've got a movie showin' on the strip.

4

John felt the sweat break out on him around two in the morning.

He lay very still, as if he were trapped in a body he no longer could control. He prayed again, and as he said the words he heard the wail of a police car's siren over on Broadway.

This time praying didn't work.

He tried concentrating on the textbook lesson he'd read today, reciting it from memory. Jesus wept. Jesus wept. Jesus . . .

It was a cruel thing, the Holy Bible.

He stared at patterns of light on the ceiling, thrown by cars passing on Vallejo. The Bible was a cruel thing. Oh, a great revolutionary work, to be sure. A miracle of language and perception. But cruel, nonetheless.

They had copped out when it came time for Jesus to have a sex life. They had simply skipped that part of Jesus' life, and picked the story up when Christ knew where his life was heading and what he had to do. They had left out anything about Jesus being unsure of himself, or needful of female companionship, or interested in anything but saving souls.

And that was a strange thing, because Jesus was Christ, yes, but Jesus had also been born human. And why had the human race been robbed of answers to questions that must've perplexed even Christ?

He knew it was said that more wars had been fought, more innocent lives slaughtered, in the name of Christ than for any other reason. So, too, it was true that religion—at least, religion as interpreted by mankind—had fashioned chains to control the sexual urge. The Holy Bible spoke of sexuality in golden tones, yes—but what about the real world, where ordinary people lusted and needed and sweated in the night for a touch of forbidden flesh? The Bible said wait until marriage. No adultery. Be strong. Have faith. Do not covet your neighbor's wife.

Fine. John understood all that.

But what did the Bible say about wanting the body of a porno star?

He was a virgin. Denial had been tough at first. Gradually he overcame all urges with his reading, his studies, his jigsaw puzzles. He poured his soul into his calling.

But something else was calling him now, something that had sneaked up from his blind side. Something forbidden, and very, very sweet.

"Dear God," he whispered, "take these thoughts away. Please . . . take these thoughts away." He knew that God did His share, but you had to meet God halfway. He concentrated on the lesson, but his memory of the pages he'd studied began to shred and fly apart. Behind the memories was another one: a pair of full red lips, and a tongue sliding slowly across the lower one in a beckoning challenge.

He couldn't sleep. Couldn't even pretend to sleep. He got up, just wearing his pajama bottoms, went to the exercise bike, and began to pedal furiously.

Sweat gleamed on his chest. Why was the heat turned up so high? He pedaled faster, and as he went nowhere he stared out the window at the huge, glowing red X.

"Dear God," he whispered, bowed his head, and prayed again, reciting a litany of Hail Marys.

But when he lifted his head again, the red X was still there.

He'd never noticed it being so bright or so large before. Maybe every time he'd looked at it, a trapdoor had bolted itself into place in his mind so the dark, seething things wouldn't creep out. But now the trapdoor's bolts were sprung, and the things within were not priestly. Not worthy! Not worthy! he shouted at himself as he squeezed his eyes shut and pedaled until his lungs rasped and sweat trickled down his face.

At two-thirty, John was pacing the floor like a caged tiger. Touching himself—relieving his tension—was out of the question. Self-abuse was one of the worst sins of all. No, no; he couldn't do that. He sat down at his jigsaw puzzle, couldn't stay seated for over two minutes. Nothing on television. He'd seen all his videotapes. The books were dry strangers. Shame and anger warred within him: shame at his lust, anger that he couldn't release it. It was building steadily inside him, pressing hotly at his groin. I'm a priest! he thought, horrified. Then: I'm a man. But a priest first. No, a man first. A priest . . . a man . . .

What would Jesus do in a situation like this?

For that there was simply no answer. And sometime just before three, John decided to get dressed and go out for a walk. In the cool air. Away from this stifling, oppressive heat.

He put on his black pants, black shirt, and white collar. Then a dark blue sweater and a beige jacket. A walk around the block would do him good, give him time to think. Maybe he could find a place that served decent coffee. So be it. John left his apartment, passed the library, the conference room, and the larger apartment where Darryl slept peacefully, went to the street door, unlocked it, and let himself out. Then locked it behind him with his key.

The morning breeze was chill. John put his hands into his pockets and, head lowered, walked briskly away from the towering white cathedral.

He went east on Vallejo, his shoes clocking on the wet pavement. A fine mist was falling, swept in from the Pacific. He passed an all-night coffeehouse, but he wasn't in the mood for coffee yet. No, no; best to keep going.

A bright redness nagged at the corner of his eye. No need to look; he knew what it was.

And he knew, deep down, what his destination really was.

He turned south on Grant Avenue. A gust of wind hit him and glanced past. He gripped his hands into fists in his pockets—and then he came to a corner where his shadow pulsed.

John lifted his face to the sizzling neon. And there he stood, facing Broadway with its gaudy signs and open doors, its music quiet now, but still rumbling like a sleepy beast. He felt heat fill his cheeks, and he stood on the corner for a long time, just staring down that fiery length of territory where even angels feared to tread.

And then he saw it, on the next block ahead: a theater marquee, one of many, but this one particularly caught his eye. The Pacifica Adult Theater's marquee announced, in glittery letters, *Animal Heat. Starring Debra Rocks. Eric Burke. Lisa DeLove. First Run!*

Go home, he told himself. For Christ's sake and the Holy Mother, go home!

His legs did not obey his mind.

They took him across the street. A few people still milled around the adult bookstores and the other movie houses, but not many. One of them saw his collar, did a double-take, and picked up his pace in the opposite direction. Two kids in black leather jackets hollered something at John, but he paid them no attention. He slowed his pace; the Pacifica Theater was coming up fast.

A middle-aged man slept in the ticket booth. And then John realized—thankfully—that there was no need to go in, because there was a big poster advertising *Animal Heat* in the display window. He could see what Debra Rocks looked like and, his curiosity satisfied, go home. That's what all this was about, wasn't it? Curiosity? He prayed to God that she had a face that would shatter glass.

But the poster didn't show Debra Rocks' face. It showed a slim, long-legged woman with black hair spilling over her shoulders, her back to the camera. She was wearing a tight-fitting leopardskin swimsuit that allowed most of her behind to show through. At her feet, their hands clawing at her legs, were three men who looked to be in the throes of insane passion.

Like me, John thought. He recognized the supple shape of Debra Rocks from his view of her at the church today; the way her body curved at the waist and swelled at the hips reminded him of a cello carved by a sensual master's hand. That impression was heightened by the tan of her flesh, as smooth as if the healthy shade had been painted on. He stared for a moment at that poster, moving to another place on the sidewalk as if his change of angle might give him a three-dimensional view of her profile. He glanced at the ticket booth; a sign said it cost five dollars to get in.

He looked at the door. It was a door just like any other, but he knew he would be damned if he walked through it. Still . . . just one peek. Five minutes in there; ten minutes at most. He burned to see the face of Debra Rocks, so he could have an image to put those ruby lips on. Her voice came to him, smoldering like a flame that would not be extinguished: *God made the world, right? He made sex too.*

True enough.

Maybe it would not be as bad in there as he feared. Maybe not. Maybe all the movie showed was playacting.

He had to see. He had to.

He took a five-dollar bill from his wallet, approached the booth, and tapped on the glass.

The man looked up, bleary-eyed, and finally focused on John's collar. "You gotta be *kiddin','*" the man said.

"One ticket." John's voice trembled.

"You really a priest? Or you just dressed up like one?"

"Give me a ticket, please," John said.

"Is this a joke? Like 'Candid Camera'?" The man glanced around, grinning, as if in search of Allen Funt.

"I'd like a ticket, please." Suddenly there was a new horror: a man in a gray overcoat lined up behind him, and John thought that it might be someone who knew him. "Come on, come on!" John said.

The man grunted and shook his head. "This beats all! Well, the pope goes in free, so you might as well." He jerked a thumb toward the door. "Hit it, padre."

John shoved the money through the booth's portal and, shivering from the wind, walked quickly into the Pacifica Adult Theater.

He heard the moaning as soon as he reached the concession stand. The sound of it, and the smell of stale popcorn, made him feel queasy. He kept going, into the darkness, but he stopped square in the doorway as if he'd run into a glass wall. On the huge screen was what looked at first like an exploratory surgery. It's a medical movie! he thought, amazed and dumbfounded. But in the next second the camera moved back and showed a nude woman atop a nude man; her back was to the audience, and her body was arching in a frenzy of action.

"'Scuse me," said the man in the gray overcoat, and John almost leapt aside to let him pass.

John's eyes gradually became adjusted to the darkness. He saw eight or nine other men sitting there, all seemingly absorbed by the on-screen movements. He took a few steps down the sticky-floored aisle, somehow got into a seat, and stared at the screen like all the others were doing.

The girl—who had shoulder-length black hair, a healthy tan, and a body like a sculptured cello—kept up her rhythm. She turned her profile quickly to the camera and then away, but it was too fast for John to see what she looked like. His heart was pounding, he felt as if his lungs had constricted, and he was brain-dazed. And then, from the right, another nude man entered the frame. He had a stick of melting butter in his hands, and he rubbed the stuff all over his fingers. As the girl continued to moan and work, the man with buttered fingers reached toward her arched behind.

A head came up from the seat directly in front of John. A man had been sitting there all along, slouched down. He turned toward John and, grinning, croaked, "It's hotter'n hell, ain't it?"

John's nerve broke. He got up, turned, and fled as Debra Rocks gave a gasping moan that penetrated his stomach like a gut-punch.

"Hey!" the ticket seller called as John reached the sidewalk and kept running. "Didn't you like the flick, padre?"

John's face was flaming. The truth—the awful truth—was that he *had* liked it.

He stopped running as soon as he was across the street from the Pacifica. His brain felt cracked open and oozing in his skull. A hundred cold showers couldn't cool him off—nor could they make him feel clean again. He felt contaminated to his soul, about to weep; but his crotch pounded, and there was no denying the power of its rhythm in his blood.

In the middle of the next block, John stopped again. To his left was a shop whose windows were covered with aluminum foil. A sign said *Vic's Adult Books. 100s of Movies. VHS, Beta. Marital Aids. Adult Novelties. MasterCard and Visa Accepted.*

The place pulled at him like a physical force. Now it seemed that a dark appetite within him had been whetted, and he could not shove it away.

He entered the store.

Hell, he discovered in another second, was not underground, a realm of burning caverns. Hell was Vic's Adult

Books, on Broadway a block south of the Cathedral of St. Francis.

Racks of magazines displayed every possible sex act and perversion, and some that John had thought before this moment must be physically impossible. Some he knew he'd be damned to purgatory for simply considering. Behind the counter, where a fat guy smoking a cigar sat watching Dr. Ruth on his portable TV, was an assortment of . . . well, there was only one way to describe them: false members, in every size and color, ribbed, warted, convoluted, ridged, smooth. John stared at them, aghast; that anyone could use a thing like that shocked him beyond belief. And, turning, John found another display: this one a wall packed with VCR tapes.

"Help you, bud?" The cigar-smoker looked up. His gaze found the white collar as John turned toward him, but his face showed no reaction. "You tomcattin', Father?"

"No. No, I . . ." He shook his head. Everywhere he looked, he felt sick—but compelled to look, too. Compelled to fill his eyes up with these forbidden sights. He took a staggering step toward the VCR tapes.

And there it was. Right there. On the row to his right, fourth from the top. *Rough Diamonds. Starring Pam Ashley and Debra Rocks.*

His hand went out with a will of its own. His fingers grasped the tapebox and pulled it from the rack. On the cover was a pretty, smiling redhead holding a palmful of diamonds. She was bare-breasted, and they were huge. The price tag read thirty-nine-ninety-five. He only had thirty dollars in his wallet, and he dared not use his Visa and sign his name.

"Half-price sale today," Vic said around his cigar. "Sale goes on till Saturday."

Oh, my Lord, John thought, and pressed his hand against his sweating forehead. Oh, my Lord . . .

"That's a good one. Nice and juicy." He returned his attention to the TV. "You ever see Dr. Ruth? She's a scream."

John wanted to put it back. Wanted to wash his hand in

battery acid. But his fingers had clamped tight, and then he turned and walked to the counter, his face pale and eyes glazed.

"Call it an even fifteen bucks," Vic told him. "I like to be a good businessman."

"Put it in a bag, please."

"Sure thing." Vic accepted a twenty and gave John five dollars change. He slipped the tape into a bag that had VIC's ADULT BOOKS stamped on it. "Hey, you might be interested in this." Vic turned a little hand-written sign on the counter around so John could see it.

The sign said: *Saturday Special! Two-thirty to Three! Debra Rocks Live in Person!*

"She's in *Rough Diamonds,*" Vic told him. "She's a real looker. Promotin' her new flick, just opened at the Pacifica. You know, she lives right here in San Francisco. Yeah, really! Don't know where, though. If I did, I sure as hell wouldn't be sittin' here watchin' Dr. Ruth, I'll tell you that!" He laughed noisily, and ashes plummeted from his cigar.

John, his hands trembling, took the bag and put it under his arm. He hurried out of the store, and only when he was walking quickly in the wind did he allow himself a full breath.

In the bookstore, Vic heard the sound of cowboy boots clumping through the back doorway, from the area where the peep shows were. "You're not gonna believe this, kid!" he said to the guy. "Just had a priest in here! No shittin'!"

The man, who wore a long brown duster and had blond crew-cut hair, strode to the counter. He'd already seen the sign announcing the arrival of Debra Rocks on Saturday, but now he stared at it as if mesmerized. "I saw her in *Super Slick,*" he said dreamily. His dark brown, hollowed-out eyes with their tattooed crimson teardrops looked into Vic's fleshy face. "I love her," he said.

"Right! You and about ten thousand other horny bastards!"

"There's a difference," Travis said softly. "She loves *me*

too." And then he turned away and walked out the door into the night.

"Freak!" Vic muttered, and turned the TV's volume up a little louder.

5

Obsession.

That's what was going on here, John thought as he took the videotape out of its bag. The bag itself was incriminating enough, and would have to be shredded to pieces before it went into the trash. His hands shook as he fumbled to open the box and slip the cassette out.

Obsession.

But no, he decided momentarily, it wasn't like that. Not really. He was simply curious. He wanted to see the face of Debra Rocks, that's all. If he could just see her face, then he could throw the videotape away too. One good look at her face, and his curiosity would be satisfied.

He turned the TV on, set the volume low, and pushed the tape into its slot. The machine automatically began to play, and the opening credits of *Rough Diamonds*—the huge-glanded redhead, dancing lasciviously—appeared on the screen. And if anyone had ever told him such a sight would be playing on his home television set, he would have thought they were totally insane. But here it was, in living color, though the tape quality was grainy and marred. Here it was, and John wondered how he was going to confess this sin.

Inwardly trembling, he pulled a chair up in front of the screen and sat down to watch.

The movie had no plot. It was something about diamond smugglers, but it made no sense whatsoever. The lighting was terrible, the camerawork was done by a palsied hack, the sound was out of sync. The redhead paraded around, displaying her flesh at every possible angle to a group of supposed diamond smugglers, and finally the three men tossed aside their booty of diamonds and climbed onto the redhead with the single-minded purpose of tramps jumping aboard a moving freight train.

At first John thought that watching the gyrations and insertions was going to make him scream and leap out of his skin, to go running through the church in his naked bones. But after fifteen minutes or so, a strange lethargy settled in. He was no longer watching human beings have sex; he was watching the slamming of meat. He thought at one point that all of them had gone to sleep, because the three men and the redhead all had their eyes closed and it looked as if their hips moved like automated machines. Even the cameraman seemed to be sleeping, because the camera ceased its shaking and stayed fixed for an interminable length of time.

John kept staring at the screen, his eyes glazed and his mouth half-open. The three men finished their duty, mercifully for the viewer. The redhead stretched and smiled as if she had just known nirvana, and John saw that she didn't shave under her arms.

Dreadful, he thought. This wasn't even sexy any longer. He reached out to press the Fast Forward.

The scene changed.

A girl with tanned skin, shoulder-length black hair, and a body that would drive an angel to tears was reclining on the chest of a nude man, both of them lying in bed. Her face was averted from the camera, but she was talking to the man and John instantly stiffened again. It was the smoky, incredibly sensual voice of Debra Rocks.

She began to lower herself to the man's crotch. The breath hitched in John's lungs, and he thought: Oh, my Lord . . .

Debra Rocks turned her face to the camera.

She was wearing a feathered, glittery mask over the upper half of her face. A Mardi Gras mask, John realized. But he could see the color of her eyes: a dusky charcoal gray. Her hair flowed in rich black waves around her tanned shoulders, and her breasts . . . oh, Lord, her breasts were as beautiful as John had hoped—had feared—they would be.

Still, the mask prevented him from seeing exactly what she looked like. And then her full red lips strained toward the man's crotch, and John thought lightning might split the ceiling and strike him dead between the eyes. But the ceiling remained solid, though John felt his own foundations starting to collapse.

The red lips of Debra Rocks worked with slow passion. The man held up an "Okay" sign to the camera, and grinned so lewdly that John wished he might see him on the street one day so he could bash his head with a brick. No, no, of course he wouldn't do that. But why did the man have to grin like that?

John pulled his chair a little closer. Debra Rocks' mouth filled the screen.

I'm going to die, John thought. Right here and now. They'll come here in the morning and find a little sticky pool with my clothes lying in it . . .

And then Debra Rocks lifted her head and said softly to the man, "I want to shave you."

Tiny beads of sweat had formed on John's upper lip. He felt them crawling down his neck. Debra Rocks sprayed lather on the man's groin and rubbed it all over. Then she took a straight razor and . . .

John jumped as the hot breath of Satan brushed the back of his neck. He realized the building's heat had clicked on, and it was hot air from a ceiling vent.

Debra Rocks, if she ever decided to give up being a porno star, might become an excellent barber.

When the sequence had ended, John pressed Rewind. He watched it again. Pressed Rewind again. And Freeze Frame on Debra Rocks' masked face.

Her beautiful gray eyes stared defiantly at the camera, her mouth parted in a whisper. John stared at that face for a long time, his heart hammering, his body damp with sweat.

And then, a bizarre thought: *I love her.*

That was ridiculous, of course. He didn't know her. Yet, again, he *did* know her. Maybe even more intimately than that grinning, freshly shaved bastard. *I love her,* he thought, and pressed his hands against his forehead and knew he had to get that trapdoor bolted down again before he lost his mind. He pressed Fast Forward to the end. Debra Rocks did not reappear.

He let the videotape rewind all the way to the opening credits, and then he turned the TV and VCR off. Purple dawn light was beginning to stain the clouds. The night was ending.

He stood in twilight at the window watching the big red X.

He felt drained, worn-out, like he'd pedaled the bike a hundred miles away from home into uncharted, unknown wilderness. And the strangest thing was that he realized the wilderness had always been there, a block away from where he lived. It was another world out there, one block away yet incalculable distance from the white walls of the church.

If Monsignor McDowell ever found out about this, the rack and iron maiden would look like a kid's toys compared to what would happen.

But still John hadn't seen the face of Debra Rocks. He thought he would go crazy if he didn't, and crazier still if he did.

He remembered the sign at Vic's Adult Books: *Saturday Special! Two-thirty to Three! Debra Rocks Live In Person!*

Two-thirty to three in the afternoon, John thought. There was no way he could set foot in that place in the daylight. Today was Thursday. Well, this was the end of it. On Saturday Debra Rocks would be at Vic's store, a short walk away, but this was the end of it.

This was the end of it.

John went to bed and tried to sleep, still dressed. Sleep eluded him as he saw the lips of Debra Rocks in his mind. Oh, to touch her skin, to run his fingers through her raven hair, to kiss those lips and lie in her warm embrace . . . oh, that would be heaven.

Sleep finally accepted him, and his thoughts melted away.

6

When he sat up, groggy and shocked, he knew at once that he was late.

The sunlight was too strong. It was ten-thirty, maybe eleven-o'clock sunlight. He was supposed to meet with

Father Stafford at nine-o'clock sharp! John looked at his wristwatch, had to blink several times to get the fog away. Ten-forty-eight. He leapt out of bed, ran into the bathroom, crashed into the doorframe, and bruised his shoulder. No time to shave, and his eyes looked like fried eggs. He brushed his teeth, gargled with Scope, and hurried out of his apartment toward the church offices. About halfway there, he realized he hadn't even paused to lock his apartment door. But that was all right; nobody was going to steal anything he had.

He burst, breathless, into Darry's office. Darryl's secretary, Mrs. O'Mears, told John that Father Stafford had left about fifteen minutes before to get ready for a gathering of the North Beach Catholic Garden Club in Conference Room Two. Mrs. O'Mears said that Father Stafford would be back in the office around eleven-thirty.

Conference Room Two was on the lower floor of the rectory. John knew he needed to make some kind of explanation about why he'd missed the morning meeting, but he caught Mrs. O'Mears looking at him strangely and he knew he was wrinkled and shoddy, his beard a light blond grizzle. He decided he'd better take a shower, shave, and get cleaned up before the monsignor caught him. He thanked Mrs. O'Mears and hurried back to his apartment.

John walked through the door and headed directly for the bathroom. He glanced quickly at the videotape player— that black box of temptation—as he passed.

His heart stopped. He swore he could feel it stop and swell like a furnace about to blow.

The VCR was gone. *Gone.*

In its place was a piece of paper. Words on it, written in ink. John picked up the paper. A note, from Darryl.

It said: "'Morning, sleepyhead! Sorry we missed connections. Thought you must be caught up in something. The VCR down in Con Room Two is on the blink. I've got thirty-eight elderly ladies who want to see a tape on crocuses and I have to borrow your machine. Your door was unlocked, so I hope you don't mind. Buy you a burger for lunch. D."

The truth dawned on John as the paper drifted from his nerveless fingers. He had not removed *Rough Diamonds* from the machine. The VCR would start playing as soon as Darryl hooked it up to the TV and switched on the power. And thirty-eight garden-club ladies would see some bulbs and sprouts they hadn't counted on . . .

"Oh, my Lord!" John almost shouted. The blood had drained from his face. He felt for a few seconds like one of those cartoon characters, his legs spinning madly and stretching his body like a rubber band as they raced for the door.

He had heard the term "hauling ass" before. Until this moment he'd never known its true meaning. He almost leapt down the stairs to the first floor, turned along a corridor, and raced toward the closed door of Conference Room Two.

He slipped, almost skidded on the linoleum. He ricocheted off the wall, and then he exploded through the conference-room door with a fury that made thirty-eight gray-, blue-and white-haired heads swivel toward him.

At the front of the room, Father Stafford had hooked the VCR to a big color television set. The TV's power was on, and Darryl's finger was poised at the VCR's on button.

"Wait!" John shouted. Most of the elderly ladies jumped in their chairs.

Darryl's finger paused, less than an inch from the button. He lifted his eyebrows. "In a hurry, Father Lancaster?"

"Yes! I mean . . . no, no hurry." He smiled weakly at the garden-club members, most of whom he recognized. " 'Morning, ladies."

" 'Morning, Father Lancaster," they answered.

"I guess you got my note," Darryl said. "I hope you don't mind."

"Me? Mind? Not a bit!" He smiled wider, but his face felt as if it were about to crack.

"Did you come to watch the show?" a little old blue-haired lady asked sweetly.

"I think Father Lancaster's already seen this one," Darryl said, and John gasped audibly as the on button was pressed.

The credits came on: *"The Crocus. Nature's Hardy Spring Beauties.* Narrated by Percy Wellington."

John stood there, stunned, as the screen filled with colorful flowers.

"I think I have something that belongs to you," Darryl said quietly as he reached his friend's side. "You ladies enjoy the tape," he told them with a pleasant smile, and then the two priests went out into the hallway.

Father Stafford opened his coat, reached into his inside pocket, and brought out the videotape that had the title *Rough Diamonds, a Cavallero Adult Film* printed on it's top. He held it between two fingers, as he might hold a dead rat. "Ring a bell?" he asked.

John's first response was to say he'd never seen such trash before—but he was already in too deep, and denying it would only make his soul heavier. He took it from Darryl, leaned back against the wall, and sighed. "Thank God you didn't show it to the garden club."

"Well, it probably would've perked up their meeting." Darryl smiled, but his eyes remained dark. His smile faded. "You want to tell me about this, John?"

"I . . ." Where to begin? He paused, took another breath. "I . . . walked over to Broadway this morning. About three o'clock. I bought the tape at a shop over there."

"Yes, go on." Darryl nodded, staring at the floor.

"I went to a movie, too. An adult movie . . ."

"I didn't think you meant a Disney flick," Darryl said.

"But I only watched a minute or two of it. Then I had to get out."

"A minute or two, huh? Did you see any . . . you know . . . ?" He let the rest go unspoken.

"Yeah. And on the tape too. Darryl, I've never in my life even *dreamed* such things went on! Maybe I'm naive, or stupid, but . . . why in the world would a place sell false penises that are at least two feet long?"

"I thought everybody was hung like that," Darryl said with mock innocence. "Aren't you?"

"I mean it!" John took a few paces away and then returned, his face furrowed with thought. "It's . . . a different world over there! Everything's for sale—and I *do* mean everything!" He shook his head. "I just can't believe such stuff goes on."

"Did you like it?" Darryl asked him.

"What?"

"Did you like it?" Darryl repeated. "Do you want to go over there again?"

"No! Of course not!" John pressed his fingers to his forehead. The truth had to be told, even if it destroyed him. "Yes," he said quietly. "I liked it." His eyes were tortured. "And I want to go back."

"Whoa," Darryl said. "I think this is getting a little heavy."

Again the opportunity to tell someone about Debra Rocks came into sight. John started to tell him, and earnestly wanted to, but suddenly he didn't want to share her. And, anyway, what was said in the confessional was private, between sinner and priest. How could he betray what had obviously meant a great deal to her? "What would you do if you were me?" John asked.

Darryl leaned against the wall and thought about it. "Well," he said momentarily, "I won't say I haven't been tempted to stroll over that way. You know, I could always say I was looking to save some souls. I could pop in and out of those movie houses and bookstores holding up my crucifix like I'm warding off vampires. But I don't. And I'm not going to. I'm a priest, but I'm a man, and I know my limitations. So I'm not going to open myself up for temptation, John."

"Meaning that those places are stronger than your power of will?"

"Not necessarily," Darryl answered. "Just that . . . I've spent my life training myself to work for Christ, and training myself to think with my mind, not with my—excuse the crudeness—dingdong. My sex organs might sleep most of the time, but every once in a while they wake up. And they say I'm the dumbest idiot who ever lived. So I take my cold showers and I read and study and pray, but I do *not* open myself for temptation. It's mind over matter."

"Those people are in our parish," John said. "It seems like . . . we *should* go over there."

"And do what? Hand out spiritual literature? Pray on the street corners? Go into the porno dens and try to save lost and burned-out souls? No, those people are too far gone to listen to anything we might say. The almighty buck and the drugs rule over there, and Christ isn't welcome."

"We ought to try. I mean . . ." He didn't know what he meant.

"And we would be consumed by the sin ourselves," Darryl told him. "We would be driven mad by what we saw. Oh, Satan's got a real good deal here, John! Satan knows those people aren't going to come to us, and wc can't go to them without . . . well, putting ourselves in dire jeopardy."

"Is that what I'm in? Dire jeopardy?"

"Yes," Darryl said flatly.

And John knew his friend had spoken the truth. "What shall I do?" John asked.

"First thing, take that tape around to the dumpster. Pull it off its reels and bury it in the trash. And for God's sake don't let the monsignor see you. Then go to your room, take an ice-cold shower, and start copying the Bible in longhand."

"Copying the Bible? Why?"

Darryl shrugged. "I don't know, but it worked for the monks."

John left the building and went around to the green dumpster. He wrenched the tape off its reels with a vengeance, getting his mind cleansed out again as he destroyed the evidence of sin. It occurred to him that he was destroying his only picture of Debra Rocks' face too, and that realization slowed his work. But he kept going, doggedly tearing the tape out. Then he threw the tape into the dumpster and shoved it down into the mass of garbage.

And there, next to his left hand, smeared with pork-'n-beans from a discarded can, was a blue leaflet that announced *Saturday Special at Vic's Adult Books! Half-Price Sale on All Used Tapes! 100s of Movies! Erotic Star Debra Rocks Live in Person Two-thirty to Three!*

"Erotic star," John thought. Somehow that sounded better than "porno queen."

He had a smear of beans on his hand. He wiped it off on the leaflet and slammed the dumpster's door shut.

7

Saturday came. Between it and Thursday the cold water streamed frequently from the shower head in John Lancaster's bathroom. Because he realized that he could destroy the tape and throw it away, but he could not erase the burning tape loop that played over and over in his mind.

He had lunch with Monsignor McDowell and Father Stafford. Then the monsignor went fishing with a friend of his, and Father Stafford went to visit his mother in Oakland. John sat down in his apartment to study a lesson on divine intervention; he read every word and every line as if he were chewing tough little bits of food, but he knew he was fooling neither himself nor God. He looked up every few minutes and watched the mantel clock as it ticked toward two-thirty.

At two-fifteen he closed his book and leaned his head forward to pray.

When he opened his eyes, he was looking at his bicycle. Of course! he thought. That was the answer! Take the ratchet-and-gear device off the bike's front tire to convert it to street use, then get on it and go for a long ride—in the opposite direction of Vic's Adult Books. Yes! That was the answer he'd been seeking!

John brushed his teeth and changed his clothes for a bike ride; he put on a pair of faded jeans, a plaid workshirt, and a brown wool sweater. No need to wear the collar today, or carry it with him. He was letting himself off-duty, for just an hour or so at least, and he hoped God would understand that he needed the break. Darryl would be back within thirty or forty minutes, so someone would be available in the church. Everything was fitting together. John put on his beat-up old Nikes—old basketball shoes—and then he took a screwdriver and removed the ratchets from the bike's front tire. Now it was ready for the street, and so was he. He put on his beige windbreaker, zipped it up, and locked the door behind him as he walked his bike out into the hallway.

His watch showed two-twenty-seven.

On Vallejo Street he boarded the bike and started pedaling west. Then north. Then west again. The afternoon was crisp and sunny—a perfect October day—but it looked as if a lot of people had had the same idea as John; the streets had a lot of auto traffic, and here and there were traffic jams. But John breezed through the knots, the wind in his hair, and kept going, pedaling steadily away from Debra Rocks.

He looked at his watch. Two-thirty-nine. She would be there by now. Signing autographs. Talking to other men, in that smoky Southern accent. Smiling at them. His pedaling got a little faster. He hit a traffic jam, turned north again, and started up a moderate hill. Two-forty-two. Oh, yes, she would be there, smiling and talking. Maybe wearing a tight red dress. Blowing kisses. Maybe licking that lower lip to drive some other fool crazy. My God! he thought. He hoped Vic would have put away all those gargantuan members, so she wouldn't be offended.

Then John had to laugh at his own stupidity, but the laugh was strained. Those awesome things would be no surprise for Debra Rocks. She probably . . . well, she probably knew what they were used for.

He pedaled on, as his wristwatch showed two-forty-four.

It was a beautiful day. Perfect for a bike ride. The wind was clean and fresh, and when he inhaled the sweet autumn air he . . .

He smelled her scent, and it almost made him go over the curb and wreck.

Two-forty-six.

His heart was beating very hard. Slow down, he told himself. Slow down, you'll kill yourself.

And it came to him with brutal clarity: if he did not see Debra Rocks before three o'clock, he would never see her again in his life. And forever after—forever after—he would thrash in the sheets and wonder what her face, framed by that rich black hair, looked like.

Not worthy! Not worthy! he shrieked at himself as tears filled his eyes. He grazed past a pedestrian and made the man leap for his life. Not worthy! he raged inside.

His willpower collapsed, not in bits and pieces, but as suddenly as the walls of a sand castle under a foaming, thundering wave. It just simply vanished.

Ten minutes before three.

John turned the bike in a quick, jarring circle and pedaled frantically toward Broadway.

His lungs gasped and heaved. He was sweating profusely under his shirt. Still his legs pumped the pedals. Faster. Faster. He ran a red light, heard a cop's whistle blow shrilly, but he hunkered down and kept flying.

Seven minutes before three.

Traffic was snarled ahead of him. He turned into an alley, raced through it and out the other side, leaving a wino grinning in his breeze. Then he was on Filbert Street, battling his way east, and then south, swerving through traffic and around pedestrians.

Four minutes before three.

I'm not going to make it, he realized. No way. I went too far to turn back. I went way too far . . .

He raced across Vallejo, a good three blocks west of the church. The next street sign said Broadway and Taylor. He swerved violently and headed east along Broadway, and he saw the big red X in the sky. He glanced quickly at his watch: two minutes before three.

A woman with shopping bags in her arms stepped out in front of him.

He yelled, "Watch out!" and swerved around her, but the abrupt motion made the bike's frame shudder and then he clamped on the brakes because he was heading straight for the display window of a Chinese grocery.

The brakes bit in, and John got the bike under control again, inches away from the smashing of glass and slivering of flesh amid hanging greased ducks. But he'd lost precious speed, and he had to build up again. There were a lot of people on the sidewalk, and cars choked the street.

His wristwatch showed one minute after three.

And that was when he skidded to a stop across the street from Vic's Adult Books.

He breathed hard, wiping his face with his sleeve. If he hadn't been riding his bike steadily for more than two years, he never would've made it. A knot of men milled around the open doorway of the bookstore, grinning and looking around sheepishly. They obscured his vision, and he couldn't see a thing. Move out of the way! he urged them mentally. Please move out of the way!

And then the knot of men untwined and parted, and a black-haired young woman wearing sunglasses and a white dress that sparkled with pearls walked sexily through the doorway onto the street.

John stopped breathing.

The way she walked said she knew she was being watched, and she enjoyed the attention. The white dress was so tight it might have been sprayed on. Her black hair had been brushed into glossy waves around her shoulders, the whiteness of the dress accenting her tan. She was slender and full-breasted, and her long legs took her to the curb with the grace of a woman who knows where she's going. Even from across the street, John could see the dark red of her pouting lips.

She's about to cross the street, John thought. She's about to cross the street and pass right in front of me!

But a white Rolls-Royce sedan slid to the curb. One of the men—a big brawny guy in a brown leather jacket—opened the door for her, and with a wave and smile at the other men who watched, she eased into the back seat. The brown-jacketed man got in with her, and so did another man in a denim jacket. The Rolls-Royce pulled away from the curb and merged with the traffic, slowly heading east toward the bay.

The men in front of Vic's Adult Books stood waving and grinning like children. Then they dispersed, and Debra Rocks was gone.

Not yet, John thought. Not yet.

He could see the big white car up ahead. It was already being stalled by the Saturday-afternoon traffic. John cast all thoughts aside except one: to follow that car and catch a glimpse of Debra Rocks' face. He started pedaling after it.

The Rolls-Royce turned on Montgomery Street, and began heading toward the Coit Tower. John lost it as it sped ahead, but he kept pedaling and found it two blocks away, caught in traffic. The Rolls turned west on Union Street, and John kept up the pace, determined not to let the car out of sight.

A block further, and John saw the sedan's taillights flare. It pulled into a parking lot, and John stopped his bike in a shadow.

The two men and Debra Rocks got out. They walked her to another car: a dark green, beat-up old Fiat convertible with silver tape holding the top together. They talked for a moment, and the man in the denim jacket lit a cigarette and gave it to her. Then the other man brought out his wallet and counted a few bills—four of them—into the girl's outstretched palm. She put them into her clasp purse—and then the man in the brown leather jacket put his hand firmly on Debra Rocks' right behind cheek.

Let her go, you bastard, John thought.

Debra Rocks reached back, grasped the man's wrist, and removed his hand.

Then she said something that made them laugh, and she unlocked the Fiat's door and slipped behind the wheel, flashing a quick glimpse of brown thigh. John heard the engine mutter, growl, and finally roar to life. It sounded a little sick. The two men walked back to the Rolls, and Debra Rocks' Fiat pulled out of the parking lot and sped away.

John pedaled out of the shadow and raced after her.

She was a fast driver, and she knew the winding, narrow streets. He would have lost her in the area of close-packed apartment buildings and town houses in North Beach, but she pulled to the curb to get a *Chronicle* from a newspaper machine. Then the Fiat went on, slower now, zeroing in on a destination.

Finally she pulled to the curb in front of a dark red building with white trim. John stopped down the block and pretended to be checking his bike's front tire. Debra Rocks got out of the Fiat, locked the door, and then entered the apartment building.

This is where she lives, John thought. It's got to be. He was maybe two or two and a half miles from the Cathedral of St. Francis, but his legs felt as if he'd pedaled twenty-five. He gave it a few minutes, still pretending to inspect his bike, and then he slowly strolled up to the dark red apartment building. It had bay windows on all three floors; as he looked up at them, he suddenly saw the bamboo blinds being raised up from the third-floor windows. On the sill were what appeared to be large clay pots holding gnarled cacti.

John stepped back, out of sight of whoever might be at that window. The blinds remained open. He was trembling, his heart slamming in his chest. From this vantage point he could look down at the bay and see the brightly colored sails of boats against the blue water. He smelled the tang of ocean air, and he wondered when he had known he was going to follow Debra Rocks home.

He climbed up the first step. Then, that one conquered, he went all the way up the steps and into the building's small vestibule. There were mailboxes with names identifying the occupants: six mailboxes, six apartments. His gaze scanned them: R. Ridgely, Doug and Susan McNabb, J. Meyer, Dwayne Miadenich, K & T Canady, D. Stoner.

D. Stoner.

Debra Rocks?

D. Stoner lived in apartment number six. That might be the one on the third floor, where the window blinds had just opened. And he was considering that possibility when he heard someone coming quickly down the stairs.

John got out just as fast, going to his bike and walking it away from the entrance. He slipped into a doorway two buildings up, and kept watch.

She came out. No longer in her white pearl-studded dress, but wearing tight, faded blue jeans, clunky boots, and a thick red sweater. Her hair was pulled back in a long ponytail, and again she wore her sunglasses. Still, John was too far away to clearly make out her features. He expected her to get into the Fiat and speed away again, but this time she dug her hands into the pockets of her sweater and began to walk briskly in the opposite direction, heading down the hill toward the bay.

He let her get a good distance in front of him, and then he swung up onto his bike and slowly followed.

She turned south on Bailey Street. Out for a walk? John wondered. Or going somewhere in particular? She had a battered-looking purse with leather fringe slung over her shoulder, and John noted how her walk had changed; it was still sexy, but in a natural way. She was not showing off for anybody, and that thrilled him even more. She walked with long strides; the walk of a woman who is used to going places and doing things for herself.

On the next corner was a small neighborhood grocery store called, appropriately, Giro's Corner. John watched as the girl went inside and the door closed behind her.

Now was the moment. He knew it. Maybe he would never be able to get so close to her again. All he wanted to do was walk past her, glance at her face, maybe get a last whiff of her scent. Then he would leave, and it would be over. He would walk past her, and know who she was, and she would never know that he had been in the confessional as she sobbed over a murdered friend. It would take just a minute. Just one minute.

He parked his bike outside the grocery store, and he went inside too.

It was a small, cramped place with a cash register in front and narrow aisles packed with groceries. It smelled of Italian bread, and at the back was a little bakery. The wooden floorboards creaked under John's shoes. A gray-haired woman with a friendly face and blue eyes smiled at him and said, "Come in!"

"Thank you." He looked around, couldn't see where the girl had gone. The aisles were piled high with canned goods, boxes, and bottles. A sign caught his eye: *Giro's Monthly Contest! Will This Be YOU?* And handwritten in red Magic Marker was *–764.*

John walked along the center aisle to the rear of the store, squeezing past an elderly woman in a brown coat and snood.

Two leather-jacketed punks, both of them shaved bald-headed, were appraising the wine selection. John realized one of them was a girl, but he tried hard not to stare; anyway, he was looking for someone else. He turned another corner, and caught a glimpse of her ponytail as she turned the corner at the end of the aisle. He walked after her.

"Marsha!" a hefty, big-jowled man in a 49ers sweater called to someone out of sight. "I found the dill pickles, finally at last!"

John eased around the next aisle. And there she was about ten feet away, still wearing her sunglasses; she was squeezing peaches, and John abruptly stopped. She glanced over at him, and he picked up the first thing that came to hand: a huge cucumber. He immediately let it drop and pretended to examine some bottled eggplant. Debra Rocks put four peaches into a plastic bag and walked on to the far end of the aisle. She inspected cartons of eggs.

John took a deep breath. He felt dizzy, alarmingly light-headed and out-of-control. And there it was, just the faintest hint of that cinammony perfume he'd smelled in the confessional. Or maybe it *was* cinammon, because there were bundles of fresh cinammon sticks on the shelf in front of him. When he dared to look up at her again, she was gone.

He heard her boots thumping on the floorboards. In a hurry once more. Going to the cash register? He walked briskly around the aisle after her—and there he came face-to-face with the bald-headed male and female punks, who slipped by on either side of him. John caught a glimpse of red through a crack between the aisles. He picked up his pace, and then he heard the woman at the cash register say, "Got everything you need today, Debbie?"

She answered, in that voice that made his bones shake, "Yeah, this'll do it. Oh, wait a sec. I need some raisin bran."

And then, as John strode quickly down the aisle toward the register, he came into contact with Debra Rocks.

8

She was there in front of him, her arms burdened with groceries, before he could stop. They crashed together, and the impact staggered them both back. The girl said, "Shit!" and dropped her carton of eggs and they smacked hard on the floor. A package of Charmin tumbled out of her grip, and a plastic bottle of Wesson Lite hit the floorboards.

John Lancaster reeled back, stumbled into a rack of paperback books, and the things went everywhere. Then, trying to keep from falling on his ass, he grabbed hold of a rack of cigarette cartons and those too flew into destruction. He did go down on his butt, and he sat there stunned and red-faced.

"You . . . dumb *shit!*" Debra Rocks shouted. "Look what you did! You broke my eggs!"

"I'm sorry. Really. I'm sorry," he babbled, his cheeks flaming. "I didn't mean to—"

"Oh, crap!" she said, waving away his apologies with an impatient hand. She glanced back at the cash register, where the two punks were buying six bottles of wine. The elderly woman with the snood had gotten in line behind them. "You made me lose my place in line!" Debra snapped. He couldn't see her eyes behind the dark glasses, and maybe that was for the best, because the anger in them might have broken his heart.

He got to his feet. "Please . . . let me help you." He picked up the carton of eggs, and yellow yolks oozed out.

"Forget it!" she said bitterly, and then she picked up her oil and Charmin and went back to get a fresh carton of eggs.

John sat there, in cigarette cartons and egg yolks. He looked down, saw ten or twelve packs of Luckies scattered around him. Luckies, he thought. Oh, yes, this was certainly his lucky day, all right! First he had followed a porno star and then he had broken her eggs and had her curse a blue streak at him. He felt disgusted with himself, totally sickened at what he'd done. Well, it was time to get up and go home. He had met Debra Rocks, and this was enough.

A Latino boy came to clean up the mess, his eyes shooting daggers at John. John got up, brushed off the seat of his jeans, and went past the cash register where Debra Rocks was angrily putting her items down to be checked. He didn't look at her, but she glanced at him and said, "You've got eggs on your ass!"

He got out fast, his head lowered with shame.

"Can you beat that?" she asked Anna, Giro's wife. "Guy busted hell out of the place and didn't even buy anything!"

"I think he must be on drugs. Better to let him go than start a scene."

"This neighborhood's drawin' a lot of creeps." She watched the total come up, and took the money from her purse. She paid the creep no attention as he began to walk the bike slowly, defeatedly, away up the slope of Raphael Street.

"How's your acting coming along?" Anna asked as she counted out the change.

"Oh . . . fine. I'm up for a bit part in a soap opera. Might go to New York next month. And I just finished a commercial."

"Really? For what?"

"Um . . . this right here." She held up the Wesson bottle. "You don't see me in it much, though. I'm just . . . like . . . sittin' at a table while the hubby and kids tell me how good a cook I am. That's a laugh." She nodded toward the half-dozen frozen dinners Anna was sacking for her.

"I'll look for it," Anna said brightly. "You know, Giro's nephew from Sacramento is coming next weekend. You remember, I showed you his picture. Handsome boy, right?"

"Oh, yeah. Real handsome."

"I can maybe introduce you, if you like. He's a popular boy with the ladies."

Her brow furrowed. "Next weekend? Oh, I'm modelin' at a car show in Anaheim! Had it set up two months ago. Sorry."

"You don't worry, I'm going to get you and Julius together! A pretty young girl like you ought to have a steady boyfriend!"

"Yeah," she agreed, picking up her groceries, "I ought to. See you next time." She took two steps, and brushed a little metal rod attached to a counter on the cash register. The counter's number had been 763. Now it clicked over to 764—and an alarm bell went off.

Debbie jumped and almost said *What the fuck is that?* but checked herself. She knew what it was, though she'd never won the contest before and never had expected to.

"Hey! Look at the number!" Anna said delightedly. "Well, it's about time you won the contest!" She switched off the bell, picked up a microphone, and turned it on. "Giro! We got a winner! You know who it is? That nice girl Debbie Stoner!"

"I've . . . never won anything in my life!" she said, still a little dumbfounded. "I mean, never."

"This must be your lucky day, then!" Anna opened the cash register and handed the girl her prize money: one hundred and fifty dollars. Giro, a thin man with curly gray hair, came up to the front with his Polaroid. "Debbie, stand over there!" He motioned toward a white background sheet taped to the wall that had GIRO'S CORNER on it and was covered with the Polaroid snapshots of previous monthly winners. "Come on, we've got to get a good picture!"

Debbie looked through the window. The man who had bumped into her was almost to the top of the hill. She saw him pause and rub his legs, as if his calves were cramping. She realized that she wouldn't have won the money if she hadn't had to go back for unbroken eggs.

"Stand right there, Debbie!" Giro directed, and she stood on a red X that had been taped to the floor in front of the other pictures. "Take your sunglasses off, now! And let's have a big smile!"

She hesitated at taking off the shades. "The flash'll hurt my eyes."

"No, there's no flash! Come on! Be proud of your beauty!"

Her hand slowly rose, and she removed the sunglasses. Her deeply tanned, lovely face had high, sculptured cheekbones, and her nose was thin-bridged and sharp. Her gorgeous charcoal-gray eyes held hints of deep blue, and they blazed with intense inner fires.

"Big smile now!" Giro urged.

Her lips, which were pale and only lightly glossed, made a pinched semismile.

"Think of something funny!" Anna said.

I could give you a smile, she thought, that would blow that camera apart. But she liked Giro and his wife, and she didn't want to fuck them over. So she let the pinched, false smile remain on her face, and Giro said, "Cheese!" and snapped the picture.

"Julius is going to fall in love when he sees this picture!" Anna said excitedly.

Debbie looked toward the bike rider again. He had gone over the top of the hill and out of sight. Her heart had started beating a little harder. She shoved the hundred and fifty dollars into the pocket of her jeans. "Listen . . . I've gotta go. You folks take care now!" She headed quickly for the door.

"Don't spend all that money in one place!" Giro told her, and she waved and left with her sackful of groceries. She began running up Raphael Street.

"Such a lovely girl," Anna commented. "Gonna make somebody a fine wife."

"Like Julius, you mean. Well, let's see what we've got here." Giro bent down to examine the box of magazines that had come in from the distributor about an hour ago. He moved aside copies of *GQ*, *Mother Earth News*, *All-Pro Wrestling*, and the *Atlantic Monthly*.

"Why do we get *that* trash?" Anna asked, and motioned distastefully toward one of the magazines.

"Because they sell, that's why." He pushed aside the six copies of *X-Rated Movie Review*. On its cover was "Today's Hottest Stars! Sunny Honeycutt! Debra Rocks! Giselle Pariss!"

The aerobics classes Debbie took five days a week paid off for her. She reached the top of the hill and saw the blond-haired man walking down the reverse slope about sixty feet away.

John's legs had stopped cramping. It was that last ride, following the speeding Fiat, that had knotted up his calf muscles. Still, they were going to be sore for quite a few days. He took three more paces, and then he got on his bike. It was going to be a painful ride home. But maybe he deserved the pain. Maybe it was God, reminding him to walk the straight-and-narrow. Not worthy! he thought, and he felt close to a sob. Oh, Jesus . . . not wor—

"Hey, you! Hold up a minute!"

Her voice. By now he would recognize it anywhere. He looked around, and he saw her approaching him, walking along Raphael between the Victorian town houses and apartment buildings.

"Who . . . *me?*" was all he could think to say.

"I don't see anybody else," she answered. She had put on her sunglasses again. She came on toward him, her ponytail swinging.

Time seemed to freeze for him. It seemed to stop like a photograph, and if he lived to be a hundred years old he would never forget the sight of Debra Rocks coming toward him in the golden October sunlight. She got within fifteen feet.

"Want a buttered finger?" he thought he heard her ask.

He almost choked. *"What?"*

"You know." She reached him, stood right in front of him. She put her hand down into the grocery bag. "A Butterfinger," she said, and offered him the candy bar.

He didn't know if he flushed crimson or went white, but he managed to say, "Thanks," and he took the candy from her.

"They're my favorite. Used to be I liked Almond Joys best, but they did somethin' to the coconut. They don't taste like they used to."

There was a sense of unreality about this. John felt as if he were perspiring on the inside of his skin. His legs were still throbbing fiercely, and he didn't know if he could pedal three blocks, much less make it back to the church. She watched as he peeled the Butterfinger's wrapper back and took a nervous bite.

"What's your name?" she asked.

"John," he said before he could think about it.

"Oh, another John," she said, mostly to herself, and she smiled slightly. Fine lines, as precise as if etched by an artist's pen, bracketed her lips. "What's the rest of it?"

"Uh . . ." What, indeed? And as his mind raced he remembered, crazily, the packs of cigarettes strewn around him in the grocery store. "Lucky."

Her smile slipped a notch or two. "You're *kiddin'*," she said.

"Why? Isn't that a good name?"

"John Lucky," she repeated. Thought about it, and shook her head. "This has been one *strange* day!"

"I couldn't agree more."

"Lucky," she said. "I like that. It kinda grows on you, huh?"

John shrugged, had the sensation that behind her dark glasses her eyes were picking him to pieces, seeing right through the pores of his skin to his soul. At any moment he expected her to say, *You're a holy guy, aren't you?*

But instead, what Debra Rocks said was, "I live a block that way," and she motioned in the direction of her building. She turned and started walking toward the corner. John just sat on his bike and stared. In another moment she stopped and looked around. "You comin', Lucky?"

He knew there were moments of great decision in life. Sometimes you were prepared for them, and you could handle them easily. Most times, though, they were like this: there without warning, and, once offered and refused, would never be offered again. The question hung in the air like a ripe fruit. Shame speared him; he thought: *I have seen your sexual organs,* and somehow that seemed so indecent, as if he were a voyeur who'd peeped his eye through her keyhole. Well, he thought, I *am* a voyeur. A wretched, unworthy . . .

"You want to come on, you're welcome," she said, and she began walking away again.

In another few seconds she heard—as she knew she would—the squeak of the bike's tires as he walked it along behind her.

9

Debra Rocks unlocked the door to her third-floor apartment, and John stepped across the threshold.

Her apartment was not seedy, or nasty, or look as if she lived out of cardboard boxes. In fact, it was nice. The living room was small, but the furniture—sofa, chairs, and coffee table—were tasteful and clean. On the walls were not posters of porno movies but framed photographs of sunrises, sunsets, and the ocean. John could see a little slice of the bay from her window; the water was reddening as the afternoon aged. The room smelled vaguely of spices—incense, he thought it must be. Or scented candles, because there were a lot of candles around. But what really amazed John was the number of potted cacti she owned. Not only were they standing like gnarled green sentinels on the sill of the high bay window, but there were at least fifteen more of varying sizes in clay pots around the room.

She set the sack of groceries on the pale green kitchen counter. "I guess you see I like cactus, huh?"

He nodded.

"They're tough," she said. "They grow even when nobody takes care of 'em." She started putting the groceries away. "You want a chain and padlock?"

"Pardon me?"

"A chain and padlock. For your bike." They'd left it down in the vestibule. "You ought to lock it up or somebody'll rip it off for sure." She slid her sunglasses up onto her head, and John stared at her face. His heart had swollen again. Oh, that face! She glanced up at him, then rummaged in a drawer and offered him a slim chain, a padlock, and a key. "Better go down and lock it up right now."

"Yes," he agreed. "I'd better." He took the chain, and felt an electric charge tingle up his arm as their fingers brushed. He walked to the door.

"You live around here, Lucky?" she asked, putting away the frozen dinners.

"Close by," he answered.

That seemed to satisfy her. John went out, and eased down the stairs on his aching legs. He stood next to his bike, chain and padlock in hand. He could see that the shadows were growing on the street. The time was becoming late. There would be Mass in the morning, and he must pray and ready himself for its spiritual rigors. It was time—past time—to leave this place and go back to the church.

She was upstairs. Three flights up. Waiting for him. Yes, *him* alone. No one else in the theater now; just he and she, and a film yet to be created.

Stop it, he told himself. Stop it, you damned fool! If you dared to make love to that woman, you would be casting both yourself and her into eternal, wandering purgatory!

But it seemed to him suddenly that most of life itself was already purgatory—a wandering over cold, heartless landscapes. Surely both he and Debra Rocks were already occupants of that netherworld.

John fastened the chain and padlock together. He locked his bike to the stairs, and then he ascended to her again.

She had opened a can of tuna and was spooning chunks onto a flat brown tray. "Do you have a cat?" he asked her.

"No. I hate cats. They make me sneeze my head off. Come on, Unicorn!" she called into another room—the bedroom, he guessed it was. "Dinner's on!" She set the tray with its tuna chunks onto the kitchen floor. "Well," she said when nothing appeared to accept the food, "he'll eat when he's hungry. You want a ham frozen dinner or turkey? I'll pop it in the microwave, just be a few minutes."

"Debr—" He stopped, before the rest of it got out. He remembered the woman at the cash register calling her *Debbie.* "Debbie," he said, "why did you ask me to come here with you?"

Something about her face had sharpened. Her eyes were hot gray pools. "How do you know my name?"

"That woman at Giro's. I . . . guess I heard her use it."

She stared at him for a moment. Then her face softened again, but there remained in it the wariness of an animal who might have smelled a trap. "Oh. I'll buy that, I guess." Again she looked up at him. "You're not going to hurt me, are you?"

"No!" he said, shocked. "Certainly not!"

"Good." She liked the way he said that; now her face lost its hardness and relaxed once more. She let her hand drift from the drawer where the knives were.

"I'd still like to know. Why did you ask me here? I mean . . . you don't even know me."

Debbie opened a ham dinner for herself and chose a ham for him too, since he didn't seem to have a preference. She shrugged. "Intuition, maybe."

"Intuition? Like how?"

"I won the monthly contest at Giro's," she explained. "Giro draws a number from a big bowl on the first Monday of every month. If you're that number customer, you win a hundred and fifty bucks. I've been goin' to Giro's for four years, and I never won the contest until today."

"What's that have to do with me?"

"Well," she went on, and as she spoke, she took the sunglasses off her head and undid her ponytail and that magnificent black hair cascaded down over her shoulders with a suddenness that almost made John gasp, "if you hadn't bumped into me I wouldn't have won. See, I would've just bought my stuff and gone. Somebody else would've been that number. But I had to go back and get the eggs, and when I went through the register, the winnin' number was me. See?" She flashed a brief smile at him, and her teeth were startlingly white against her tan.

"I think so."

"And then, you havin' the name Lucky and all. I mean . . . it's like a sign, you know?"

"A sign of what?"

She looked at him, disappointed that he didn't seem to grasp her meaning. "A sign," she said, "that everything's gonna go right for me from now on. That's why I came after you. I couldn't let you just walk on out of my life. And I knew it for sure when you told me your name."

"Oh." John felt a new heaviness inside him. "I see."

She opened the refrigerator and checked to make sure she had enough white wine. "My birthday's November third. What's yours?"

"March eleventh," he said, and he went to the window to look out and think about what was happening here at what felt like the speed of light.

"See? I *knew* you weren't in Giro's by any old accident!"

"What?" He turned toward her.

"We're soul mates!" she said. "Scorpio and Pisces! Two water signs!" She frowned slightly at his blank expression. "Don't you read your horoscope?"

"No, I don't."

"Well, we're soul mates. Take my word for it." She got two of her nicest wineglasses out of a cabinet.

He had to ask the next question, and as soon as he did he damned himself for it: "Debbie . . . what do you do?"

She poured the glasses full of wine. "My job, you mean?"

"Yes. Your job."

"I'm an actress," she said with no hesitation. "Commercials and stuff. I do modeling too." She went right on, though he didn't wish to hear any more. "I do a lot of TV work. I did a commercial for this wine right here. Gallo. That's why I drink it."

His heart hurt, a deeper hurt than anything he'd ever experienced in his life. The false cheer of her voice almost squeezed the tears out of his eyes. "Here y'go," she said, and offered him a glass. He took it, sipped, and was afraid to look at her for fear of what he might see—or what his own face might show. "Know what? I'm up for a movie part right now. Believe it!" Her voice was now full of genuine excitement, and John thought that at least this part of it might be true. "My agent, Solly Sapperstein in L.A., got a callback from my first readin'. They want me to go back and read again on Thursday. It's Bright Star Pictures, and they've done some real bitchin' flicks. Ever see *Destruction Road?*"

"I don't go to movies very much," John told her.

"Man, you must be from another planet!" She laughed, the sound like a stream flowing over smooth warm stones. She watched Lucky sip his wine, and she admired his profile. "So what do you do?"

"I'm a . . ." He paused. Tell her the truth, you gutless sonofabitch! "I'm . . . in public relations," he said.

"Yeah, me too. Kind of." She strode back into the kitchen. "You want some dinner now?"

"Yes," he said. "That would be good."

"Sorry I can't cook worth a shit. I just pop the fuckin' frozen dinners in and that's about it. Don't taste worth a fuck, but—"

"Please don't curse," John said.

Debbie abruptly halted with a frozen dinner in each hand. Her back was to Lucky. Something about what he'd just said bothered her, but she couldn't get a handle on it. Had somebody said that to her just recently? Where had it been? She couldn't remember. The toot was burning out her memory cells. Well, fuck it! She looked at him, standing there in the slanting golden light, his shadow thrown across her floor. "You're weird," she said.

There was a scuttling noise. John stared down at the kitchen floor. A land crab the size of a dinner plate was moving across the linoleum tiles toward the tray of tuna chunks.

"There's my baby Unicorn!" Debbie said. She put aside the TV dinners, gently picked up the huge crustacean, and kissed its plated back. "I call him Unicorn 'cause he's always so horny." She laughed, but Lucky didn't seem to get the joke. "Well, *I* thought it was funny," she said, and lowered the crab to its food. "Eat 'em up, babe!"

When the TV dinners were ready, John and Debbie sat at the little circular table in her kitchen and ate. She ate fast, as if afraid someone was going to jerk the food away from her. He watched her lips move, and his crotch began to stiffen with the memory of her masked face in *Rough Diamonds* and what her mouth was doing. He shifted uncomfortably, and asked her where in the South she came from.

"Louisiana. Town called De Ridder. Between Merryville and Sugartown." The way she said it let him know she didn't want to talk about it.

He shifted again. His legs were beginning to ache once more, the muscles knotted. He rubbed his calves and winced.

"Come on," she said when she'd finished her food. "Let's fix that right now."

"Fix what?"

"Your legs are hurtin', aren't they? Been ridin' that bike too much. Come on, get up."

He did.

"Shuck your pants off," she said, and went into the kitchen.

"No. Listen . . . wait a minute." He watched her return with a bottle of Wesson oil. "What are you going to do?" His voice trembled.

She blinked. "Give your legs a massage. Work those kinks out. Come on, shuck your pants and you can lie down right here on the carpet." She got a pillow from the sofa and laid it down for his head. Then she knelt, waiting.

"I'm all right," John said. He swallowed hard. "Really."

"No you're not. You're hurtin'. I can tell."

He looked at her strong brown hands, then at the bottle of Wesson oil. Get out of here! he urged himself. Right now! But he stood where he was, and he said, "You don't have to."

"I want to," Debbie told him, and patted the pillow. Then, before John could react, she reached up and unzipped his trousers. He sprang back as if fire had licked his crotch. Debbie laughed softly. "Wow!" she said, amazed. "You're *shy*, aren't you?"

"Listen . . . this is wrong. I've got to tell you—"

"I'll tell *you*," she said firmly. She began to unbuckle his belt. "It's *right*." And then he stood and squeezed his eyes shut while she tugged his trousers down to his knees. Now he was only a pair of Jockey briefs away from total, soul-searing damnation.

Debbie patted the pillow again. "Come on, put your head here." She unscrewed the bottle, poured a little oil into the palm of her right hand, and rubbed both palms together. John felt his insides twist into a lump of Silly Putty. His willpower was water, and hers was flame; commingled, there would be steam. But his legs *were* hurting. What would be the harm in a massage that would last at the most two or three minutes? He could control himself; he could rein in his sensual urges.

He hoped.

He lay down on his stomach, his cheek against the pillow, and she said, "Cute ass," and began to knead the knotted muscles of his calves with her warm, slick fingers. The first touch made him jump, and she laughed softly and said, "Relax." Her hands dug down into the core of his soreness, fingers rippling in the muscles. There was a lot of pain for the first minute or so, but gradually her hands kneaded away the pain and got down to the pleasure.

She felt Lucky tremble under her hands. He was sure a strange dude. She'd never met anyone quite like him. He looked fine, but why was he so shy? Gay, maybe? No, she could tell those things. She liked the way he said "Pardon me" instead of just "Huh" when he didn't understand about the chain and padlock. He was . . . God, it was corny, but Lucky was a gentleman. She didn't see many of those; the breed was almost extinct.

She was working hard. "Lucky?" she said. "Would you take off my sweater for me? I don't want to get oil on it."

John slowly sat up. Debbie lifted her arms. His fingers burned when he touched her red sweater. Quickly, before he could change his mind, he pulled the sweater up over her arms and head. Underneath, she wore nothing but a black lacy bra, and over the rise of her jeans her stomach was hard and flat. Her shoulders and stomach gleamed a little with the sweat of her effort. "Thanks," she said, and then John lay back down again with an inner groan, and her fingers began to work his calves once more.

"Just relax," she urged him, her smoky voice gentle. "You're too stiff!"

Oh, Lord, John thought. Oh Lord oh Lord oh Lord oh . . .

Debbie leaned her weight on his legs, her hands sliding across his flesh.

John closed his eyes. He couldn't stand much more of this. Oh, God, he couldn't take it! But he didn't tell her to stop, nor did he try to get up. Her hands felt so good, so soothing; the pleasure was in his brain now, and he felt all his muscles unkinking. If this wasn't paradise, it might be the closest earth had to offer. Even the memory of the porn scenes began to fade from his mind, and his brain relaxed. He thought about nothing but sensation, the sheer pleasure of warm flesh pressing yielding flesh.

He opened his eyes.

The pressure of her hands was no longer there.

He lifted his head from the pillow—and found himself looking into the face of the huge land crab, or as much of a face as the armored creature had. He sat up, startled, and the crab shot with surprising speed under the sofa, where it folded itself up and glowered at him.

John looked out the bay window. Night had fallen, and lights gleamed. The lamps were on in Debbie's apartment, and some of the scented candles—vanilla and strawberry—burned. He looked at his wristwatch, bleary-eyed. It was seventeen minutes before nine o'clock. He had slept for almost four hours!

He stood up. His pants were still down around his ankles, and instantly he tripped on them and fell to the floor again.

"Lucky?" Her voice came from the other room. "You okay?"

"Yeah. Yeah, fine." He struggled to pull up his pants, zip his zipper, and fasten his belt. This was madness! Insane, sinful madness! He had to get out of here!

He looked at the floor. On the carpet lay Debbie's red sweater, her blue jeans, wool socks, and the boots she'd been wearing.

"Lucky, will you come in here a minute?" she called.

He pressed his hand to his face. The crab scuttled past his

feet and into the kitchen, crawling onto the last few tuna chunks.

"Lucky?" she urged.

He was midway between her bedroom door and the way out. He took two steps toward the way out—and then he stopped, his body trembling like a lightning rod. He smelled the electricity of his own need. At least he could tell her good-bye, he decided. He shouldn't sneak out like a thief in the night. He turned and walked to the bedroom door, stood at the threshold, and peeked around the corner.

Debbie was sitting at her dresser, applying mascara while she watched herself in the mirror. She wore only the lacy black bra, black underwear and garters, and dark hose with black flowers on them. Her lips were wine-red with freshly applied lipstick, and her cheeks had a rouged glow against her tan. "Hi." She put down the tube of mascara, one eye done, and smiled at him. "You must've been pooped."

"I was." His voice sounded strangled.

"I let you sleep. I hope that was okay."

"Yeah. Fine." He darted a glance at her breasts and his face bloomed red.

"Do you like to dance?"

"Pardon me?"

There it was again. The etched lines around her lips deepened. "You know: dance. Guess you haven't heard of dancin' on your world, huh?"

"No . . . I mean . . . I don't dance."

"Well, you can fake it. I want to take you somewhere." She began making up her other eye. "The Mile-High Club. It's just a few blocks away."

"A club? No . . . really. I don't go to clubs."

She had to ask it: "Lucky, are you gay?"

"No!"

That was emphasized firmly enough. "Bisexual?"

"No!"

This would be the worst possibility. "How about neuter?"

He paused, mulling that one over. "Maybe," he finally said.

"Oh, you're kiddin' me now! Nice-lookin' guy like you

can't be neuter. It'd be too much of a fuckin' waste." She finished her other eye, then picked up a brush and began to stroke her black mane back over her shoulders. John watched, transfixed; her face was becoming the face of Debra Rocks now, yet there was still something in it that was much softer, much less self-involved than the masked face he'd seen at work in *Rough Diamonds*. She stood up, walked to her bed, and picked up the black leather skirt that was folded there; she slipped into it and tugged it up over her thighs and rear. "Gainin' some weight," she fretted, though she looked perfectly slim and trim to John. She put on a silver-glittered blouse. "Lucky, would you get me my jacket from the closet?" She motioned to it.

John opened the closet door. Inside was a variety of jackets—cloth, mottled camouflage, leather, feathered, leopardskin. "Which one?"

"Guess."

He knew. He took the leopardskin jacket off its wooden hanger. But he noted something else hanging there: a man's dark blue blazer, with a striped tie looped around the hanger's neck. He gave the leopardskin jacket to her, and she said, "See? I told you we were soul mates." She slipped it on as if God had molded that particular leopard just for her. She caught his gaze and misinterpreted it. "Oh, it's not real. I wouldn't buy a real one. Anyway, somebody gave this to me."

"Oh." The man who fit that blue blazer? he wondered.

Debbie put on a pair of black high heels. She walked out of the bedroom, with John following. "You're gonna like the Mile-High Club," she told him as she went into the kitchen. "It's hot. You can go there and dance and nobody fucks with you." She opened an apple-shaped cookie jar on the kitchen's counter and began to take out some vanilla wafers, Oreos, and Lorna Doones. "If you don't want to dance, you can just hang out. No pressure." She reached down deep into the jar, and her hand emerged with a little cellophane packet of white powder. "I like a club with hot music. Helps you go for the burn." With a speed born of much practice she brought a small mirror, a razor blade, and a short straw out of a drawer, then carefully sifted some of the powder from the packet onto the glass and formed two thin lines with the blade. "I like the people there, too. They leave you alone when you want to be left alone." She held her hair back as she sniffed up a line of what John had realized was cocaine.

"Please . . . Debbie, don't do that," he said quickly.

She looked up, a little smear of white at one nostril. "Do what?"

"That. What you're doing."

"Oh." She smiled slyly. "Don't worry, babe. I'll leave some toot for you." She offered him the mirror and cocaine.

He shook his head. "I don't use drugs."

Debbie stared at him, puzzled. "How do you *live?*" she asked, and then she shrugged and inhaled the second white line. When she was done, she opened her black clasp purse, took out a little gold box, and sifted some more of the drug into it. Then put the gold box back into her purse and returned the remaining bit of cocaine in its packet to the cookie jar.

"Ready!" she said, her eyes ablaze with chemical fire.

They went down the stairs. In the vestibule, John paused at his bike—but then Debbie's hand slid into his, the electric touch destroying his fleeting thought that he was walking on a dangerous edge. She led him to her Fiat, and after he'd gotten in she started the sputtery engine and pulled away from the curb.

About four seconds later, the headlights of a battered gray Volkswagen van parked down the block came on. The van left the curb and followed the Fiat at a steady distance. The van had an Oklahoma license plate.

10

The Mile-High Club was another dimension of hell. It was a cavern with black-painted brick walls, and hanging from the ceiling on thin wires were hundreds of plastic airplane models. They swung in the breeze of frenzied motion from the dance floor, and it took John a few minutes to figure out what was peculiar about the models: they all looked scorched, melted, burned-up, and wrecked. And on huge videoscreens, in accompaniment to slamming rock drumbeats and grunting bass guitars, were played over and over scenes of airplane-crash bulletins lifted from TV newscasts. As flames, wreckage, and death filled the screens, John felt Debbie take his hand.

"I want you to meet somebody!" she shouted over the pulsing thunder, and pulled him through the gyrating bodies. Strobe lights flashed, and a small spotlight at the ceiling swiveled to track a particular couple for a few seconds before its cold eye searched for fresh amusement.

John was shaken to the core. He saw women with crew cuts and muscles that would have made a 49er blanch with fear. He saw a man in black panty hose, and another man dancing with him cheek-to-cheek. He saw a leather-jacketed kid with six gold pins in his nose, whirling like a dervish on the dance floor. He saw a black woman kiss a white woman on the mouth, and then the wet gleam of their tongues as the spotlight caught them.

His knees almost gave way, but if he fell on that dance floor he knew he'd be trampled under combat boots, spike heels, and gladiator sandals. His hand tightened around Debbie's, and she led him out of the confusion. Booths were crowded with shadowy figures, black light sparkling on Day-Glo-daubed, blown-up black-and-whites of airplane-crash pictures. She led him toward a booth and waved at somebody.

Four people were intertwined in a booth, legs and arms pretzeled together. "Big Georgia!" Debbie called. "I want you to meet my new friend! This is Lucky."

John found himself staring at a beautiful, big-boned, red-haired woman who wore black eye shadow and lipstick. Her hair was the color of flame, and cascaded down over her breasts and shoulders. Big Georgia looked him up and down, starting with his crotch, and stared him forcefully in the eyes. She licked slowly along her pouting lower lip. "He looks like he enjoys sufferin'," she said.

Except it was a man's husky voice, with a Deep South drawl.

"Lucky's all right," Debbie explained. "He's my good-luck charm."

"Any friend of Debbie's is a rear end of mine," Big Georgia said, and batted his eyes at John. Then he turned his attention to Debbie. "Honey, you are lookin' *soooo* fine! You use those diet pills I gave you?"

"Oh, yeah. They were bitchin'.'"

"You got any more weight to lose?"

"Yeah." Debbie patted her flat stomach. "A little bit right here."

"Try these, then." Big Georgia reached down into his beaded purse and the black-nailed hand came out with a little bottle. "They'll melt that bad shit right off you, honey."

John felt himself slipping into a trance, as if his mind had become a dial tone. Debbie immediately shook a small white pill into her mouth and sipped from the glass of chablis Big Georgia offered. The man sitting next to Big Georgia had a hand on a breast, and on that hand was a large tattooed spider.

"You workin', honey?" Big Georgia inquired, and Debbie said quickly, "Yeah! Commercials! You know. Like the other TV work I've been doin'.'"

"Oh." Big Georgia glanced at John, and the redhead's heavy-lidded eyes narrowed with comprehension. "I like to do a little TV work myself."

John realized Debbie didn't want him knowing about the porno movies, though Big Georgia certainly seemed to understand her true line of work. They talked on, just chitchat about fashions and shoes and such, and then John had a new sensation.

Someone was staring holes through him.

He was certain of it. And it was no one at the booth, either; they were all either bored silly or listening to Debbie and Big Georgia. He looked to his left and looked to his right. Just shadows, merged and moving.

He turned and looked toward the dance floor.

A tall, lean figure stood there at the dance floor's edge, silhouetted by the explosion of strobe lights.

A spotlight swept past, brushing the figure's face. A man, John saw it was. Maybe. Anyway, whoever it was had blond crew-cut hair and wore a long coat. The man—presumably —just stood there, hands resting on his hips. Maybe one of Debbie's friends, John thought. He sincerely hoped not.

When John's attention went to Debbie again, she was just putting the little gold box back in her purse. "Let's dance!" she told him eagerly, flecks of white on her upper lip.

"No. Really, I can't—" But she was already pulling him toward the dance floor. He saw that the man with the blond crew cut had vanished.

"Work his ass, Debbie!" Big Georgia hollered. Then, in a quieter voice to his companion, "I know I'd like to."

Debbie guided him into the midst of the bodies that crashed and thrashed under the spinning lights. The music was deafening, and Debbie shouted something at him but he couldn't hear a syllable of it. Then she stepped back, elbowing room for herself, put her hands behind her hips, and began to grind with a sensuous rhythm that would have knocked Lazarus dead again. All John could do was stand there and stare at her hips, as a high-pitched singer moaned about somebody dressed in peach and black and you've got the look.

John felt insane, standing at the center of insanity. The strobes flashed and the spotlights swept back and forth, and then the singer was wailing about slamming and ramming. Debbie grasped John's hips and tried to get him shaking, but he had the movements of a swamp log.

Somebody shoved John aside.

A man stepped in front of him and began to thrust his pelvis energetically at Debbie. John saw a guy with curly black hair and a face like a chiseled Italian statue, wearing skintight jeans and a white sweater. Debbie glanced at John, then back to the new dancer—and in that instant John saw her face change.

The hardness poured back into it—but it was a sexy, ruthless hardness, and it made her mouth curl and sneer with cruel lust. Her tongue flicked along her lower lip, she arched her back and moaned, and her hands swept upward through her black hair, disrupting it into wild waves. Her eyes blazed with a fire that John feared would explode his bones if she ever turned its heat directly on him. He stepped back, stunned, and he knew he was seeing Debra Rocks emerge from the skin of Debbie Stoner.

The Italian guy pumped his hips, and Debra Rocks slid down his legs like a cat, her face level with his crotch.

A spotlight zigzagged across the crowd and locked on them. The other dancers melted back, as if they too had been scorched, and a ring of people gaped and shouted as Debra Rocks turned her power to full burn.

She was lying on the floor now, her body writhing, and the Italian guy was on top of her, right over her mouth, in a dancing display of oral lust. She came up off the floor, back arching with supple strength, pressing her thighs toward the man's face. He grasped her hips, picked her up, and she locked her legs around him. They spun and twisted in the blue-tinged light, Debra Rocks gripping his hair and flicking her tongue across his forehead. The drumbeat rhythm was a primal call, animal to animal, and John saw her eyes flare with desire, her offered tongue straining toward the Italian's. The heat of her glare blinded John as if he had looked at an atomic-bomb blast.

The place was going crazy, people hollering, clapping, and stomping to the beat. The floor shook, in danger of becoming the Mile-Low Club. Debra Rocks was on her feet again, her hips going around and around as she urged the Italian on. He clung to her legs, his tongue darting at her black flowers. Sweat glistened on her face, and on his too, and they locked fingers and Debra Rocks ground her crotch over the man's gasping mouth.

John felt a tide of sickness in his stomach. Someone shoved him further away from the inner ring, and he staggered back. Collided with another body, and heard God's name taken in vain as he was pushed off the dance floor like a loose sack of yesterday's news.

He saw a sign on the wall—PEE, followed by an arrow. He

thought he was going to throw up, and he had to get to the men's room fast. He hurried in the direction of the arrow, down a black corridor and through a red door, and there were the urinals and toilet stalls. He staggered into one of the stalls, closed the door, and leaned over the toilet. Cigarette butts floated in murky water before his face. He was shivering, covered with cold sweat, and he waited for what was going to happen as the brutal blast of drums made the walls tremble.

He heard the red door open and close. Heard the sound of boots clocking on the slick linoleum. The footsteps stopped.

Outside the stall, Travis slid the Colt .45 from his holster. His eyes were as dead as ashes, and they had watched this man enter the bathroom alone. Travis extended his arm, aiming the Colt at the center of the stall's door. He eased back the hammer; it made a solid, powerful *click*.

John heard it and looked up from the toilet bowl. What was that noise?

The cowboy's finger tightened on the trigger.

"Man, that's one hot bitch!" somebody said, coming through the red door. His companion belched beer and said, "I'd lay her down and fuck her bowlegged, I swear it!" as he unzipped his pants en route to a urinal.

Just that fast, Travis considered the options. He would have to kill all three of them. Where was the back door here? How could he get out? In a split second he'd made his decision.

The pearl-handled pistol spun around his finger and slid back into the holster, and the two men who'd just entered with beer-swollen bladders hadn't even seen a blur.

Travis knew there would be a next time.

He abruptly turned and stalked out of the bathroom.

John hadn't thrown up yet. His stomach still raged, but he wasn't going to be sick after all. Still, he waited to make sure all was clear in his digestive tract. Cold sweat sparkled on his face, but that began to subside too. He drew a few deep breaths to clear his head, but the toilet's odors didn't exactly help. He wiped his face with a piece of tissue, and then he left the stall and returned to the hellish den beyond.

Debbie was nowhere to be seen. And neither, John realized with mounting alarm, was the Italian stud. The dance floor was jammed again, the bodies moving like a hydra. John searched for Debbie, and found himself heading back toward the booth where Big Georgia held sway.

"Where'd Debbie go?" he asked, still light-headed.

"She was lookin' for you. Thought you'd left her. So she left too." Big Georgia shrugged, and smiled mischievously. "And not alone."

"Oh." The bottom of his stomach seemed to fall away, and an immense pit opened. "I was just . . . gone for a few minutes!"

"What Debbie can do in a few minutes you wouldn't want to know." Big Georgia leaned forward, showing those pendulous breasts. She smiled sweetly. "Would you like a Southern girl, you big hunk of damn Yankee?"

John decided it would be expedient to be gone with the wind. He made his way out of the Mile-High Club and, at the curb, stood in the chilly dark staring at the empty space where Debbie's Fiat had been. The breath whistled from his lungs like air from a punctured tire. Down deep, somewhere underneath the heart, he felt a knife-twist of pure agony.

Well, what did I expect? he asked himself. True love? He had eaten the apple, and was left was a seed-clogged throat. Even the very air around the Mile-High Club seemed fouled. To inhale much of it would poison the soul.

Damn, he thought, and began walking in search of a cab. *I thought she liked me.*

About four blocks south of the club, he finally hailed a cab that would stop to pick him up. "Where to?" the cabbie asked. John hesitated only a second, then gave him the address—or close to it—of Debbie's apartment building. The only thing to do now was to unlock his bike and get back to the church. He felt like a mangy mutt with a scalded ass.

He reached into his pocket for the padlock's key.

His fingers couldn't find it.

Well, the key had to be on him! He searched his other pocket. No padlock key. It occurred to him that it might have fallen out on the dance floor at the Mile-High Club, but to go back to that wretched sin den would make his blood curdle. Anyway, if anybody at that place found a key on the floor, they'd probably swallow it. He searched both pockets again; the key was not in his jeans.

"You lose somethin'?" the driver asked.

"I've got my wallet," John assured him. That was still in his back pocket—but the key, el zippo. He sat back, as the cab got closer to Debbie's neighborhood, and wondered what to do. He couldn't bring himself to ascend those stairs and knock at her door. If a grinning Italian stud's face peered out, John would lose his Catholic manners. But he remembered putting that key in his right pocket! Why wasn't it there?

"Hold it," John said. The driver slowed down, smelling trouble. "Forget that first address. I need to go to the Cathedral of St. Francis, on Vallejo and—"

"Yeah, I know where it is. Pretty place." The driver swung south, and John was headed home.

He decided he would have to deal with this problem tomorrow. Oh, Lord, tomorrow was Sunday! He was adrift in time, because his Saturday nights were usually spent in prayer and meditation. He stared out the window and caught his reflection in the glass. He wondered how he was going to sleep tonight, but he already felt the tingle of cold water on his flesh.

I'm possessed, he told himself, simply and frankly. I am totally possessed, and if my bed starts rocking tonight I'm going to blast through the wall and keep on running.

He sighed, and shook his head. He could still feel a little oil behind his knees.

11

"Now you can tell your friends you been fucked by the best," the young, nude, and muscular man said as he sat on the edge of the rumpled bed and lit a cigarette. "Paulo D'Anthony, Italian stallion, hung and ready!"

"You mean dumb and reedy," she muttered.

"Huh? What'choo say, baby?"

"Oh, Pauuuulo," she crooned, glancing quickly at her imitation Lady Rolex.

"That's what I thought you said." He inhaled cigarette smoke and then puffed out thick rings. "Baby, you're good. You're real good." He stuck his finger into one of the rings and churned it around. "But I can teach you a lot more tricks, baby. Just hang with me." He got up, walked—a little sorely—into the bathroom of his cluttered apartment. He gave a cigarette cough, then began urinating without closing the door.

Debbie sat up. Her clothes were all over the floor, scattered by the whirlwinds of passion. Or what masqueraded as passion on a drug-drowsed Saturday night. Damn it! she thought, running fingers through her damp, tangled hair. What kind of pill had Big Georgia given her? It must've been the pill that made her lose her mind and follow this pizza squeezer to his apartment! Paulo was a great dancer and he had a sexy body and he drove a gray Mercedes convertible, but . . .

He left me, she thought. Why did he leave me?

Big Georgia had said she saw him walk out. That big bitch oughta have her clock cleaned for handin' out Spanish fly and callin' it a diet pill, she fumed. The coke, the wine, the pill . . . all of it had combined to land her right here, getting drilled by a strand of spaghetti. She had to get dressed and get out of here; she couldn't stand sleeping in any bed but her own. She got her panties and bra on. Forget the hose, they were all ripped up anyway. Brutus Beefcake was in there gargling now, like he was trying to sing opera underwater. She picked up her blouse, put it on, and hurriedly buttoned it.

And from out of nowhere, she smelled his scent.

Maybe it was on her hands, she decided. There was still some residue of oil in the skin between her fingers. Maybe Lucky's smell was caught in that. She couldn't identify his aroma, but it smelled clean. The nearest thing she could think of was a brand-new copy of *Cosmo* that nobody had even touched yet.

While Little Caesar was pronging her, a storm of half-remembered faces had swept through her mind. So many men, so little time: that had been her motto. And not just in the business, either. She liked sex; she enjoyed its funk and bump and pulsing heat, and afterward she liked to recline on a man's body like a queen on a muscular throne. But there were so many faces, most of them without names. Or fake names at best, names like Bart and Glenn and Ranger and Ramrod. If they didn't have huge ones, a lot of them would be grooming poodles.

It was funny, though. Real funny. Tonight, while Nero the Zero had been whispering some kind of gibberish in her ear, she had thought most clearly of Lucky. His face, while he'd been sleeping after the massage. He'd looked . . . so peaceful lying there. That's why she hadn't awakened him; she just sat down and stroked his hair, and had a memory of home.

It was all in black and white, like one of those classic movies they shouldn't ought to colorize. She had been sitting on a grassy slope, with the town behind her and the huge white clouds floating in the sky, and she was picking dandelions and watching the wind blow them west. West, over the Louisiana forest toward the hills of California. Where those dandelion umbrellas would finally land, she didn't know, but her hometown was too small for all of them. Her hometown grew mills and water tanks, railroads and rust. Dandelions would not root in iron; they needed the California sun.

And what she'd never realized, until that memory of home with the silk of Lucky's hair under her fingers, was that she'd come to California as a dandelion blown on the wind, but her soul had grown its own iron.

Why did Lucky walk out on me? she asked herself. Nobody did that to Debra Rocks; *nobody*.

And maybe the fit of anger that had coursed through her had helped bring her to this bed too. Well, Lucky would come back, she knew. Oh, yeah, he'd be back.

If he wanted his bike, that is. While he'd been asleep, she'd taken the padlock key out of his jeans pocket and hidden it. This wasn't the first time she'd started out with one guy and ended up with another, and she'd wanted to be prepared in case Lucky got lost in the shuffle. Such things happened.

She heard the noise of a tape being popped into the cassette player in Paulo's bathroom. About four seconds later, the theme music of a *Rocky* movie—"Eye of the Tiger," she thought it was—blared from the tinny speaker, and Paulo leapt through the bathroom's door wearing only a black velvet G-string and flexing his muscles.

"Double biceps shot!" he yelled, and flexed. "Look at these quads, baby!" Another exaggerated pose. "Crunched abs!" He made his stomach muscles stand out like a washboard.

"Oh, no," Debbie said. "Oh, no!" She couldn't help but giggle—and then the floodgate broke and she hollered with laughter. Paulo had combed and sprayed his hair into a stiff helmet of curls, and he was making such ridiculous faces as he shot his muscle poses that he looked like he was agonized with hemorrhoids.

"Stop it! Stop it!" Debbie shouted, holding her aching stomach as she laughed. "You're killin' me!"

He shot one more flex that made his thigh muscles bulge enormously, and then he finally realized why she was laughing. "Hey! Bitch! I'm showin' you my muscles here! Pay some respect to a bodybuilder!"

Her laugh stopped fast. "Don't you call me a bitch, chump! And stop tryin' to show off! I've seen better in the monkey house at the zoo!" She got up, really angry now—at herself, this dork, Big Georgia, and Lucky too—and pulled on her skirt.

"Where you think you're goin'? Huh?" He moved toward her, crowding her. "Where you think you're goin'?"

"Don't touch me. I'm goin' home." She picked up her clasp purse and slid her hand into it.

"When *I* say you go home is when you go home. Me. Paulo D'Anthony." He reached to grab her elbow. "Hear it, bit—"

Her hand flashed out of the purse and popped another finger; this one was long and steel-blue, and its point rested lightly on Paulo's throat.

"Okay," Paulo said, wide-eyed. "So you can go home already."

"Turn off that damn music. I hated that movie."

Paulo backed away from the switchblade, grinning weakly, all his muscles suddenly turned to fleshy dumplings. When he'd reached the bathroom and turned off the tape, he sneered. "Y'know what's wrong with you? You ain't had a good fuck in so long it made you go crazy!"

"Ha," Debbie said softly, folded the switchblade up, and returned it to her purse. She put on her heels, secure that he wasn't going to crowd her again. She left the bedroom, and Paulo followed her like a puppy, but at a respectful distance.

"You don't have to go, baby," he whined. "Come on. You want money? I'll give you money."

"No thanks."

"Coke. I've got a real strong connection, baby. Get you all the blow you need."

"I've got my own dealer." She picked up her leopardskin jacket where it lay on the floor, the first stop of the sex express.

"Shit!" Paulo said bitterly, his fragile ego starting to fall to ruins. "You don't know a real man when you see one!"

"Do tell," she said, shrugging into her jacket.

"Hey." Paulo's voice was softer now, and something in it was desperate. "Don't leave me alone, okay?"

"You're a sweet kid. Have a good life," she said, and she had her Fiat keys in her hand as she went through the door out into the hallway.

He followed her, still G-string-clad. Now his face was swelling with rage. She was waiting for the elevator to come up. "You *suck,* you know that?" he shouted, oblivious of his neighbors at almost three-thirty in the morning. "You suck *big* ones!"

"That lets you off, then," she answered calmly. The elevator doors slid open.

He couldn't let her go without one last angry shot. "You ain't nothin' but a fucked-up two-bit *whore!*"

She paused, her back to him and spine stiff, her hands holding the doors from closing. Slowly her head turned. Her beautiful face was as tight as metal, and the fierce fire in her gray eyes struck Paulo dumb. "Better get your mama to pop those pimples on your ass," she said tautly, and let the doors hiss shut behind her.

Paulo stared at the sealed elevator, his face slack and a pulse beating at his temple. He had the urge to go after her, to chase her in the street, but he let it go. There was no use. A woman like that didn't belong to anybody, and never would. Well, the bitch just didn't know what she was missin'. He pulled his chest up again and swaggered into the apartment, shut the door, and locked it.

A shadow disengaged itself from the other shadows at the far end of the corridor, near the stairwell. There was the steady noise of bootheels approaching Paulo's door.

Paulo opened his refrigerator, popped a beer, and swigged half of it down. The doorbell buzzed. Now, who the hell could that be? Probably some dumb-ass neighbor called the cops, wants to make a big thing about the noise. Hell, life was noise!

He stormed to the door, reached out, and put his hand on the lock. Hold it, he thought. Can't be too careful around here. He peered through the door's spyhole, saw a blond crewcut guy he didn't know. "Who're you?"

The guy smiled coldly. "You lookin' at me, man?"

"Yeah, I see you." Freaky tattoos at the corner of the guy's eyes. "What do you want?"

"She's my date," the guy said.

"Huh?" Paulo saw the freak lift something. There was the glint of metal. The spyhole went dark. "Hey, what're you tryin' to—"

The gun went off, and the bullet blasted through the spyhole's glass and into Paulo's right eye. It went through the back of his skull in a grisly shower of bone, brains, and curly black hair. The second bullet caught Paulo over the heart as he staggered back, and blood exploded from Paulo's nose and mouth as his aorta ruptured. He slammed down on his back, his body continuing to twitch even though his brain knew nothing more of movement.

The cowboy had already reached the stairwell and was descending to the street.

At the curb, Debbie was pulling away in the green Fiat. She thought she'd heard a faint, muffled backfire, maybe from a car on the next street over. She headed for home and a good hot bath.

After two or three minutes, a gray Volkswagen van rounded the corner and drove in the direction of Debbie's apartment. There was a scream from the floor where Paulo had lived.

12

Sunday passed, a day of torture.

John was busy at the church all day, and that night he went into his apartment and read about the temptations of Christ. There wasn't much in the lesson that cooled his fever. He looked up D. Stoner in the telephone book; of course, as he'd known it would be, her number was unlisted. He popped the *Road Warrior* into the VCR and sat down to watch it for about the eighth time. It was one of his favorite movies, but he couldn't take it all the way through and it popped out again. He drew the blinds on the huge red X. He wasn't interested in roaming Broadway's dens; he needed only to see Debbie.

Not Debra. She scared him, but she drove him crazy too. That sight of her, dancing wildly at the Mile-High Club, still remained behind his eyes. He'd gotten maybe three hours of sleep between the time he'd witnessed that dance and the time for early Mass. He felt as if the gears of his brain had gone into overdrive and were beginning to spark and smoke with friction.

Sunday night he slept a grand total of four hours, give or

take. He thought he must have awakened every ten minutes to her smoky voice calling his name: not John, but Lucky.

On Monday he had a meeting with Monsignor McDowell at ten o'clock. He pulled it off as best he could, but McDowell said he looked tired. Was he taking vitamins? John said no, and McDowell gave him a bottle of One-A-Days. At lunch he had a meeting with Mr. Richardson and Mrs. Lewandoski, co-chairpersons of the upcoming November fund-raising drive. He hung in to that one too, as figures and prospections were bandied about. He found himself writing LUCKY on his notepad.

It wasn't until after three that his schedule was clear. Father Stafford was in the confessional this week. John went to his apartment, removed his collar, put on his jeans, a dark green flannel shirt, and a gray pullover. He sneaked down to the street, praying that the monsignor wouldn't catch him. He hailed a cab two blocks away and gave the driver her address.

He told himself that all he wanted was his bike. But he knew better.

Debbie's Fiat was not parked anywhere in sight. In the vestibule, his bicycle was still chained to the stairs. John walked up to her apartment.

Taped to the door was an envelope that had LUCKY on it. He sat down on the top step, opened the envelope, and began to read the handwritten letter.

It said: *Lucky. I knew you'd come back. At least, I hope you have. The key's inside, in the cookie jar. Hope you're not mad. Ha Ha.*

I have a modeling assignment today (Monday) and I should be back around six. Why did you run out on me?

Me run out on *her?* he thought. A little ember of anger—or jealousy—stirred. He read on.

I need to talk to you. About important stuff. Please be here at six. Okay? I'll give you back your bike. See ya.

It was signed *Your Soul Mate.*

He stared at the two words that made him feel queasy. *Modeling assignment.* He knew what that must mean.

He was wondering where to kill the time for two hours or so when he heard someone coming up the steps. A heavy footfall, making slow progress. A gray-haired, balding man in a dark blue suit was coming up, gripping hard to the railing. He had the face of a weary basset hound, his gray eyebrows meeting between his eyes. He wore black horn-rimmed glasses, and he stopped for a second when he saw John.

"Can I help you?" the man asked.

"I'm waiting for someone."

"Number six?" He nodded at the door.

"That's right." A little alarm bell began ringing in John's mind.

"You're Lucky. Right?" The thick eyebrows lifted.

"Right. How did you know?"

"Debra told me." Not Debbie, John realized the man had said. "She said you might show up. I'm here to feed her crab." He brought a key from his pocket and unlocked her door. "You can come in, if you want."

John entered. The man closed the door. He trudged into the kitchen and went to the cabinet where the cans of tuna were.

"I'm kind of at a disadvantage here," John said. "You seem to know who I am. Who're you?"

"Joey Sinclair," the man said as he used a can opener on the tuna. "I'm Debra's manager." He glanced at John over the rim of his glasses.

John grunted. He had seen the crab, up on the windowsill sunning itself amid the pots of cacti.

"Joey Sinclair and Sons," the man added. "It's a family business." He scooped the tuna out onto the tray with a fork and set it down. Unicorn didn't budge.

John had realized that was probably the man's blue blazer and tie in the closet. And those were probably the man's sons who'd escorted Debbie in the white Rolls.

"Harbor sewage," Sinclair said, wiping his hands on a rag. "Tuna smells like harbor sewage, doesn't it? Guess that's why her crab likes it so much."

"I've never met anybody who kept a land crab as a pet before."

"Me neither." Sinclair smiled slightly, but smiling seemed like a real effort for his heavily lined, large-jowled face. "Debra's a real unusual girl. She tells me you're in public relations."

"That's right." Careful, he thought.

"With whom?"

"Well, I . . ." He was stuck. Joey Sinclair was watching him with old, sharp eyes. John knew a man named Palma, a member of the church, who was an account executive with an advertising company called Chambers, McClain, and Schell. So that's the company he named.

"Uh-huh." Sinclair went directly to the telephone book. John's mouth had gotten dry, and his heart was pounding. "Let's see here." The man was turning the Yellow Pages. "Chambers, McClain, and Schell." He tapped the listing. "On Pine Street. That's expensive office space." He picked up the telephone and started dialing with a gnarly finger.

When Joey Sinclair had dialed four numbers, John said, "Wait."

The man stared at him, finger poised. "There's something you've decided to tell me?"

"Yes. I . . . I'm not working in the office anymore. I'm free-lancing."

"But they'll know your name there, right? John Lucky?" He pressed the fifth number.

John took a breath, held and slowly released it. "No," he admitted. "They won't."

"Oh, my. I'm sorry to hear that." Sinclair gently returned the phone to its cradle. Then he turned toward John, and his eyes looked like the business end of pistol barrels. "Harbor sewage," he said. "I smell it now worse than ever." He approached John and slowly circled him. "Where do you live, John Lucky?"

John didn't answer. There was no need to try to fool this smart operator.

"I knew I smelled shit when Debra told me about you."

His voice had gotten ugly. "Debra's usually a pretty good judge of character; I'm surprised she fucked up on this one. You think you're real cute, don't you?" Sinclair stepped between John and the door. He suddenly looked a lot bigger and meaner than he had when he'd come up the stairs, as if anger had nourished him. "I know what you are."

"You do?" His voice shook.

"I do. A priest . . ."

John thought his heart was going to explode.

". . . might be what you need right now, fuckhead," Sinclair continued. "To give you the Last Rites."

He's Catholic, John realized. His heart was still slamming.

"So tell me why I shouldn't go down to the car and get my son and let's do a little boogie on your brainpan, Mr. Vice Cop?" Sinclair shoved John with rough, surprising strength. The crab scuttled quickly past John's feet, almost tripping him up.

"Listen . . . wait . . . I'm not a cop."

"Uh-huh." Sinclair shoved him again, and John staggered back against the kitchen counter. "You ain't got anything on Debra or me, or anybody else," Sinclair said. "I run a clean modeling agency. It's just that I came up here and found you prowling around my ladyfriend's apartment. So I decided I'd better pull my gun, because you looked dangerous." He opened his coat, reached in and drew a wicked little .38 revolver from a shoulder holster. John lifted his hands, stepped back, and almost knocked the cookie jar off the counter.

"I'm tired of being hassled by you vice fuckheads." Sinclair raised the pistol and took aim at John's skull. John had the sensation of flinching inside his skin; his hands lifted to protect his face. He heard the *click* of the hammer drawing back, and he thought: *I've heard that sound before.*

"Please . . . all I want to do is . . . just get my bike keys and go." John grasped the cookie jar, his hands shaking, opened it, and reached inside. No keys, just cookies. He turned the cookie jar over on the counter and everything dumped out—including three cellophane packets full of cocaine, right there in full view.

"Oh, shit," Sinclair whispered, and now it was his voice that trembled.

A silence stretched. John saw the padlock key lying next to an Oreo, and he snatched it up.

"Hey, I'm a big kidder, huh?" Joey Sinclair said, and his grin showed a row of sparkling white capped teeth. "Bet I had you going, right? Look." He flipped the .38's cylinder open and shook it. No bullets fell out. "An old man and his toys!" Sinclair said, his eyes bright and scared. "My sons don't let me carry bullets. They don't want their senile old daddy to shoot his own cock off, right?"

The center of power had taken a violent and startling shift. John watched, amazed and stunned, as Joey Sinclair laid the gun down on the counter and lifted his hands in supplication. "I'm senile as hell! Ask anybody!" He glanced at the cocaine packets and then back to John, who hadn't moved a muscle. "We can make a deal, right? You know, if Debra goes to the slammer, she's not going to look so good when she comes out."

It finally dawned on John what the man was talking about. He said, "I'm not a vice policeman."

Sinclair looked like a man who'd been tickled with a feather and kicked in the crotch at the same time. "Huh?" Some of the meanness started to return to his eyes. "What kind of cop are you, then? A narc?"

"No. I'm . . . not a policeman at all."

Sinclair lowered his hands. His mouth worked for a few seconds, but made no noise. John could see the wheels turning behind his eyes. Sinclair picked up the .38. "Okay, I'll bite. You're one of Rio's boys, right? That sonofabitch is still trying to steal my business, is that it? Never! Rio couldn't make a decent fuckflick if Cecil B. deMille came back from the dead and wanted to direct it!" He stabbed a finger at John. "And you're not stud enough to take Debra away from me, either!"

"I don't know anybody named Rio," John said. The key

was in his hand. He was ready to go. Why, then, did his legs not start moving?

Again Joey Sinclair was struck silent. His heavy-lidded eyes slowly blinked. "So that's it. Yeah, I know your type. You're either a private dick trying to dig up dirt on her, or you're a rotten little hustler on the make. Which is it?" He didn't give John time to answer. "I think you're a hustler. Hell, if you were a private dick you'd have your ass covered. Anyway, Debra's not fucking anybody's husband right now. Yeah, you're a hustler. God knows she's had her fill of *them* too! I should've spotted you for a hustler right off." He returned the pistol to his shoulder holster. "Maybe I *am* getting senile."

John didn't care to debate that point. He headed for the door.

"Where do you think you're going?" Sinclair asked sharply.

John stopped with his hand on the knob. "Out of here. I'm going down to get my bike, and I'm—"

"You're staying right here until Debra gets home," Sinclair said, glowering. "If you were a vice cop or one of Rio's boys, I would've kicked your ass out. You might be a lousy hustler, but . . . Debra thinks you're her good-luck charm."

"What?"

"You heard me. *Lucky.*" He sneered it. Then shook his head, stepped over the feeding land crab, went to the refrigerator, and pulled out two bottles of beer. He threw one of them to John. "She begs for trouble," he said, almost to himself. He popped the beer open and swigged it. "Debra believes in the supernatural. She's . . . like . . . a real spiritual girl." He wiped a froth of beer from his lips. "On Thursday she's got a callback reading for a legit flick in L.A. You're going with her."

John felt his jaw drop like an anvil. "I . . . can't . . ."

"I know you can't pay for it, punk," Sinclair said. "You probably haven't got ten bucks to your name. I'm buying the tickets. You'll get some money to take her to lunch too. I'll make the reservations. Somewhere classy." He looked at

John, eyes narrowed. "You own a coat and tie?" He grunted with disgust when John didn't respond. "Damn hustler! Okay, I'll spring for a suit too! What're your sizes?"

"I . . . wear a size forty coat. Long. I . . ." His mind spun. "Size thirty-two waist. Thirty-three length."

"What about your collar?" Sinclair asked.

"My . . . collar?"

"Yeah. You know, the thing that goes around your neck. What size collar, stupid?"

"Fifteen."

"It'll be a blue suit. You can pick it up here on Thursday morning. Nine sharp. And don't wear those damned basketball sneakers. Wear black shoes, and make sure they're polished. Your plane leaves at ten."

"Why . . ." John waited for his senses to stop reeling. "Why are you doing this?"

"Because I want Debra to do good at her audition. She's been wanting to get a shot at legit for a long time. My associate Solly Sapperstein's been trying to find a movie for her. Of course, the legit boys don't know Debra's . . . uh . . . past experience. She'll be auditioning under the name Debbie Stoner." He chugged down the rest of the beer and dropped the bottle into the trash. "If she's confident, she'll do good. And she'll be confident if she thinks she's got her lucky-charm boy with her. If she gets the job, maybe I can start managing some legit actresses. You never know."

"Does she . . . does she have a chance to get the part?"

"They called her back. That's a good sign." He belched. "I met Debra in L.A. about six years ago, at my other office. She was working the topless clubs, doing a few loops and bits on the side. That was before she got her nose fixed. I did it for her."

"You did a good job."

Sinclair looked at him and scowled. "I didn't *do* the surgery, stupid. I paid for it. Anyway, it did a lot for her confidence. My wife showed her how to do her makeup and hair."

"Your *wife?*"

"Yeah. She's about Debra's age." He noted the hustler's

strange expression. "My third wife," he explained. "Not the mother of my sons." He opened the refrigerator again, found a carrot, and chewed on it. "Debra's worked hard. She deserves a good shot. You're going to make sure she gets it. Right?"

And John said it, quietly: "Right."

"Good boy. Now, listen up." Joey Sinclair walked to John and stopped, and John saw the deadly darkness in the other man's eyes. "Debra's got potential. Real potential. Maybe she's not as good a judge of character as she thinks she is, but I'm going to tell you something, and you'd better understand it." He leaned his face close to John's. "I've seen your kind in every gutter I ever stepped over. You don't give a shit for anybody in the world but yourself. Well, I understand that. Maybe I'm like that too. But . . . you hurt Debra in any way—you make her shed *one* tear—and I'll start right here . . ." He placed his finger on John's forehead. ". . . and I'll split you open down to here." He jabbed John's testicles. "Get it?"

"Got it," John answered.

"You're stupid, but you're not dumb." He crunched on the carrot, and then he said, "Nine o'clock Thursday morning. I'll send the Rolls. Be here." Joey Sinclair walked to the door, opened it, and left without a backward glance.

13

John stood at the bay window in the golden afternoon light and slowly he sank to his knees.

He could say a hundred thousand times "Hail Mary, Mother of Grace," he realized, and still the storm inside him would not be stilled. How had he come to this place, weak and on his knees in the apartment of a porno star? Oh, Holy Father . . . this was more than his soul could withstand . . .

He sensed a stealthy movement beside him, and looked to his right. The crab had joined him. It hunkered down on the carpet and just sat there.

John clasped his hands before him, closed his eyes, and offered his face to the sun. He began to pray for guidance, for the tumult in his soul to be soothed, for his blood to stop its fiery racing through the avenues of his veins. He must be delivered from this tangled web of ev—

There was the click of a key turning in the lock. The door came open, and there she was.

He twisted his head around, but didn't have time to leap to his feet. Debbie wore her jeans and a bulky pale blue sweater. Her face looked a little used and tired, as if she'd gone several nights without decent rest. Her hair was damp—from a shower or bath? he wondered—and it was pulled back again into a raven ponytail.

She smiled, and it was like the sun emerging from gloom. "I saw the note was gone!" she said. "Uncle Joey must've let you in, right? I knew you'd come back! Lucky, I'm so glad to see you!" She closed the door behind her.

John stayed where he was, frozen in an attitude of prayer.

She bent over and kissed him on the forehead. Her lips seared his flesh. Then she got down on her knees beside him, facing the sun. Their arms rubbed. "I like to meditate too," she said. "It's a kick." She closed her eyes, and began to intone, "Ommmmmmm . . ."

I'm going to scream, John thought. I'm going to scream so loud the windows will explode.

"Do you believe in reincarnation?" she asked him suddenly, her gray eyes soft and inquiring.

"I . . ." His tongue tangled.

"I've read all of Shirley MacLaine's books," she went on. "I had a dream once where I was an Egyptian queen, and I was watchin' them build the pyramids. It seemed like a real place. I mean . . . it was cosmic. So that's why I read her books." She turned her body toward him and took both his hands in hers. The golden light streamed around them and merged their shadows. "You know what she says? That people who loved each other in past lives always meet again. Somehow or other, they always get together. But sometimes you can miss your lover, and that's why people live unhappy lives. So you've just got to hang in there, and maybe in the next life you'll find your soul mate again. Do you believe that?"

He couldn't lie about something like this. "No," he said quietly, and he saw the disappointment well up in her eyes.

But it was quickly gone, like a little cloud past the sun. "I don't either, not really," she said. "But it would be nice to pretend, wouldn't it?" She took his silence for agreement. "Anyway, I've found my soul mate this time around!" She squeezed his hands. "Lucky, I'm so glad you came back!"

"I couldn't stay away," he said, before he could think about it. And added, "You had the padlock key."

"Yeah. Guess I pulled a fast one on you, huh? Forgive me?"

How could he not? "Of course."

She got up and stretched her body. "Wow, I've had a day! Hi there, Unicorn! Uncle Joey come by and feed you yet?" She saw the tuna chunks, and also the spilled cookies and packets of cocaine on the counter. "You do that?" she asked him.

"Sorry. I was looking for the key. I was going to clean it up."

"Aw, I'll get it." She went to the counter, put everything back into the jar but one packet of cocaine. She began to get out the mirror, straw, and razor blade again.

At once John was on his feet. Debbie formed two lines on the glass with the razor blade, and leaned forward with the straw to her nostril.

Before she could inhale, John reached out and grasped the straw away. She looked up, puzzled. "Hey! What're you—"

"I don't want you to do that anymore," he said. He snapped the straw and dropped it into the trash. "That shit . . . that stuff . . . isn't good for you."

"Oh, it's good shit," she said. "It's fresh. I got it yesterday." She lifted the mirror to her nose and inhaled first one line, then licked her finger, put it into the other line, and worked the powder into her mouth and gums.

Hopeless, John thought. He felt as strong as a wrung-out rag.

"How come you left me?" she asked. Her gaze had

sharpened. "At the Mile-High Club. How come you walked?"

"*I* didn't leave. I went into the bathroom. When I came out, that transves . . . I mean, Big Georgia said you'd gone." He avoided her eyes. "With that guy you were dancing with."

"Oh." It came clear to her. That Big Georgia wanted every man she saw! "Oh, he wasn't anybody," she said, putting her drug paraphernalia away. "Just a good dancer." She frowned and touched between her legs. "Gee, I'm kind of hurtin'." Quickly she realized Lucky didn't yet know about her line of work, and she turned away. "I . . . did some modelin' at a gym today. You know, leotards and like that. I had to do a lot of stretchin'."

My soul, John thought, is the size of a cinder.

Debbie picked up Unicorn and took him to his sandbox in the bathroom. Then she caught her reflection in the mirror, and she stood staring at herself for a moment. Her lipstick was smeared, and there were dark circles under her eyes.

I have to tell him, she thought. I can't lie to him anymore.

She tried to shove that thought away, but it lodged in her like a thorn. If he listened, and ran out . . . well, he wouldn't do that. Lucky was her soul mate, right? Believe it. And anyway, what kind of man would run out after she told him what had to be said? If there was any such man on earth, she hadn't met him yet. She ran a finger lightly over her lips; they were a little swollen.

It was time. Now or never.

She went to a closet in the bedroom, opened it, and reached to the top shelf, having to stand on her tiptoes. Her body felt like a well-used glove. She grasped the brown leather photo album, brought it down, and went out to Lucky.

He was sitting in a chair, facing the window, with his head in his hands. He looked as if he'd had a rough day too. She came up behind him, and when she touched his shoulders, he jumped.

"I didn't know you were there," he said.

"You're tight. Your shoulders. Lot of stress in there, huh?"

"Oh, yeah." Much of it had come from Joey Sinclair. He felt her fingers work deep into the stiff muscles, and he closed his eyes and tried to relax.

"I have to tell you some things," she said after a long pause. Her fingers kept kneading Lucky's shoulders with slow, steady power. "I'm an actress. Remember, I told you that before?" He nodded. "Well . . . I've got a different name, too. An actress name."

His eyes opened, but he kept his head lowered.

"Debra." She hesitated. Four or five seconds went past. "Rocks," she said, almost like an afterthought. "Get it? Debbie Stoner? Debra Rocks?"

"I get it," John said softly.

"I came up with that one myself." Her fingers kept working, but Lucky's shoulders didn't seem to be getting any looser. "Have you . . . like . . . ever heard of me?"

"No," John said, and his heart clenched. He heard her release a breath she'd been holding.

She placed a brown leather photo album in his lap, and then she turned away, walked into the kitchen, and poured herself a glass of white wine.

He stared at the leather as if it covered a secret door. Beyond this point, he thought, there lie monsters.

His fingers were damp. He opened the book.

On the first page, under a thin sheet of plastic, was a postcard-size picture of a movie poster. The movie was titled *Carny Girls,* and showed a man and woman passionately kissing against the neon blaze of a carnival's midway. *Starring Tawnee Wells, Debra Rocks, and Cyndy Funn,* read the credit line.

John turned the page.

The next facsimile movie poster announced *Closest Encounters. Starring Paula Angel, Heather Scott, and Debra Rocks.* He turned the page again.

Wild and Wet. Starring Cheri Dane and Gina Alvarado. Special Guest Star Debra Rocks.

Another turn of the page.

347

Darkest Africa. Starring Debra Rocks and Black Venus.

Oh, my Lord, John thought. He felt as if his lungs were being squeezed by the weight of heaven.

Super Slick was the next poster. *Starring Cheri Dane, Debra Rocks, and Easee Breeze.*

There were no actual depictions of sexual acts on these posters, but the poses, challenging stares, and red-lipped pouts were provocative enough. The bodies of the women were sleek and tanned, their faces and hair perfect. But there was something robotic about their expressions, as if they were staring at their own reflections instead of a camera lens, and mesmerized by what they saw. Even the face of Debra Rocks had that same blankness about it, a scrubbed sensual nothingness.

Cox Fox was on the following page. *Starring Raven Xaviera and Debra Rocks.*

His heart stuttered. Debra Rocks—Debbie Stoner—had just walked into the room and stood beside his chair. He dared not look up at her. He kept turning pages: *She's Willing; Acapulco Gold; Sweet Wet Honey; California Surfer Girls . . .*

"You . . . must be very tired by now," John said, his voice like the sound of air through a dry husk.

"I won't do more than three guys at the same time," she said quietly, as if reciting the terms of a contract from memory. "I won't do bondage, or S-and-M. I won't do animal acts, gangbangs, golden showers, or chocolate drops. I won't do enemas or bi-threeways or TV-threeways. I like to have location control too. No greasy garages or woods. I'm real allergic to ragweed and poison oak."

He came to the last poster, after what seemed like twenty-five or thirty of them: *Animal Heat.*

"That's my new one. It just opened on the strip."

He closed the book, and he sat there unable to say a word.

Her hands—oh, Lord, where had those beautiful hands been?—came down and took the book from his lap. He heard her walk back to her bedroom. Heard a closet door open and close. He felt lifeless, a puppet with broken strings.

"So what would you like for dinner?" she asked momentarily. There was just a hint of a nervous edge in her voice. "Ham or turkey?"

He stood up. It was time, now, for him to cast off his disguise as well.

But when he turned toward her he saw her not as a porno actress, a sex queen, a girl who survived by selling glimpses of false lust to unworthy strangers. Maybe he wanted to see her that way, so he could turn his back on her once and for all and grasp heaven's ladder again for his torturous climb out of the basement. Maybe he did . . . but he could not.

He saw Debbie Stoner standing there, ponytailed and weary-looking. And there was fear in her eyes too; a sharp, awful glint of it.

"You're gonna stay for dinner, aren't you, Lucky?" she asked.

I love you, he thought. *Oh, dear God . . . I love you.*

"Ham," he said. "That would be fine."

She quickly turned away and took the dinners out of the freezer.

"Some guys might make a big deal out of it," Debbie said as they sat at the kitchen table and ate their food. She'd lit candles, and the air was scented with vanilla. "You know. What I showed and told you." Lucky hadn't spoken much since he'd found out. She wasn't sure he was all with her any longer, but at least most of him was still here. "I mean . . . it's a job. Like anything else. Only . . ." She shrugged. "There's not much of anything else I can do real well." She ate a few more bites. "About the Mile-High Club," Debbie ventured. "She goes a little crazy when the spotlight gets on her."

"Her?" He looked up from the tasteless ham. "Who?"

"Debra Rocks. My actress self. See . . . sometimes I kind of feel like I can turn her off and on, like a switch in my brain. When the director says 'Action,' you've got to be right there, ready to go, because time's money and . . . well . . ." Another shrug. "I'm a star."

"How did you . . ." He stopped, altered his voice a little so the question wouldn't sound so accusatory. "How'd you get into acting?"

"First off, I like sex. I mean, not twenty times a day like you might think. But it's okay. I'd *better* like it, huh?"

He couldn't suppress a quick smile.

"There you go! A smile makes you handsome." She stared at the side of his head. "You've got nice lobes."

"Pardon me?"

"Nice earlobes. They're sexy. You need to have a pierced ear. I can do it for you, if you want."

"No, I don't think so." That would be all the monsignor would need to see.

"How'd I get into acting?" she repeated, returning to his question after her brief avoidance of it. "I always liked attention, I guess. I thrived on it. I used to be a majorette. De Ridder High School. When I got out there and twirled, I could hear how quiet people got. Especially the guys. I knew I had a good body. Well, I wasn't too pretty otherwise."

"I can't believe that," John said. "I think you're beautiful."

"Nose job. Plus my hair was short and I didn't wear it so good. Plus I had a lot of baby fat, but still I had a nice body. When you crave attention like I did, you do stupid things." She stuck her fork into her ham a few times. "I had to get married when I was seventeen. I had two miscarriages." She was silent for a moment. "He knocked me around some. Busted my nose and three ribs. Bastard was a truck driver. He went out on the road just before Christmas, high on coke and drunk too. Skidded across the interstate and went through the guardrail. Scratch one truck driver. Then all of a sudden I was a bad girl."

"What about your parents?"

"I lived with my ma and grandmomma. My dad didn't come around, and my ma . . . well, she kinda craved attention too. She still lives there, but I guess she's older now. I went back home for my grandmomma's funeral, but nobody recognized me. I just stayed one day." She pushed the aluminum tray aside. "I loved my grandmomma. She was good to me. She'd say, 'Debbie, you better stop readin' them movie magazines! You don't want to wind up in California, no ma'am!' But . . . I always thought California was a place where it was easy to be loved. You know? Everybody in California was always smilin' and dressed up so nice, and they all looked like they had money and lots of friends." She took a quick sip of wine. "I was wrong."

"Not everybody can be a star," John said.

Debbie laughed, and there was some bitterness in it. "Try tellin' that to a nineteen-year-old Louisiana girl standin' in a bus station with ten dollars in her purse. I mean . . . I *am* a star!" she said, catching herself. Then her eyes hazed over again. "I could dance. Couldn't sing worth a shit, though. And I had the country-girl look. You know? I swear to God, I got out of a lot of scrapes by the skin of my teeth. But then . . . bein' wild got to be excitin'. And gettin' *paid* for it too? Not a whole lot, but still . . ." She shook her head. "It's a crazy world."

"Do you send any money to your mother?" John asked.

"Fuck, no!" she said with a snort. "She'd just drink it up! And not Gallo white wine, either! She goes for the rotgut!" Debbie looked into Lucky's eyes. There was some pain in them; why was that? "How old do you think I am?"

He was reluctant to say, and he shook his head.

"Twenty-six. I'll be twenty-seven next month. That's old for this business. Younger ones ride the buses in every day. They start them off at eighteen, but those girls are just like me: by the time you fuck for a camera, there's nothin' you haven't done." She played with the stem of her wineglass. "Sometimes I feel real old, like old inside. You get old and start puttin' on weight, they pair you up to scabs and the action gets rough. That's why I've got to get this part down in L.A. on Thursday. I've *got* to." Her eyes blazed with determination.

"Joey Sinclair told me about the audition," John admitted. "He told me about . . . the work you do, too."

That threw her for a loop. "You mean . . . you already knew about me? Uncle Joey told you?"

"Yes. Not in detail. Just that the audition is important to you."

She didn't know whether to be angry at him, for saying he'd never heard of Debra Rocks before and making her spill her guts, or pleased that he had waited for her. She chose the second. "Then you're gonna go to L.A. with me? To bring me good luck?"

"I'll go with you. I don't know about the luck."

"Great!" She clasped his hand excitedly. "If you're with me, I'll get the part! I know I will!"

He saw it then, and he understood it. That's what this was all about; Debbie thought he was lucky for her, and his presence would somehow assure that she got the role in a legitimate production.

"Would you like to take a bath?" she asked him.

"Uh . . ." His gears were stripped again. "Uh . . . I don't . . ."

"It's a nice big bathtub. Come on, I'll show you." Debbie stood up, still clasping his hand, and pulled him to his feet. John resisted just a little bit, but not very much.

It was an old claw-footed white tub. She turned on the hot water and poured in some bubblebath for him that had the cinammony-perfume smell he remembered. The bubbles boiled up, white and frothy, under the flow of steamy water. She rubbed his tense shoulders. "You're just full of kinks, aren't you? Go ahead and get in, a good bath'll do you wonders."

"I'd better not." He watched the water stream in. He couldn't remember the last time he'd relaxed in a bathtub; his apartment's bathroom was large enough for only a shower stall.

Debbie reached in and swirled the water, making the bubbles plump up. "I'm gonna go wash the wineglasses out. Go ahead, enjoy." She kissed his cheek, her fingers caressing his chin; then she left him alone and closed the door. Alone, that is, except for Unicorn; the crab sat in a big detergent box full of sand over in the corner.

John sighed with relief. She wanted him to bathe by himself. Well, maybe that would be all right. Still, her touch and the idea of this bath had made his crotch stiffen and pound again. The smell was maddening, and deep down he relished the thought of wallowing in her scent. Steam welled into his face. He pulled his sweater off. Stop it! he told himself. He began to unbutton his shirt. No! You can't! He shrugged his shirt off. The lathery bubbles had boiled up in waves. He unbuckled his belt, and he knew he had crossed the line.

He slipped into the hot water and winced as it embraced his testicles. He laid his head back against the porcelain, felt his muscles untense, smelled steam and cinammon.

In another moment the door opened, and she came in, nude.

He sat bolt upright, sloshing water out. Debbie had undone her hair, and it had fallen loosely around her shoulders. She had an all-over tan, and her body was magnificent. She was holding a straight razor and a can of Foamy. "I want to shave you," she said.

"No!" he shouted. "For God's sake, no!"

"You need a shave," she said, somewhat taken aback. "I felt your beard when I kissed you."

"Huh? Oh. *That* beard." He touched the fine blond grizzle on his chin; he must've forgotten to shave this morning. His schedule was off, and his habits gone awry.

"You're crazy," Debbie said, and stepped into the water facing him.

14

She sat down straddling his lap, her smooth thighs pressed up against his sides. "I'm not gonna *bite* you," she said, because Lucky looked as if he were about to leap up to the ceiling and cling there like a cat. "You *are* shy, aren't you?" She shook up the can and squirted a gout of lather into her palm. "Well, that's really refreshin'." Slowly, with tender attention, she began to smear the lather over his cheeks, chin, and throat. "Don't worry," she told him when he flinched again. "I used to be a barber. No foolin'. That was one of the jobs I had in L.A." She leaned forward slightly, the razor ready, and her breasts brushed the hair on his chest.

He dared not move, even as her breasts pressed against

him, because she began shaving the left side of his face with long, slow strokes.

"You married, Lucky?" she asked him as she worked on his upper lip.

"No," he said carefully.

"Got a girlfriend?"

"No." He saw her look at him strangely. "I mean . . . I used to. What I mean is . . . we might be breaking up soon."

"I figured you had to have a girlfriend. If you're not gay, and you're not bisexual, and I *know* you're not neuter, then you had to have a girlfriend." She focused on his chin and gently shifted her position. Her body was slick with bubblebath. "Is she pretty?"

"Who?"

"Your *girlfriend*. Man, you've got a concentration problem! Hold still, now."

He did, as best he could. The razor slid over his throat like a feather. "Yes," he said. "Very pretty."

"What does she look like?"

"She . . . kind of looks like you," he said.

The razor stopped. "You're so sweet," Debbie told him, looking into his eyes. "I swear to God, how come I never met anybody like you before?"

"I guess . . . we don't move in the same circles."

She started shaving the right side of his face, smoothly, slowly. "Well, we've hooked up now. Better late than never, huh? Believe it."

He concentrated on staring at her eyes, shutting away the damp heat of her breasts against his chest and the firm pressure of her thighs on either side of him. The fire was still down in her eyes, but it was on a low burn now. Debra Rocks was sleeping.

Debbie finished the shave and washed the blade off in the bubbly water. Then she put the razor up beside the sink and slipped her arms around Lucky's neck. "You can fuck me now," she said softly.

"Please . . . don't use that word."

She frowned slightly. "What word?"

"You know. *That* word."

"Oh. You mean fu—" He put a finger to her lips, and she kissed it. "Okay. Just for you I won't, Mr. Shy." Her hand slipped down through the suds to his crotch. And lingered there.

She blinked slowly, staring at him. "Tell me one thing: why do you still have your underwear on?"

"I think bathtime's over," John said, and he worked loose from her and got out, the water streaming from his soaked Jockey shorts. He grasped a towel and wrapped it around himself.

"Wait a minute. Hold on." She lifted a finger, as if trying to mark a sentence in the air where things had slipped out of her control. "Are you turnin' *me* down?"

"No. I'm just . . ." Think fast! "Like I said, I haven't broken up with my girlfriend yet."

"Wait. Just wait. You're sayin' you're not gonna fu . . . not gonna be with me because of your other girlfriend?"

"That's right." He scooped up his jeans and got into them, wet Jockeys and all. He tried as best as he could to keep his eyes averted from her body.

Debbie laughed and smacked the water with her palm. "You are *weird!* I'm offerin' to you on a platter what a thousand guys would die to have, and you say no! Man, I was right! You're not from this world!"

"I'm not a thousand guys," he said, putting on his shirt. "I'm me."

"I thought you said I was beautiful."

"You are. But . . ." He pulled on his sweater. "This isn't right."

"Who says?" Her voice had taken on a hint of acid.

"You told me you were hurting when you came in from . . . uh . . . your work today. So the only reason you want me to make love to you is that you want to make sure I'll be back on Thursday." He saw her face tighten as he hit the truth nerve. "I told you I'd go with you to Los Angeles, and I will. Trust me."

She was silent for a moment, and then she also got out of the tub. John handed her a towel, which she wrapped around her body as gracefully as if it were yet another piece of sexy clothing. "Sorry," she said quietly. "Debra almost got out." She watched as he sat on the edge of the tub to put on his socks and sneakers. "I've never met anybody like you before. You know what I want. What do *you* want?"

The question was as blunt as a baseball bat, and it swung hard against John's brain. "I don't know," he admitted, and that was the truth too. He laced up his sneakers. "I think I'd better go now. Thanks for the dinner. And the shave too." He touched his smooth chin.

Debbie followed him to the apartment's door. "Listen . . . you can at least leave me your telephone number, can't you? If . . . like . . . I wanted to call you?"

John hesitated. He had his own private line, of course, but there was another problem to consider: if Debbie heard his voice without seeing his face, might she remember the voice of a priest in a confessional? "I move around a lot," he said lamely. "I'm hardly ever at home."

"Okay." Again there was a spark of pain in her eyes; she wasn't used to being rejected by a man, and it hurt like hell. "Then you take my phone number and you call me whenever you . . . like . . . get the urge." She went to a desk, opened a drawer, brought out a little card, and gave it to him. On it was printed simply D. STONER and a telephone number. He tucked the card into his jeans pocket.

She caught his arm as he started through the door. "Lucky? You do . . . like me a little bit, don't you?"

John looked into her face—that beautiful face with its smoldering gray eyes—and he thought: You just don't know. "I like you a lot," he answered, and she smiled and let him go.

Halfway down the stairs, it occurred to him to stop and check his pocket for the padlock key. It was right there where he'd put it. He went down to his bike, unlocked the padlock, and wrapped the chain around the handlebars. Then he walked the bike out onto the dark street, got on—his wet underwear wasn't going to make this a pleasure trip—and began pedaling toward Vallejo Street.

A battered Volkswagen van pulled away from the curb a block up from the apartment building and followed.

The first tendrils of fog were beginning to drift in from the bay. John crested a hill and could see the fog-smeared lights on the Golden Gate Bridge; then he started down again, pedaling at a slow, easy pace and wondering how he was going to get away from the church all day Thursday.

A van brushed past him, dangerously close, and John had to swerve violently away. He went up onto the curb between two parked cars, and he shouted, "Watch it!" as the van rounded the corner ahead and disappeared.

Somebody was drinking and driving, he thought. That was much too close. He pedaled on the sidewalk, past multicolored Victorian houses, and then he swung back onto the street again.

The van rounded the corner behind him, and followed as he turned south.

Monsignor McDowell would absolutely freak out if he had an inkling of what had happened tonight, John mused. That is, what had *almost* happened. Well, the monsignor would freak out, nonetheless. He swerved to avoid a series of potholes. The streets in this area weren't in such good shape, and some of the ornate streetlamps had burned out. Patches of fog rolled like ghost breath across the pavement.

He felt heat on the back of his neck.

He swiveled his head—and saw the van, right there, bearing down on him.

With a shout, he cut the handlebars to the right and narrowly missed crashing into the side of a parked Toyota; he skimmed past it, and the van skimmed past him by bare inches. He hit the curb, jarred up over it with a bounce that shook his teeth, and then he skidded to a stop just short of a wrought-iron fence.

The van went on about twenty yards. And then its brake lights flared. It stopped dead in the middle of the street.

John's heart was pounding, and he smelled the electricity of his own fear. That van again. Its driver was drunk or crazy. In either case, John didn't care to stick around. He saw the entrance to a narrow alley just ahead, and he pedaled toward it.

In the van's darkness, Travis slipped three bullets into his

Colt and clicked the cylinder shut. Then he laid the gun on the stained seat beside him and drove on, turning sharply right at the next corner and picking up speed.

As John came out of the alley, he saw the van roar around the corner and come after him.

His first thought was *Oh, Jesus.* He stayed on the sidewalk, veered away from the van, and started pedaling fast. Faster. Faster.

The van's tires jubbled over potholes, then hit smooth pavement again. Its engine snorted and popped like the ravenous, saliva-damp mouth of a hungry beast.

John's legs pumped furiously, his body thrust forward, head over the handlebars. His eyes were wide and glittering, and he knew now that he was a long way from home.

The van pulled up level with him. There was a flash and *crack!* from its interior.

John thought he heard a hornet zip past his head; he was aware of heat, the tang of scorched metal, his hair standing up at the back of his neck. He heard the glass of a window explode in the wake of his bicycle, and three seconds later he realized he'd just been shot at.

Maybe he peed in his pants; he didn't know, since he was already soaked, but his bladder certainly gave a lurch. Another alley entrance was ahead; he veered into it, his rear tire skidding, and as the alley took him, another bullet ricocheted like a scream off the red bricks.

John shot out of the alley's far side, swerved right, and sped across the street. Cold sweat had surfaced on his face. My God! he thought, amazed. My God, why would anybody want to kill *me?*

An engine roared. The van tore around the corner, coming out of the low-lying fog, and raced toward him.

John's foot slipped off a pedal. He lost control of the handlebars, and then he was going up onto the curb, trying to drag his feet against the pavement. He skidded into a group of garbage cans around a burned-out streetlamp, and there he fell off the bike into the embrace of Hefty bags.

Travis slowed the van, lifted the Colt, and wedged his arm up on the driver's door. The barrel glinted, steel-blue. He saw the man—the sonofabitching Satan who was trying to steal his date—get up on his knees and reach for his fallen bicycle. The bike rider looked up, and Travis grinned. He had a clear shot. Right between the eyes.

He squeezed the trigger.

The van's front-left tire hit a pothole.

John saw the flash of gunfire. And there was a *clang!* of metal against metal and sparks leapt off the streetlamp's pole right in front of his face.

The van went on maybe fifteen yards before its brakes squealed. It stopped, and Travis shouted, *"Shit!"* and reached back to his gunbelt for more bullets.

John scrambled onto his bike, turned in the opposite direction from the stopped van, and started pedaling frantically down a hill.

Travis got another bullet into the Colt, and then he glanced into the sideview mirror. He thrust the gun out, taking aim at the rider's back by the mirror's reflection. But in the next second the bike rider descended the grade and vanished into a pocket of fog. Travis slammed his fist down on the steering wheel, and he started to back up, but here came another car behind him. Travis pulled his gun hand back in. The driver stopped and honked his horn.

Travis started to get out and kill him, but that would be a waste. Anyway, a siren was wailing. Most likely whoever owned that broken window had called the cops. If that Satan showed up again, he'd be sorry as dust, like they said in Oklahoma. Travis shot the car's driver a bird, and then he sped on, turned left at the next corner, left again, and headed for safety.

15

"You're not taking your vitamins," the monsignor said sternly. "You look like you need some iron."

"No, sir," John said. "I'm fine."

"I know when somebody needs iron." McDowell opened a desk drawer and brought out a bottle of Iron Plus tablets.

"Here. I take 'em all the time. A man gets to a certain age, he needs a lot of iron."

"Yes, sir," John said, and put the bottle in his pocket.

"Okay, let's get down to business." McDowell opened a schedule book. "As you know, Father Stafford and I are going to the state Catholic convention in San Diego. We're leaving Saturday morning and we'll be back on Wednesday."

John blinked. "I . . . thought I was going to be a delegate too."

"No, I decided to take Father Stafford along. I don't think you're up to politics, do you?" His thick brows lifted.

"No, sir, I suppose I'm not," he had to agree. His bones were still trembling from what had happened last night, and he'd been able to sleep, fitfully, for only three hours.

"Right. So you'll be manning the helm, so to speak. I expect you to be up to the task."

John nodded, without fully hearing him. "Up to the task" meant strict office and consultation hours, duty in the confessional, on call and available at all hours for whatever might come up. That meant also, he realized, that from Saturday to Wednesday it would be impossible to see Debbie.

The hand of God had finally jerked him back to reality.

"Don't nod. Say 'yes,'" McDowell insisted.

"Yes, sir," John answered.

"All right. Take this." He handed John a list of functions and meetings scheduled between Saturday and Wednesday. They were all low-level priority, but required a Catholic presence. "I'll have more information for you on Thursday. Be here at ten o'clock."

"Yes, sir." He stood up, and that's when it hit him. "Ten o'clock? This Thursday?"

"There's a problem?"

The walls seemed to spin around him. John clutched hold of the monsignor's huge black desk. "No," he said finally. "There's no problem."

"Okay, good. Have a nice day."

John somehow got out of there, and he went straight to his apartment and took an iron pill. He stayed at the church all day, reading, studying, and praying with a vengeance. He didn't glance at the red X even once, though he knew exactly where it was all the time. He wanted to fill his mind up with crisp holiness, because it had an inclination to wander in two directions: toward the memory of Debbie, shaving him in a bubblebath with her breasts pressed against his chest, and toward the memory of gunfire.

He'd almost called the police when he'd gotten home. But of course there would have been complications. The police might have come here to see him, and the monsignor would find out, and want to know where he'd been riding his bike at that time of night. Complications best avoided.

Whoever had shot at him was crazy or high on drugs. It had been a chance encounter. John was alive, though the first bullet had come so close he'd found slivers of glass in the back of his sweater when he got home. Leave it at that.

On Wednesday afternoon, when his work and studying were done, he took off his collar, put on some casual clothes, and walked his bike down to the street. He had to lean over and pretend to be adjusting something on his bike, because Garcia, the maintenance man, went past him and said, "'Afternoon, Father." Then, when Garcia was out of sight, John got on his bike and pedaled away.

He didn't intend to go to Debbie's. Maybe he didn't. But that's where the wheels took him. Her Fiat wasn't at the curb. He drove past Giro's, wandered around the sinuous streets for about an hour, and then back to Debbie's. Still no Fiat. A working day, he thought. He felt a jab at his heart, and he went home.

He was wide-awake at six o'clock on Thursday morning, listening to the clock tick.

Monsignor McDowell expected him in his office at ten o'clock. That was when he would be on an airplane to Los Angeles, the lucky charm of a porno star who hoped today would be her big break. He got out of bed and took vitamins, and then he stood under the shower and just let it drench him. After his shower, he sat down and polished his black shoes.

The clock ticked on, and at a quarter to eight he dressed in jeans, shirt, and sweater and took his bike to the street. It would take him only fifteen to eighteen minutes to reach Debbie's apartment if he pedaled at a steady pace, but he wanted to get out early, before Darryl and the monsignor were in their offices.

He locked his bike to her stairs and went up to her.

She answered the door with a smear of white powder at her nostrils. "Lucky!" she said breathlessly. When she hugged him, he felt how she was trembling. She pulled him in, her hand clenched around his with desperate strength. "It's good you got here early, you can help calm me down. You want some coffee? I can't cook worth a shit, but I can make bitchin' coffee. It's black. You like yours black?"

"Black's fine."

She poured a cup for him, but she was shaking and the cup clattered on the saucer as she brought it to him. "I'm kind of nervous," she apologized. "I didn't spill any on you, did I?" He said no. "Uncle Joey told me he was bringin' you a suit. He said you and he had a real . . . how'd he put it . . . communion."

"Yes," John said, "I think we understood each other." He watched as Debbie drank down a cup of coffee, took a bottle of some kind of pills from a cupboard and popped two of those, and generally behaved like a pinball knocked between flippers. She went into the bedroom, emerged a few seconds later having taken off her white gown; now she had one leg in hose and one leg bare, her breasts fully exposed. "Do I sound hoarse?" she asked him. "I think I sound hoarse. My God, if I'm gettin' a cold I'll just *die!*"

"You sound fine," he assured her, averting his eyes from her breasts.

She struggled with her black bra, couldn't get the clasps done. "What time is it? Lucky, what time is it?"

"Eight-twenty-six."

"Damn it, I can't get this fuckin' thing on! I can't . . ." He heard her voice choke. "I can't . . . do anything right!"

He got up, walked to her, gently took the back of her bra, and clasped it. She was trembling, and she kept running her hands through her hair like fleshly brushes. "Shhhh," he whispered to her, and he put his arms around her from behind. "Come on, settle down."

Still shivering, she leaned her head back against his shoulder. The waves of her black hair floated before his face, and he could feel her heart beating—like a trapped bird trying to fly—through his hands. Lucky had a gentle touch, she thought, and she let his heat soothe her freezing bones. "I'm torn up," she said. "Just hold me, okay?"

He tightened his grip on her, and he smelled the perfume of her hair. He kissed the soft nape of her neck, his lips stinging, and then he rested his head against hers.

"Damn, I've gotta get ready!" she remembered, and she pushed out of his arms. She raced into the bedroom again, where John could hear her tearing through the closet.

Unicorn came scuttling to his feet, passed him, and climbed up into a cactus pot, where it busied itself digging into the sand.

At seven minutes before nine the door buzzer was pressed, and John answered it because Debbie was still in the throes of decision between a skirt-and-sweater outfit or her red dress. At the door stood a broad-shouldered, dark-haired young man who had the same chilly, heavy-lidded eyes as his father. "You Lucky?" he said, and John nodded. "This is for you." He thrust forward a dark blue suit, white shirt, and a paisley-print tie on a hanger. "To *borrow*," he added ominously. The young man bulled his way past John. "Hey, Debra!" he shouted toward the bedroom. "Pop's in the car! Move your ass!" Then his gaze locked, disdainfully, on John. "Well, put it on, cockface! You think you're supposed to just stand there and *look* at it?"

John took off his clothes and struggled into the suit; struggled because it was at least a size too small, and the shirt was starched as if it had been fashioned from platinum. He forced the gruesomely tight collar buttoned and put on the necktie. Had to tie it once, twice, a third time before Sinclair's son said, "Shit! Don't you know how to tie a fuckin' *tie?* C'mere!" He jerked John toward him by the paisley, roughly untied it, and started over again. "Debra!" the young man hollered. "Pop's parked in the handicapped zone!"

"I'm ready," she answered as she emerged from the bedroom.

Both John and the young man stared at her.

She had chosen her red dress, the same curved glimpse of fire John had seen when he'd come out of the confessional. Her makeup was perfect, her black hair glossy and brushed back from her face, cascading softly over her tanned shoulders. Her face had the glow of life and energy, and her gray eyes were level and steady; she was in control.

Debbie put on a light red jacket, got her clutch purse, and went to the door. Sinclair's son opened it for her, and John followed them down the stairs in his too-tight slacks.

The interior of the white Rolls reeked of cigar smoke. Joey Sinclair's other son was behind the wheel, and Sinclair himself sat in the huge expanse of the rear seat. "Debra, you're stunning," he said as he kissed her hand. Then, to John: "Hey, Lucky! You must be putting on a little weight!" John smiled grimly, and Sinclair dug an elbow into his son's side and laughed like a foghorn.

"This is the deal," Sinclair said as they drove to the airport. "Solly's meeting you in L.A. You've got reservations at Spago's at one-thirty." He glanced at John. "That's a *classy* place," he said, for Lucky's benefit. "Your audition's at three-thirty. Solly'll get you there on time. Then he'll get you back to LAX. Your plane leaves at eight-forty. I wanted to give you plenty of time, if the Bright Star boys want to take you to an early dinner." He took Debra's hands between his own. "Let's look at you. Open your mouth. Brush your teeth good? Want a mint? Chuck, give her a mint!" The young man instantly handed her a pack of Clorets. "Your hands are like ice," Sinclair said. "You toot some blow?"

"A little bit." She put on her sunglasses.

"Good. It'll keep you charged." Sinclair's head suddenly turned, and he stared forcefully at Lucky. He had felt the damn hustler watching him. "What're you lookin' at, you little fuckhead?"

"Joey!" Debbie said, a little sharper than she'd intended. "Please . . . Lucky's my friend."

"Oh, I know what he wants." Sinclair dug out his wallet and opened it, exposing a thick pad of green. He counted out four one-hundred-dollar bills, and then he slapped them down on John's knee. "That's Debra's play money. She sees something she wants, she gets it."

"Thank you, Uncle Joey," she told him, but she was staring out the window.

John and Debbie were sitting on an airplane within twenty minutes. At two minutes before ten, the jet's engines whined, and shortly afterward the shuttle-service craft began to taxi toward the runway.

Debbie grasped John's hand. "I get scared on takeoff," she explained.

He squeezed her hand, and he was looking at his watch as it ticked dead on ten o'clock and he knew Monsignor McDowell was glancing at his own watch.

The plane took off and headed south.

As they flew, Debbie took off her sunglasses and told him what movie she was auditioning for: "It's called *The Rad Brigade*. Rad for Radiation. See, it's a sci-fi movie about after a nuclear war, and these teenagers get all mutated and have super powers and stuff. Then they have to . . . like . . . fight the bad mutant gang. I'm up for the part of Toni, the hooker."

John couldn't help it; he smiled slightly and shook his head.

"It's a big part!" Debbie said. "Toni's a mutant too, see. Like . . . her boobs glow in the dark. But she protects the Rad Brigade from the Blaster Bunch, and she's a hero. Or heroine. You know what I mean."

He was afraid he did, and he figured the less he said about it, the better, so he kept his mouth shut.

The immense crazy-quilt sprawl of Los Angeles crept under the plane. Debbie put her sunglasses back on, took

John's hand, and held it tight. "You're gonna be lucky for me," she said. "I know you are. I knew it from the first minute we met. Scorpio and Pisces. Soul mates. I'm gonna do good, aren't I?"

"You'll do great," he told her, and he kissed her hand and rested it against his cheek.

The plane landed with a jolt. Solly Sapperstein—a thin, gangly man in his early forties, wearing a sharkskin suit and a brown Beatles-hair toupee—was waiting at the gate. He talked loud, with an abrasive northern accent, and kept looking everywhere else but at Debbie as he talked to her. To John he paid no attention at all. They went out to the huge crowded parking lot and got in Solly's black Cadillac, which had rusted scrapes along the sides.

Spago's, on Sunset Boulevard, was essentially a stratosphere-priced pizza parlor. The pizzas had things like goat cheese and rabbit livers on them. Debbie ordered only a salad, and kept her sunglasses on. John decided to go the salad route too, but Solly ordered a pizza with duck sausage and double garlic.

"So! Debra!" Solly said with a big-toothed grin. "I caught *Animal Heat* last week. You're hot, babe, totally nuclear."

"Thank you," Debbie said quietly, and she shifted a bit in her seat.

"You see it?" Solly asked John. Before John could decide what to say, Solly blasted on: "Got a guy in there with a schlong from here to Encino! If I had a schlong like that—whoa, baby!"

"Please keep your voice down," John told him, feeling as if he had gravel churning in his stomach.

"What's *his* problem?" Solly inquired of Debbie. "You did good in that flick, kid. Put on a real good show. You bring some of that fire into your reading today, you'll walk off with the part."

Debbie removed her sunglasses. Her eyes were building up to a blaze again; Debra Rocks was peering out. "Isn't there anybody I can fuck to get it?" she asked.

"No, babe. Not these guys. They're pros, and they don't play that game." He shrugged apologetically. "They put up five, six million bucks, they want to make sure they're getting acting talent, not . . ." He stopped himself, cleared his throat, and took another bite of pizza. "They don't play that game," he repeated.

Debbie put her sunglasses back on, shielding the eyes of Debra Rocks. She stared out the window, and John watched her scrape the polish from her thumbnail. He placed his hand over hers. "Take it easy," he said.

"Yeah, listen to your boyfriend," Solly advised.

It was a long drive to where the audition was going to be held. John sat in the back beside Debbie, his arm around her, and every so often he felt her shake as if electricity had pulsed through her. All during the flight and lunch he'd been glancing at his wristwatch and thinking about what he would've been doing at church; but now all that was forgotten, and he concentrated on comforting her.

The Bright Star studios, in Burbank, looked like a warehouse in need of paint. But the parking lot held BMW's, Mercedeses, and Jaguars, so John knew this must be the place.

"Stay with me," Debbie whispered, her voice quavering. They got out and followed Solly Sapperstein's quick stride into the building.

16

It was a quiet place, like a center of power. Solly announced who he was to the receptionist, and that he and Miss Debbie Stoner had an appointment with Mr. Carmine. The woman asked them to take a seat, and she pressed a buzzer and relayed Solly's message.

As they waited, Solly touched Debbie's shoulder and leaned across John to whisper, "I got your credits all fixed up. Not to worry, babe."

"Thanks," she said, her hands clasped in her lap.

Credits fixed up, John thought. What did that mean? Credits? As in movie credits? He looked at Debbie, and the scrunched-up, tense way she was sitting made him remember something that knocked a soft breath out of him: the Bright Star studio was auditioning Debbie Stoner, not Debra Rocks. They didn't know.

"Mr. Sapperstein? Miss Stoner?" the receptionist said. Debbie jumped. "Mr. Carmine will see you now. Room E, down the corridor to the right."

"This is it," Solly said. They stood up, and Debbie cleared her throat. She reached for Lucky's hand and pulled him close as they walked.

"Oh, I'm sorry, Mr. Sapperstein," the receptionist said as they started to pass her desk. "Just you and Miss Stoner."

John felt her nails grip into his skin.

"What's that mean? We're three people here," Solly said, smiling. "See? One, two, three."

The woman checked her appointment sheet. "I have down Mr. Solly Sapperstein and Miss Debbie Stoner for Mr. Carmine at three-thirty. Two names."

"Well . . . listen. He's her boyfriend. You know. Moral support."

"We've had this problem before, and Mr. Carmine is very specific." The woman's voice was cool, professional, and totally in charge. "No boyfriends, girlfriends, live-ins, or anyone in an audition but a legal representative. Those are the ground rules."

"You can bend the rules. Just a little? Huh?" Solly was dancing on ice. He glanced weakly at Debbie. "Sorry, babe. Lucky stays here."

"No! Solly . . . listen!" She grasped his hand with cold fingers. Behind her dark glasses, her eyes had panicked. "No! Lucky's got to be with me, all the way!"

"What's the big deal?" Solly shrugged and worked his hand away from her. "Lucky can sit right in here and wait. Then you can come out and give him the good news."

Debbie shook her head adamantly. "No! He's got to be with me!"

"Would you resolve this situation, please?" the receptionist prodded. "Mr. Carmine is waiting."

"It's all right," John told her. "I'll be right in here."

"No! Lucky . . . I want you in the audition! You've *got* to be there!"

John glanced at the receptionist; she was sharpening a pencil, grinding it around and around. Then he took Debbie's sunglasses off, and the abject fear in her eyes ripped his heart. He put his hands on her shoulders. "Listen to me." She started to speak, and he said, "Listen. You're an actress, aren't you?" She nodded, terrified. "Then go in there and *act*. Do the best acting you've ever done in your life, and know that I'm in there with you, all the way."

"I . . . can't . . ."

"You *can!*" John told her, and waited until he saw it sink in.

"Let's go, Debbie," Solly urged.

"Go on," John said softly. There was something else you were supposed to say. What was it? Oh yes. "Break a leg."

Debbie stared into his eyes, trying to draw strength from his center. It seemed as if he was the only thing solid in a slippery world. And then Solly tugged at her, and she knew that her chance was on the line. And on her own shoulders, too. She drew a breath, held it—then let it go and followed Solly down the corridor and to the right.

John walked back to a chair, sat down, and started reading a *Time* magazine. His own palms were wet.

Room E was a cluttered little soundstage, the dreary gray walls covered with cables and other equipment. Three men sat at a long table, and the one in the center—a young, fresh-faced man in a Hawaiian shirt and khakis—stood up as Solly and Debbie entered. His expression was a bit irritated, because he didn't like to be kept waiting. "Mr. Sapperstein? Miss Stoner? Good to see you again. You already know Mr. Katzenwaite." He indicated the gray-haired man on his left. "This is Mr. Royer." He motioned to the bearded man on his right. "Mr. Sapperstein, if you'll sit down back there, please?" Carmine nodded toward a chair at the rear of the room. "Miss Stoner." A motion to the chair in the middle of the room.

"Go for it, babe," Solly whispered, and left her alone.

On Debbie's chair was a script: *The Rad Brigade*. She picked it up and sat down, her legs like rubber bands and the pounding of her heart making her entire body shake.

"Just relax now, Miss Stoner," Carmine said. "We want to get a good reading from you, just sort of see what you can do. As I'm sure Mr. Sapperstein has told you, we were very impressed with your first audition. We think you've got a real grasp of Toni's character." He looked over at Royer, who had opened the girl's résumé and was skimming it. She'd done three films—sword-and-sorcery costume pieces—in Italy for Avanti Productions, and she had an impressive list of European modeling credits. "So let's begin, shall we?"

Debbie couldn't stop shaking. Damn it! she thought. God, I need some blow so *bad!*

"Just loosen up," Carmine advised; she was sitting as if on cactus needles. He picked up his copy of the script and paged to a place he had marked. "Let's start off with page thirty-nine. That's Scene Eight, where Gato meets Toni. I'll read Gato's part. Ready?"

"Yes." She wasn't sure he'd heard her. "Ready." Her voice sounded hoarse and unsteady. Straighten up, damn it! she thought. You're a professional!

"Starting from the top of page thirty-nine," Carmine said, sitting down again. "Okay, so what does it all mean, hotpants?"

"'It . . .'" Read it with *feeling*, dummy! "'It means, little boy, that . . . the Blaster Bunch won't let it go at this. Fuck, no. They're . . . going to come after you with all their guns blazing, and by the time they're finished with you, they—'"

"Wait, wait," Carmine interrupted. "Miss Stoner—Debbie—we'd like for you to emphasize your Southern accent, not try to mask it. Just go with it. Start again."

She nodded. "'It means, little boy, that the Blaster Bunch won't let it go at this. Fuck, no. They're gonna come after you with all their guns blazin', and by—'"

"Would you stand up, please?" Katzenwaite asked. "We'd like to see how you stand and deliver the lines."

"All right." She stood up and smoothed her dress. "'It

means, little boy, that the Blaster Bunch won't let it go at this.'" She looked up, trying to put some Scarlett in her face.

"'Fuck, no. They're gonna come after ya'll with all their—'"

"Not 'ya'll,'" Carmine said. "'You.' Just read the lines as they're written, please."

"Sorry." She cleared her throat, walked around the chair to get the blood circulating in her legs. Then took her spot and began again. This time they let her get beyond the third line. "'And if I were you, I wouldn't stick around. I'd find me a nice deep hole to crawl into.'"

"'Is that an offer?'" Carmine read, his own delivery flat and rushed.

"'If you've got the cash, I've got the sl—'"

"Hold it, please." Carmine was staring past her toward the door. "Who is that?"

She looked around with a gasp, hoping to see Lucky. Instead, it was another guy, this one wearing a black shirt with red polka dots. "It's Keith, Bill. I've got something you might want to see. Like right now."

"We're auditioning in here."

"Right *now*," Keith said, and he walked into the room, past Debbie, and toward the long table. He was carrying a satchel.

"Oh, for Christ's sake!" Carmine threw up his hands. "Debbie, pick it up, please, and go on."

"'. . . the slash,'" she continued, really putting a Southern drawl into it. "'I can take you places you ain't never dreamed of, little boy. I can grow you up in a real quick—'" She glanced up, and that's when she saw Keith pop open the satchel and slide the magazines out on the table in front of Carmine, Katzenwaite, and Royer.

"'—hurry,'" she whispered, and felt the world cave in on her head.

Carmine had put aside the script. He was looking at the magazines. One of them was a *Hustler,* one was an *Erotic Stars in Review,* and another was a cheapie she'd done a couple of years ago titled *Hot Cowgirl.*

Carmine stared at a picture in the *Erotic Stars* magazine. He showed it to the other two men, then whispered something to them. Debbie jumped as Solly placed his hand on her shoulder. "Steady, steady," he whispered.

Carmine looked up at her, his face pinched with anger. "This audition is over."

She couldn't make anything but a soft, stunned moan. Solly stepped forward, a frozen grin on his face. "Hey, chief! Hold on a sec! You're not gonna jerk the rug out from under us, are you?"

"You're damned straight I am, *Mr.* Sapperstein." Carmine shook his head incredulously. "You're either crazy or you've got iron balls, my friend. You know, your reputation had preceded you here. Was it last April you tried to pass off a stroke actress to Vista Pictures for a *family* film? We've got a research and legal department to check people out, Mr. Sapperstein. They don't just sit on their asses and draw fifty grand gratis."

"Listen . . . come on. Bill, right? Be a pal, Bill. Look at Debbie." He pushed his hand into her back to make her stand up straight. "She's got presence, Bill. Star quality. Yeah, maybe she's raw, but you put the time and money into her and you can develop—"

"We can develop a lot of money blown on coke," Royer told him. "We're not in the business of financing drug habits for porn stars. We're working with millions of bucks here! You think we're going to toss it to . . ." He glanced at the magazine again. "Debra Rocks? Man, you're crazy to have even brought that in here!"

The pressure of Solly's hand on her back was hurting her. That pain stirred up other, worse pains, until she was aflame with pain, suspended in a universe of it. She clenched her hands into fists at her sides and listened to these men talking about her as if she were a *thing*.

"You can use her," Solly insisted. "Let the word leak who she really is. It'll boost your box office."

"Yeah, and destroy all our artistic integrity," Katzenwaite said. "Forget it."

"This audition is over," Carmine repeated, and he picked up his script and started to stalk away.

Her voice cracked out like the sound of a whip on bloody flesh: "No, it is *not!*"

All of them stopped—Carmine, Katzenwaite, Royer, and Keith—and they stared at what stood before them.

She had felt the fire of Debra Rocks leap from her pores, and she saw that awesome heat scorch their faces. Even Solly stepped back, because her eyes blazed with determined power and the scared little Southern girl who had been there just a second before had vanished. Everyone jumped when she threw the script to the floor. Her backbone was as rigid as an iron bar, and as she walked toward the table she was all tiger and suffocating steam.

Debra Rocks picked up the copy of *Hustler*, flipped it open to her nude centerfold, and pushed the pink right up into Carmine's face. "Don't you like it, Billy?" she asked, velvet-on-steel. "Oh, come on and tell me how much you like it."

"Miss . . . Stoner," he said, his eyes wide. "There's no need to—"

"The name is *Rocks.* Oh, you know there's a need, Billy. You know it." She licked her finger until it glistened, and then she ran that finger across his lower lip. Their saliva intermingled. "What're you thinkin', Billy? Thinkin' . . . hard thoughts?" Her megawattage gaze wandered to Royer. She took a step forward and hooked two fingers up his nostrils. "You got a coke sniffle, baby? You like a little blow now and then? Oh, big man, I can show you places to lick coke from that you never dared dream about." Another step, and she was in front of Katzenwaite. "Oh, let's you and me talk artistic integrity, baby. Like stirrin' up horny teenagers and makin' 'em think they're dead if they're not fuckin' by fifteen." Her hips made a slow, grinding circle. "Look at it, Katzy. Think about it." Her fingers flicked over her thighs. "You're standin' real close to the fire, Katzy. Ohhhhh . . . slide the wood in and let it burnnnn . . ." She drifted to Keith, picked up *Hot Cowgirl,* and opened it to a photograph that she knew was in there. "See that guy on top of me, Keithy baby? He was twelve inches, and I took him alllll in. Every." She grasped his hand and sucked a finger into her mouth. "Single. Inch," she said, and spat his member out.

Keith moaned softly. Carmine's hand had gone to his crotch.

Debra Rocks backed toward the doorway, her fingers beckoning them to follow if they dared. Katzenwaite looked as if he were about to leap over the table, and Royer's face had frozen into a strained rictus. Solly staggered back and bumped into the wall. "I'm in a new movie," she said huskily. *"Animal Heat.* It's in one of those theaters with reallllll sticky floors. Now, when I walk out that door, you're all gonna be thinkin' how soon can you get to that theater, and how soon can you be lickin' your lips over what was just starin' you in the face. You remember my name, and you call it out when you get lonely. Hear, ya'll?" And with a sultry, soul-killing smile, she said, *"Now* the audition is over," turned her back on them, and walked proudly through the door.

Solly hurried after her, and caught up with her long-legged stride. "Whoa, baby!" he exclaimed, his cheeks slick with perspiration. "That was some job!"

Her face had tightened. The fire in her dark-hollowed eyes had dimmed, but it had burned a little more of her insides away. "I'm an artist," she said, staring straight down the long chilly corridor. "My paintbrush is a man's cock."

John looked up from his magazine and saw them coming. Instantly he could tell that things had gone wrong. He stood up. Debbie strode past the receptionist, stuck a bird-finger right into the woman's face, and kept going through the door. John followed, knowing the luck had run out.

"Where to? You want a drink?" Solly asked as he pulled the Cadillac out of the parking lot.

"No. Just drive."

"What happened?" John asked. "You look—"

"You should've been in there with me!" she snapped, and something in her eyes went savage. "If you'd been in there, everything would've gone all right!"

"They found out about Debra Rocks," Solly explained. "Perverts must've combed the porn shops."

"The part sucked, anyway," Debbie said coldly. "They wanted me to play a slut." She popped open her clutch purse. Her hand slid in and came out with a small gold box. Then she pulled out a straw. Her hands were shaking, and a sheen of sweat glistened on her face. "I don't need the bastards," she said. "I don't need any of 'em!" She started to slide the lid of the gold box open.

John had had enough. There was no way in Heaven or Hell that he could sit beside her and watch her snort up that crap again. His hand flashed out, grabbed the box away from her. Before she could move, John opened his door and flung it out. There was a puff of white on the roadside, and then they had left it behind. Debbie stared at him openmouthed. "You're killing yourself with that stuff," he said, his face aflame with anger. "I don't want you to—"

"You *bastard!*" she screamed, and attacked him.

It wasn't a halfhearted attack. It was a clawing, shrieking, frenzied attack that drove John against the door and made Solly swerve the car and shout, "Hey! Cut the crap!" But Debbie was listening to no one now but her inner demons. She swung her fingers at Lucky's eyes, grabbed his hair, and banged his head against the doorframe. She clutched at his throat, dug her nails in, hammered at his face and head with her fist, all the time screaming and cursing. Solly kept jerking the wheel, looking back over his shoulder to make sure the wild bitch didn't jump his ass too; the Cadillac lurched drunkenly down Olive Avenue.

She punched John on the side of the face, a glancing blow, and that was it. He grabbed her wrist, shoved her back with his other hand, and threw his body on top of her, forcing her down against the seat. Her knees pounded at his ribs, but he got those down and then she reached up for his eyes, her face twisted with fury. He dodged just before he lost his vision, and she grabbed his collar and started trying to bang his head against the roof. "Stop it!" he shouted, gripping her wrists. "Debbie, stop it!"

He didn't know exactly when it happened. But suddenly her arms were around his neck, trying to pull his mouth down on hers, and her body was hot and thrashing and the lips in her tormented, lust-puffed face moaned, "Hurt me, Lucky. Hurt me, hurt me, I want you to hurt me . . ."

John recoiled, breaking her grip. She sat up, reaching for him, saying, "Hurt me, hurt me."

"I don't want to hurt you!" he said. "I love you!"

And there it was, spilled out like a glassful of forbidden wine.

Her hands stopped short of clawing his suit jacket off. Her face was frozen between a sneer and a moan. It stayed that way for a second or two—and then he saw her lower lip tremble, and a single tear streaked down her left cheek.

"You . . . should've been with me," she whispered brokenheartedly. "Why weren't you with me?"

The tears came then, and she sobbed as if someone had delivered a brutal blow to her stomach. She reached for him, a drowning figure reaching for a life-ring, and he put his arms around her and pulled her close. She wedged her head against his neck, and her tears soaked his collar.

"Hanky?" Solly offered one over the seat, but it had green flecks on it and John said, "No. Thanks anyway."

He put the handkerchief away. "Lucky, where you want me to drive to? I mean, it's a big place."

"I don't care," John answered. "Just somewhere pretty."

As Debbie continued to sob, her hands clutching at John's shoulders and her body bowed in defeat, John did what he had been unable to in the confessional. He gently stroked her hair, hugged her body tightly against his, squeezed his eyes shut as her sobs racked his own body. Finally, her despair quietened if not exhausted, she lay silently beside him, her head on his shoulder, and stared at the world through swollen eyes. John took off his paisley tie and offered that to her as a handkerchief, but she didn't move to accept it.

"Malibu comin' up!" Solly told them, and his exuberance clued John that the man might have started out as a tour-bus driver.

John had never seen Malibu before, but he'd heard a great deal about it. The late-afternoon light, however, didn't reveal what he'd expected. The beaches of Malibu were gray, and the houses looked to John simply like oversize weather-beaten shacks. Debbie perked up a little bit, lifted her head, and said, "I used to live there," pointing to a dreary beach shack, one of what looked like hundreds jammed together on the continent's edge. Then Debbie lay back against him again, drained by memories.

Solly kept driving, as the red sun began to sink. The beach had eroded, and cracks had winnowed across the highway. Finally Solly slowed, turned the Cadillac, and headed back to L.A. "That's the beach," Solly said. "Where to next, chief?"

Debbie spoke up: "Forest Lawn."

Solly laughed uneasily. "That's a cemetery."

"I know it's a cemetery, numb nuts." Her voice was still weak, but it was regaining power. "Take me there."

"Okay, okay. You don't have to be rude." And Solly drove toward her destination.

17

By the time they reached the particular plot Debbie guided Solly to in the huge expanse of Forest Lawn Cemetery, the sun had sunk low. The orange light had faded to purple, and now edged into blue.

Debbie said, "Stop here," and she got out and walked through the headstones and ornate markers to the grave she sought. She stood over it, just staring down, and didn't move when John reached her. He saw a name on a little bronze plate in the ground: Lynn Phillips. John saw also that she'd died in mid-August of this last summer, and she'd been twenty-three years old.

"Lynn was my roommate for a while," Debbie explained. "We were best friends. I mean . . . we didn't have sex or anything. We were like sisters. Pals." She sighed, a pained sound. "I helped her pick out her name: Cheri Dane. Know why? 'Cause she was hooked on cherry Danishes. She used to go out to the Farmers Market and bring back a sackload. So we really had a laugh over that name, because we knew all across America guys were turned on by a girl named after a cherry Danish." She smiled faintly, but it didn't stick.

"What happened to her? Drugs?"

"No!" Debbie looked sharply at him. "Cheri was clean! Well . . . she was gettin' that way. No, somebody got into her apartment, over in Santa Monica. Whoever it was . . . tied her up and drowned her in her bathtub." She shrugged, but it was to hide a shudder. "The cops never found out who it was. I don't think they looked too hard. You know what they call us? Freak fodder. I'm beginnin' to believe it."

"Why is that?"

"Oh . . . another friend of mine hit the dirt last week." It was said with false bravado and masked a core of hurt. "Janey McCullough. And the real gut-clencher is that we all had a hit together: *Super Slick*. At least, it was a hit in the business. It played everywhere, and did six high figures in videotape. Not that we saw very many of the bucks. I mean, somebody's gettin' rich, but it's sure not us." She stared down at the marker. "Lynn, how many times did I tell you? If you don't know the face, don't let 'em into your place. Hell, she would've given the devil a thousand bucks and waited for change." Debbie saw a bouquet of fresh flowers on another grave a few yards away; she went to it, picked some of the flowers out of the vase, and sprinkled them around Lynn's marker. "There you go, babe," Debbie said. "Let's get you pretty."

John glanced at his wristwatch. "We'd better go, maybe grab a sandwich somewhere before we catch our plane."

Debbie walked away from the grave, and then she abruptly stopped again. She looked around, to all points of the compass. "It's the blue world now," she said in a hushed and respectful voice.

"What?" He hadn't fully understood her.

"The blue world," she repeated. "Listen." She put her finger to her lips.

He did. The cemetery was an oasis of silence. Dying light flared on the towers of buildings off in the haze, but cool blue shadows had pooled around the headstones and monuments, and even the air itself had turned to indigo. A solitary car moved along one of the cemetery's streets, and the twilight breeze stirred a palm tree's fronds.

"See?" Debbie said quietly. "When everything turns blue, and the whole world seems to be holdin' its breath. That's the blue world. My grandmomma and me used to sit out on the porch in the twilight, and we'd rock in the glider and she'd sing me these songs her momma sang to her a long time before. Songs like that don't change; just people's voices do." She turned her face and smiled, and John saw she was looking to the southeast.

"Grandmomma said the blue world was the entrance to the night, but it wasn't anything to fear. Oh, no! She said the blue world came back again, at dawn, and then it was the way out of the night. She said . . . the blue world was God's way of sayin' there would always be a new day." Debbie looked at him and gave a bitter grimace. "I was raised a Baptist. Isn't that a big damned hoot?"

John didn't hoot; he didn't speak either. He just let her go on, and watched her face as she drifted back into time.

"I haven't thought about that for . . . it seems like forever," she said. "The blue world. Maybe . . . I just stopped lookin'. I don't know." She walked to a monument, leaned against it, and traced her fingers over the carved white marble. "It's strange, huh? People live and die every day, and you never know a thing about 'em. Everybody just goes on about their business, like a big boilin' pot. I mean . . . we're all in it together, aren't we?" She gazed at Lucky, her eyes glittering in the blue half-light, and then she looked away. Her fingers tightened on the marble. "I've gotta get out of this," she said. "I've gotta . . . figure things out. Somethin' went wrong. It went wrong, and I don't know where it went wrong." She lowered her head, and John heard her choking on a sob. It was the same sound of a lost, crying child that he'd heard in the confessional, and his heart yearned to give her peace. He started toward her, to rest his hand on her shoulder and tell her his name was not Lucky but John Lancaster, and that he was a Catholic priest.

"Don't touch me," she said as he reached out. "Okay? Don't touch me just yet."

John stopped. He pulled his hand back, and the moment spun away like a dead leaf.

"I'm sorry." She reached out and grasped his fingers. "I'm a bitch sometimes." She examined his face and touched a place on his left cheek that made him wince. "I bruised you," she said. "Hell, maybe I ought to get into foxy boxin' and oil-wrestlin', huh?"

"I wouldn't be surprised."

"Listen . . . I'm not mad at you. I knew me gettin' that part was a real long shot. It wasn't you that screwed me up. You're still my Lucky, right? Soul mates?"

"Right," John said.

She nodded. "Believe it." She paused, staring toward the grave of her friend. The blue world was passing now, and night's edge was coming over the horizon. "Come on," she said, and tugged him toward Solly's car. "I'll buy you a burger."

At eight-forty-six their jet was taking off from LAX. It turned above the hazy fire of the metropolis and arrowed north.

By ten o'clock they were leaving San Francisco International, heading along the Bayshore Freeway in Joey Sinclair's white Rolls-Royce.

Sinclair lit a cigar, and the flame painted his face. His eyes glared at John for a moment; then his attention drifted to Debbie. "Solly called me after you left L.A.," he said in a subdued voice. "That Solly." He shook his head and puffed blue smoke. "You put him up to bat, and he can't hit nothing but foul balls."

"It wasn't Solly's fault," Debbie told him. She had her sunglasses back on, staring at the red circle of Uncle Joey's cigar. "They found out, that's all."

"Yeah." Sinclair sat without moving for a long time, his eyes half-closed and the cigar's fire glowing and waning. The lights of San Francisco gleamed ahead. John saw Sinclair's hand slip to Debbie's knee, and the older man patted it gently. "Don't worry, baby. You're a star. I snap my fingers, you've got a flick opening in three hundred theaters. What more could you want?"

She didn't answer. Her dark glasses caught a spark of neon, and John saw her stare at her hands, clenched into fists in her lap.

"Chuck? See our friends upstairs, please," Sinclair told his son when they'd parked in front of Debbie's building. A light rain was falling, the street like black glass. Debbie got out, but as John started to, Sinclair's hand closed on his sleeve. "Hey, Lucky," the man said quietly and forcefully. John had no choice but to pause. "You queer?" Sinclair asked.

"No."

"You got AIDS?"

"No."

"Good, 'cause Debra likes you. I can tell. She gets hot for a guy, it shows on her face. You ever done any film work?"

"No," John said, his throat dry.

"Doesn't matter. How about this deal: you and Debra in a movie together? It'd just be a bit part for you, but we'd do some photo spreads and get 'em in the glossies like *Chic* and *High Society.* Then we'd let it leak that you two are fucking each other in real life." He removed the cigar. "See the beauty of it?"

John could do nothing but just stand and stare at him, his mouth partly open, as waves of disgust crashed through him.

"Yeah, I thought you might go for that idea. You think about it and let Uncle Joey know." He released John's sleeve. "I want the suit back, but you keep the money," Sinclair said. "Call it a down payment, right?" He laughed and shut the door, and a little stinking whiff of cigar smoke floated past John's nostrils before the rain shredded it.

Up in Debbie's apartment, Chuck looked at John as he came through the door and said, "Off. The duds. Now." John started to walk back to the bathroom, but Chuck caught his arm. "You deaf, Lucky? Take 'em off. I gotta go."

John stripped off his borrowed suit, and in another moment he was standing in his underwear and socks. Chuck put the clothes back on their hanger and called, "I'm gone, Debra! See you tomorrow, babe!" He went out the door, and it thunked shut behind him.

"Tomorrow?" John heard water running in the bathroom. He walked in and found her vigorously brushing her teeth, stripped down to her hose, panties, and bra. "What's tomorrow?"

"Working day," she said, her mouth full of green foam. She spat into the sink. "We're shootin' in Chinatown. Want to go with me, kinda hang out?"

"No." He steadied himself against the bathroom door. Unicorn was in his sandbox, listening like a flat sphinx. "I've got to get dressed and go—"

"No!" Debbie said suddenly, her eyes widening. She spat the rest of the toothpaste foam out. "Lucky, no! You're gonna stay the night with me, aren't you?"

"I can't. Really. My . . . uh . . . other girlfriend—"

"Screw your other girlfriend!" she said. "I mean . . . *don't* screw her. Lucky, I need you to be with me tonight. I don't want to be alone. Okay?"

"Debbie . . . I . . ."

"I've got fresh sheets," she told him. "Look. Let me show you." She took his hand and pulled him into the bedroom before he could brace his legs to resist. The bed was made—one of the tasks she'd done when she'd been zipping around this morning—and now she threw back the spread to show him the crisp pale blue sheets. "I put these on 'cause I kinda thought they went with your eyes and, you know, we could celebrate."

"I don't think there's much to celebrate."

"Yes there is!" She paused, thinking. "Our plane didn't crash."

He laughed in spite of himself, and she put her arms around him and held tightly. "If you don't want to fu . . . if you don't want to, like, be disloyal to your girlfriend, I can understand that. I don't *like* it, but I understand it. Just come to bed with me and hold me, Lucky." Her hands gripped into his shoulders. "Okay? Just hold me?"

"Okay," John said, and this time nothing in him screamed that it was wrong.

He got into bed, still wearing his underwear, and she slid in beside him with her hose, bra, and panties on. "This'll be like a pajama party, huh?" she asked him excitedly. He put his head on the pillow, and her head with its long black hair found his shoulder. Then she twisted her body around to face him, her hands stroking his chest. "We must've met in another life," she said. "That's why I feel so good around you. Maybe we were lovers in ancient Egypt, huh? I want to do you, Lucky."

"What?"

"I want to do you." She touched his left earlobe. "You know. I want to pierce your ear for you."

"No, thanks."

"It'll be sexy! Come on, let me! I'll put ice on it to get it numb, and—"

"No!"

"Either you let me pierce your ear," she said defiantly, "or I'm gonna go to my cookie jar and have a white taste."

He looked at her; she wasn't fooling. Oh, my dear Lord . . . ! he moaned inwardly. He closed his eyes. Opened them again. She was still waiting for his answer. "Will it hurt?" he asked.

"Sure. That's what it's all about." Then she smacked him on the stomach. "No, dummy! The ice deadens your earlobe, and I'll burn the needle before I use it." She got up and hurried to the kitchen, where John could hear her scooping ice into a plastic bowl. He looked down at the floor. Unicorn had scuttled beside the bed and settled himself into a corner; the damned crab looked as if it were smiling in expectation of quite a spectacle.

Debbie returned with the bowl of ice, a cold wet cloth, and a needle. She lit a match and held it under the needle's tip as John pressed two pieces of ice on either side of his lobe. Then she straddled his chest. "Okay, turn your head this way. You feel that?" She pinched his earlobe, and he said, "Yes. No. Wait. No, I didn't feel it."

"Good. Hold still, now, this'll just take a sec." She leaned forward, the needle ready.

He remembered a dentist saying that to him, just before the pain almost blasted his molars out.

The needle touched his flesh. John grasped hold of Debbie's thighs. "Little sting," she said, and then the needle slid in.

This, then, must be love.

Tears squeezed from his eyes, and he bit his lower lip. "Easy, easy," she whispered. "Almost done." The needle was in, and she was drawing it all the way through the lobe. She caught the drops of crimson on the cold cloth. "One more time through," she told him. The needle entered the raw-edged hole. She let it stay there, half-in and half-out. "I knew a guy with five studs in one ear," she told him. "You want to go for two?"

"No!" he said quickly, before that idea locked in her mind. "One's plenty."

"Well, I think you're gonna look real good." She leaned forward, her hair brushing his face, and worked the needle gently in and out for a moment. "Got to make sure it doesn't clot up. You know, the hole'll grow shut real soon if you don't keep it open." She removed the needle, and her hand went to her hair and shoveled it back. John could see that there were three studs in each of her earlobes. She took one out of her left lobe. "Wear this one. It's a real diamond. A rough diamond, I mean. But it's got a shine to it, see?" She showed him its hard glint, then pushed the stud into his ear—a new level of pain—and capped its sharp little point on the other side. "All done," she told him.

Hail Mary, Mother of Grace, he thought. I didn't scream.

She caught one of his tears on her fingertip, and she licked it off. Then she put the torture equipment away and rested her head against his shoulder, her fingers gliding back and forth across his chest.

Sometime during the night, when rain thrashed against the bay windows, John awakened to the sound of her crying.

She had turned away from him, her back pressed against his side, and she was sobbing—muffled, horrible sounds—into a pillow. When he shifted his position a half-inch, her crying immediately halted on a strangled note.

He lay where he was, his eyes closed and burning, and Debbie Stoner sobbed her soul out.

18

A knock at the door. An impatient knock, John thought. He went to the door and opened it.

Father Stafford stood there. "Well, the prodigal returns! John, where in the world *were* you yesterday? McDowell was tearing the place apart looking for you!" Darryl's gaze was suddenly riveted, and John knew why. "John . . . tell me what that is in your ear."

"A rough diamond," he answered, and he went back into his bathroom to finish splashing cold water on his face. It was eight o'clock on Friday morning, and John had returned from Debbie's apartment barely thirty minutes before.

"Oh." Darryl stood in the doorway. "Great. Well, that explains everything. You disappear all day—and night—without warning, and suddenly you're back with a pierced ear. Would you explain—" He stopped, and looked quickly to his left. John felt a leap of terror, because Darryl had just glanced at the apartment door and John heard someone else walk in.

"Father Lancaster," the monsignor said quietly. He pushed Darryl aside. "You missed our conference yesterday morning. I knocked at your door and there was no answer, so I had Garcia unlock it. Strange to say, you were not here. Neither were you in any of the other places I checked. Would you mind enlightening me as to your whereabouts?"

"I . . ." His heart boomed. What to say, when there was no explanation? Or, at least, not an explanation the monsignor would care to hear. "I . . . was with a sick friend."

"Oh!" McDowell glanced at Darryl, his face expressing cynical sympathy. "John was with a sick friend! All day and all night, without a word, and not even a telephone number in case we had an emergency. Now, isn't that a fine picture of responsibility?" He glared again at John, and behind the monsignor's back Darryl made a throat-slashing gesture.

"My friend needed me." John felt a touch of anger redden his cheeks. His heart was pounding hard.

"What if *we* needed you? Don't you think you have a duty to— What is *that?*"

"That what?"

"That. That! Right there! In your ear! What is that in your ear?"

McDowell was shouting, the harsh voice like explosions off the bathroom tiles. John touched his diamond stud, but of course there was no way to hide it. "Take it out!" McDowell commanded. "Take it out, this minute!"

The voice hurt his eardrums. It was a voice without sense or reason, just the snort of a bull about to charge a scarlet flag. John felt his face redden a deeper shade, which simply served to make the old bull's eyes flare wider. And as he looked into those eyes and saw the callous stone behind them, John was aware of a jam in the river of his obedience, like logs crashing together and damming a flow that had always run the safe, well-ordered route.

"No, sir," he said, surprisingly calm about it now that he'd made his decision. "I won't take it out."

McDowell gasped, absolutely gasped. John thought his eyes had bulged, and the small purple veins on his nose— wine veins, John had always thought of them—swelled. "You *will!*" McDowell thundered. "Or I'll jerk it out myself!"

"If having a pierced ear makes me less of a priest," John said, "you can flush yourself down the toilet and I'm walking out of here."

Now even Darryl looked stricken, as if he was on the verge of a heart attack.

McDowell moaned, shivered, and stuttered like a furnace about to blow.

"This is my apartment. You had no right to come in here when I was absent." He wanted to stop; he knew he had to stop, but his mind was casting out the long-stifled thoughts. "I was with a friend all day yesterday and last night. I'm sorry I couldn't let you know where I was, but I just couldn't. Does that make me less of a priest too? Can't I have friends? Can't I . . . have *freedom?*"

"You've gone mad," McDowell managed to say.

"No, sir. I've gone sane. Look at us! Three blackbirds in a golden cage! And we sit in here and study and read and do *not* connect with *that!*" He emerged from the bathroom, passing McDowell, and pointed through his window. "The real world. Where everybody isn't a saint, sir. Oh, we're full of great advice and platitudes! We speak, and medieval iron falls out of our mouths! We've *got* to come to grips with the world, sir! With real people! Flesh and blood, not . . . marble statues and numbers on a damned budget sheet!"

"Holy Lord," McDowell breathed, retreating. "I think we need an exorcist."

"And that's just what I mean!" John said. "We've got to stop putting all the blame on Satan, and start understanding why there's evil in *humans.* And when we do come eyeball-to-eyeball with Satan, we shouldn't blink and run back to the church! No! We ought to have guts enough to follow the devil to hell and fight him on his own turf!" He looked from the monsignor to Darryl and back again, his eyes anguished. "If *we* don't, who will?"

Darryl lowered his face and put his hand to his forehead. He guessed now what had sparked this tirade: John's visit to the porno parlors of Broadway.

"I'm sorry," John went on. Then corrected himself. "No, I'm not sorry. That's how I feel. I'm not sorry at all."

"I am," the monsignor said, recovering his icy composure. "You're in serious need of counseling, John. Serious need. At ten o'clock I'll have a list for you of functions and meetings you'll attend while Father Stafford and I are at our convention. When we return, you and I are going to have an in-depth discussion about your future at the Cathedral of St. Francis." He started to stalk out, then halted. "Can I trust you to attend those functions and your duties as a priest in this parish, or shall I contact Bishop Hagan?"

"You can trust me," John told him, and McDowell strode quickly away.

"Your can is in the jam," Darryl said. "Have you flipped your lid, John? This isn't like the old you!"

"The old me is dead," John answered. "And thank God for it. I was deaf, dumb, and blind."

"And now you think you can see?"

"Now I'm not afraid to look."

Darryl started to respond, but the words crumpled to ashes before he could get them out. Their residue left a bad taste in his mouth. "I don't know," he finally said, and threw up his hands. "I just don't know." He walked away, befuddled and furiously trying to sort it all out.

John closed the door and returned to the bathroom. He took a One-A-Day and an iron pill. His eyes looked like red jellyfish. He'd slept hardly at all after awakening to hear her crying, but he hadn't moved again all the long, rainy night. He'd known she didn't want him to see her like that, defenseless and beaten, holding a pillow and sobbing into it. He wasn't going to be able to see her today; nor tomorrow, nor any day through Wednesday. He yearned to tell her who he really was, but for that he needed to be with her, in person. It would be a shock, to say the least. No, no; she wasn't ready for that yet, and neither was he.

He went to the window and peered out at the wet street. How was he going to stay in contact with Debbie—look after her, as it were—and still carry out his duties here? It was impossible! His first responsibility was here, yes, but still . . . there was no telling what she might get into if he wasn't around.

Right. She's a big girl, jerk! he told himself. She got along for twenty-six years without you, didn't she? Yeah, he thought, and look at the mess she's in. He feared she would do something rash, because she was torn up about not getting the movie part, or that she was going to overdose on cocaine, or . . . well, the list of what-ifs was endless and scary. I need to be in two places at once, he thought. Or at least I need another set of eyeballs.

Eyeballs. Hold it.

John went to the Yellow Pages. He found the listing for Detective Agencies, wedged between Designers, Underground Earth Houses, and Devotion for the Day. Then he looked through the agency listings until he found one close to the church; it was Investigations Unlimited, and its address was about four blocks north. The ad said the agency specialized in Missing Persons, Marriage and Business Suspicions, Runaways, Surveillance and Photography, Bodyguarding and Security. At the bottom of the ad was "The Hoss Is the Boss."

Well, John thought, it was worth a shot. He particularly liked the Bodyguarding and Security part. He dialed the number.

A gruff, throaty voice answered on the third ring. "Investigations Unlimited. The Hoss Is the Boss."

"I'd like to make an appointment, please. For today, if possible."

"Hold on a minute. Let me check with my secretary." There was a pause. Then: "How about thirty minutes?"

"No . . . it'll have to be this afternoon. Say one or one-thirty?"

"One it is, friend. Got you down on my schedule book in red ink. What's the name?"

"Father John Lancaster."

"Oh. I see," the voice said carefully. "I'm Hoss Teegarten. You come on in at one, I'll take care of you pronto."

John hung up. Sat there for a moment wondering how he was going to pay for this. Well, he still had three hundred and sixty-two dollars of Joey Sinclair's money. It would be put to good use after all. Then John looked up Florists, and he called one with an address in North Beach and ordered a dozen red roses to be delivered to the apartment of a Miss Debbie Stoner.

19

On Greenwich Street, a creaking elevator took John up to the fifth floor of a building that had so many patched earthquake cracks in it he was amazed it hadn't slid apart like slices of cheese on a slick platter.

The office of Investigations Unlimited had one of those frosted-glass doors straight out of *The Maltese Falcon,* and John felt a little like a hunched Peter Lorre as he rapped on the glass. He expected to hear a Bogart snarl.

Instead, there was nothing but an erratic *thump . . . thump.* Then a pause. Another *thump.* And another one, quickly following. He knocked on the glass again, louder. Still a *thump.* A silence. *Thump . . . thump.* Followed by the squeal of a chair's springs.

John turned the door's handle and opened it.

It was a single small room with a desk, a file cabinet, and stacks of newspapers, letters, and other papers in cardboard boxes. There was no secretary, and the window was grimy. A coffee cup and an ashtray full of cigarette butts sat on the desk; a cigarette was still smoking. John craned his neck in and looked for signs of life.

A fat man in a red-striped shirt and overalls was plucking darts out of a taped-up, perforated photograph of Jim and Tammy Bakker. He had a Walkman on his cueball-bald head, and even from this distance John could hear cranked-up rock music. The man suddenly looked toward the door, his electric-blue eyes widening. He had a curly, unkempt ginger-hued beard. His gaze skidded toward the grinning dartboard and then back to John. "Friends of yours?" he asked.

"Certainly not." He hesitated, about to turn and leave.

"Come on in!" Hoss Teegarten said with a broad smile. He stuck Tammy right between the eyes. Then he stripped off the Walkman—The Doors' "Riders on the Storm" pounded out—and popped the tape out. "Sit down, Father," he said, motioning with a big hand toward a dusty green chair. "Right there in front of my desk!"

John entered reluctantly. The place looked like a crazed rat's nest. Teegarten made a show of straightening papers that he then unceremoniously dumped into a box. He had three chins and a round moon face with a nose like a tulip bulb. His beard hung down over his chest. "Sit down! Please!" Teegarten insisted, and John eased himself into the little-used chair.

"You're a little early, aren't you? I didn't expect you until one." Teegarten sat down, and the chair yelled.

"It's six minutes after one," John said patiently.

"Oh. It is?" He shook his wristwatch violently, then gave a weak smile. "Cheap watch."

"I think I'm in the wrong place." John started to rise.

"Now, hold on, Father! Just one minute, okay? Tell me who this is." He swiveled laborously around. Behind him was a rack with a multitude of hats. He plucked a huge cowboy hat off and put it on his head. "Who do I look like?"

The Pillsbury Doughboy, he thought, but of course he didn't say it.

"Hoss!" Teegarten said. "You know! From *Bonanza*! Everybody always says I look like him. Dan Blocker. He died, but he was Hoss. That's me too."

"I think I'd better get back to the church." John got up and went to the door.

"The Cathedral of St. Francis, you mean? Where you've been a priest for going on four years? And before that you were a priest at a small church in San Mateo for three years? And before that you were at the Grace of St. Mark Catholic Church in Fresno? Is that right?"

John stopped, hand on the knob. He turned slowly toward Hoss Teegarten.

The fat man leaned back, dangerously, in his chair and cupped his hands behind his Hoss-hatted head. "You were born in Medford, Oregon, your parents moved to Fresno when you were twelve years old. Neal and Elaine Lancaster still live there, do they?"

"Yes," John said.

"And your dad owns part of a Ford dealership. Anything else I ought to know?" He grinned.

"How did you . . . get all that information?"

"It's amazing what you can do over the phone, if you put your soul into it. I called the bishop. Hagan's his name, right? I talked to his secretary, Mrs. Weaver. Bet you didn't know you were talking to an eccentric old rich dude who wanted to donate some heavy cash to a young priest who helped his wife cross a busy intersection while her arms were all full of shopping bags." He wiggled his eyebrows up and down.

"What was the point of going to all the trouble?"

Hoss laughed huskily, took off his hat, and sat up. "I don't have such a great office, do I? Don't have a whole lot of clients either. So I wanted you to know: you've got a job for me, I'll do my damnedest . . . uh . . . darnedest."

John stood there thinking it over.

"You want to tell me how I can help you, Father?" Teegarten urged.

John returned to his chair. He refused a cup of watery coffee from Teegarten and said, "I'd like someone watched. Protected, really. You do bodyguarding, right?"

"Plenty of it," Teegarten said, smoking a fresh cigarette.

Somehow John didn't believe him, but he plowed on. "It's a girl. Her name is Debbie Stoner." He gave him her address. "She's . . . an actress."

"Oh, yeah? What's she in?"

John traced a scratch on the desk. "She's . . ." Go ahead, he told himself. "She's . . . an erotic actress."

"You mean porno," Teegarten said, and the O puffed a smoke ring.

"I want you to watch her. Protect her. I don't know what I want . . . but . . ."

"You want her to have a guardian angel," Teegarten supplied. He smiled beatifically.

The deal was struck. Teegarten agreed to keep tabs on Debbie from tonight until Wednesday morning. He would follow her—at a discreet distance, of course—and let John know where she went, whom she saw, and who went in and out of her apartment. Also, if she went to any clubs or discos—like the Mile-High Club—he would be nearby to keep an eye on her. And if she got in any trouble? "I don't have a brown belt for nothing," he said.

Teegarten gladly accepted the three hundred and sixty-two dollars as a first payment, and then he put on his Sherlock Holmes deerstalker hat.

John got out before his better judgment overcame his need to be in contact with Debbie, if only through the eyes of Hoss Teegarten.

And as John left the office and stepped into the rickety elevator, Giro's wife, Anna, plucked the photograph of Debbie Stoner off the display of contest winners. "This is her, Julius!" she said, beaming at the stocky dark-haired young man who stood before her. "Now, have you ever seen a more beautiful face than this?"

"Yeah, she looks fine. She's a fox, huh?"

Giro grinned and slapped him on the back. "Since when do you know about foxes? He's my blood, Anna! Watch out for him!"

"Aw, Uncle Giro," Julius said, embarrassed by all this attention. He'd been dreading this visit for two months, ever since his father had made the arrangements for him. Uncle Giro and Aunt Anna had a nice apartment, up on the floor above the grocery, but Uncle Giro snored and Anna talked his head off when all he wanted to do was go out and score a little San Francisco action. He knew the story: they said a cable snapped every time a virgin crossed the Golden Gate Bridge, and it sure didn't look to him as if it were in any danger of collapse.

"She's a sweet girl!" Anna told him. "You should count your lucky stars you should ever meet such a sweet girl!"

"Does she live in the neighborhood?"

"Anna, he's got that gleam in his eye!" Giro said. "Look at his brain turn!"

"She's cute." Julius stared at the photograph. He had a

good eye for faces, and she really did look nice. Maybe it *was* the right decision to come to San Francisco, after all.

"She goes back with the rest of the winners!" Anna told him; she took the photograph and returned it to the display. Then a customer came in who wanted some marinated mushrooms, and Giro went back to get them for him. Anna had to tend to the register for a kid who was buying a Rolling Stone and a pack of Life-Savers.

Julius drifted to the magazine rack.

Now, here was the hot stuff! he thought, and instantly picked up a *Cavalier*. Paged quickly through it, found nothing of real interest. But next to it on the rack was another magazine, entitled *X-Rated Movie Review*. "Wow!" Julius breathed softly. He picked up the magazine and this time slowly turned the pages, taking in all the action.

Good lookers, all. Where'd they get these foxes? They must grow 'em on trees in L.A., he thought. Whore orchards. He ate the tanned, lush, straining bodies with his eyes. And the names: Cyndy Funn, Paula Angel, Tiffany Glove, Debra Rocks, Heather . . .

Wait a minute. Wait. Just. One. Minute.

This face he'd seen before. Hadn't he? It was . . .

Julius blinked. This had to be a mirage. Sure. It had to be.

But it was not. He took the magazine to the display of contest winners, and he snatched the picture Anna had been showing him off the wall.

He held the two pictures, one Polaroid, one pornoid, together for comparison.

His heart fell to his penis.

"Aunt Anna?" he called quietly. Then, louder: "Aunt Anna? Would you come over here for a minute?"

20

At four-forty-nine, Debbie Stoner pulled her green Fiat to the curb just down from her apartment building and put on the parking brake. She got out, a little stiff-legged. For such a skinny guy, he'd been . . . well, interesting.

Her skin seemed to be still hot from the camera's lights. It wasn't much fun, under those burning lights, grinding and smiling while a director was saying move this and move that and the makeup guy was fretting about a pimple and the sound guy was saying somebody was whistling as they breathed. But she'd thrown herself into her work today with grim energy, because she'd learned one thing from her experience at Bright Star studios: this was as far as she went.

Lucky would be over tonight. Of course, he hadn't exactly said he would be, but he hadn't said he wouldn't be, either. She had another club she wanted to take him to, called the Golden Spike, over on Polk Street. If Lucky had liked the Mile-High Club, he was going to really get a kick from the Spike.

She started up the front steps. Hold it, she thought. What about dinner? The frozen eats were gone. And she wouldn't mind a nice bottle of white wine, either. Lucky liked white wine. That clinched it; she started walking toward Giro's, a pretty girl with her hair in a black ponytail, dressed in jeans, boots, and a white cableknit sweater.

"Hi, Anna!" Debbie said as she breezed through the door. Anna was counting out change for an elderly man and woman, and Debbie was past her before Anna could have a chance to answer. Debbie went on into the aisles, picked out a medium-expensive bottle of wine, and saw Giro behind the bakery's counter. "Giro! Hi!" she called. He stood there staring at her, expressionless.

Must've been a bad day, she thought. "Hello! It's me! Debbie Stoner! Your contest winner!"

Giro turned his back.

Debbie sensed a movement behind her; she swiveled around, and there was Anna.

The woman's eyes looked as if they'd sunk into her face, and her entire face seemed to hang like a fleshy sack on the bones. She didn't smile, and not smiling made her face look hard and wrinkled.

"Anna?" Debbie said. Something was very wrong. "What is—"

Anna lifted a can of Lysol spray, and without a word began to douse Debbie's sweater.

Debbie stepped back, stumbling into the wine rack. Bottles clacked together and tumbled to the floor.

Anna sprayed Lysol into Debbie's hair, sprayed it into her face and into her open mouth as the girl cried out, "Anna! Please . . . stop it! Stop it!"

And then the shout came, blasting from Anna's mouth: "You dirty little *whore!* Get out of here! Get out of our store, you tramp!" She reached out, grabbed a handful of Debbie's hair, and flung her along the aisle. "You've been laughing at us all this time, haven't you! Laughing at two old fools! Get out! Get out, and go to Hell!"

Debbie tripped on a rolling wine bottle, had the sting of Lysol in her eyes and its chemical foulness on her tongue. She fell, and went to the floorboard on her knees. Now other customers were peering into the aisle, and they saw Anna take a broom from a rack of household items and begin vigorously, vengefully, sweeping the floor around the fallen girl. "Get out, you piece of trash!" Anna shrieked. "We saw those pictures! We know who you really are, you whore! Get out! Get out *now!*"

Debbie struggled to rise as the broom whacked at her and knocked her down again. And now, in the midst of dust and a cloud of Lysol, Debbie cleared her eyes and realized what must have happened. Somewhere . . . somehow . . . Giro and Anna had found out there was a woman named Debra Rocks, and that she had Debbie Stoner's face.

"Get *out!*" Anna shouted, her voice rattling the bottles. She swung the broom, and it hit Debbie on the side of the head.

Debbie scrambled up, tripped and staggered, slammed into a display of canned soup; then she got her balance and, the broom swinging behind her, ran for the door.

"You stay away from here, you little piece of nothing!" Anna raged as the foul whore ran up the hill. Oh, those pictures in that magazine were enough to make a decent person sick! And they *had* made Anna throw up, which was why her face was so pasty and loose. One more swing of the broom, through the settling Lysol cloud, and then Giro caught her shoulders. "It's over," he told her. "Anna, it's over."

Anna sobbed, clutched both hands to her mouth, and Giro—a good husband—pressed her to him.

Debbie ran. She crossed the street, almost ran headlong into a gray Volkswagen van slowly cruising past, and fell over the curb, skinning her palms. She moaned—the sound of a wounded animal—as she got up and staggered on, the tears streaming from her eyes and the brutal world in a kaleidoscopic haze.

Her nose was flowing, her stomach pounded with pain, her right palm was bleeding. She crashed into somebody walking on the sidewalk, and the middle-aged man shoved her aside like a garbage bag. She careened into a wrought-iron fence, fighting a scream.

You whore.

You trash.

You little piece of nothing.

She ran into her building, and fell on the stairs going up, twisting her ankle. But she pulled herself up with the willpower of Debra Rocks and climbed the stairs, blinded and hurting.

She fumbled with her keys, dropped them, finally jammed the right one into the lock, and burst into her apartment. Unicorn zipped away from under her feet, almost tripping her again. And then her pained ankle gave way and she did fall, crashing over the coffee table and scattering scented candles. She lay on the carpet clutching her ankle and rocked herself as she cried and moaned.

You whore.

You trash.

You little piece of nothing.

And then a new voice surfaced like jagged ice from her memory: *This audition is over.*

A sob racked her. Hang on! she told herself, her teeth gritted. Tough it out! Tough it . . . !

But suddenly she didn't feel so tough.

The tears flowed down her cheeks and dripped from her chin. Her stomach cramped, her heart ached, her soul yearned . . . for something. Call it peace.

This audition is over.

You got one shot, she knew. One shot. If you missed the target, the bus only went in one direction. No! she thought as she squeezed her eyes shut. No! You're a star! You're Debra Rocks!

She opened her eyes; they were blurred by tears, but she was looking inward. Her lip curled in a sneer. Debra Rocks *sucked.*

She was a fantasy, Debra Rocks was. A made-up, tight-dressed, high-heeled fiction. A pumping machine. A mask that held a false smile as the flesh of a stranger entered her. A pair of thighs with no shame, a pair of breasts thrust toward greedy teeth. Debra Rocks was not Debbie Stoner; but what was Debbie Stoner without Debra Rocks?

I screwed up, she thought. Her fingers gripped the carpet, and another sob forced the breath from her lungs. I screwed up . . . somewhere . . . I screwed up . . . and it all got away from me.

Her mind was taking a dangerous turn. It was opening itself up to a burst of agonizing light. She couldn't allow that; Debra Rocks wouldn't allow it. Where was Lucky? I need him! she almost screamed. Where was Lucky?

With his other girlfriend, she thought. The one he's so loyal to.

Got to call somebody. Got to call somebody, and get some action going. She got up, hobbling and crying, and went to the telephone. Uncle Joey and his sons had left for Vegas this afternoon, on business, and wouldn't be back until Thursday. Kathy Crenshaw—Cyndy Funn—had gone to Miami with Mitch, her boyfriend. Mike Laker was in Big Sur on a weekend shoot. Gary Sayles had gone back to his wife, and Bobby Barta was in prison on a three-to-five. She had already looked up the name of John Lucky in the telephone book, and come up empty, but now she grasped the book and flipped through it. Thousands of names went by, and she knew none of them.

Through the rising terror, a line came to her from that movie where the three guys chased ghosts: *Who ya gonna call?*

She screamed—a mixture of rage and pain—and hurled the telephone book. It slammed into a cactus pot, and sand flew. Unicorn skittered under the sofa.

She opened the cookie jar and had her white taste.

But even that served not to damp the fires, but to feed them. They were lonely flames, and they burned cold. I can go out to a club, she decided. Sure. If I can't dance, I can just hang out. Take your pick: the Mile-High, the Spike, Cell 60, Lobotomy, Advance Vision, the Tombs, the Certain Death . . .

She found herself in the bathroom staring at her swollen, scarlet-eyed face in the mirror. White crystals glittered at her nostrils, and her hair stank of Lysol. And of one thing she was certain at that moment when the dark basement of her soul collapsed into even deeper darkness: there was no God.

Her gaze ticked toward the sink, and there found the straight razor.

This audition is over.

She went to the medicine cabinet, opened a bottle, and took two pills. They were little blue pills, and they were supposed to help you get mellow.

She stared at the straight razor. It looked sharp and clean; it looked like a ticket out of this.

Because she knew what was ahead: you just got older, and keeping the weight off was tougher, and the younger ones came in by bus everyday to San Francisco, Los Angeles, and New York, and in offices or bedrooms new stars were being made right now, at this very moment. For her there would be a downward spiral now, because this was as far as she went. There would be guys with bad teeth and zits on their asses, guys with rough thrusts and mean eyes, and sooner or later—sooner or later—she would say yes when somebody brought out a rope and alligator clips.

I want to start all over, she thought. Tears hung from her chin and dropped into the sink. I want to start all over, and next time I want Debbie Stoner to be a star.

She went to the bathtub and turned on the hot water, without bubblebath.

But of course she wouldn't be Debbie Stoner in her next life, she thought. No, she would be . . . somebody beautiful. And she would meet her soul mate again too, and next time Lucky wouldn't have another girlfriend. Next time he would be hers, and she would be loyal to him too.

She picked up the razor and ran her finger across the road home.

She shrugged off her sweater, and then she started to unzip her jeans as sweet steam filled the bathroom.

The door buzzer went off.

Lucky, she thought. It was Lucky! But still she hesitated, her hand clenched around the razor. Lucky was here, yes, but he wouldn't stay. He'd leave her again, and the loneliness would pierce even deeper next time. Run, she thought. The razor glinted. Run home while you can still get there . . .

The buzzer went off again.

Debbie lowered her head. Two tears fell from her face into the hot water. And then, her hand trembling, she returned the razor to the sink, shut off the water, and limped to the door. She checked the spyhole. Her heart fell; it wasn't Lucky. It was a black kid.

"What do you want?" she asked him in a weak and whispery voice.

"Miss Debbie Stoner?" the kid said. "Got something for you from North Beach Florist." He held up the long white box so she could see.

She opened the door, took the box of flowers from him, and tipped him five dollars because she didn't have any ones. Then she sat down on the floor, as Unicorn emerged cautiously from beneath the sofa, lifted the box's lid, and stared at the dozen red roses.

There was a card, what Lucky must've either written or dictated. It said: *Debbie. Hi! I'm not going to be able to see you or call you for a few days. But I'm thinking about you. There's something I need to tell you, and I hope you'll understand. People do crazy things, don't we? Stay out of trouble! I love you. Lucky.*

She picked up the roses, not minding the sting of their thorns, and crushed them against her. Her head bowed, and her back trembled.

Unicorn came up beside her and sat in silent company.

That night she had a dream: it was in black and white, like one of those old movies they shouldn't ought to colorize. She was standing on a hill, with Lucky beside her and the concrete towers of San Francisco at her back. The sky was full of drifting white clouds, and as Lucky put his hand on her shoulder, she lifted a dandelion. The wind blew it to pieces, and the dandelion's white umbrellas spun away, toward the green, forgiving forests of Louisiana.

She knew then: dandelions could not grow in concrete.

And as Debbie dreamed, a vase full of bruised roses beside her bed, Hoss Teegarten sat in his beat-up brown Chevy just down the street. He lifted his automatic-shutter Nikon and, to check the mechanism in this meager light, aimed the lens at the doorway of the red brick apartment building and squeezed off a half-dozen shots.

21

"Father Lancaster?"

John had been speaking to Mr. and Mrs. Winthrop. Now he turned around and saw, standing in the center aisle of the Cathedral of St. Francis, Hoss Teegarten in his overalls, a loud red-checked shirt and a black Hell's Angels motorcycle cap.

Sunday Mass had ended perhaps ten minutes before, and

John had been talking to members of the parish, his face composed and serious—a priest face. Now his priest face slipped right off like melting wax, and Teegarten said, "Hiya, Fatheɾ."

"Hello," John answered, getting at least a modicum of his composure back. "One minute, please." He continued his conversation with the Winthrops, and didn't even mind how they kept being distracted by his pierced ear. He shook hands firmly with Mr. Winthrop and then the man and his wife left the church. John and Teegarten were alone except for a few people still on their way out.

"Got you a few things." Teegarten held up a coffee-stained manila folder. "Want to take a look?" Without waiting for a response, the fat man went to the foremost pew and plopped himself down.

"I think we'd better do this in my—"

"What's wrong?" Teegarten asked. "You ashamed of something?"

That jabbed him. "No," he said, and sat down beside the man. Teegarten had a hint of body odor, but it wasn't too bad.

"I wanted to make sure I got you, so I came on in after the Mass," Teegarten explained. He began to open the folder with his pudgy fingers. "I think you'll understand why it couldn't wait." He sifted out a group of grainy black-and-white photographs, all shot with an infrared lens and blown up to eight and a half by eleven. "Recognize this place?" He offered John the photograph on top; it was a simple shot of the doorway of Debbie's apartment building.

"Yes," John said. "That's where she lives."

"Uh-huh. Incidentally, she's led a pretty quiet life for the last couple of days. She went out to the Supersaver Grocery on Montgomery Street Friday night around seven-thirty. I followed her, natch. She came out with her groceries and went straight home."

That was strange, John thought. Why had she driven all the way to Montgomery Street, when she could have walked to Giro's?

"She must be a late sleeper," the man went on. "She

didn't leave her apartment until about three yesterday afternoon. She drove over to the Wharf and ate a clam chowder from a vendor. Then she strolled around Ghirardelli Square for about an hour. She went up to that dessert place and had a chocolate-mousse cheesecake."

Chocolate-mousse cheesecake, John thought. It slowly sank in. That thing was surely loaded with calories. Wasn't she paranoid about gaining even an extra ounce of weight?

Or, at least, she *had* been before yesterday afternoon.

"She's a fine-looking lady," Teegarten said. "I don't know what I expected, but she's different. You've got good taste, Father." John glared at him, and Teegarten smiled meekly. "Just kidding, don't get your collar wrinkled. Take a look at . . . let's see . . . here. The fourth picture." He slid it into John's lap. "See anything there?"

It was another picture, as they all seemed to be, of the same angle facing Debbie's apartment building, taken at night. Except now there were wisps of fog across the pavement, and most of the lights had gone out in the windows.

"No, I don't see anything."

"Well, neither did I, at first. Look here." He pointed to the extreme right edge of the photograph. "See him?"

And then John did: a figure, standing in the misty fog near the building's front steps. He couldn't tell anything about the figure at all, just that there was a shape mostly consumed by darkness.

"That was Saturday morning, about one-thirty. This was Sunday morning, around one." Teegarten slid the next photograph over.

In it, the figure had almost emerged from the fog. It was still a dark, hazy shape, but now it was definitely a human being. A man, tall and slim. At least, John thought it was a man; the hair was very short. Then again, that didn't really say much.

"It's a man, all right," Teegarten said, as if reading his thoughts. He offered the next photograph, and in it the man—wearing a long, loose coat of some kind—had stridden out of the fog. He was standing in front of the building, arms hanging at his sides. His face—a gray blur—was tilted upward.

John felt his breath catch, as if his lungs had iced up. He knew.

"Yeah," Teegarten said. "I think he's looking up at the window of number six." He pushed several more pictures over for John's inspection. In them, John could see the tall blond man edging closer toward the apartment steps. Then the man actually started up them, and was about to enter the building.

And then the last photograph: the man was standing almost at the entrance, and his face—still a cloudy blur, the features indistinct—was turned, directly it seemed, toward the lens of Teegarten's camera.

"I stopped shooting to put on a zoom lens," Teegarten explained. "I wanted to get his face good and clear. But right after that shot, he turned and walked away. He went around the corner, too fast for a fat gut like me to catch up with."

"So you think he saw you?"

"Saw me? Naw! I was hunkered down in my car with what looked like a basket of dirty laundry over my head. A car was coming. It must've spooked him, and he took off. Listen, when the Hoss wants to pull a camouflage job, he does it up right!"

"How long was this man standing there?" John asked, staring at the final photo. There was something oddly familiar about the figure—the stance, the coat . . . something—but he couldn't figure out what it was.

"Wasn't more than three minutes. But three minutes is a long time. You either go where you're going or you don't in three minutes. That dude didn't want to be seen. A quiet creeper."

"You mean . . . he wasn't looking for an address? Or just walking around late at night?"

"Nope," Teegarten said. He took the pictures back and returned them to the folder. "I think he knew the address already. And I think he knew who he was looking for."

"Debbie," John said, an ashy taste in his mouth.

"You win the seegar." He sealed up the folder. "Father Lancaster, it seems you're not the only one keeping tabs on . . ." What had he called her? ". . . this erotic actress."

John sat back and stared up at Christ awrithe on the Cross.

"I'll be back in the trenches tonight." Teegarten stood up. "With my trusty Nikon. We'll see if our friend comes calling again."

"And if he does?"

"If he does, I think we ought to get the cops in on it. Three nights in a row and you don't call it creeping anymore." He paused.

"What . . . do you call it?" John asked.

"Stalking," Teegarten told him. He clapped John hard on the shoulder. "Leave it to the Hoss, Father! That guy goes into the building, I'll get on his ass real quick. Fat gut and all." He walked away a few paces up the aisle, then remembered something and halted. "Hey, Father! Where'd you get that ten-speed?"

"Bay Cycle, over on Pacific Avenue." He was still stunned. *Stalking,* he thought.

"I watched you pedal off after you left my office. That's real good exercise, huh? I was thinking about maybe getting me a ten-speed. You can change the gears so the hills won't break your ass?"

"Yes," John said hollowly.

"That's good. I've got a lot of ass to be broken. Well, maybe I'll get me a bike and some of those tight black pants that look like sprayed-on rubber. That'd be a whopping sight, wouldn't it?" This time the priest didn't answer, and Teegarten knew the information had burrowed down to a deep place. "Don't worry," Teegarten said firmly; then he walked on along the aisle, pushed through the heavy oak doors and out into the misting rain of a gray Sunday.

John leaned forward and put his hands to his face. Don't worry. Stalking. Don't worry. Easy to say, but it was an impossibility. Oh, my God . . . oh, Holy Lord . . . if someone *was* stalking Debbie . . .

No, not Debbie, he realized. Someone was stalking Debra Rocks.

He remembered what she'd said at Forest Lawn, about the death of her friend in Los Angeles: *The cops never found out who it was. I don't think they looked too hard. You know what they call us? Freak fodder.*

And it seemed now that yet another freak had just crawled out of the woodwork.

"Father?"

John quickly looked up.

Garcia stood there. "I don't mean to bother you during your prayer, Father, but do you want me to lock the doors?"

John hesitated. It was customary to lock the doors on Sunday afternoon, because of the gilded icons, the candleholders, and other expensive fixtures. Garcia waited for him to speak.

"No," John said finally. "No, leave the doors unlocked." If someone came in and made off with a heavy candleholder or two, they surely were in more dire need of money than the Catholic Church. John stood up, leaving Garcia blinking in puzzlement over the failure to turn a key that had been turned every Sunday for at least the nine years of his employment as a maintenance man. John went directly to his apartment, where he sat down in a chair, attacked a volume on the nature of evil, and tried desperately not to consider picking up the phone and calling Debbie.

Stalking, he thought. That word rattled in his brain like a cold stone, or a bullet.

Rain ticked on the window's glass, and beyond it the red X was a savage smear. The afternoon passed on.

22

By twelve-thirty on Monday morning Hoss Teegarten had been sitting in his Chevy, watching Debbie Stoner's apartment building, for over four hours. Her green Fiat was at the curb, and the lights of number six were on. He could look up, from under his camouflage cover of what appeared to be old newspapers, and see the shapes of cacti in her window. His butt had gone to sleep, but he was born to be a couch potato anyway. Or a car eggplant, at least.

Rain speckled the windshield. He had the driver's window rolled down, and his hand ready with the Nikon. But so far there was no sign of Blondie. A few cars had passed by, but they were on their way somewhere else. Now the street was deserted of movement, just the low tendrils of fog beginning to roll up from the bay at about knee-height over the pavement.

He yawned. Stifle it! he thought. Got a long time to sit here. At times like these he wished he could afford to hire an assistant. Tonight had been another slow one; at around six-thirty, Debbie Stoner had walked down the hill to a Chinese restaurant. She'd taken her time, sitting in the window and watching the rain as she ate. He had some nice pictures of her face. What was a beautiful girl like that doing in porno? His not to question why. He himself used to ride with the Hell's Angels, when he was twenty-one and seventy pounds lighter. Oh, those were the days! he mused. Now he'd bend a hog's frame into a chrome street-scraper. Got to cut out the spaghetti and meatballs, he vowed for the fourth or fifth time that day. Get hooked on sushi, maybe.

He eased up a little bit, put his elbow on the doorframe, and squeezed off a couple of shots just to get the camera warmed up.

There was a metallic *click*.

And it did not come from the Nikon.

A gun barrel slid up into the window, right into Teegarten's face.

"No sounds," the man who'd crawled up beside the Chevy whispered.

"Is that real? That's not real, is it?" Teegarten babbled.

"Shut." The man's blond-crew-cut head rose into view. "Up."

"I've just got a camera, see? Just a camera. I'm just sitting here—"

"In deep shit," the cowboy told him, and Teegarten saw the red teardrops tattooed at the outer corners of his eyes. "You took my picture, didn't you?"

"Me? No. I never saw you before!" His voice shook, along with his chins, and he knew that the cowboy knew.

"Hands on the wheel. Do it. Grip tight." The cowboy walked around the car, the Colt's barrel still aimed through the glass at Hoss Teegarten, and then he slid smoothly into the passenger side and closed the door. The barrel pushed into the fat man's blubbery side. "Drive," Travis said.

"Oh . . . come on." Jesus! Teegarten thought. Oh, Jesus . . . this guy's not kidding! "Listen . . . I'm nobody. I'm just a private dick, right? Come on, give me a break."

"I'll break you, all right. Drive."

By the time he scrambled out of the car, Teegarten realized, he'd be a fat Swiss cheese. He swallowed, cold sweat on his face and sparkling on his scalp. He started the engine and guided the Chevy away from the curb. "Where . . . do you want me to drive to? Around the block?"

"I'll show you. Turn right at the next corner."

Teegarten did. He could crash into another car, he thought. He could run up on the curb, or go right into a store's window. He could yell like bloody hell at a stoplight. But he did none of those things, because he wanted to live. "I'm Hoss Teegarten," he said, his voice shaking. "Like Hoss in 'Bonanza.' Right? What's your name?"

"Death," Travis said, and the car drove on.

They crossed Market Street and headed along Fourth Street toward the warehouses and wharfs of China Basin. "Give me a break," Teegarten kept saying, his palms slick on the wheel. "Okay? I'd give you one. I used to be a Hell's Angel. Can you dig it?"

"You're not one anymore, though, are you?" Travis asked. "Turn left here. Now straight and another right at the light."

Warehouses brooded on either side. The streets were empty, as if the city had turned her face away. They went on three more blocks, near the basin now, and Travis said, "In this alley and stop."

Teegarten did. A bead of sweat ran from his forehead and

dangled on the end of his nose. "Cut the lights," Travis told him, and Teegarten obeyed with a soft, terrified moan. Then Travis got out and came around to the driver's side. He opened Teegarten's door for him. "Walk." He motioned— not with his gun hand—toward a doorway in the alley's ugly wall. "Hold it." Teegarten froze on the edge of getting out, his breath rasping. "Give me the keys."

And the way the cowboy said that told Teegarten he would have no further use for them.

Travis put the keys in his jeans pocket. "Now, walk, Moby Dick."

Teegarten entered the doorway. He smelled damp concrete and the tang of salt rust on metal. There was no light, not even a hint of it, and four paces behind him Travis ordered, "Stop." The cowboy bent down and found the flashlight that he knew was hidden beneath an old orange crate three paces right of the door. The light came on, spearing into Teegarten's back. "Keep walking."

"I can't . . . I can't see where I'm going." But he had no choice. He walked, his legs loggy, and his heart hammered behind his breastbone and his eyes bulged with terror. The warehouse—deserted, it appeared, for some time—was full of cavernlike rooms and corridors. "Turn left," Travis said. They came in another moment to a staircase, going down.

"Oh, no. Please . . . listen . . ."

A hand shoved him forward, and Teegarten grasped at the iron railing before he tumbled like Humpty Dumpty. He went down into darkness. "I've got money," he said. "Got a bank account. Crocker Bank. I swear to God, I'll get you all the money I've got!"

"I think," Travis said softly, "I hear a ghost talkin'."

The lower floor was puddled, and water dripped from corroded pipes overhead. Teegarten kept going, shoved along at the point of the flashlight. He splashed through a puddle and stepped on something that squished under his left sneaker.

"Right. Into there." Travis motioned with the light; it swept across the concrete and toward an archway about ten feet ahead.

Teegarten caught his breath. He had seen something on the floor, in the sweep of that light. It had looked like a mangy dog, its head shot away, and beside the carcass a little mound of gray hamburger. He heard the hungry buzz of flies, and now he could smell rot. He hesitated, trembling— and then the Colt's barrel pressed into his spine. Its chill eagerness forced him through the archway and into a realm of the damned.

Dead rats, each dispatched with a single shot that had blasted their carcasses to pieces, lay around Teegarten's feet. He walked on, stepping on mangle, and then abruptly stopped again as the light glanced past his shoulder and fell on something else that lay ahead.

It was a dead man, old and skinny. Wearing gray trousers and a tattered purple sweater with brown blotches. No, no, Teegarten realized. The brown blotches were not part of the sweater's natural color. Flies clung to the bullet holes in the corpse's chest, and spun like a dark blizzard over the gaping face.

"Walk to the wall," Travis commanded. "Go on, Moby Dick." He chuckled. "Moby Dick. Get it?"

Teegarten trudged forward in a zombie daze. The wall was of dark, wet bricks, and there was a chair. Around the chair were more brown blotches.

"Sit," Travis said.

Teegarten did. The chair creaked. He was sitting not facing the cowboy but with the wall on his right. He stared into darkness, and every time he trembled, the chair groaned again.

A match flared. The cowboy was lighting candles set around the room, stuck with wax to paper plates. The match went out, and Travis struck another one and kept lighting candles until all fifteen of them were burning.

"Please don't kill me," Teegarten whispered, and a tear crawled from his right eye.

"My name is Travis," the cowboy began, and Teegarten winced because he didn't want to hear a name, he didn't want to know anything, all he wanted to do was go home and pull the covers over his skull. "I'm from Oklahoma. Ever been there?"

"No. Please . . ."

"Hush. I'm talkin'. Oklahoma's the big country. Everythin's wide open. I used to be in the rodeo. You want a cigarette, Moby?"

"I . . . want to . . . go home."

An unlit cigarette was pushed into Teegarten's mouth. Then there was the clocking noise of the cowboy's boots as he walked back toward the archway. He stopped, and when he spoke again his voice echoed: "Don't move, now. This is my best trick." He holstered his Colt and took a gunfighter's stance. "Keep your chin up!" Travis said.

A drop of sweat rolled into Teegarten's eye. He shivered, and started to scream.

The Colt came out of the cowboy's holster in a blur, and its barrel spat fire.

The bullet ricocheted off the bricks beside Teegarten's head and blasted the side of his face with clay splinters. The tip of the cigarette burst into flame, and an instant later the flame went out.

Smoke trickled between Teegarten's clenched teeth.

Travis spun the Colt around his finger and lodged it home again. "There you go. Pull on that coffin nail. Don't spit it out now, I don't wanna have to light you another one."

Teegarten's teeth met through the filter.

"I used to be with the rodeo," Travis went on. "Did I say that? I was a trick shot. You gimme anything, I can hit it. Don't matter. I kinda like the movin' targets best." The toe of his cowboy boot prodded a dead rat. "Sit up straight, Moby! We got some jawin' to do."

The fat man trembled, swallowed, bellowed smoke through his nostrils.

"So why were you sittin' there takin' pictures in front of my girlfriend's apartment?" Travis asked, kneeling down between two candles. "You can take the cigarette out for a second."

Teegarten removed it, but his lips remained in a tight O.

"I don't know . . . anything about your girlfriend, man. I was there to watch somebody for a client. A priest. Yeah, this eccentric priest, rides around on a ten-speed. He wanted me to watch—"

"Whoa," Travis said quietly. "A ten-speed. Bicycle?"

"Yeah. Yeah. A bicycle. He wanted me to . . . like . . . keep tabs on this girl who lives in apartment number six. Her name is—"

"Debra Rocks," Travis interrupted coldly. "She's my girlfriend."

Oh . . . *shit,* Teegarten thought. His mind skipped and lurched.

"I believe I've met a bike rider before. He ran me a little race. A *priest?*" He paused. "Oh, that's wicked." He held his gun hand palm-down over the candle's flame on his right, and slowly worked the fingers. "What's his name, and what church is he at?"

"His name is . . . is . . ." The detective's heart pumped. "His name is Father Murphy, at the Church of St. Nicholas."

Travis kept clenching and unclenching the long pale fingers. "What street?"

"Valle . . . Jones Street," he corrected. "Jones and Jackson. It's a big white place."

"Ain't they all?" Travis asked as the flame began to scorch his palm. His face was devoid of expression. He looked up from the candle. "Saint Nicholas. Ain't he Santa Claus?"

"I swear to God," Teegarten gasped, "if you let me go . . . I won't say a thing. Nobody'll ever know. I swear it. Okay?"

"You'll know," Travis answered. He removed his hand from the fire. "Put the cigarette back in your mouth, Moby." He stood up.

"No . . . please . . ." He caught back a sob, and pushed the scorched cigarette into his mouth when he felt the awful force of the cowboy's silence.

"Hold still, now. Real still. I don't think I believe there's a Santa Claus church." His hand flashed to the Colt and wrenched it smoothly from the holster in an eyeblink. The gun boomed, more brick splinters hit Teegarten's face, and the cigarette was clipped in half. Teegarten wet his pants, his mouth clamped on the smoking butt.

"'It's the Cathedral of St. Francis!" he shouted. "I swear it! The Cathedral of St. Francis, on Vallejo Street!"

"Okie-dokie. Is that the priest's real name, or is he made up too?"

Teegarten choked on smoke, and tasted hellfire.

He heard the Colt's hammer click back.

"Lancaster," Teegarten moaned, tears trickling down his face. "Father . . . John Lancaster. That's his name."

"Good," Travis said, and pulled the trigger.

The bullet smashed into the fleshy bulb of Teegarten's nose and took it away in a splatter of blood and flesh fragments. The shock threw him off the chair and against the bullet-pocked bricks; he cried out in agony and grasped his bleeding face.

"Shucks." Travis blew smoke from the barrel's tip. "I missed." The Colt spun around his finger, was returned to the well-used leather. "Stop cryin'. I hate that sound. I'm gonna tell you a story now," he decided. "Once upon a time there was a cowboy who had so much love in him it busted his heart. Just—boom—blew it all to pieces. So Dr. Fields —oh, yeah, him, the bastard—said shut him away so he can't never love nobody again. And I was doin' so damned good before I heard that music. On a radio at night. Out there in that big country, where all the music floats in and tangles up in the air. Now, I told Bethy to behave. I swear I did. Oh, she was a willful thing!" He rubbed his hands together, trying to dry the palms. "Willful. I said you want me to cry blood, I'll show you I can, by God, and then I went and had him do it. You know. The guy on Tenth Street out by the fairgrounds."

Hoss Teegarten held his face as if trying to keep the rest of his dangling nose from falling off. His eyes were bright and staring with pain, and he began crawling away from the blotches of his own blood.

"I think he had a needle that made me sick," Travis wandered on, through the haunted land. "Bethy and those red shoes, I swear!" He blinked, watching the fat man crawl. "No," he said, and he pulled his gun out and shot the detective through the left knee. Then, as Teegarten sobbed and howled and sobbed some more, Travis opened the Colt's cylinder and began to reload with bullets from his holster. "I always had a thing for blonds, but I like me brunettes too. Hell, redheads I won't kick out of bed for eatin' crackers. Cheri Dane and Easee Breeze were blonds. Debra Rocks is a brunette. You see *Super Slick?*"

Teegarten kept crawling, desperate and insane now, dragging his ruined leg across the wet concrete.

"There's a scene where they all looked at me. Right at me. The three of them, together. And when they opened their mouths I heard that music, and I knew right then that California wasn't such a long way from Oklahoma. See, the movie was made in California. So I came here. I mean, to Los Angeles first. Cheri Dane went to the openin' of her new movie. *Girl Trouble.* But that's not near as good as *Super Slick.* So I followed her to her place, just like I followed Debra Rocks when she was at that bookstore. Oh, they try to change cars and all to shake you, but once ol' Travis gets his heart set . . ." He watched the wounded man crawling, and then he lifted his reloaded gun and put a bullet squarely through the right elbow.

"I found out from this guy in a theater that he saw Easee Breeze in person at a place right here in San Francisco. So I came on to find her. I loved her, see. Like I loved Cheri Dane. And like I love Debra Rocks. I mean . . . they love me too, 'cause I figured out the music." He clicked the hammer back. "I knew what they were really sayin', all the time." He took aim. "They were sayin', 'Travis, come make us cry blood.'"

The gun went off.

Hoss Teegarten lurched and fell on his face, his skull pierced at the right temple.

"And that's the end of that story," Travis said. He spun the Colt gracefully and sank it away. The barrel's warmth bled through his jeans. "That wicked, wicked priest. We're gonna have to do somethin' about him, ain't we? She's my date." He went around blowing out the candles, but before he extinguished the last one he walked to his sleeping bag, surrounded by hamburger wrappers, and picked up a coil of rope. Then the final candle went dark, and he followed the flashlight's beam out.

23

The telephone rang.

John almost fell out of bed in his haste to get to it. He grasped the receiver. "Hello?"

"Howdy."

Whose voice was that? John had been expecting to hear from Hoss Teegarten . . .

"This Lancaster? Father John Lancaster?"

"Yes. Who is this?" Rain was still tapping at the window.

"Somebody who wants to see you."

John glanced at his wristwatch on the small bedside table; he couldn't make it out, so he switched on the lamp. Three minutes before two. "It's a little early for games, isn't it?"

"Not this game. The time's just right. I've got a message for you from your girlfriend."

"My . . ." His heart seized up. "Who is this?"

"I can bring the message to you, if that's what you want."

"Just tell me now."

"Oh, I can't do that." The voice sounded as if the man might be smiling. "No, sir. You got a place we can meet . . . say, in about ten minutes?"

"The sanctuary," John said. "What's this about?"

"The sanctuary," the man repeated. "I like the way that sounds. Safe. Listen, you a Catholic?"

"Of course I am."

"You Catholics . . . like . . . have a little box you go into, don't you? Thing about the size of a closet? You go in there and listen to people tellin' you what all they've done wrong?"

"A confessional, yes."

"And you don't see each other's faces, do you? It's like one box talkin' to another box."

"Roughly speaking."

"That's where I want you to be."

John frowned. *"What?"*

"In your box. In ten minutes. That'll be . . . two-oh-seven. Whoops. Two-oh-eight. Then you leave the front door open, and I'll come and get in my box. They're right out where you can see them, ain't they?"

"Yes," John said cautiously. His skin was beginning to crawl.

"Well, that works out pretty as pink. You be there, and I will too. Oh. Hold on, now. Let's get this straight up front: what I've got to say to you is between you and me. There ain't gonna be nobody else there, right?"

"I—"

"If there's anybody else there, I won't come in. I won't tell you what your girlfriend in apartment number six with that pretty long black hair wants you to know. You be there alone, now." The man hung up.

John's first impulse was to call the police. But for what? Someone was coming to confessional; maybe the time was strange, but . . . And anyway, John wanted to hear what the man had to say. He was shaking like a wild leaf; if this really was a message from Debbie, had she found out about him? Oh, my God . . . had Teegarten told her?

Mysteries, mysteries.

John hurriedly put on his jeans. His black shirt with its stiff white collar was lying nearest to hand, so he put that on and buttoned it up. Then a thick beige cardian pulled out of the closet. He slipped on his sneakers, without socks, and ran from his apartment to the sanctuary.

He checked the doors; they were still unlocked. The lights were low in the sanctuary, saving electricity, and he decided to leave them that way. He checked his watch. Almost time. This was ridiculous, but he had to find out what was going on. He walked to the confessional booth, entered it, and sat down on the velvet cushion to wait.

Two-oh-eight.

Two-oh-nine.

Two-ten.

And John sat alone, feeling like more of a fool every passing second.

Two-eleven.

Two-twelve.

He heard the hinge creak quietly as the front doors were pushed open. He sat up straight, his heart pounding, and put his hand on the latch.

"Which one you in, Father?" the man's voice called.

"This one. Here, on your left." He started to open the latch and peer out, but the man said, "You stay in there, now. Got somethin' real important to tell you."

John's fingers burned to open the door, but he sat listening to the sound of boots coming across the marble. Had he heard that sound somewhere before?

The footsteps halted. "You nice and snug in there, Father?"

"Come on and let's get this over with!" John said, his nerves about to snap. "What do you want to tell me?"

"I want to confess," the man said, and John heard him enter the confessor's booth.

"Look. It's late. Just tell me, all right?" What was that smell? John thought. A strange, pungent odor . . .

"I know all about your girlfriend, Father. A big fat dick told me." The man bent down, and in the low light John could see a pair of pale lips at the screen.

A burnt smell, John thought. That's what it was. "Meaning?"

"Meanin' your ass is cooked, Father John. I heard the music, not you."

"Music?" Was this guy nuts, or what? "What music?"

The man laughed quietly. "Sure, you know what I mean. All you guys know the secret. That's why you went after Debra."

"I'd like to know who you . . ." He stopped. *Debra,* the man had said. Not *Debbie*. His eyes widened.

"She's my date," the man said.

There was a metallic *click.*

Gunpowder, John thought. That's what I smell.

He jerked his face back from the grille and instinctively lifted his right hand in a gesture of protection because he remembered hearing that *click* when he was inside a toilet stall, and now he knew what it—

The gun went off, a gout of fire blasting through the grille. The palm of John's open hand exploded, blood spraying across the opposite wall. Pain seared him, and as he grabbed his wrist and fell off the velvet cushion the pistol went off a second time.

This bullet creased across the front of John's throat, shocking his larynx like a punch. He grunted with pain and slid to the floor as the third bullet passed through the confessional over his head in a shower of wood splinters.

Travis peered through the broken grille, could see the bastard lying there and blood all over the wall. The bastard's collar was turning crimson. Got him right in the neck, he thought. Bleed to death real quick. The priest's eyelids were fluttering, but he was a goner for sure. "She's my date," Travis repeated, and he holstered his Colt, got out of the confining little closet, and ran for the doors. Then out into the rain, toward Moby Dick's Chevy parked up on the curb.

He pulled away, heading for his girlfriend's place.

And two minutes later, Father John Lancaster burst out of the confessional and fell to the hard marble, his bleeding hand clasped to his chest. He squeezed the wrist with the other hand, trying to constrict the veins and stop the ghastly flow. His face had gone white, and blood crept down his throat over the crimson collar. His first thought was to scream for help—not that anyone was around to hear him—but when he tried that, his voice came out as a pained croak.

Oh, my Christ, he thought. Oh, Holy Mother . . . I've got to get up.

Bleeding. Bleeding all over the floor. The monsignor was . . . going to . . . split a gut. . . .

His consciousness ebbed, came back again, ebbed and

returned. Pain throbbed up his wrist and through his shoulder; his hand felt as if it had been caught in a freezer, but his face was on fire.

She's my date, the maniac had said.

My date.

"Oh, Lord," he gasped, but it came out as the grunt of a wounded beast. Got to get up . . . got to get up . . . *now.*

He got to his knees. His head was starting to clear a little, but dark pain still sought to drag him under. The smell of blood was sickening, and his palm kept oozing though he squeezed his wrist with all his strength.

Get up . . . get up . . . damn you, get up!

That maniac was stalking Debbie . . . no, stalking Debra Rocks. But Debbie was the one who wore her face.

John stood up, wavered on his feet, clenched his teeth, and staggered through the door that led him into the administrative wing. A telephone, he thought. Got to get to a telephone. The first office was locked. So was the second. His own office was locked, and his keys were in his apartment. He staggered on, leaving a trail of blood drops.

In his apartment, he couldn't make his fingers close around the telephone's receiver. They jittered and jumped, but would not obey. Nerve damage, he thought. He lifted the receiver with his left hand and jabbed at the O button with his elbow. Circuits clicked and whirred. "Operator."

He wanted to say *I need the police,* but nothing would come out. Sweat broke from his pores. "I . . . need . . ." he croaked.

"Is someone there?" the operator asked. "Hello?"

"I . . . need . . . the . . ." His bruised larynx refused to let the words come out as anything but a harsh moan.

"Hello? Is anyone . . ."

Blood was trickling down John's right wrist, and he knew at that moment that if he did not get to Debbie she was doomed.

He looked at his bicycle, next to the door. The operator hung up.

He had to make it. He had to, wounded or not. By the

time he got to the police, she might well be raped or . . . worse, much worse. Anybody who used a gun like that wasn't going to be satisfied with rape. And now John had to pull whatever guts he had up from his shoes and reach Debbie, because the clock was ticking and time was fast running out.

He went to his black pants, hanging over a chair. He yanked the belt out and tied it as tightly as he could stand around his right wrist, using his left hand and his teeth. Then he shook the cobwebs out of his head, and he thought of Debbie coming face-to-face with that maniac—that killer, possibly—and he jumped on his bike and pedaled furiously down the hall to the stairs.

Blood spotted the floor behind him.

He went through the street door pedaling, out onto Vallejo and into the drizzle. The chilly air served to knock some of the sluggishness out of his legs, and he pedaled harder. His right hand twitched, the palm a red oozing mass and the rest of the hand bone-white. He sped across Broadway and into the night.

24

He went up the stairs, all the way to number six, and there he buzzed her door.

Debbie opened her eyes. What was that? Somebody at the door? She waited, not sure she'd heard anything at all but a wish. And there it was again: the buzzer.

She sat up in bed. "Lucky," she whispered.

John was pedaling hard, but the world had slowed down. The streets were made of black, gleaming tar, and the air had thickened. He took a corner fast, and suddenly the tar let his tires go and he was slung into a group of garbage cans.

Debbie put on her white robe, stepped over Unicorn— who liked to scuttle around in the darkness—and flipped on lights as she hurried to the door. On the kitchen counter was an airline ticket, and it was good Lucky had come because there were a lot of things she needed to say to him.

She started to open the door, in a rush to see his face. But at the last second she stopped herself and peered through the spyhole.

It was a guy with a blond crew cut, wearing a rain-damp canvas coat. He was studying his hands.

"What is it?" she asked, her voice sharp now that she realized it wasn't him after all.

The guy looked up at the spyhole. He smiled, and she could see weird tattoos at the outer corners of his eyes.

Up again, and speeding onward.

Hurry! he told himself. His legs were cramping. Forget the pain. Hurry, damn it! His vision kept going in and out, but now he had control of himself and he wasn't going to lose consciousness again. Still, he had a long way to go yet. He grabbed the belt with his teeth and gave it a tightening jerk. Then, his head over the handlebars, he raced toward North Beach.

"Howdy," Travis said. His heart was thudding. Oh, she was so beautiful, so . . . within reach.

"You want me me to call a cop?" she asked warily, ready to spring back from the door.

"No! Oh, no!" His smile went crooked. "I've got a message for you from your boyfriend."

"My boyfriend?"

"Sure. You know. Fa . . ." He paused. "John."

"John?" How many Johns did she know? she thought. This guy must be cracked! But then it dawned on her. "John. You mean Lucky?"

That seemed to turn a light on, he decided. "Lucky," he repeated thickly. "Yeah, he's sure lucky, knowin' you and all."

Still, something wasn't right. Debbie could smell it. "How do you know him?"

"Oh, we go way back. We're just like this." He held up a hand with two intertwined fingers.

Debbie still didn't open the door. If you don't know the face, she thought, don't let 'em into the place. "What's the message?"

"Let me in and I'll tell you."

"No. Sorry. Tell me from out there."

"I don't think you want your neighbors hearin' this."

"They're heavy sleepers. Let's hear it, Jack."

"Travis," he told her with a pained expression. "Travis, from Oklahoma."

"Okay, great. What's the message, Travis?"

He paused, studying his hands again. The warped wheels went round and round. Finally he looked up into the spyhole and gave her his best smile. "Your boyfriend's a priest."

Her mouth slowly opened. Her face contorted; then she shook her head and grinned. "Travis, you're crazier'n a one-legged grasshopper!"

"Father John Lancaster," he went on. "The Cathedral of St. Francis. It's on Vallejo. A big white place."

She whispered, "No." Then, louder: "Hell, no! What kind of joke is this, man?"

"He's got blond hair. Kind of tall and slim," Travis said. "Like me. Oh, yeah: he rides around on a ten-speed."

Debbie stared out at Travis for a moment. Her mouth worked, would release no words. Nothing she could consider saying would express what she was feeling: a war between tears and hysterical laughter. The Cathedral of St. Francis was where she'd gone to ask a priest to pray for Janey McCullough. And the priest in the confessional . . .

"Oh, no," she said softly, as if slapped by a feather. "Oh, no."

She remembered now: *Please don't curse*. That had been said to her in the confessional, and repeated in her apartment while she was in the kitchen with a frozen dinner in each hand.

"Oh . . ." It was a pained, stunned, world-crashing gasp. ". . . *no*."

"Open up. I'll tell you everythin'," Travis said.

Her hand drifted to the latch. Hung there, as Debbie shook her head and tried to make the room stop spinning.

She turned the latch, opened the door, and the cowboy boots clumped across the threshold.

A hill rose before him. It had never seemed so large, so damned monstrous, before. The earth was playing with him, he thought. Hills were rising to block his way. He shifted down to low gear, and fought the bicycle up it, his legs screaming for relief but the fresh pain cleaning all the haze out of his head. Her building was just a couple of blocks to the east now, and when he got up this hill he would take a sharp right and . . .

God, help me! he begged. Tears had filled his eyes. God, help me!

"A priest," Debbie whispered. That word made her throat feel raw. "I talked to him when I went to the church. He was in the confession booth. Right there, beside me. And I never knew. I never knew."

"Now you know," Travis said. "It's a hell of a kick, huh? You got any beer?"

"Beer? No. I've got wine. Oh, Jesus." She felt faint, had to grasp hold of the kitchen counter. "I've got wine. I think I need a drink myself." She turned toward the refrigerator, and that was when he came up behind her, slipping the rope out from around his arm, and clutched it around her throat.

She grasped his hands as the rope tightened, and she started to let out a scream, but his face got up right against her ear and the mouth whispered, "I love you, Debra. Even better than I loved Cheri and Easee."

The scream faltered and stopped on a choke. The impact of what he'd just said, coupled with the realization that her lucky charm—her soul mate—was and always had been a Catholic priest, made her knees buckle.

His right hand left her throat. She heard the rustle of his canvas coat, and her body arched to wrench away from him, to reach the knife drawer and sink a dagger into his black heart. But she didn't have time, because in the next second something slammed against the back of her skull and the kitchen floor came up like a bad dream.

John reached the top of the hill. And a police car sped past him, descending in the opposite direction. He started to lift his arms, but the car was going somewhere fast and he had no voice to make the officers understand. He looked away, his face grim and determined, and kept pedaling. It was up to him now. Up to him. God was in his heaven, and the angels were abed. It was up to him.

He took the sharp right, misjudged, and ran up over the curb with a spine-jarring bump. The handlebars shivered out of his one-handed grip, and the frame made a noise like guitar strings snapping. Suddenly he had no traction; his pedals were slipping, without engaging the tires. The chain, he realized with an inner shriek, had come off the gear wheels. Without hesitation he threw the bicycle aside in front of a Vietnamese restaurant and ran for Raphael Street.

Debbie opened her eyes. She was in a world of white, and her stomach muscles had cramped with tension. Pain throbbed, a dull bruise, at the back of her head. She trembled, about to throw up, and that was when she realized she was roped.

Not just roped. Bound and hog-tied, with expert knots. She was still in her white robe, but it was open and had ridden up over her hips. Her hands were tied at the wrists behind her, and the tough rope came up around her throat and head and was knotted above her face to . . .

She moaned; there was a washrag jammed into her mouth.

. . . to the bathtub's faucet. She was lying in the bathtub, her face about six inches under the waterflow.

"Now we're all ready," Travis said, coming into view above her. He knelt down beside the tub, as Debbie thrashed and tried to get her ankles hooked around the towel rack. No use, she knew after a couple of tries. No use. . . .

"Remember, in *Super Slick?*" Travis asked her excitedly. "You and Cheri did that scene in the tub with the two guys? That was hot, Debra. I couldn't get that scene out of my mind, it was so hot. It was . . . like . . . it was just branded right in there. I put Cheri in a tub too. I'm kind of like a director, huh?"

She thrashed on, knowing it was useless but not ready to give up. Her head remained tautly secured under the faucet.

"Easee's best scene was when she was on her knees doin' that black guy. I did the best I could with that one." His hand went to the hot-water tap. "I loved you. I loved all of you. And I knew the music was for me. It called me to California." His hand twisted, and Debbie thrashed anew but she wasn't going anywhere. He added cold water to the flow so it wouldn't burn her, and now the water was streaming forcefully into her face. She was able to turn her head maybe a half-inch or so, but the pain killed her neck and the water was still going up her nostrils. The washcloth soaked through and seemed to expand in her mouth. Gonna drown me, she knew. Oh, sweet Jesus . . . he's gonna drown me! She blew water out of her nostrils and fought for a breath; she got a gulp of air, but the water was too strong. It went up her nostrils and down her throat.

"There you go," Travis said. "We'll wait a couple of minutes now."

The door's buzzer went off.

Travis stood up fast.

The door's buzzer went off again. Then again. Then somebody was leaning on it.

"I don't like that sound," Travis told her, as water burst from her nostrils and she battled desperately for a breath. He walked into the front room, his hand going to the holstered Colt.

Outside, John took his finger off the buzzer. She should've answered by now. Her Fiat was at the curb. If she could have answered, she would have. He braced himself and kicked at the door, just below the knob. It was sturdy.

Travis started to ease the gun out, his eyes narrowing and his tongue flicking across his lower lip.

John kicked the door again, aiming at the exact same spot. It burst inward, and he barreled through.

And there he stood, the blond man in the long canvas coat. Something was coming up, gripped in his hand in a blue-steel blur, and John saw the man's face tighten with shock. John didn't hesitate; the pistol was rising fast. He lunged across the threshold and right at the maniac.

The gun cracked, and the bullet zipped over John's shoulder and took a chunk out of the doorframe. But then John's left hand had gripped the gun-arm wrist, and his momentum took them both crashing over the coffee table and to the floor.

Travis clawed at John's face, almost getting his fingers hooked in the priest's eyes, but John averted his face and drove a knee hard into the man's groin. Air whistled between Travis' teeth. John's fingers tightened on the gun-arm wrist, trying to keep it pinned to the floor, knowing if that gun got free, he was dead.

He heard water running, back in the bathroom.

Oh, no. Oh, God, no!

A fist slammed into the side of his head and knocked him off. John kept his grip on the wrist, stars wheeling through his brain. And then another blow hit him on the forehead, as Travis roared with rage, and this time John fell backward and lost his hold.

The Colt came up, started to take aim into John's face.

John kicked the man's inner elbow. The gun went off, smashing a cactus pot, and then the man's fingers spasmed open and the Colt sailed out, slamming against the wall and landing on the carpet.

Travis twisted like a snake, crawling madly after his gun.

John landed on his back, bellowing the wind out of him and hooking his left arm around the man's throat, trying to keep him from reaching the Colt. Travis thrashed and strained, fingers grasping, the gun's barrel carpeted inches away.

As the two figures struggled, so did Debbie Stoner. Water was gushing up her nostrils now, and coming through the washrag into her mouth. She was gasping, searching for air in the torrent. She blew water from her nose, but more of it came back. She was filling up with water, and there was no escape from the flood.

Travis reared back and slammed his elbow into John's ribs. John, teeth clenched, hung on and squeezed, but Travis was thrashing again, wildly, and John couldn't keep his grip. Travis lunged forward, and his right hand grasped the Colt's barrel. He drew it to him like a true love.

John released the man's throat and smashed him in the face with his left fist, a blow with the strength of near-madness behind it. Travis's upper lip exploded, and two teeth went into his mouth. But Travis was twisting around again, throwing John off him, and the gun was coming up in a quick, deadly arc.

John leapt for the wrist, got his fingers around it as the Colt fired. The hot flash of the bullet seared his face. There was a noise like a hammer knocking the wall, and plaster dust bloomed beside the picture of a Malibu sunset.

Travis grabbed John's hair, yanking his head back, trying to wrench the priest off his gun hand. But John hung on doggedly, and when the gun went off again it blew a hole through the bay window's glass.

They struggled at close quarters. Travis's fingers twitched on the Colt's handle, and four inches of gleaming, serrated blue steel slid out in front of John's face.

Travis slammed his fist into John's stomach. Then again. John's fingers weakened, his eyes going glassy and sweat glistening on his face. The knife blade slowly descended toward John's bleeding throat.

John got a leg between them, and lodged his knee into the maniac's chest. Travis was on top of him now, his weight bearing down.

John knew there was no other way. In seconds either the knife would go into his neck or the barrel would fire a bullet into his brain. He arched his body upward and cracked his skull into the man's nose.

Travis howled and fell back, blowing blood. John scrambled away, his grip lost and his strength almost gone. Travis shook his head violently, blood dripping from his chin, and then he brought the Colt around to take aim and blow the priest to hell.

John saw the gun coming. There was no way to stop it. No way.

His gaze ticked to a thorny cactus in a small clay pot on his left. He grasped the pot and lifted the cactus off the floor.

Travis' head had almost turned, eyes glittering. The Colt was about to find its target.

John swung out with the cactus.

And raked it across the other man's eyes.

Travis screamed and recoiled, blinded. He rolled away, the bridge of his nose and his cheeks scoured with thorn gashes, his eyes punctured and oozing. He got up on his knees, screaming, and then to his feet. John saw Unicorn racing around the room, madly searching for cover in the frenzy. Travis lurched to right and left, the Colt extended and finger on the trigger. The barrel stared into John's face for a second, then veered away about two feet and fired into the wall. John lay flat, his heart hammering, as Travis screamed, "Where are you! Where are you!" and took a backward step, the Colt swinging to the left again.

He stepped on the crab as it sped across the room under his feet.

Travis went backward, off-balance. The Colt fired a sixth time, the bullet breaking glass in the kitchen, and its recoil sealed the man's fate.

He went back, back, over the sill, and into the bay windows.

The glass shattered behind him, and his mouth opened in a panicked zero. His fingers caught at broken edges and left smears of red, and then he was going out the window and his scream went down with him all the way.

There was a *wham!* and the scream stopped.

John got up, staggering to the smashed window, and looked down. The man lay on the dented roof of a car, belly-up, and his head had snapped backward through the windshield. He still gripped the Colt. A death grip.

Lights were coming on across the street. People were peering out their own windows. Someone screamed out there. And then a man wearing glasses and a terry-cloth robe came into Debbie's apartment, followed by a young blond woman, and both of them stopped dead at the splintered doorway.

Debbie! John thought. Oh, dear Lord!

He ran to the bathroom, as Unicorn started burying itself in the sand from an overturned cactus pot.

She was still alive, and still fighting for life. John got the taps turned off, and she blew and gurgled water and sobbed hysterically around the sopping gag. He wrenched at the rope with his left hand, got a crucial knot loosened from around the faucet. She saw him then, her eyes bloodshot and half-drowned, and she saw the bloody collar around Lucky's neck.

He lifted her up, out of the white tomb, and crushed her to him, getting the rag out of her mouth so she could draw a full breath. Her head pressed against his shoulder, and he held her as she moaned and cried.

"Shhhhh, Debbie," he told her in his mangled voice, as he rocked her shivering body. Whether she understood any of it, he didn't know. "It's all right, Debbie. It's all right, my child. Shhhhhh. It's all right. Shhhhhh, my child."

He held her until the police came.

25

There were many days when San Francisco might be called the most beautiful city on earth, and this was one of them. The bay glittered in the golden sunlight of late October, and sailboats advanced before the wind. In the blue sky, airplanes brought some people here, and also took some people home.

That was Debbie Stoner's destination.

Father John Lancaster waited with her at her gate for the plane to New Orleans. They sat side by side, and as the bustle of a busy airport went on around them their movements were slow and precise, the movements of two people who have already arrived.

She wore her traveling clothes: jeans, a pale blue blouse, and a white sweater that really accented her tan and the clear gray of her eyes. It was a light sweater, one that could be worn in a Southern climate. She wore no sunglasses, and the stripe of light that lay across her hands did not hurt her sight.

John wore his own traveling clothes; he was continuing his journey, and his white collar was fresh and not starched quite so stiffly. Around his right hand were the wrappings of bandages, and another small bandage covered the bullet crease at his throat.

Debbie sighed; her first sound in more than a minute. She looked up at him and then away, quickly. He waited, and he realized he was dreading something: the call that would be coming any minute, the call that would take her out of his life forever.

"I still don't know what Uncle Joey's gonna do," she said quietly. "I left a message on his machine, but . . . well, you never know about Uncle Joey."

"I'm sure Uncle Joey can take care of himself." His voice was still a little croaky.

"You sound like a frog," she said, and gave him a quick nervous smile. He returned it, and then they both looked away from each other again.

"I've got a long way to go," she said finally.

"Not so far. New Orleans, first. Then you can rent a car to—"

"You know what I mean," she said. "I've got a long way. I don't know if I can go the distance."

"You won't know unless you try."

"Right." She nodded, and looked at her hands. She'd taken off her false red fingernails. "I'm scared," she said softly. "I . . . I'm not the same as I used to be. I mean . . . going home . . . it's scary."

"I guess that's part of going home, isn't it?"

"Yeah. But I don't know where I fit in anymore. I mean, my ma sounded glad to hear from me, and she says she's tryin' to kick the bottle, but . . . it's not gonna be easy."

"No," John agreed, watching her beautiful face. There were many questions behind it; they were questions that Debra Rocks wouldn't have asked herself. "Nothing worth a damn is easy."

"Guess not." She was silent for a while longer. The loudspeaker paged somebody, and she jumped a little bit, all needles and pins. "I've got to kick the cocaine," she said. "I know that. That place in New Orleans—"

"It's a good place," John told her. That face, that face! Oh, how it hurt his eyes to look at her. "They'll take good care of you. But that won't be easy either. They've got the facility, but you'll have to work at it."

"I always worked," Debbie said. "I'm not afraid of a little work." She smiled, and he thought it was a different smile; part of her was already facing southeast, maybe looking from the edge of the blue world, about to pass into day.

The loudspeaker's metallic voice announced, "United's flight 1714 to Dallas, Memphis, and New Orleans will soon begin boarding. All passengers with small children or who need extra care . . ."

"That ought to be me," Debbie said nervously. "I feel like a little kid who needs a lot of extra care."

John stood up. It was almost time. Debbie stood up too, and they walked together toward the gate.

"I might not stay there. Home, I mean," she told him. She glanced at him, looked away again because she thought his face was like a blaze, and if she looked too long she'd start to cry. "It's a small town, and I think I've outgrown it. But . . . it seems to me that that's where I've got to go. To find out what happened to Debbie Stoner. I think I left her back there, a long time ago, and she's due her chance too, don't you think?"

"I do think," he agreed. His throat caught. The wound was still hurting, that was it.

"Well, I . . . I've got to give it my best shot. Got to—" Her eyes saw something behind John, and they widened with stunned surprise.

"You fuckhead!" Joey Sinclair's voice growled. "Hey,

Lucky! I'm talkin' to you! I got your message, Debra! What the hell kinda shit is—" He grabbed John's arm roughly and twisted him around.

"Hello, Uncle Joey," John said calmly, and saw the man stare at his collar.

Joey Sinclair was flanked by his sons, two slabs of tough beef. But suddenly Sinclair himself was shrinking, as if he were melting into his suit, and his face took on the color of spoiled cheese. He took a backward step, slamming so hard into one of his sons he almost toppled the boy.

"You're a . . . *priest,*" Sinclair whispered, strangling. "When did you become a priest?"

"I've always been a priest."

"Always? Always?" He had shriveled, and John thought the man was going to become a gnarled little dwarf right there in front of his eyes. "Always?" He seemed to have that word caught in his throat. "Like . . . always?"

"Like always," John told him.

"You mean . . . I called a *priest* a fu . . ." He stopped, diminished, and his eyes bulged with inner pressure.

"Miss Stoner is going home," John said, and put his hand firmly on Joey Sinclair's shoulder. "Is that all right with you?"

"Oh, yeah! It's fine! You got the ticket yet? I'll buy the ticket! First class!"

"Economy is good enough," Debbie said.

Sinclair choked a little more, and then his gaze—softer now, and still frightened—fixed on Debbie. "You're . . . you've always been a good kid. A hard worker. Star quality!"

"Stars burn out," Debbie told him in a quiet and reasoned voice. "I think I want to just be a person now."

"Oh, yeah! Just be a person! That's fine enough!" His scared gaze skittered to John. Then back to Debbie, and it lingered. "Listen . . . Debbie. You . . . be the *best* person. You hear me?"

"I hear you, Uncle Joey."

"Yeah, and you tell anybody gives you trouble that you've got high connections! Understand?"

She smiled, and nodded.

Then Sinclair regarded John again, still astonished, still cheese-faced. *"Always?"*

"Always. I'm at the Cathedral of St. Francis, on Vallejo. You come by sometime, we'll have lunch. I've got high connections."

"Yeah. Sure, Father! Sure! High connections!" He grinned and dug an elbow into Chuck's ribs with a force that made the boy wince. "High connections! He's a funny man!"

"Good-bye, Uncle Joey," Debbie told him, and she took his hand and squeezed it.

"'Bye, kid. Father . . . I guess I'll be seein' you."

"Sooner or later."

"Yeah! Yeah, right!" He grinned again, and then he had to grasp hold of his sons' shoulders and be supported as they left the gate.

"Now boarding United's flight 1714 to Dallas, Memphis, and New Orleans," the loudspeaker announced.

They walked closer to the door that led to the aircraft. Debbie had the ticket gripped hard in her hand. Passengers with carry-on luggage were passing back and forth, the airport full of noise.

"I guess it's time," John said, and he stared at the floor.

She took a deep breath. "Father . . . she wants to say good-bye."

He looked up. "What?"

"Debra Rocks wants to say good-bye," she repeated, and he saw it happen.

The fire came out of her; it leapt from her and engulfed him. Her eyes blazed with passion, and suddenly she was reaching for him and her arms went around his neck. Her lips, soft and burning, fastened on his, and he smelled cinnamon-scented bubblebath and thought he was going to swoon.

Her mouth opened, and her tongue pushed between his lips and entered his, sliding smoothly over wet, yielding flesh.

She locked her hands around his neck, her fingers going

into his hair—and then she lifted one leg and put it around his hip. Then the other leg, and they were clamped together and kissing like the true meeting of souls.

"United's flight 1714, now board—" The loudspeaker's voice halted.

The airport went silent but for the noise of carry-on bags hitting the floor.

Her tongue swirled, teasing and ferocious, inside his mouth. They clung together, John oblivious of everyone and everything but this moment, a carving in time. Her tongue tickled the roof of his mouth, brushed past his tongue. Then began to ease out, and she sucked on his lower lip before she let it go.

Then she was unlocking her legs from around his hips, in the silence of the airport, and as her feet touched the floor she was Debbie Stoner again, a young girl with a plane to catch.

"That was Debra saying good-bye," she told him, damp-eyed. "I don't think she'll be around much anymore. Now this is just me." She hugged him, and put her head against his shoulder. Her raven hair floated against his face, and for the rest of his life he would remember its silk. "Thank you, Father," she whispered. "Thank you . . . for loving me."

His eyes filled up, and he had to let her go. She took a few paces and stopped, and when she looked back her face was streaked with tears. "Soul mates?" she asked.

"Believe it," he answered.

"Pray for me," she said, and she went out that door leading home.

A middle-aged woman with rouged cheeks and a pinched mouth sauntered up to him and looked at him with livid disgust. "And you call yourself a *priest!*"

He said, "Yes, ma'am. I do."

He stayed until the plane took off. Sunlight flared silver on its wings. New Orleans wasn't so far away, he thought. The telephone wires went there and back, and so did the mail. Not so far. Well, we'll see . . .

In his apartment, he began working on a new jigsaw

puzzle, of a green Southern landscape. It wasn't too hard to imagine her in it.

Maybe someday he would get a letter, he thought. And in that letter she would say Debbie Stoner was doing just fine, and she'd met someone nice, someone who would love and respect her and wonder where Debbie Stoner had been all his life.

On that day, he thought his heart might break a little bit. Because he loved her.

But it would be a happy day.

Darryl came to the door. "John? Somebody wants to see you in the sanctuary." He glanced, still a bit uneasily, at the crab in its sandbox over in the corner.

"Thanks." He got up from his puzzle and hurried out.

She was waiting with Monsignor McDowell. She was a pretty blond girl, maybe nineteen or twenty, and behind her makeup her eyes were still fresh enough to be scared.

"Are you . . . Father Lucky?" she asked.

"You can call me that," he said, casting a quick glance at the monsignor.

"My . . . name is Kathy Crenshaw." She shivered, and John saw needle marks on her arms. "Debbie Stoner told me about you." She reached out, a trembling hand, and her face collapsed. "Can you . . . help me?"

"We'll see," he answered, and he took her hand. They sat together, in a pew, while Father Lucky listened, and the rough diamond in his pierced ear threw a spark of light.

Monsignor McDowell stood nearby for a moment, and then he walked to the doors and opened them.

Dear Readers:

I wanted to take this opportunity to introduce you to my next novel, *MINE*, which will be published in hardcover by Pocket Books in May.

I sat down to write a ghost story. When I finished, I'd written *MINE*. Not exactly what I'd started out to do, and certainly not a ghost story in the traditional sense, but a ghost story all the same. *MINE* is the story of a past era, and a walking dead woman haunted by the specters of what used to be.

Mary Terror, a woman lost in time, yearns for the days of radical militancy and the underground presses, an era of black-light posters, roach clips, strawberry incense and psychedelic dreams. She remembers like the touch of an old lover the violence of those times—the clashes with "the pigs" on college campuses, the Weather Underground's bombings, the rage of the Black Panthers, the cold calculations of the Symbionese Liberation Army. Her own angry band of brothers and sisters—the Storm Front—is long gone, destroyed by the police in a shootout in 1972 that also took the life of her unborn child. Mary Terror escaped the inferno, and she's lived alone, on the run from the murders of her past, since 1972. She talks to God in her room, and listens to his commands at thirty-three and a third revolutions per minute. She waits like a coiled-up snake, an arsenal of guns around her, and she sniffs the air for the bitter, hated scent of pigs. Mary Terror is insane. Mary Terror is deadly.

And Mary Terror wants a baby.

What happened to those children of the sixties who learned the language of hatred, who swore oaths upon their bloodstained manifestos and vowed to never surrender? What happened to those soul survivors, when the clock of hours ran out on their day and the night came on fast and brutal and lonely? What happened to them, when the world stopped watching?

Most of them changed. Took off their bell-bottoms and cut their hair and merged into the stream that leads always into the future. Most of them married, had families, and now fret about rap music and their kids getting into drugs. Most of them went on.

But Mary Terror, with blood on her hands and darkness in her heart, has a different destination. Back into the twisted maze of the past, back into the domain of bombs and guns and highways heading toward a dream of glory across a haunted land.

Mary Terror is going to go back, in a search to recapture her youth and the days of the Storm Front, the best days of her life.

And this time she's going with a baby in her arms.

Even if the child is not her own.

So, a ghost story? Yes, I think *MINE* is. The ghosts of a time and place. The ghosts of what used to be, whispering from the yellowed pages of a *Rolling Stone*. Mary Terror's journey, into that land where the past and present meet in a violent and inexorable collision, is about to begin.

Robert R. McCammon

(On the following pages you will find a special preview excerpt of MINE.)

Pocket Books Is Proud to Present
A Spine-Tingling Preview
Excerpt from
Robert R. McCammon's
Next Novel

To Be Published in Hardcover
By Pocket Books
May 1990

Pocket Books Is Proud to Present
A Spine-Tingling Preview
Excerpt from
Robert R. McCammon's
Next Novel

MINE

To Be Published in Hardcover
By Pocket Books
May 1990

uniforms of the nurses on the maternity ward at St. James Hospital had dark blue piping around the

Dr. Bonnart laid David on Laura Clayborne's stomach. She pressed the baby close, feeling his heat. He was still crying, but it was a wonderful sound. "Shhhh, shhhh," Laura said, as her fingers stroked the baby's smooth back. She felt the little shoulder blades and the ridges of his spine. Skeleton, nerves, veins, intestines, brain; he was whole and complete, and he was hers.

She felt it kick in then. What other women who'd had babies had told her to expect: a warm, radiant rush through her body that seemed to make her heart pound and swell. She recognized it as a mother's love, and as she stroked her baby she felt David relax from rigid indignance to soft compliance. His crying eased, became a quiet whimper, and ended on a gurgling sigh. "My baby," Laura said, and she looked up at Dr. Bonnart and the nurse with tears in her eyes. "My baby."

"Thursday's child," the nurse said, checking the clock. "Far to go."

The voice of God was singing in Mary Terror's apartment, at thirty-three and a third revolutions per minute. She was sitting on the bed, using a dark blue marker on the white extra-large uniform she'd rented from Costumes Atlanta on Friday afternoon. The uniforms of the nurses on the maternity ward at St. James Hospital had dark blue piping around the collars and the breast pockets, and their hats were trimmed with dark blue. This uniform had snaps instead of buttons, as the real uniforms did, but it was all she could find in her size.

As she worked on the uniform, Mary began to think about her pickup truck. It was fine for around here, but it wasn't going to do for a long trip. She needed something she could pull onto a side road and sleep in. A van of some kind would do. She could find a van at one of the used-car dealers and trade her pickup for it. But she'd need money, too.

Mary walked into the kitchen, opened a drawer and got a knife with a sharp, serrated blade. A knife used for gutting fish, she thought. She laid it on the countertop, and then she returned to the bedroom and the work on the nurse's uniform.

She was long finished with the job by the time she heard Shecklett coughing as he passed her door. Mary stood at her door, dressed in jeans, a brown sweater, her windbreaker, and a woolen cap. She listened for the clicking of Shecklett's keys as he slid the right one into his door. Then she went out into the cold, her .38 gripped in her right hand and the knife slipped down in her waistband under the windbreaker.

Shecklett was a gaunt man with a pockmarked face, his white hair wild and windblown and his skin cracked like old leather. Shecklett barely had time to register the fact that someone was beside him before he felt the gun's barrel press against his skull. "Inside," Mary told him, and she guided him through the door and slid the key out of the lock.

Mary closed the door and turned the latch. "Kneel," she told him.

"Listen . . . listen . . . wait, okay? Is this a joke?"

"You've got money," Mary said flatly. "Where is it?"

"Money? I don't have money! I'm poor, I swear to God!"

She eased back the Colt's hammer, the gun aimed into Shecklett's face.

"Listen . . . wait a minute . . . what's this all about, huh? Tell me what it's all about and maybe I can help you."

Mary was tired of wasting time. She took a breath, lifted the Colt, and brought it down in a savage arc across Shecklett's face. He cried out and pitched onto his side, his body shuddering as the pain racked him. Mary knelt down beside him and put the gun to his pulsing temple. "Shit time is over," she said. "Give me your money. Got it?"

Shecklett blinked up at her, his eyes beginning to swell. "Oh God . . . please . . . please . . ." Mary lifted the Colt again to hit him in the mouth, and the old man flinched and whined. "No! Please! In the dresser! Top drawer, in my socks! That's everything I've got!"

Mary picked up the wad of socks he'd indicated. She closed the drawer and gave the socks back to him. "Show me."

Shecklett unwadded them, his hands trembling. Inside the socks was a roll of money. He held it up for her to see, and she said, "Count it."

He began. There were two hundred-dollar bills, three fifties, six twenties, four tens, five fives and eight dollar bills. A total of five hundred and forty-three dollars. Mary snatched the cash from his hand. "That's not all of it," she said. "Where's the rest?"

Shecklett held his hand to his nose, his puffed eyes shiny with fear. "That's all. My social security. That's all I've got in the world."

"There's no more, is there?" she asked, training the Colt on him.

"I said there wasn't."

"Take off your clothes," Mary ordered.

"Huh?"

"Your clothes. Off."

"My *clothes?* How come you want me to—"

She was on him before he could utter another word. The gun rose and fell, and the old man dropped to his knees with his jaw broken and three teeth loose. Moaning with pain, he began to take his clothes off. When he was finished, his bony white body nude, Mary said, "Get up." He did, his eyes deep-sunken and terrified. "Into the bathroom," she told him, and she followed him in. "Get in the bathtub on your hands and knees.

"Head down. Don't look at me," she said. Shecklett's skinny chest heaved, and he coughed violently for maybe a minute. She waited until his coughing was done, and then she slid the knife from her waistband.

"Swear I won't tell a soul." His chest heaved again, this time in a sob. "God, please don't hurt me. I never did anything to you. I won't tell anybody. I'll keep my mouth shut, I swear to—"

Mary picked up a washrag from the sink and jammed it into Shecklett's mouth. He gasped and gagged, and then Mary leaned over his naked body. She thrust the knife into one side of Shecklett's throat, her knuckles scraping the sandpaper of his skin. Before Shecklett could fully realize what she was doing, Mary cut his throat from ear to ear with the serrated blade, and crimson blood fountained into the air.

Mary sat on the edge of the tub and watched him die. There was something about him that made her think of a baby, swimming through a sea of blood and mothers' fluid to reach the light.

The uniform was ready. Before the day was done, she would be a mother.

An olive green Chevy van with rust holes in the passenger door and a cracked left rear window pulled to the loading dock behind St. James Hospital. The woman who got out wore a nurse's uniform, white trimmed with dark blue. Over her breast pocket her plastic tag identified her as Janette Leister. Next to the name tag was pinned a yellow Smiley Face.

Mary Terror spent a moment pulling a smile up from the depths of her own face. She looked fresh-scrubbed and pink-cheeked, and she'd put clear gloss on her lips. Her heart was hammering, her stomach twisted into nervous knots. But she took a few deep breaths, thinking of the baby she was going to take to Lord Jack. The baby was up there on the second floor, waiting for her in one of the three rooms with blue bows on the doors.

She came around a curve and found herself about twenty paces behind a female pig with a walkie-talkie, going in the same direction as she. Mary's heart stuttered, and she stepped back out of sight for a minute or two, giving the she-pig time to clear out. Then, when the corridor was clear, Mary started toward the stairwell again.

As she ascended past the first floor, she faced another challenge: two nurses coming down. She popped her smile back on, the two nurses smiled and nodded, and Mary passed them with damp palms. She was on the maternity ward, and there was no one else in the corridor between her and the curve that led to the nurses' station.

Mary heard a soft chime that, she presumed, signaled one of the nurses. The crying of babies drifted through the hallway like a siren song. It was now or never. She chose room 24, and she walked in as if she owned the hospital.

She was nervous. If this one didn't work out, she might have to scrub the mission.

She thought of Lord Jack, awaiting her at the weeping lady, and she went in.

The mother was asleep, her baby cradled against her. In a chair by the window sat an older woman with curly gray hair, doing needlepoint. "Hello," the woman in the chair said. "How are you today?"

"I'm fine, thanks." Mary saw the mother's eyes start to open. The baby began to stir too; his eyelids fluttered open for a second, and Mary saw that the child's eyes were light blue, like Lord Jack's. Her heart leapt; it was karma at work.

"Oh, I drifted off." Laura Clayborne blinked, trying to focus on the nurse who stood over the bed. A big woman with a nondescript face and brown hair. A yellow Smiley Face button on her uniform. Her name tag said Janette something. "What time is it?"

"Time to weigh the baby," Mary answered. She heard tension in her voice, and she got a grip on it. "It'll just take a minute or two."

David was waking up. His initial response was to open his mouth and let out a high, thin cry. "I think he's hungry again," Laura said. "Can I feed him first?"

Couldn't chance a real nurse coming in, Mary thought. She kept her smile on. "I won't be very long. Just get this over with and out of the way, all right?"

Laura said, "All right," though she yearned to feed him. "I haven't seen you before."

"I only work weekends," Mary replied, her arms offered.

"Shhhhh, shhhhh, don't cry," Laura told her son. She kissed his forehead, smelling the peaches-and-cream aroma of his flesh. "Oh, you're so precious," she told him, and she reluctantly placed him in the nurse's arms. Immediately she felt the need to grasp him back to her again. The nurse had big hands, and Laura saw that one of the woman's fingernails had a dark red crust beneath it. She glanced again at the name tag: *Leister*.

"There we go," Mary said, rocking the infant in her arms. "There we go, sweet thing." She began moving toward the door. "I'll bring him right back."

"Take good care of him," Laura said. Needs to wash her hands, she thought.

"I sure will." Mary was almost out the door.

"Nurse?" Laura asked.

Mary stopped on the threshold, the baby still crying in her arms.

"Would you bring me some orange juice, please?"

"Yes, ma'am."

"She had dirty hands," Laura said to her mother. "Did you notice that?"

"No, but that was the biggest woman I ever laid eyes on."

Mary Terror, her index finger clasped in the baby's mouth, strode through the corridor toward the loading dock's door. The baby began to cry just before Mary reached the exit, but it was a soft crying and the noise of the laundry masked it. She opened the door. The wind had picked up, and silver needles of rain were falling. She pushed the hamper out onto the loading dock and scooped the infant out still wrapped in a towel. Then she hurried down the concrete steps to her van, which she'd traded for her truck and three hundred and eighty dollars at Friendly Ernie's Used Cars in Smyrna about two hours before. She put the crying baby onto the floorboard on the passenger side, next to her sawed-off shotgun. She started the engine, which ran rough as a cob and made the entire van shudder. The windshield wipers shrieked as they swept back and forth across the glass.

Then Mary Terror backed away from the loading dock, turned the van around, and drove away from the hospital. "Hush, now!" she told the baby. "Mary's got you!"

Don't miss MINE, *the new Robert R. McCammon novel of terror, to be published in hardcover by Pocket Books, May 1990, available wherever hardcover books are sold.*